D1127272

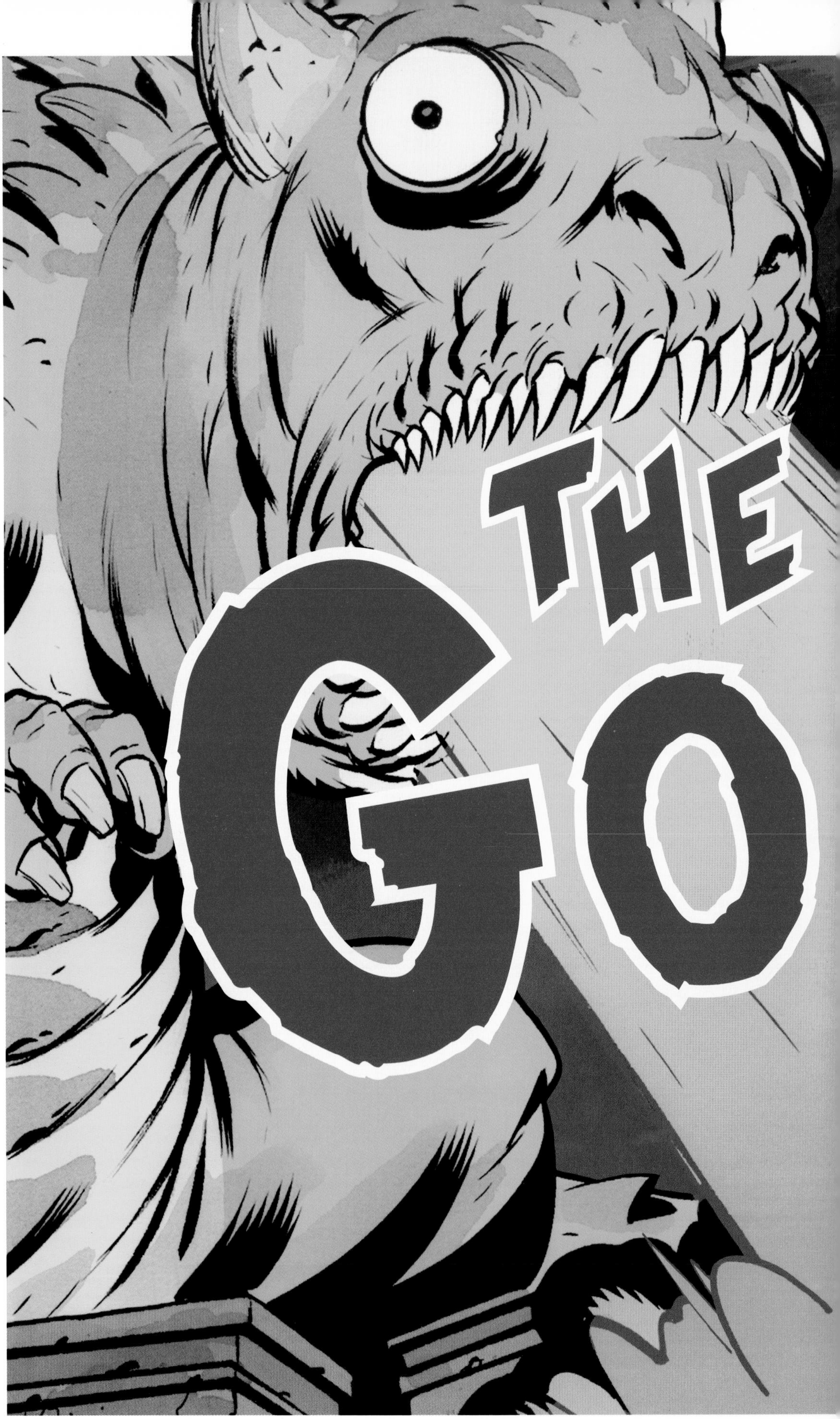
THE
GO

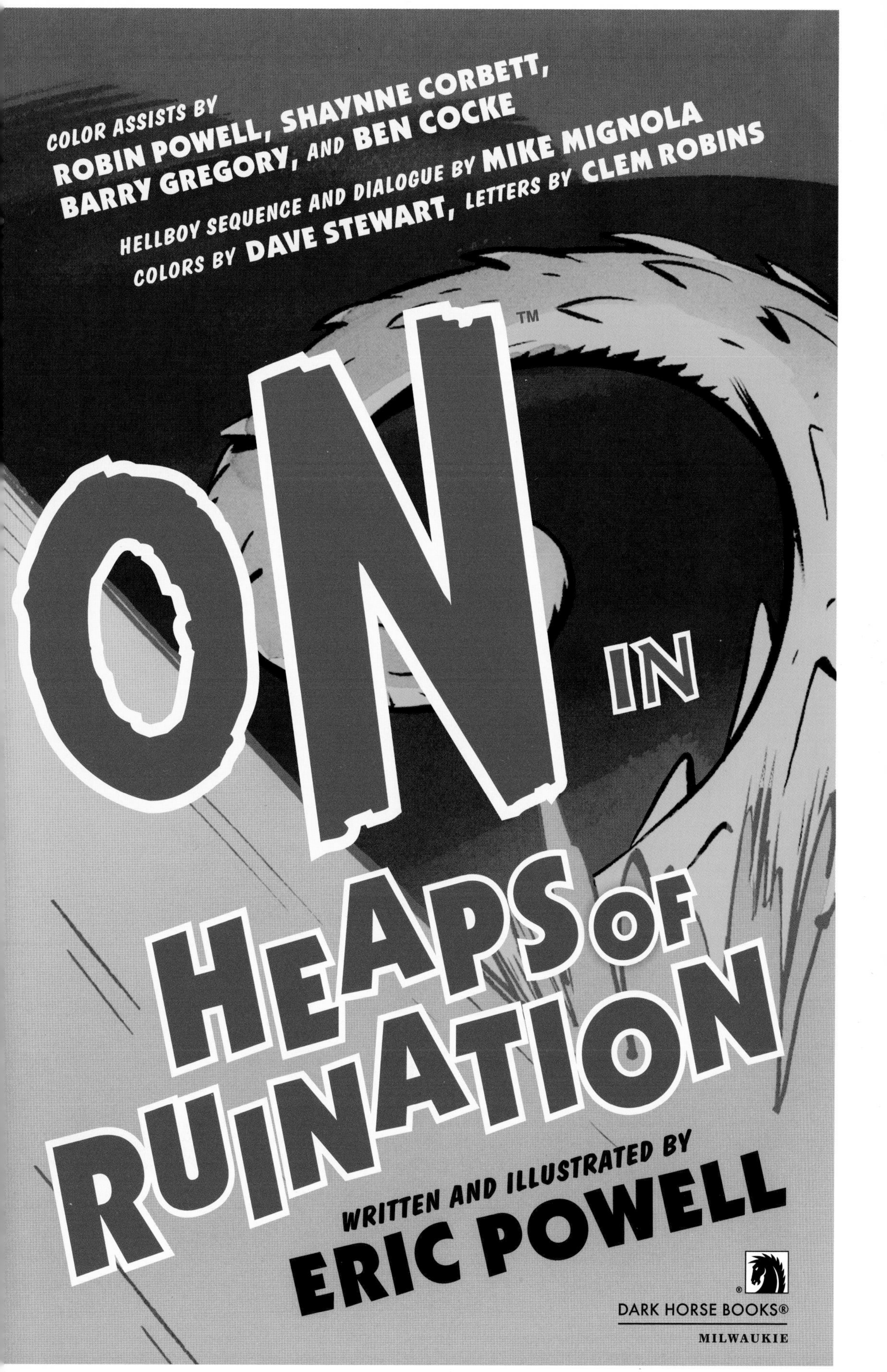

COLOR ASSISTS BY
ROBIN POWELL, SHAYNNE CORBETT,
BARRY GREGORY, AND BEN COCKE

HELLBOY SEQUENCE AND DIALOGUE BY MIKE MIGNOLA
COLORS BY DAVE STEWART, LETTERS BY CLEM ROBINS

THE GOON™ IN HEAPS OF RUINATION

WRITTEN AND ILLUSTRATED BY
ERIC POWELL

DARK HORSE BOOKS®
MILWAUKIE

First edition:

editors SCOTT ALLIE & MATT DRYER

Second edition:

editor SCOTT ALLIE

assistant editor BRENDAN WRIGHT

designer AMY ARENDTS

president & publisher MIKE RICHARDSON

Neil Hankerson *executive vice president* • Tom Weddle *chief financial officer* • Randy Stradley *vice president of publishing* • Michael Martens *vice president of book trade sales* • Anita Nelson *vice president of business affairs* • Micha Hershman *vice president of marketing* • David Scroggy *vice president of product development* • Dale LaFountain *vice president of information technology* Darlene Vogel *senior director of print, design, and production* • Ken Lizzi *general counsel* • Davey Estrada *editorial director* • Scott Allie *senior managing editor* • Chris Warner *senior books editor* Diana Schutz *executive editor* • Cary Grazzini *director of print and development* • Lia Ribacchi *art director* • Cara Niece *director of scheduling*

THE GOON™: HEAPS OF RUINATION

The Goon™ & © 2011 Eric Powell. All rights reserved. Dark Horse Books® and the Dark Horse logo are registered trademarks of Dark Horse Comics, Inc. All rights reserved. No portion of this publication may be reproduced or transmitted, in any form or by any means, without the express written permission of Dark Horse Comics, Inc. Names, characters, places, and incidents featured in this publication either are the product of the author's imagination or are used fictitiously. Any resemblance to actual persons (living, dead, or undead), events, institutions, or locales, without satiric intent, is coincidental.

This volume collects issues #5–#8 of the Dark Horse Comics ongoing series *The Goon*.

Published by
Dark Horse Books
A division of
Dark Horse Comics, Inc.
10956 SE Main Street
Milwaukie, OR 97222

DarkHorse.com

To find a comics shop in your area,
call the Comic Shop Locator Service toll-free at (888) 266-4226.

First edition: May 2005
Second edition: September 2011
ISBN 978-1-59582-625-1

10 9 8 7 6 5 4 3 2 1

Printed by Midas Printing International, Ltd., Huizhou, China.

INTRODUCTION
by FRANK DARABONT

Ever since I first laid eyes on *The Goon*, something had been tickling my brain . . . let's be fair and call it a weird—though oddly *pleasing*—sense of déjà vu.

Don't get me wrong. *The Goon* is a wildly original work in comics, a unique and singular creation by Eric Powell, a hugely talented new voice making an important mark. Still, I *do* recall feeling that tingle of déjà vu the moment I saw the *Nothin' But Misery* collection beckoning to me from a shelf at my local comic-book shop. Something about that glorious cover painting (Goon knocking the head off a rather surprised-looking zombie), as well as the interior art, made that tingle happen. It happened again that night when I brought the book home and read the stories (and found myself delighted—indeed, floored—by Powell's off-kilter, hilarious world). The tingle I felt wasn't *familiarity*, exactly . . . more like a vague sense that I'd known these guys all my life, that Goon and Franky were old friends I'd somehow lost track of and forgotten.

How could this be, considering that *The Goon* is, as I've said, fresh and original and all those other good things? How could something be entirely new, yet still give me that Rod Serling vibe that I'd stumbled into a place I'd visited before and reencountered people I'd known, perhaps in a previous life? It was a puzzler, all right, and I'd been trying to put my finger on it ever since.

The answer finally came to me the other day when I was down in my basement working on my treadmill (nothing like exercise to get the mind wandering). The solution had been lurking there in my hindbrain like an air bubble at the bottom of a pond, and it finally broke loose and rose quietly to the surface where I could see it.

Folks, I've developed a theory about *The Goon*, and though some of you may laugh in my face, I will take courage in hand and share that theory with you today.

It has to do with Eric winning the Eisner Award for Best Single Issue. Mind you, it's no small cheese winning an Eisner—it's the comic industry's most coveted and meaningful honor. It's given to people in comics who keep the bar raised high, and has been won by the likes of *Hellboy* creator Mike Mignola and *League of Extraordinary Gentlemen* scribe Alan Moore. That's some rarified company to be in, and if you can make that kind of cut, you know you're doing something right. More to the point, consider the legacy the Eisner Award suggests—well, to risk stating the obvious, it's named after *Will Eisner*, isn't it? In the pantheon of comics, Mr. Eisner sits atop Mount Olympus. This is the gentlemen who created *The Spirit*, after all, which has inspired generations of storytellers to take pen and brush in hand, and remains to this day a high-water mark to which all aspire (in the film world, this would be like having directed *Battleship Potemkin* or *Citizen Kane*.) And so I'm thinking, as I'm sweating away on my treadmill, that winning an award named after Will "I am Zeus" Eisner has got to be just about the most thrilling honor a young comic-book creator like Eric Powell can receive.

And as I mused upon this, that air bubble in my brain pond started to rise, and I began to perceive a deeper connection between Powell and Eisner than I had previously allowed for—and thus did my theory take shape.

I certainly *had* noted, even upon my first exposure to *The Goon*, that Eric Powell's art, though very much his own, owes a debt of inspiration to Eisner. Check Eric's line work, the shading, the compositions, the expressions on the characters' faces—I guarantee you Eric spent at least a part of his childhood peering over every page and panel of *The Spirit*, the circuits in his young head going *clickety-clack* and lighting up with "gee, I wanna do that when I grow up" inspiration. This is no different than any of us who grow up to become storytellers for a living; those inspirations are there to be soaked in, cherished, and used as fuel someday. I have a whole list of inspirations myself, those keenly felt treasures that give us a big kick in the pants when we're kids and help propel us into following our dreams in our adult lives. In my case, Frank Capra had a lot to do with it. So did Stanley Kubrick. So did Stephen King, Ray Bradbury, and Harlan Ellison. So did

seeing *THX 1138*—still George Lucas's best and most personal work, in my opinion—when I was twelve. The list goes on, but I won't bore you—this intro's about Eric, not me. The point is, there I was the other day, sweating on my treadmill, thinking about Eric Powell's *The Goon* and Will Eisner's *The Spirit*, when I finally realized why *Goon* had given me that nice shiver of déjà vu:

I think Eric Powell's *The Goon* takes place in a part of Central City that Will Eisner never *quite* showed us (though it was just around the corner, and he did take us down some of the same mean streets and alleys). And I'm convinced that Goon himself is a tough customer that Eisner's intrepid criminologist, Denny Colt—who struck fear into the hearts of most criminals as "The Spirit"—probably butted heads with more than once in his crime-fighting career, but never managed to bring down. (Note that I said *most* criminals—Goon probably slapped the Spirit around pretty good and even threw him through a wall.) Perhaps Goon and the Spirit even developed a grudging admiration for each other over time, and left each other alone. Maybe they even found themselves fighting on the *same* side once or twice, much to their surprise. I'm guessing Mr. Eisner just never got around to telling us those particular tales, because he was understandably distracted by all those sultry femme-fatale hotties like P'Gell and Sand Saref that kept sashaying after our boy Denny.

Yes, the more I've thought about it, the more certain I am that if we could visit Lonely Street, we'd find it just a stone's throw from Wildwood Cemetery. (I mean, take another look at the boneyard where the G-men find Labrazio's headstone right after the Goon lops off Fishy Pete's limbs with a chainsaw—just *try* and tell me that's not Wildwood . . . come on, you *know* it is.) If we exited the road to where the docks are, we'd find ourselves in Goon's neighborhood . . . ducking zombies and car-hugging giant squids, I have no doubt.

I think what Eric Powell has done in creating *The Goon* is given us the flip side of *The Spirit*: shown us how the other, less fortunate half lives—you know, the guys who aren't James Garner handsome and *don't* get the chance to flirt endlessly with Ellen, Commissioner Dolan's sexy and pampered daughter. I'm talking about those *other* guys, the pug-uglies we often glimpsed in the Spirit's adventures but never really got to know, the disposable guys who dwelt on the murkier side of the law, did all the dirty work and heavy lifting, and spent the off hours in those sleazy dives along the waterfront. (Those are the very same dives the Spirit would often poke his head into, but—lightweight that he was—never stick around and do whiskey shooters until he passed out and went *flumpf* facedown on the floor.)

So there's my theory—that *The Goon* amounts to a perfect companion piece to Will Eisner's *The Spirit*—submitted, as Serling would say, for your approval. I think Eric has created the yang to Eisner's yin, made those disposable pug-uglies indispensable, and brilliantly filled in for us the other half of the Spirit's world. Go ahead and laugh if you must, but I think I'm onto something here. I think it explains that tingle of déjà vu and the reason Goon and Franky seemed like old, forgotten friends to me—because in a sense, they are. I swear I caught glimpses of them years ago when I was a kid reading those excellent Warren reprints of *The Spirit*, the pair of them darting around the corners of dark alleys lugging a safe on their shoulders or bags of loot under their arms while Denny Colt went zipping by in hot pursuit of bigger fish like the Octopus, or a sexy dame like Silk Satin, or . . . hell, maybe even on the trail of Labrazio. All of which makes Eric winning the Eisner Award not only deserved, but—to my mind—oddly and sweetly *appropriate*.

Part of my thrill in writing the intro to this volume is that it contains the most talked-about and fun crossover of the year—of course I'm talking about Goon meeting Hellboy. (And if you've read my intro to the Hellboy anthology *Odder Jobs*, you're certainly aware what a rabid Hellboy fan I am, and what a genius I think Mignola is.) But, hey, as much as I loved Goon hooking up with Hellboy, you know what I'd give anything to see? I mean *anything*? (Even my naked pictures of Ingrid Bergman?) That's right, bub . . . I'd *love* to see the Spirit stumble into Nort's sleazy bar with a herd of Eric Powell zombies snapping at his heels, trying to chew his ass off.

How about it, Eric? I think it's the least you could do for us, having taken home the Eisner.

Okay, so maybe I'm dreaming. And maybe I'm projecting bigtime about *The Goon* being the flipside of *The Spirit*; perhaps I'm just conflating the two because I love them dearly, and both have a uniquely Damon Runyon period flavor. But, dammit, I don't *think* I'm wrong. And even if I am, what the hell . . . If you can't make a geeky fanboy of yourself writing an intro, then what's the point of doing one? Tell you what—when you get to write the intro, you can subject the rest of us to whatever crackpot theory *you* want to float. Right now *I've* got the floor, so siddown and shaddup, 'cause I ain't done talkin' yet. (Sorry, all this talk of Goon is bringing out *my* Damon Runyon.)

Before I hand over the reins to the estimable Mr. Powell, let me just say again how much I adore what he's created here. For starters, he's got a thing for flesh-eating zombies (which I share), and he draws them funnier than anybody I've ever seen. *The Goon* is a true American original—a delirious medley of strange characters, stranger creatures, wild-ass (and often truly creepy) storytelling, art so excellent and perfectly matched to the tone of his stories as to be flabbergasting, and writing so hilarious that it sometimes comes close to making me pee my pants. ("*¡Lagarto Hombre!*," which we are fortunate to have in this collection, is one of the funniest things I've read this year, a hilarious tip of the hat to every "giant monsters beating the crap out of each other like drunken WWF wrestlers" movie ever made.) And make no mistake; Eric's just getting better as he goes—"The Vampire Dame Had to Die," also in this collection, starts out being fall-down funny (I love the way he skewers the overwrought Anne Rice goth types), then surprises us with the fascinating and extremely delicate trick of becoming unexpectedly and genuinely *moving* in its last few pages.

Yeah, boys and girls, this Powell guy's *good*. He's the real deal, doing pitch-perfect work, and I'm making a safe bet he'll be taking home a few more Eisners before he's through.

Frank Darabont
Los Angeles, CA

CHAPTER 1

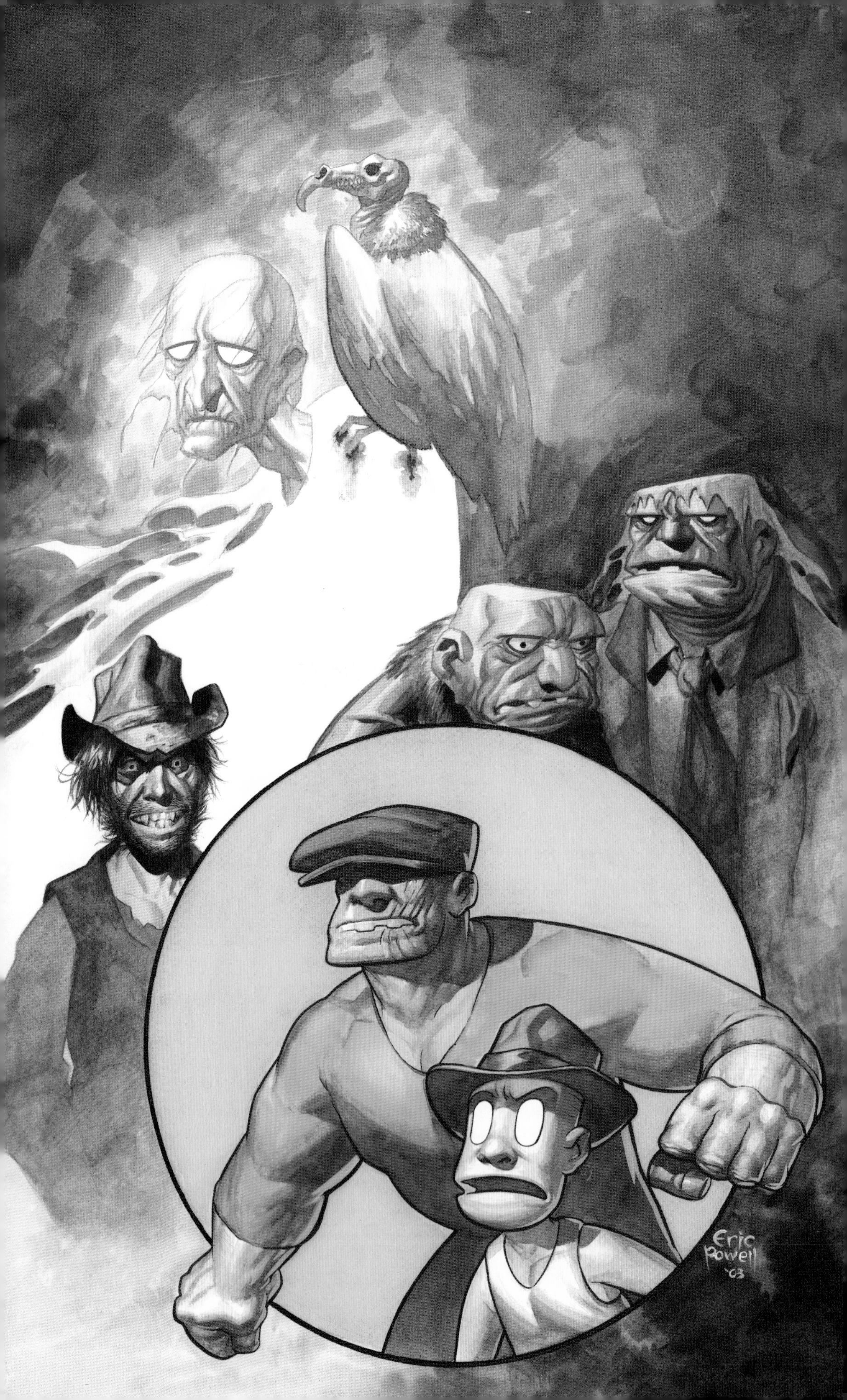
Eric Powell '03

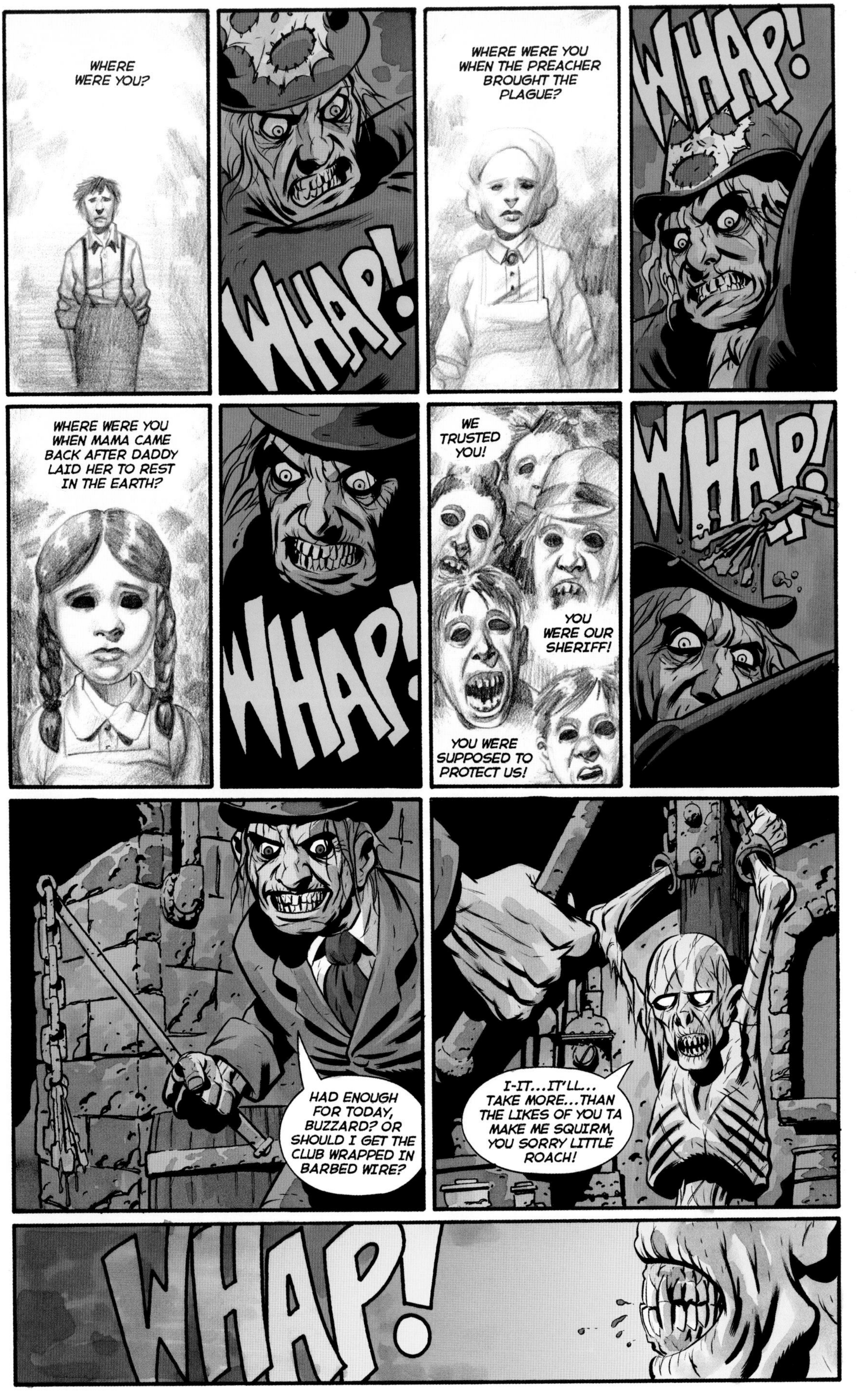

WHERE WERE YOU?
WHAP!
WHERE WERE YOU WHEN THE PREACHER BROUGHT THE PLAGUE?
WHAP!
WHERE WERE YOU WHEN MAMA CAME BACK AFTER DADDY LAID HER TO REST IN THE EARTH?
WHAP!
WE TRUSTED YOU!
YOU WERE OUR SHERIFF!
YOU WERE SUPPOSED TO PROTECT US!
WHAP!
HAD ENOUGH FOR TODAY, BUZZARD? OR SHOULD I GET THE CLUB WRAPPED IN BARBED WIRE?
I-IT...IT'LL... TAKE MORE...THAN THE LIKES OF YOU TA MAKE ME SQUIRM, YOU SORRY LITTLE ROACH!
WHAP!

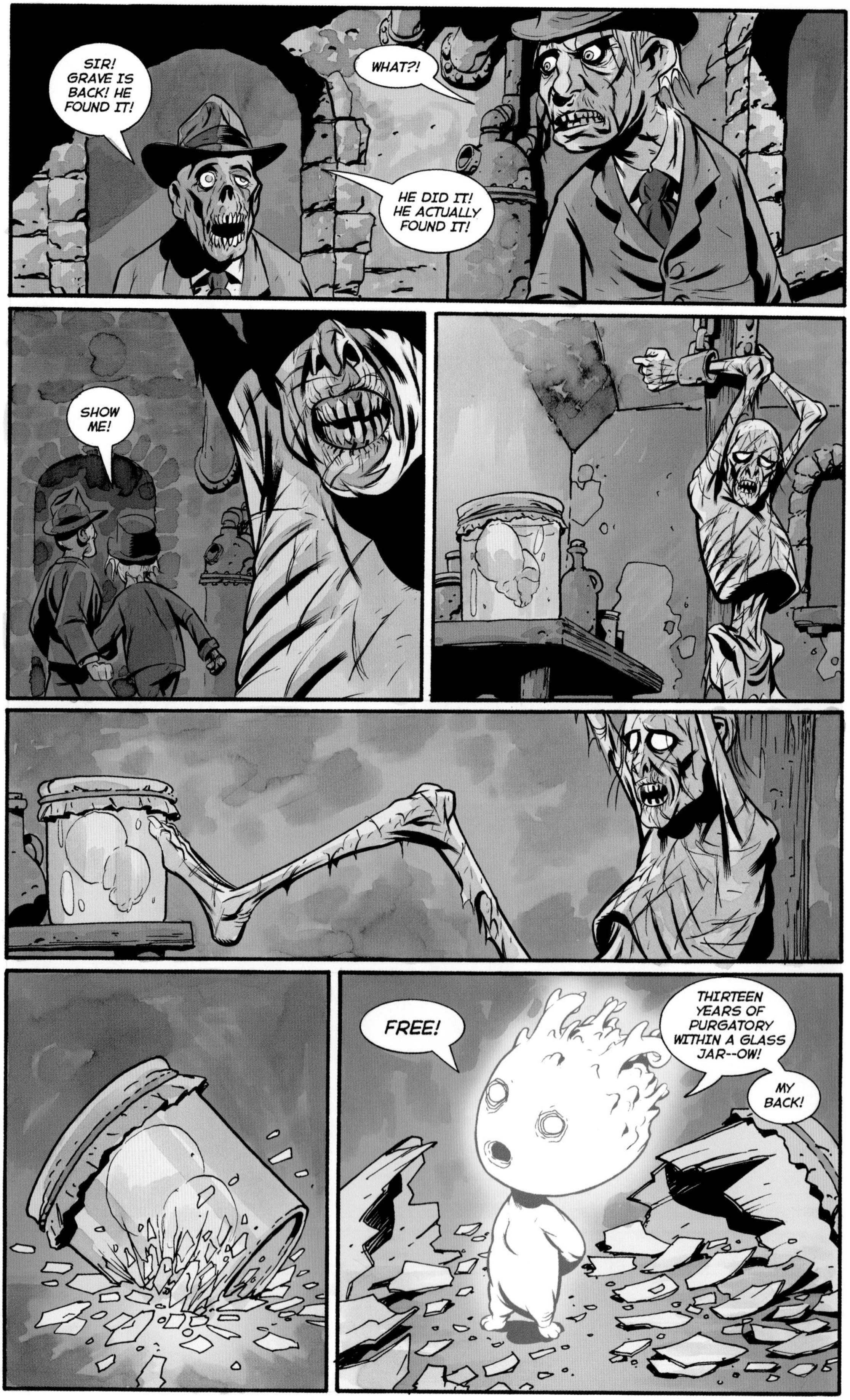
SIR! GRAVE IS BACK! HE FOUND IT!
WHAT?!
HE DID IT! HE ACTUALLY FOUND IT!
SHOW ME!
FREE!
THIRTEEN YEARS OF PURGATORY WITHIN A GLASS JAR--OW!
MY BACK!

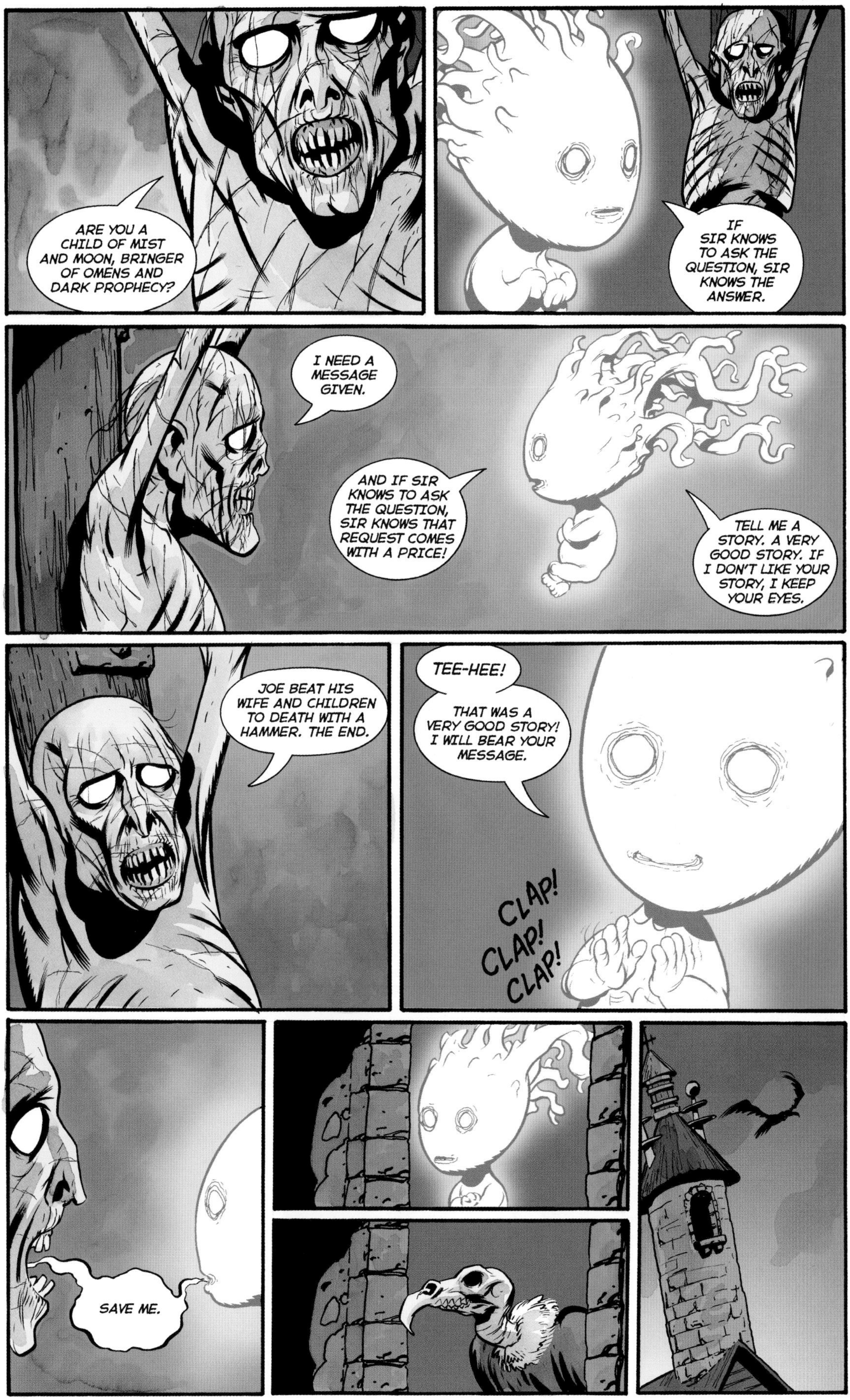
ARE YOU A CHILD OF MIST AND MOON, BRINGER OF OMENS AND DARK PROPHECY?
IF SIR KNOWS TO ASK THE QUESTION, SIR KNOWS THE ANSWER.
I NEED A MESSAGE GIVEN.
AND IF SIR KNOWS TO ASK THE QUESTION, SIR KNOWS THAT REQUEST COMES WITH A PRICE!
TELL ME A STORY. A VERY GOOD STORY. IF I DON'T LIKE YOUR STORY, I KEEP YOUR EYES.
JOE BEAT HIS WIFE AND CHILDREN TO DEATH WITH A HAMMER. THE END.
TEE-HEE!
THAT WAS A VERY GOOD STORY! I WILL BEAR YOUR MESSAGE.
CLAP! CLAP! CLAP!
SAVE ME.

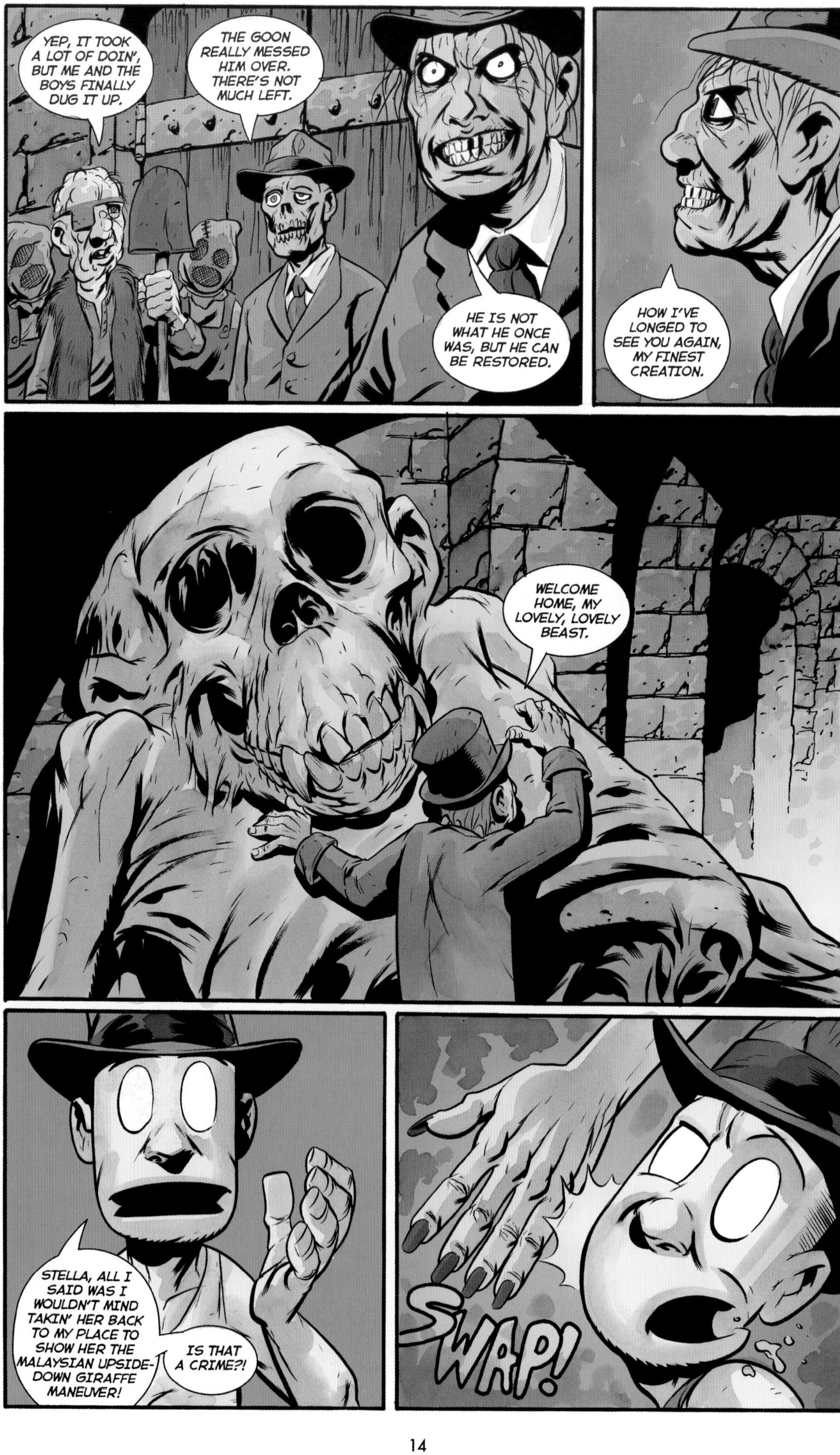
YEP, IT TOOK A LOT OF DOIN', BUT ME AND THE BOYS FINALLY DUG IT UP.
THE GOON REALLY MESSED HIM OVER. THERE'S NOT MUCH LEFT.
HE IS NOT WHAT HE ONCE WAS, BUT HE CAN BE RESTORED.
HOW I'VE LONGED TO SEE YOU AGAIN, MY FINEST CREATION.
WELCOME HOME, MY LOVELY, LOVELY BEAST.
STELLA, ALL I SAID WAS I WOULDN'T MIND TAKIN' HER BACK TO MY PLACE TO SHOW HER THE MALAYSIAN UPSIDE-DOWN GIRAFFE MANEUVER!
IS THAT A CRIME?!
SWAP!

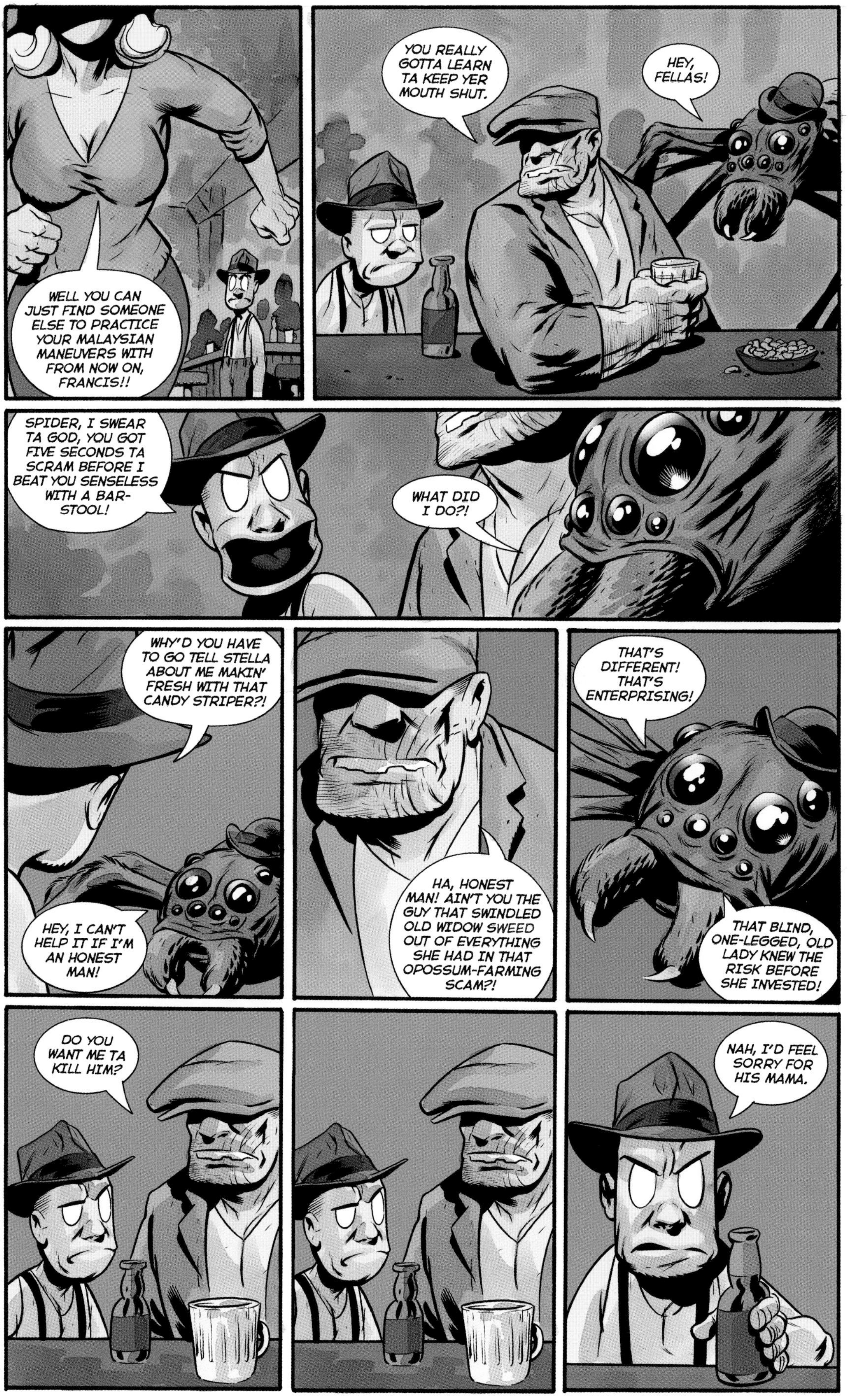

WELL YOU CAN JUST FIND SOMEONE ELSE TO PRACTICE YOUR MALAYSIAN MANEUVERS WITH FROM NOW ON, FRANCIS!!
YOU REALLY GOTTA LEARN TA KEEP YER MOUTH SHUT.
HEY, FELLAS!
SPIDER, I SWEAR TA GOD, YOU GOT FIVE SECONDS TA SCRAM BEFORE I BEAT YOU SENSELESS WITH A BAR-STOOL!
WHAT DID I DO?!
WHY'D YOU HAVE TO GO TELL STELLA ABOUT ME MAKIN' FRESH WITH THAT CANDY STRIPER?!
HEY, I CAN'T HELP IT IF I'M AN HONEST MAN!
HA, HONEST MAN! AIN'T YOU THE GUY THAT SWINDLED OLD WIDOW SWEED OUT OF EVERYTHING SHE HAD IN THAT OPOSSUM-FARMING SCAM?!
THAT'S DIFFERENT! THAT'S ENTERPRISING!
THAT BLIND, ONE-LEGGED, OLD LADY KNEW THE RISK BEFORE SHE INVESTED!
DO YOU WANT ME TA KILL HIM?
NAH, I'D FEEL SORRY FOR HIS MAMA.

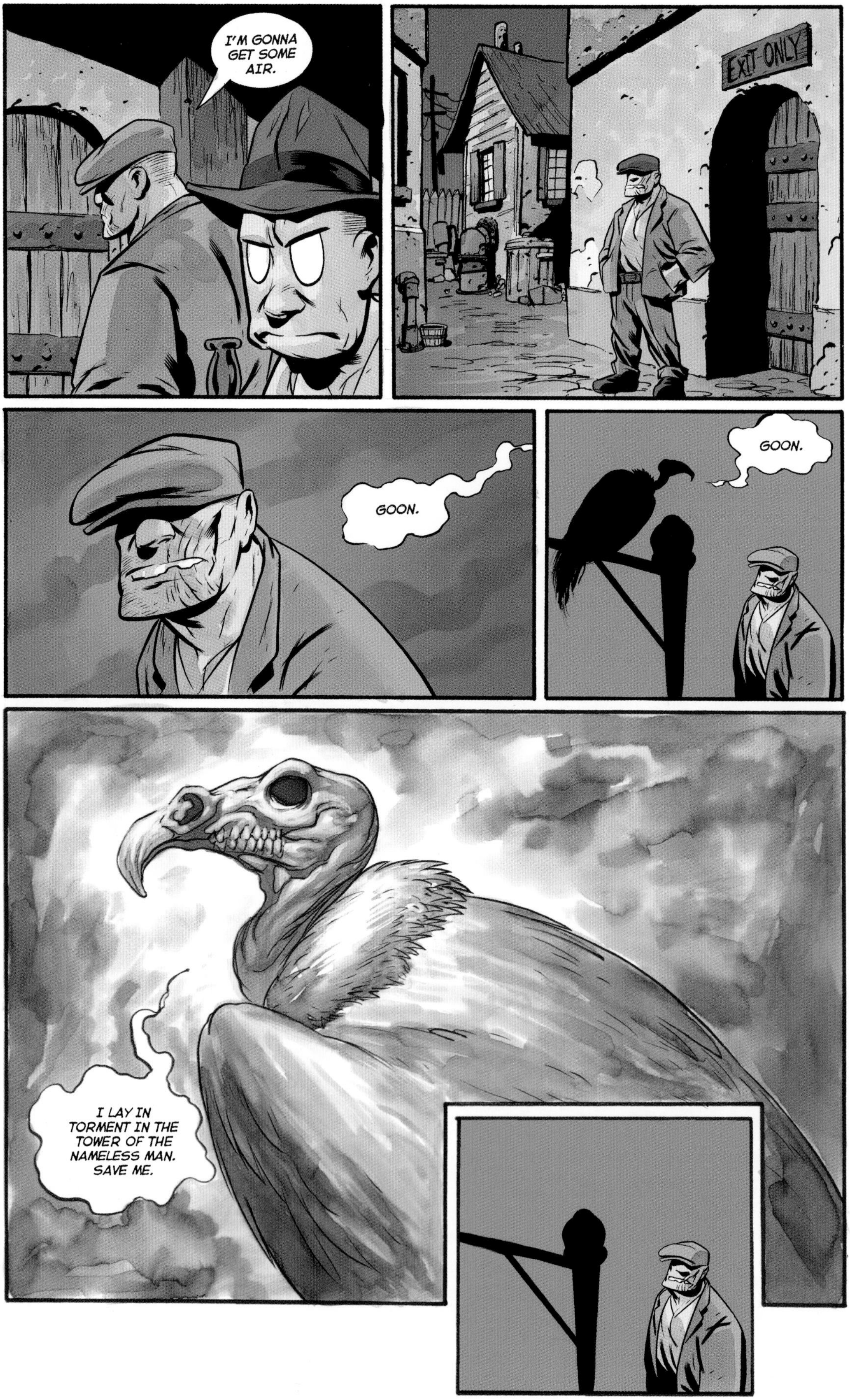
I'M GONNA GET SOME AIR.
EXIT ONLY
GOON.
GOON.
I LAY IN TORMENT IN THE TOWER OF THE NAMELESS MAN. SAVE ME.

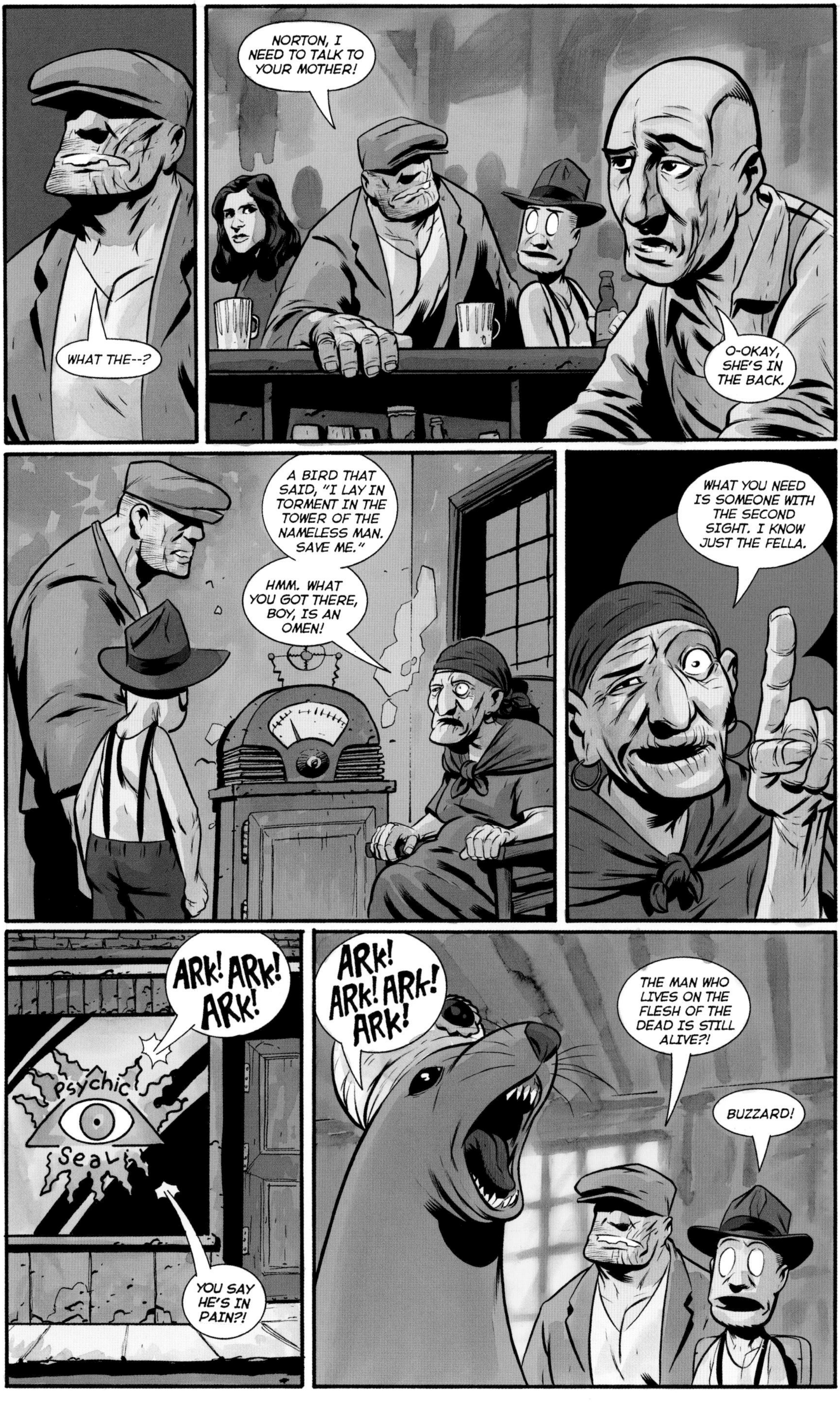
WHAT THE--?
NORTON, I NEED TO TALK TO YOUR MOTHER!
O-OKAY, SHE'S IN THE BACK.
A BIRD THAT SAID, "I LAY IN TORMENT IN THE TOWER OF THE NAMELESS MAN. SAVE ME."
HMM. WHAT YOU GOT THERE, BOY, IS AN OMEN!
WHAT YOU NEED IS SOMEONE WITH THE SECOND SIGHT. I KNOW JUST THE FELLA.
ARK! ARK! ARK!
Psychic Seal
YOU SAY HE'S IN PAIN?!
ARK! ARK! ARK! ARK!
THE MAN WHO LIVES ON THE FLESH OF THE DEAD IS STILL ALIVE?!
BUZZARD!

ARK! ARK! ARK! ARK!
HE'S BEING TORTURED IN THE TOWER OF THE NAMELESS MAN, THE ZOMBIE PRIEST?!
ARK! ARK! ARK!
THAT OLD FREAK IS STILL ALIVE?! WHAT ARE WE GONNA DO?
WE GOTTA GET 'IM OUTTA THERE!
ARK! ARK! ARK! ARK!
YEAH, WELL WE DIDN'T ASK YOU!
ARK! ARK! ARK! ARK! ARK! ARK! ARK!
DON'T NOBODY TALK ABOUT MY MAMA!
GET 'IM!!

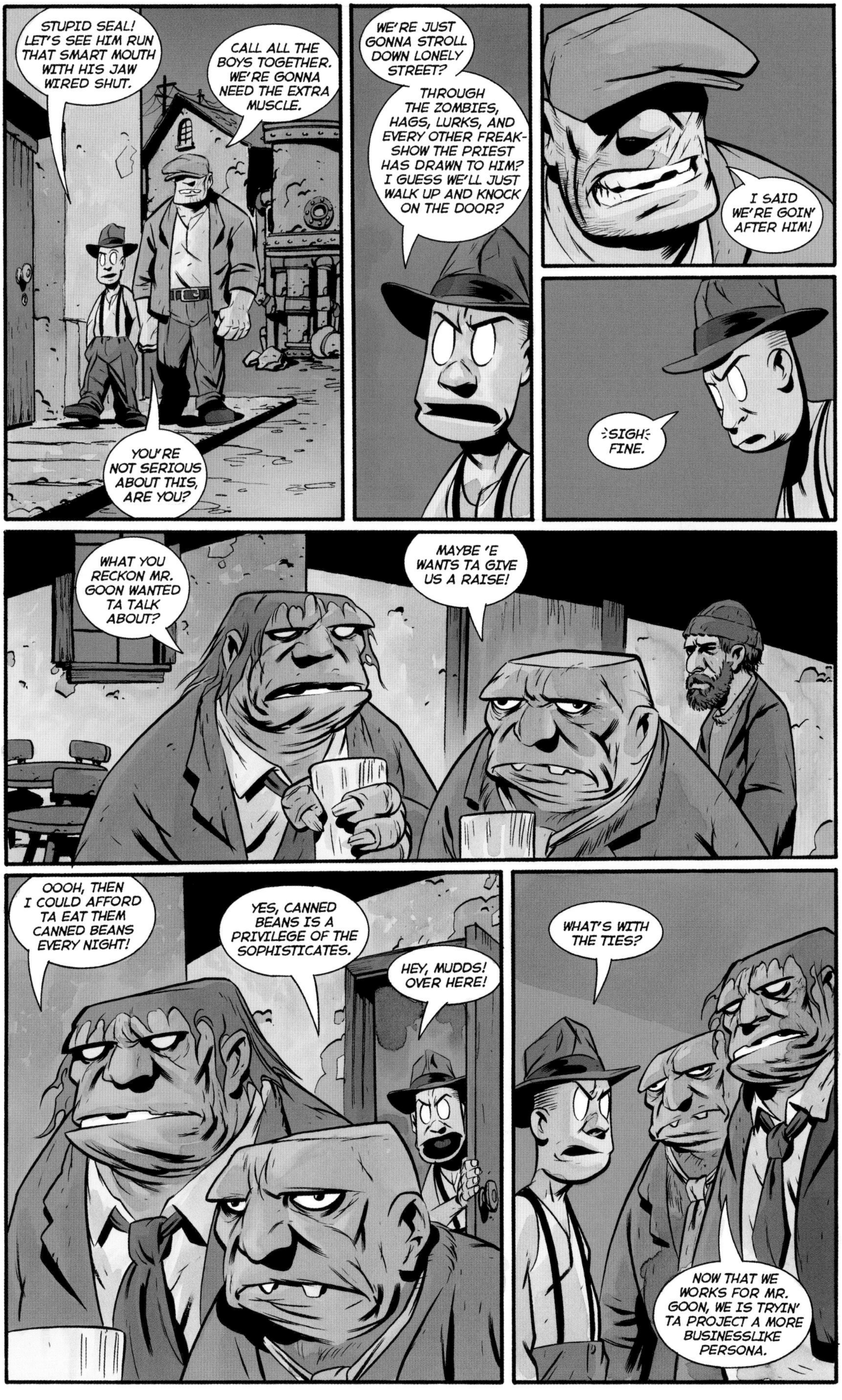

STUPID SEAL! LET'S SEE HIM RUN THAT SMART MOUTH WITH HIS JAW WIRED SHUT.
CALL ALL THE BOYS TOGETHER. WE'RE GONNA NEED THE EXTRA MUSCLE.
YOU'RE NOT SERIOUS ABOUT THIS, ARE YOU?
WE'RE JUST GONNA STROLL DOWN LONELY STREET?
THROUGH THE ZOMBIES, HAGS, LURKS, AND EVERY OTHER FREAK-SHOW THE PRIEST HAS DRAWN TO HIM? I GUESS WE'LL JUST WALK UP AND KNOCK ON THE DOOR?
I SAID WE'RE GOIN' AFTER HIM!
SIGH FINE.
WHAT YOU RECKON MR. GOON WANTED TA TALK ABOUT?
MAYBE 'E WANTS TA GIVE US A RAISE!
OOOH, THEN I COULD AFFORD TA EAT THEM CANNED BEANS EVERY NIGHT!
YES, CANNED BEANS IS A PRIVILEGE OF THE SOPHISTICATES.
HEY, MUDDS! OVER HERE!
WHAT'S WITH THE TIES?
NOW THAT WE WORKS FOR MR. GOON, WE IS TRYIN' TA PROJECT A MORE BUSINESSLIKE PERSONA.

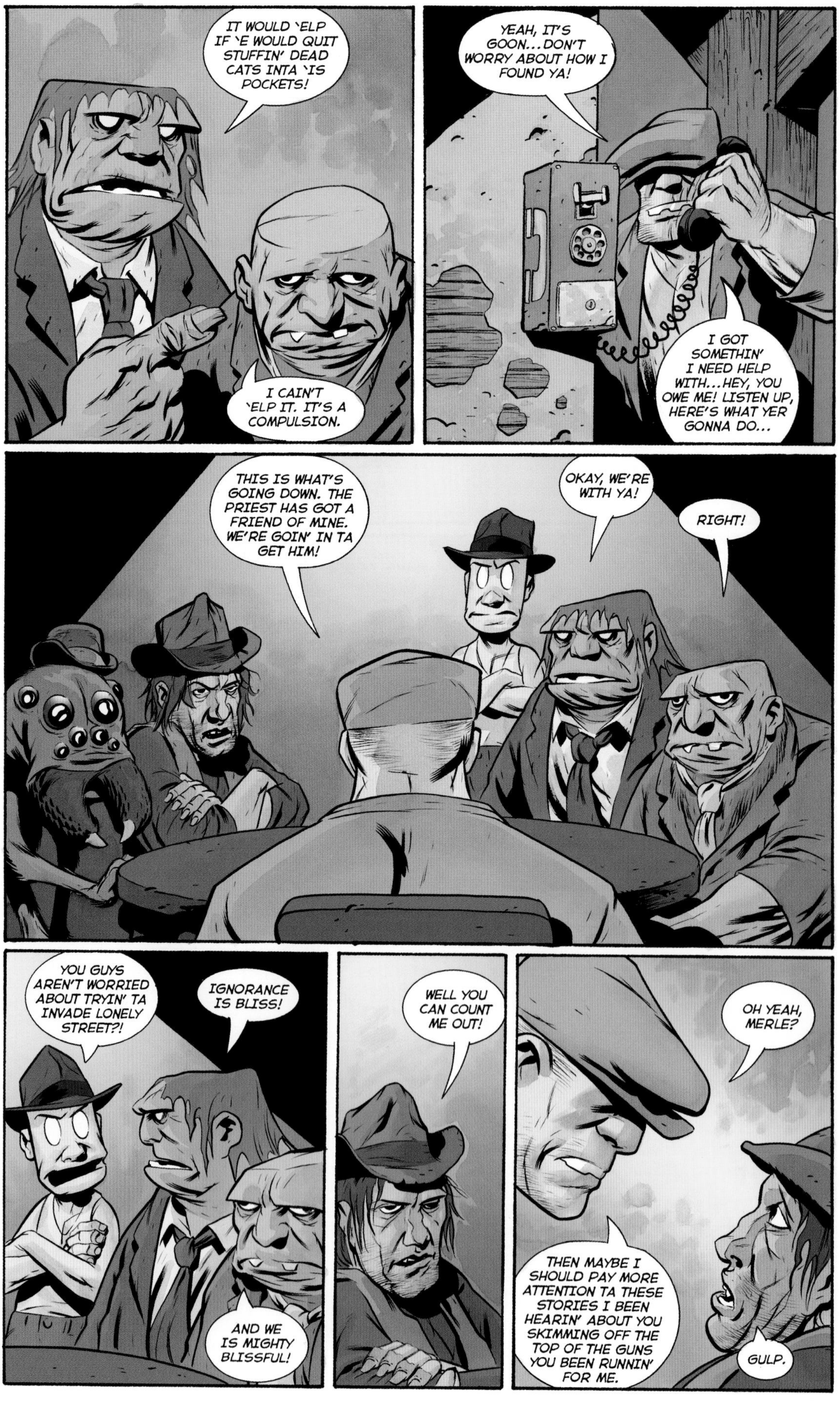
IT WOULD `ELP IF `E WOULD QUIT STUFFIN' DEAD CATS INTA `IS POCKETS!
I CAIN'T `ELP IT. IT'S A COMPULSION.
YEAH, IT'S GOON... DON'T WORRY ABOUT HOW I FOUND YA!
I GOT SOMETHIN' I NEED HELP WITH... HEY, YOU OWE ME! LISTEN UP, HERE'S WHAT YER GONNA DO...
THIS IS WHAT'S GOING DOWN. THE PRIEST HAS GOT A FRIEND OF MINE. WE'RE GOIN' IN TA GET HIM!
OKAY, WE'RE WITH YA!
RIGHT!
YOU GUYS AREN'T WORRIED ABOUT TRYIN' TA INVADE LONELY STREET?!
IGNORANCE IS BLISS!
AND WE IS MIGHTY BLISSFUL!
WELL YOU CAN COUNT ME OUT!
OH YEAH, MERLE?
THEN MAYBE I SHOULD PAY MORE ATTENTION TA THESE STORIES I BEEN HEARIN' ABOUT YOU SKIMMING OFF THE TOP OF THE GUNS YOU BEEN RUNNIN' FOR ME.
GULP.

BESIDES, ALL I WANT YOU TO DO IS BE A DIVERSION.

I JUST WANT YOU TO DRAW THE ZOMBIES OFF WHILE THE MUDDS, FRANKY, AND ME STORM THE TOWER.

YOU EXPECT ME TA HANDLE ALL THE ZOMBIES ON LONELY STREET?!

DON'T WORRY ABOUT IT. YOU'LL HAVE HELP.

WHAT ABOUT SPIDER?

SPIDER'S USELESS.

HEY!!

EVERYBODY DO WHAT YOU GOTTA DO TO GET READY. WE'RE GOING TONIGHT!

I'M SORRY!

SHERIFF, WHY DIDN'T YOU COME HELP ME WHEN DADDY GOT THE FEVER AND DIED? I WAS ALL ALONE.

DADDY WAS DEAD, BUT HE GOT UP. HE GOT UP AND CAME AFTER ME, SHERIFF.

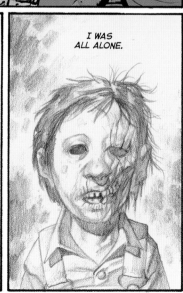

I WAS ALL ALONE.

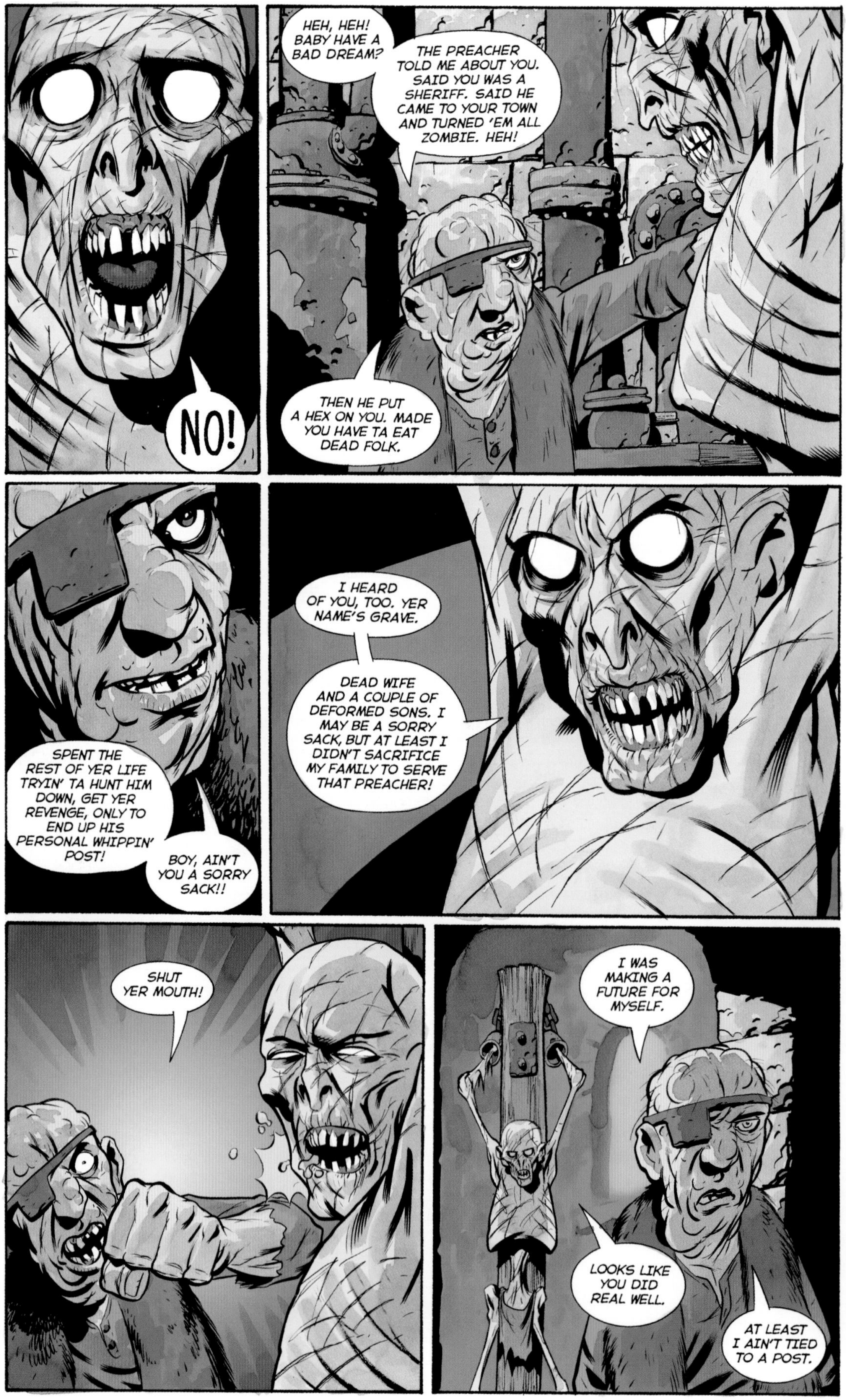
NO!
HEH, HEH! BABY HAVE A BAD DREAM?
THE PREACHER TOLD ME ABOUT YOU. SAID YOU WAS A SHERIFF. SAID HE CAME TO YOUR TOWN AND TURNED 'EM ALL ZOMBIE. HEH!
THEN HE PUT A HEX ON YOU. MADE YOU HAVE TA EAT DEAD FOLK.
SPENT THE REST OF YER LIFE TRYIN' TA HUNT HIM DOWN, GET YER REVENGE, ONLY TO END UP HIS PERSONAL WHIPPIN' POST!
BOY, AIN'T YOU A SORRY SACK!!
I HEARD OF YOU, TOO. YER NAME'S GRAVE.
DEAD WIFE AND A COUPLE OF DEFORMED SONS. I MAY BE A SORRY SACK, BUT AT LEAST I DIDN'T SACRIFICE MY FAMILY TO SERVE THAT PREACHER!
SHUT YER MOUTH!
I WAS MAKING A FUTURE FOR MYSELF.
LOOKS LIKE YOU DID REAL WELL.
AT LEAST I AIN'T TIED TO A POST.

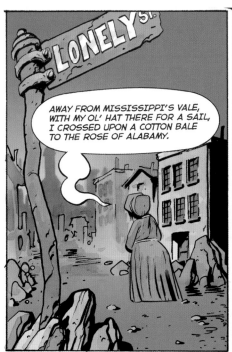

AWAY FROM MISSISSIPPI'S VALE, WITH MY OL' HAT THERE FOR A SAIL, I CROSSED UPON A COTTON BALE TO THE ROSE OF ALABAMY.

OH, SWEET ROSIE, THE ROSE OF ALABAMY. A SWEET TOBACCO POSEY IS MY ROSE OF ALABAMY.

THAT GUY BETTER SHOW UP, GOON!

YOU BOYS WOULDN'T DARE DREAM OF CHEWIN' ON LITTLE OL' ME, WOULD YA?

WOULD YA?!!

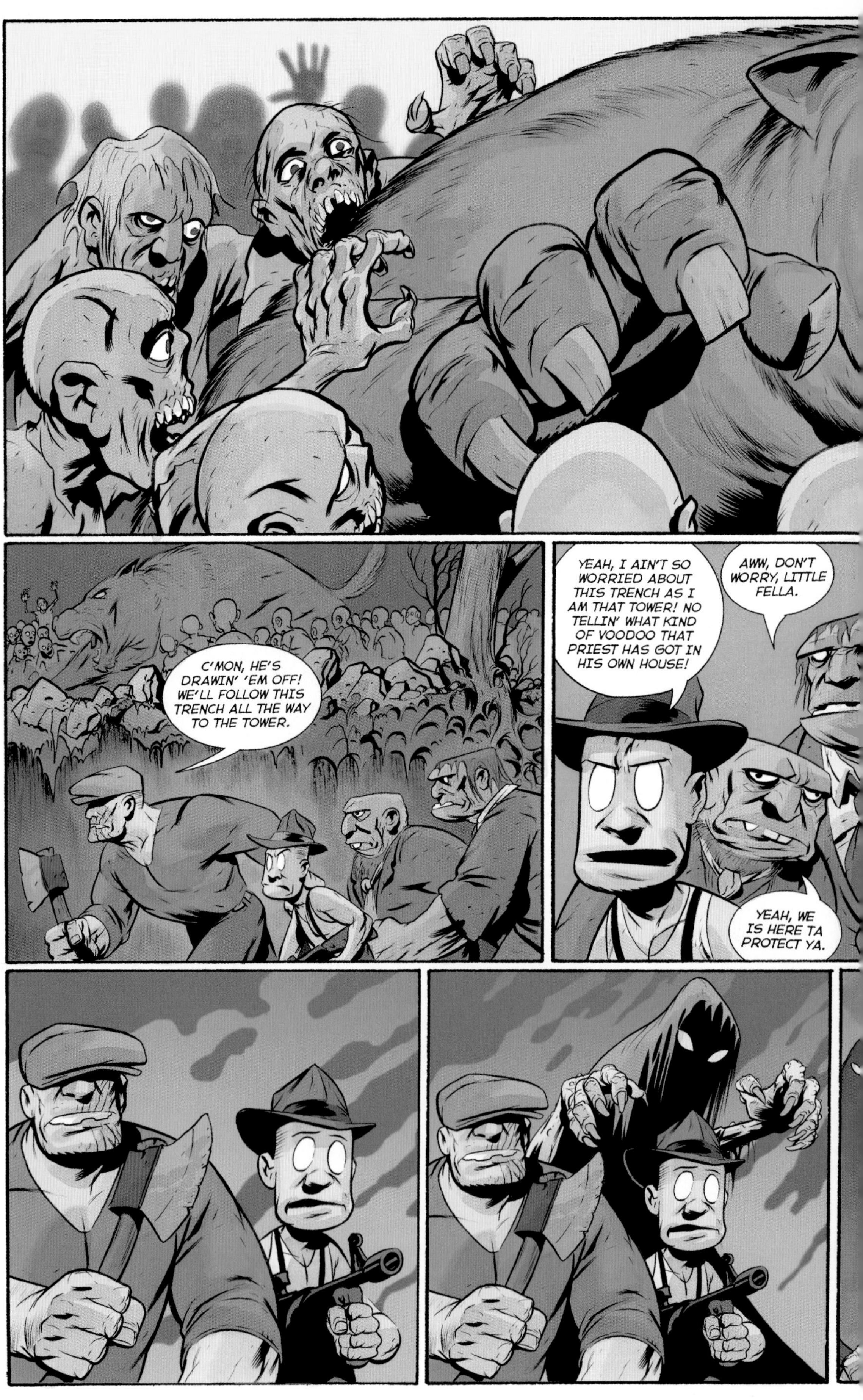
C'MON, HE'S DRAWIN' 'EM OFF! WE'LL FOLLOW THIS TRENCH ALL THE WAY TO THE TOWER.
YEAH, I AIN'T SO WORRIED ABOUT THIS TRENCH AS I AM THAT TOWER! NO TELLIN' WHAT KIND OF VOODOO THAT PRIEST HAS GOT IN HIS OWN HOUSE!
AWW, DON'T WORRY, LITTLE FELLA.
YEAH, WE IS HERE TA PROTECT YA.

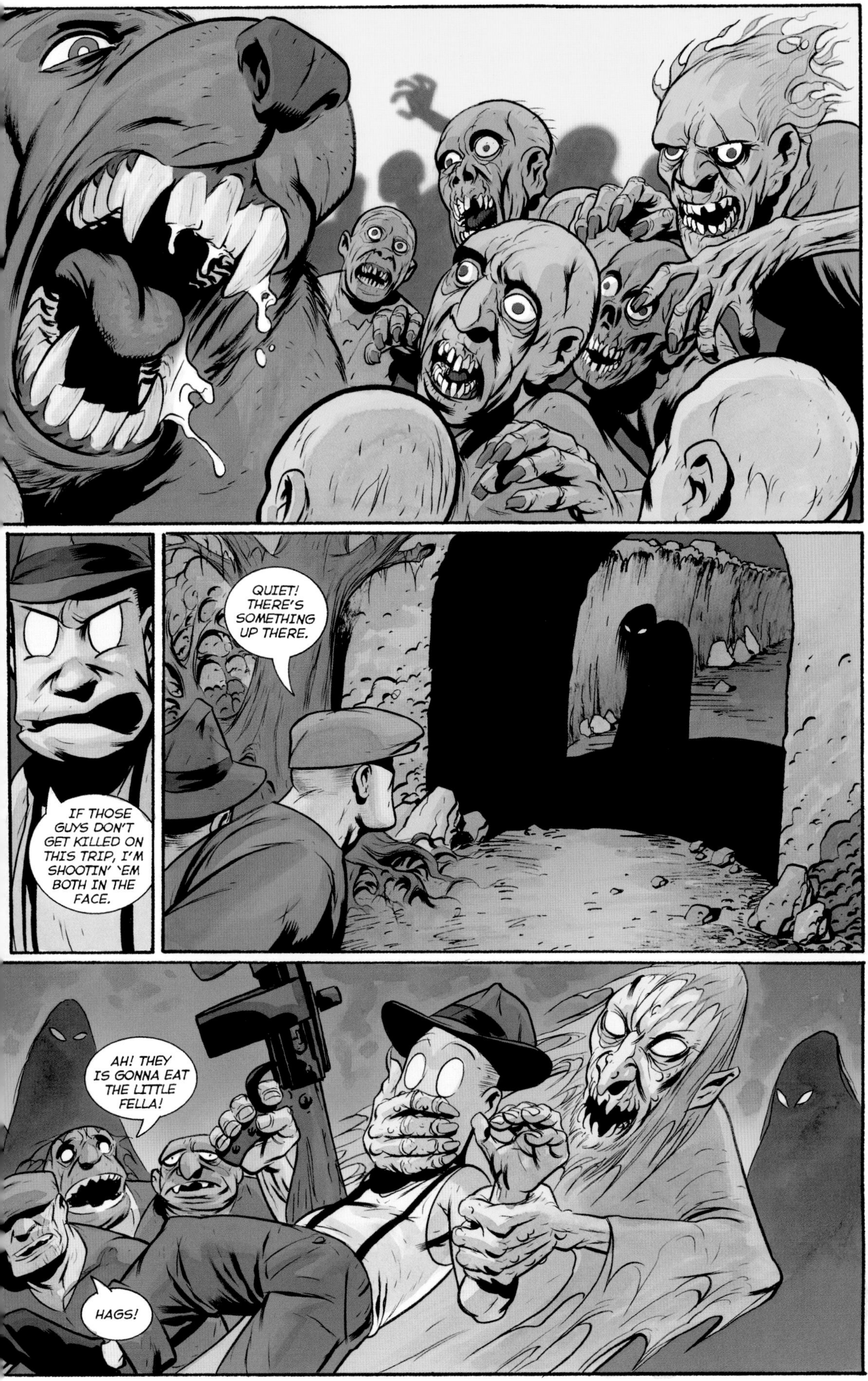
QUIET! THERE'S SOMETHING UP THERE.
IF THOSE GUYS DON'T GET KILLED ON THIS TRIP, I'M SHOOTIN' 'EM BOTH IN THE FACE.
AH! THEY IS GONNA EAT THE LITTLE FELLA!
HAGS!

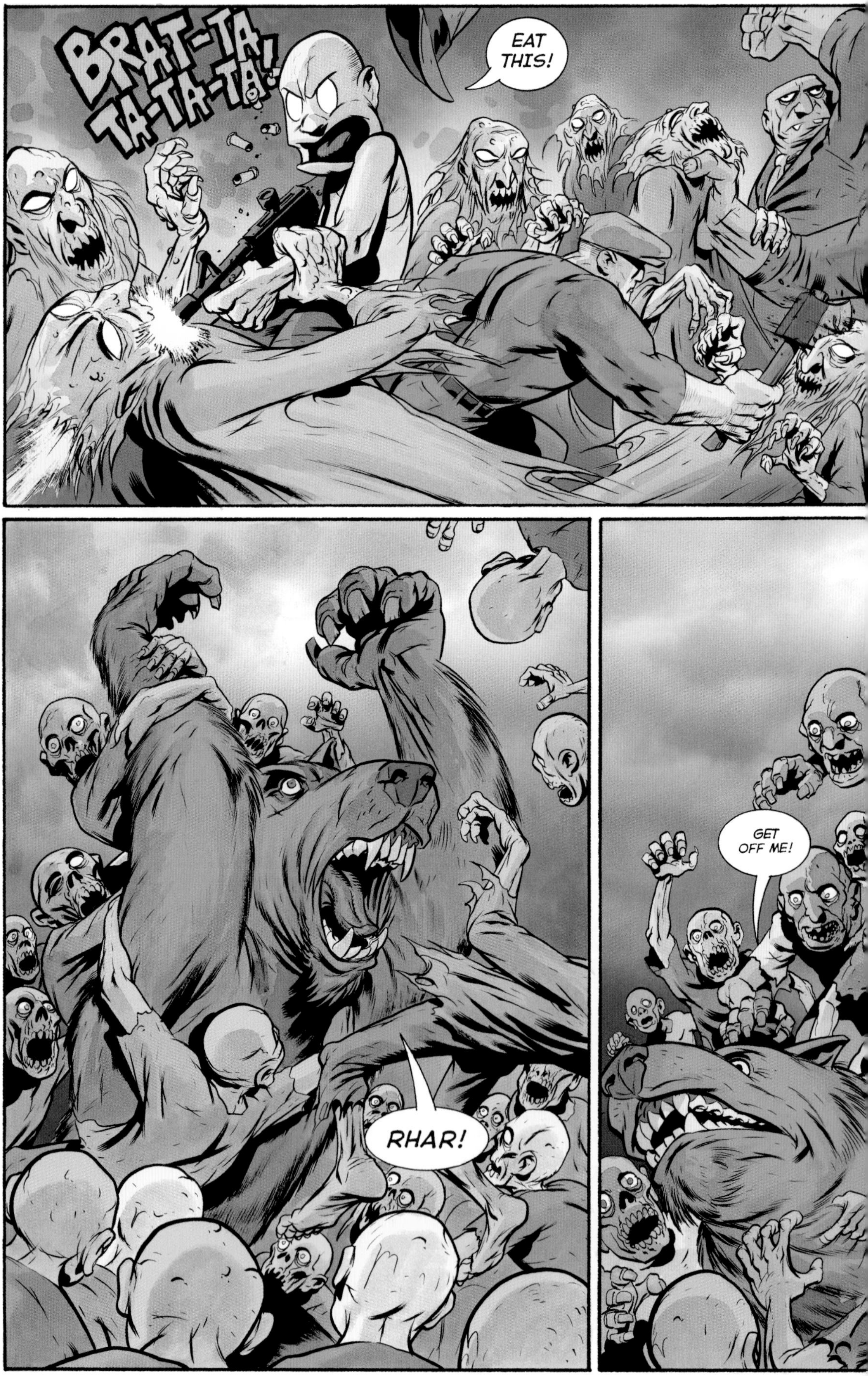
BRAT-TA TA-TA-TA!
EAT THIS!
RHAR!
GET OFF ME!

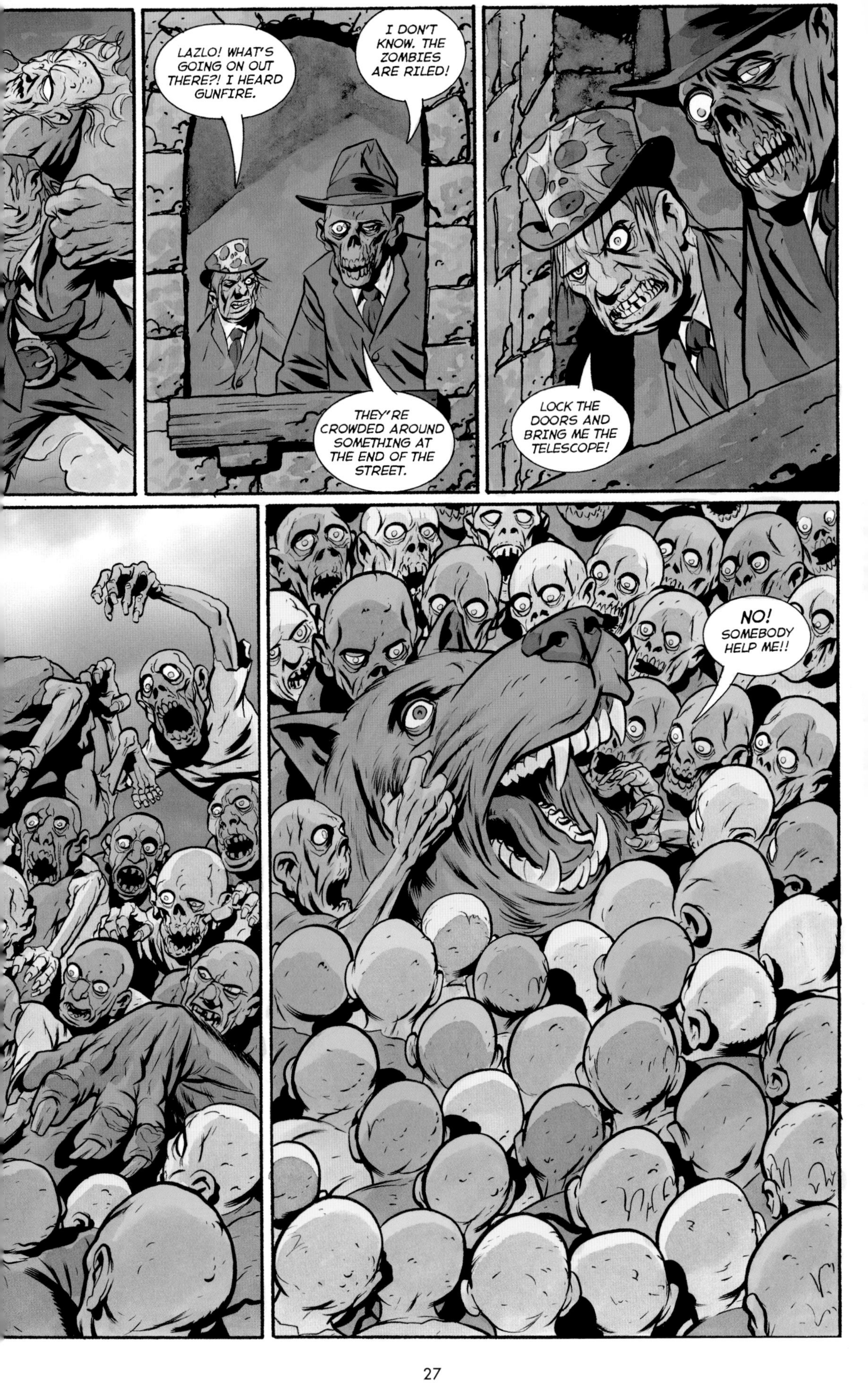
LAZLO! WHAT'S GOING ON OUT THERE?! I HEARD GUNFIRE.
I DON'T KNOW. THE ZOMBIES ARE RILED!
THEY'RE CROWDED AROUND SOMETHING AT THE END OF THE STREET.
LOCK THE DOORS AND BRING ME THE TELESCOPE!
NO! SOMEBODY HELP ME!!

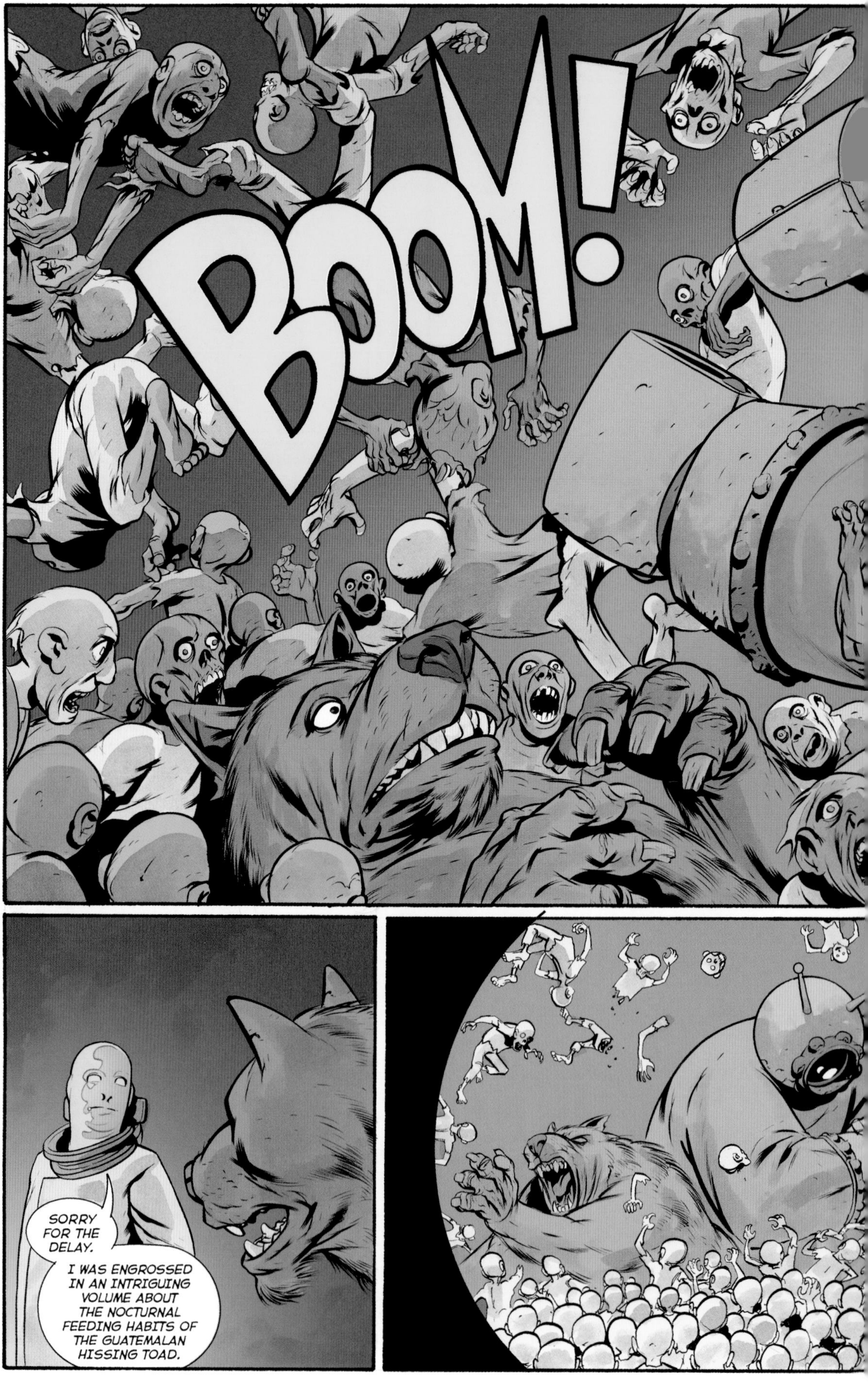
BOOM!
SORRY FOR THE DELAY.
I WAS ENGROSSED IN AN INTRIGUING VOLUME ABOUT THE NOCTURNAL FEEDING HABITS OF THE GUATEMALAN HISSING TOAD.

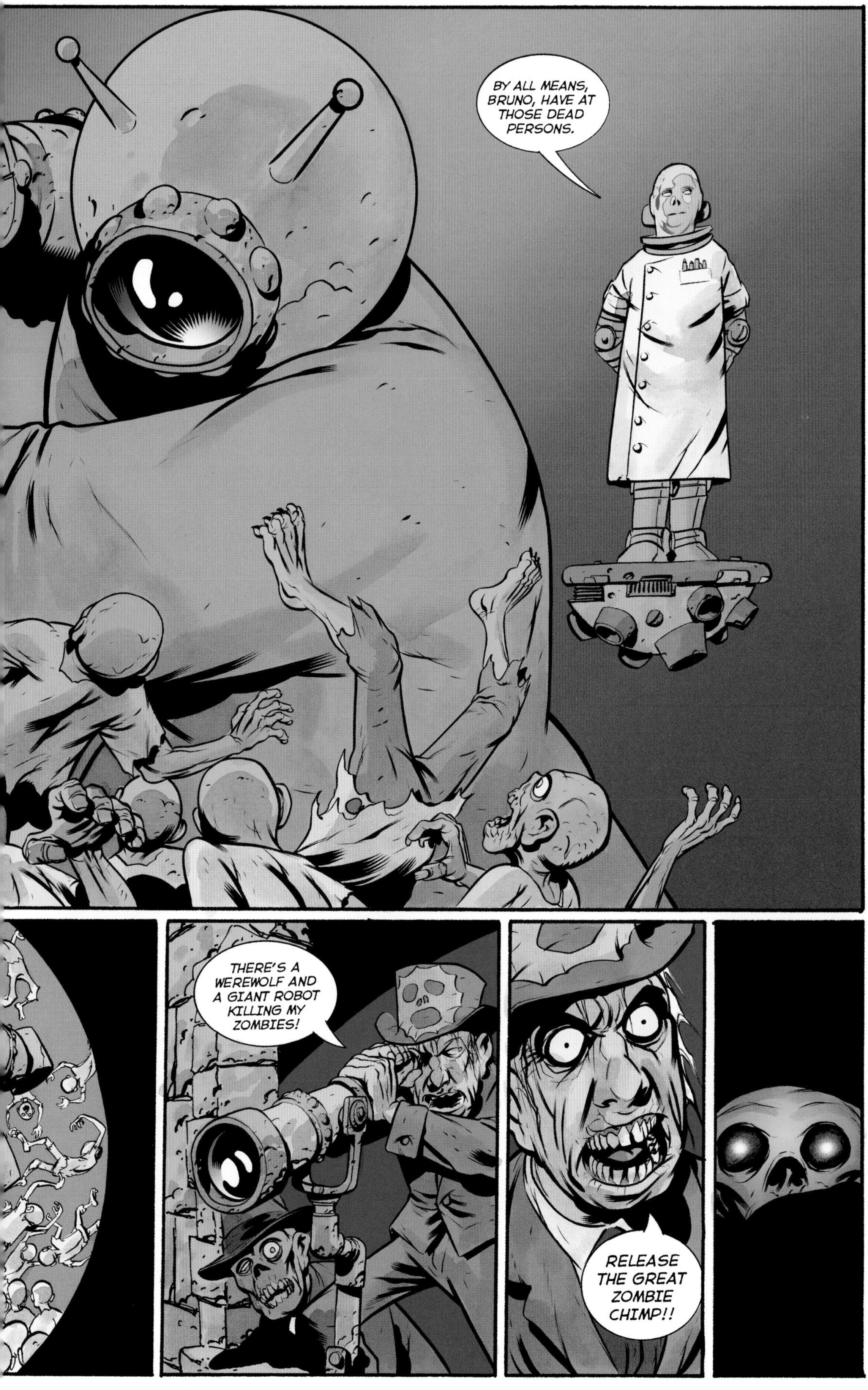

BY ALL MEANS, BRUNO, HAVE AT THOSE DEAD PERSONS.
THERE'S A WEREWOLF AND A GIANT ROBOT KILLING MY ZOMBIES!
RELEASE THE GREAT ZOMBIE CHIMP!!

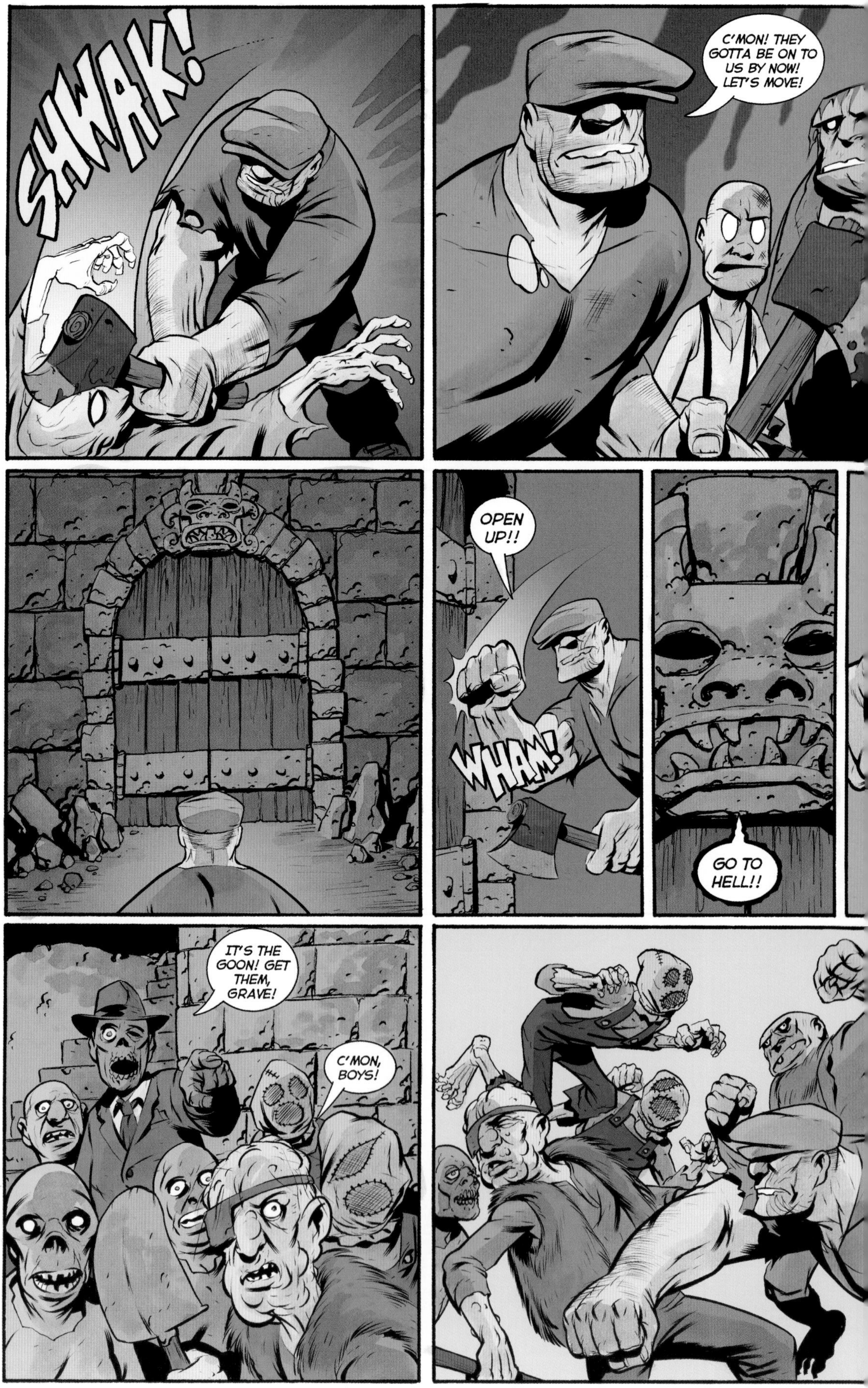
SHWAK!
C'MON! THEY GOTTA BE ON TO US BY NOW! LET'S MOVE!
OPEN UP!!
WHAM!
GO TO HELL!!
IT'S THE GOON! GET THEM, GRAVE!
C'MON, BOYS!

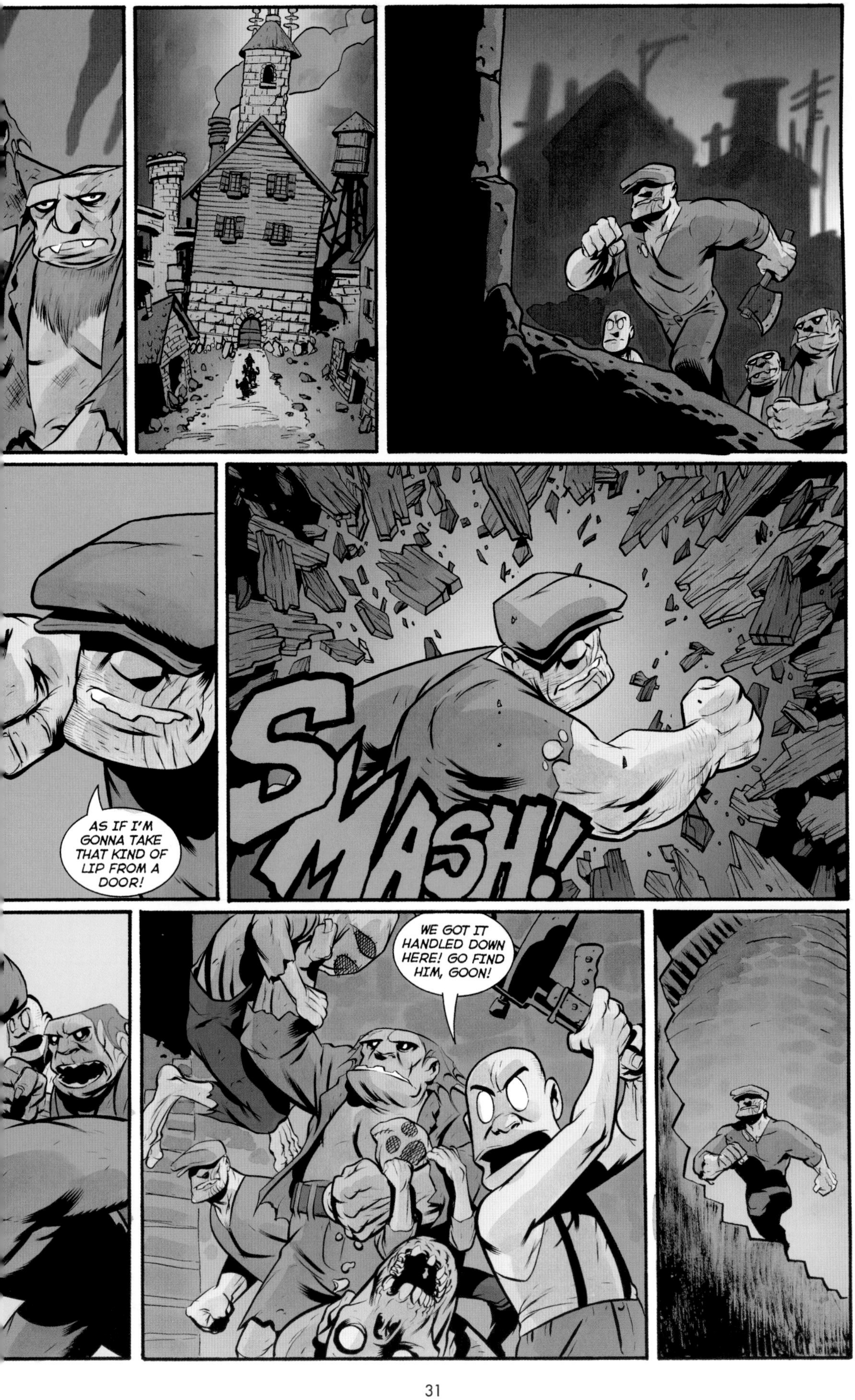
AS IF I'M GONNA TAKE THAT KIND OF LIP FROM A DOOR!
SMASH!
WE GOT IT HANDLED DOWN HERE! GO FIND HIM, GOON!

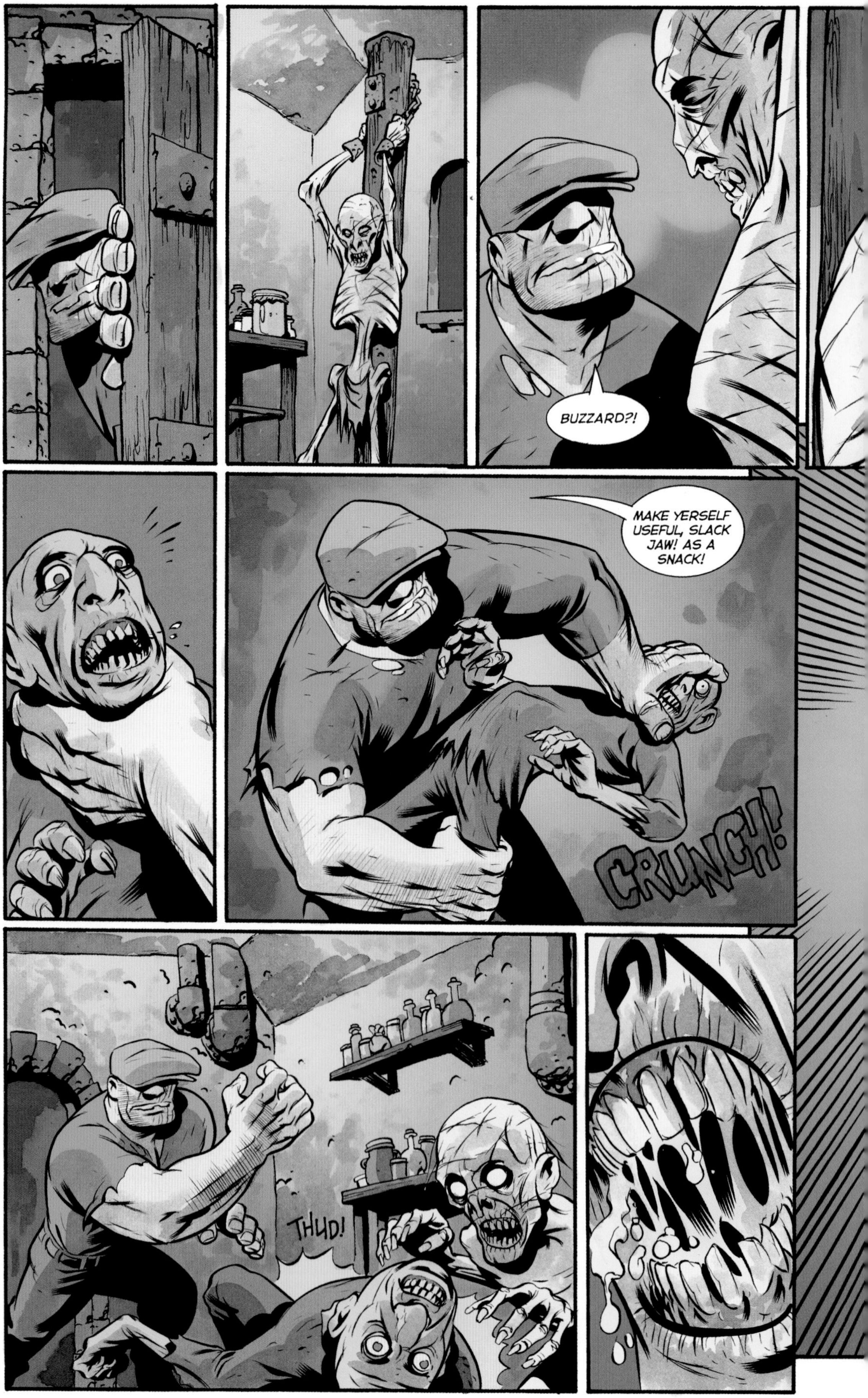
BUZZARD?!
MAKE YERSELF USEFUL, SLACK JAW! AS A SNACK!
CRUNCH!
THUD!

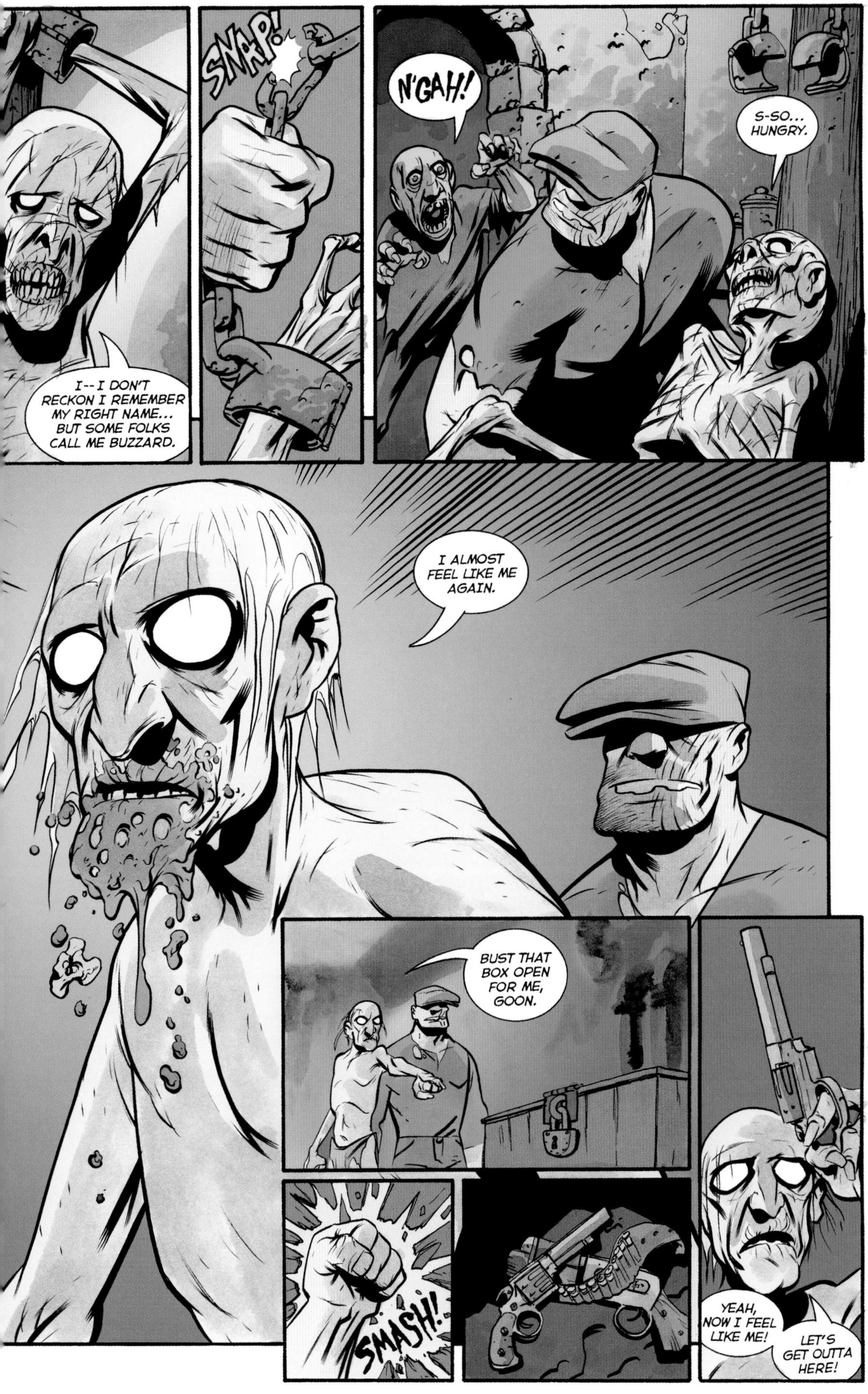
I-- I DON'T RECKON I REMEMBER MY RIGHT NAME... BUT SOME FOLKS CALL ME BUZZARD.
SNAP!
N'GAH!
S-SO... HUNGRY.
I ALMOST FEEL LIKE ME AGAIN.
BUST THAT BOX OPEN FOR ME, GOON.
SMASH!
YEAH, NOW I FEEL LIKE ME!
LET'S GET OUTTA HERE!

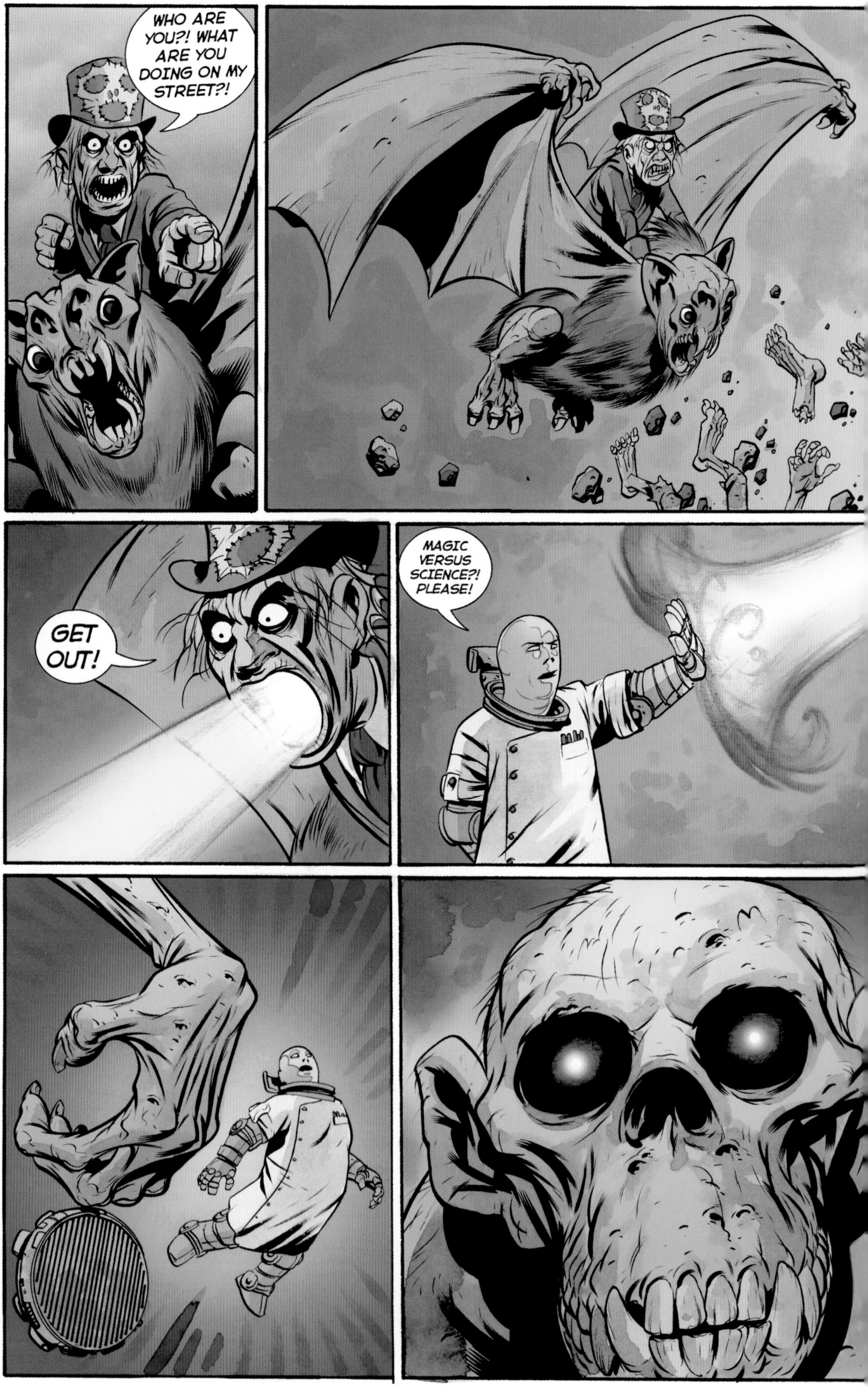
WHO ARE YOU?! WHAT ARE YOU DOING ON MY STREET?!
GET OUT!
MAGIC VERSUS SCIENCE?! PLEASE!

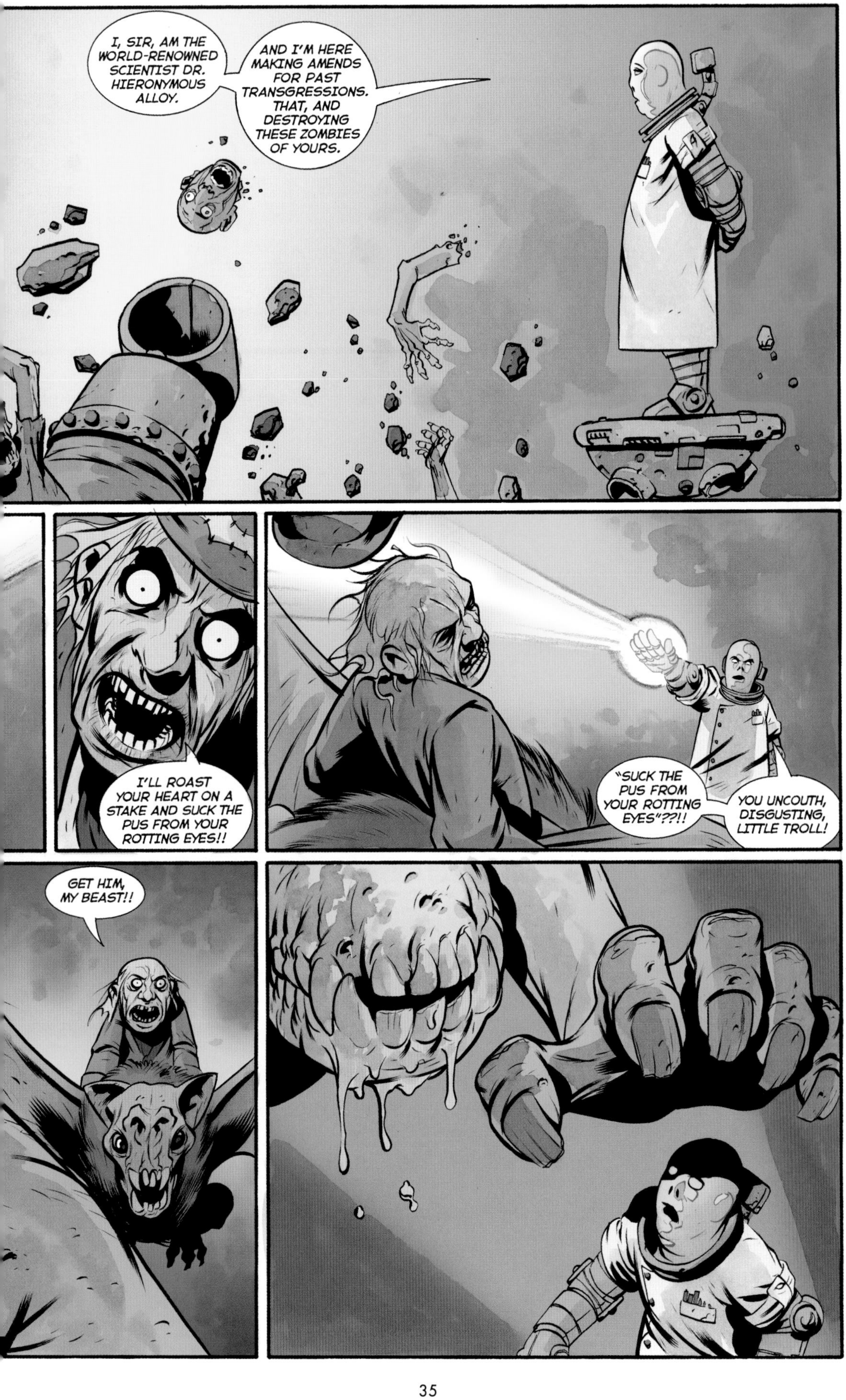
I, SIR, AM THE WORLD-RENOWNED SCIENTIST DR. HIERONYMOUS ALLOY.
AND I'M HERE MAKING AMENDS FOR PAST TRANSGRESSIONS. THAT, AND DESTROYING THESE ZOMBIES OF YOURS.
I'LL ROAST YOUR HEART ON A STAKE AND SUCK THE PUS FROM YOUR ROTTING EYES!!
"SUCK THE PUS FROM YOUR ROTTING EYES"??!!
YOU UNCOUTH, DISGUSTING, LITTLE TROLL!
GET HIM, MY BEAST!!

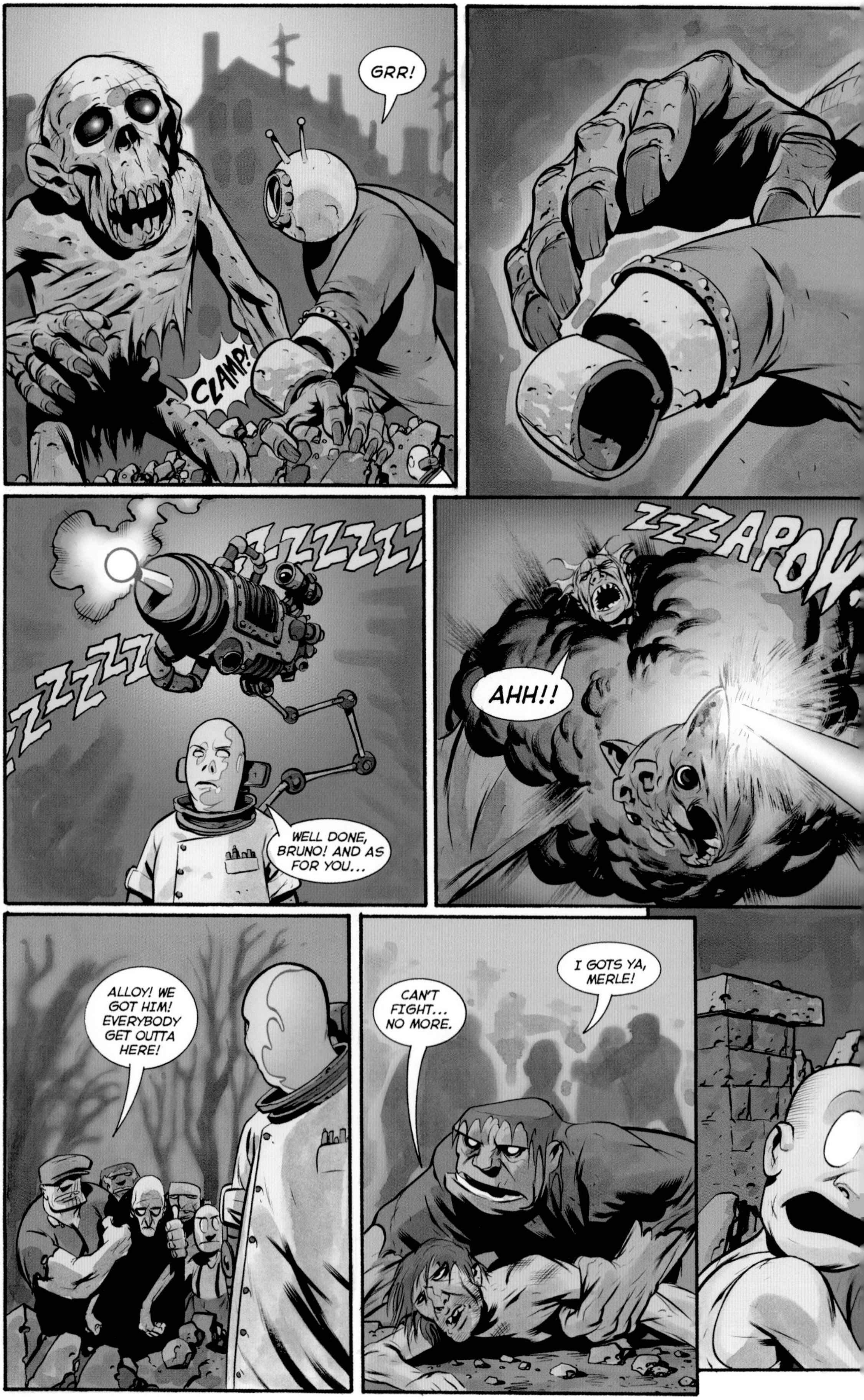
GRR!
CLAMP!
ZZZZZZZT
ZZZZZZZT
WELL DONE, BRUNO! AND AS FOR YOU...
ZZZAPOW
AHH!!
ALLOY! WE GOT HIM! EVERYBODY GET OUTTA HERE!
CAN'T FIGHT... NO MORE.
I GOTS YA, MERLE!

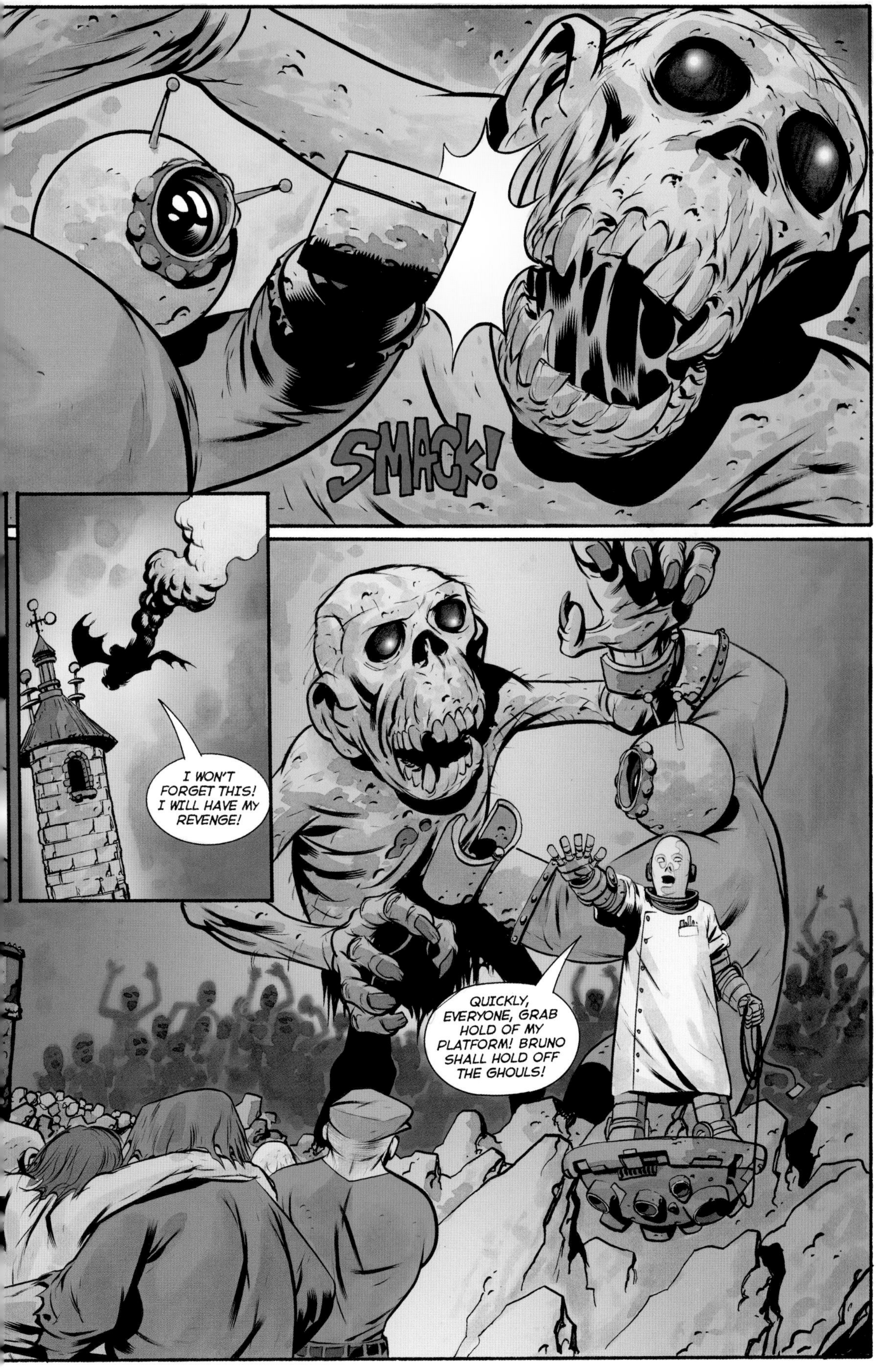
SMACK!
I WON'T FORGET THIS! I WILL HAVE MY REVENGE!
QUICKLY, EVERYONE, GRAB HOLD OF MY PLATFORM! BRUNO SHALL HOLD OFF THE GHOULS!

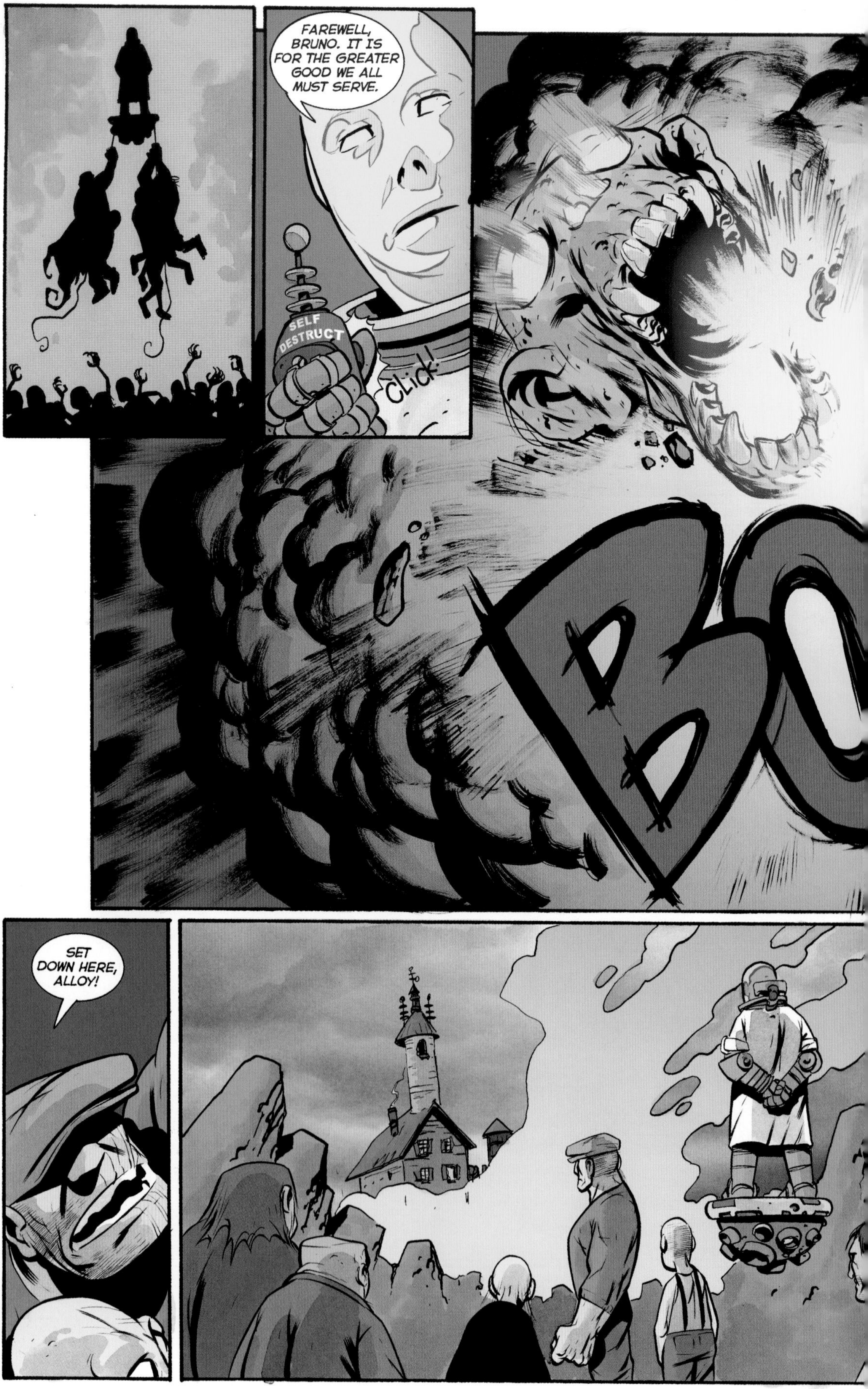
FAREWELL, BRUNO. IT IS FOR THE GREATER GOOD WE ALL MUST SERVE.
SELF DESTRUCT
CLICK
SET DOWN HERE, ALLOY!

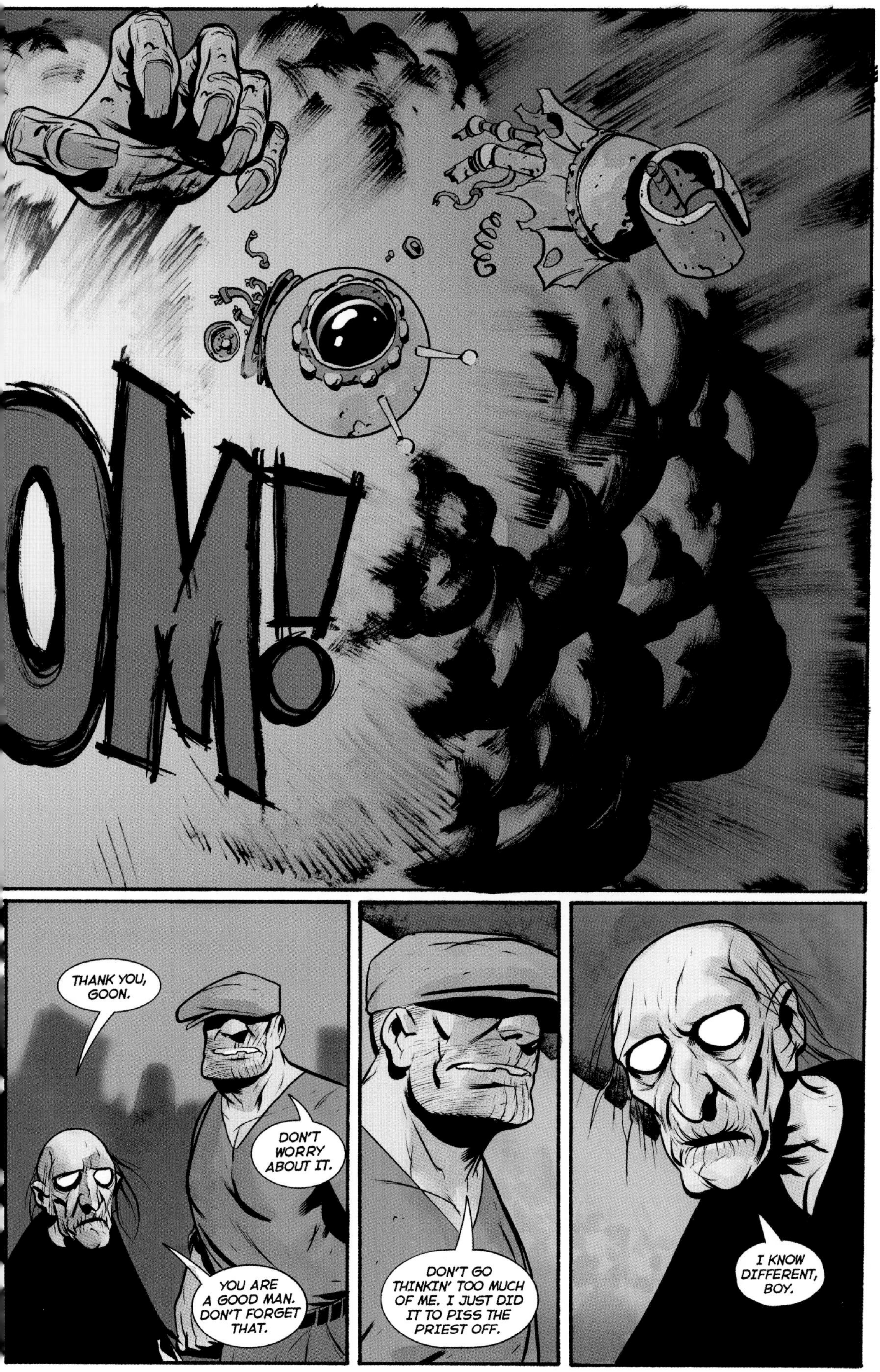
OM!
THANK YOU, GOON.
DON'T WORRY ABOUT IT.
YOU ARE A GOOD MAN. DON'T FORGET THAT.
DON'T GO THINKIN' TOO MUCH OF ME. I JUST DID IT TO PISS THE PRIEST OFF.
I KNOW DIFFERENT, BOY.

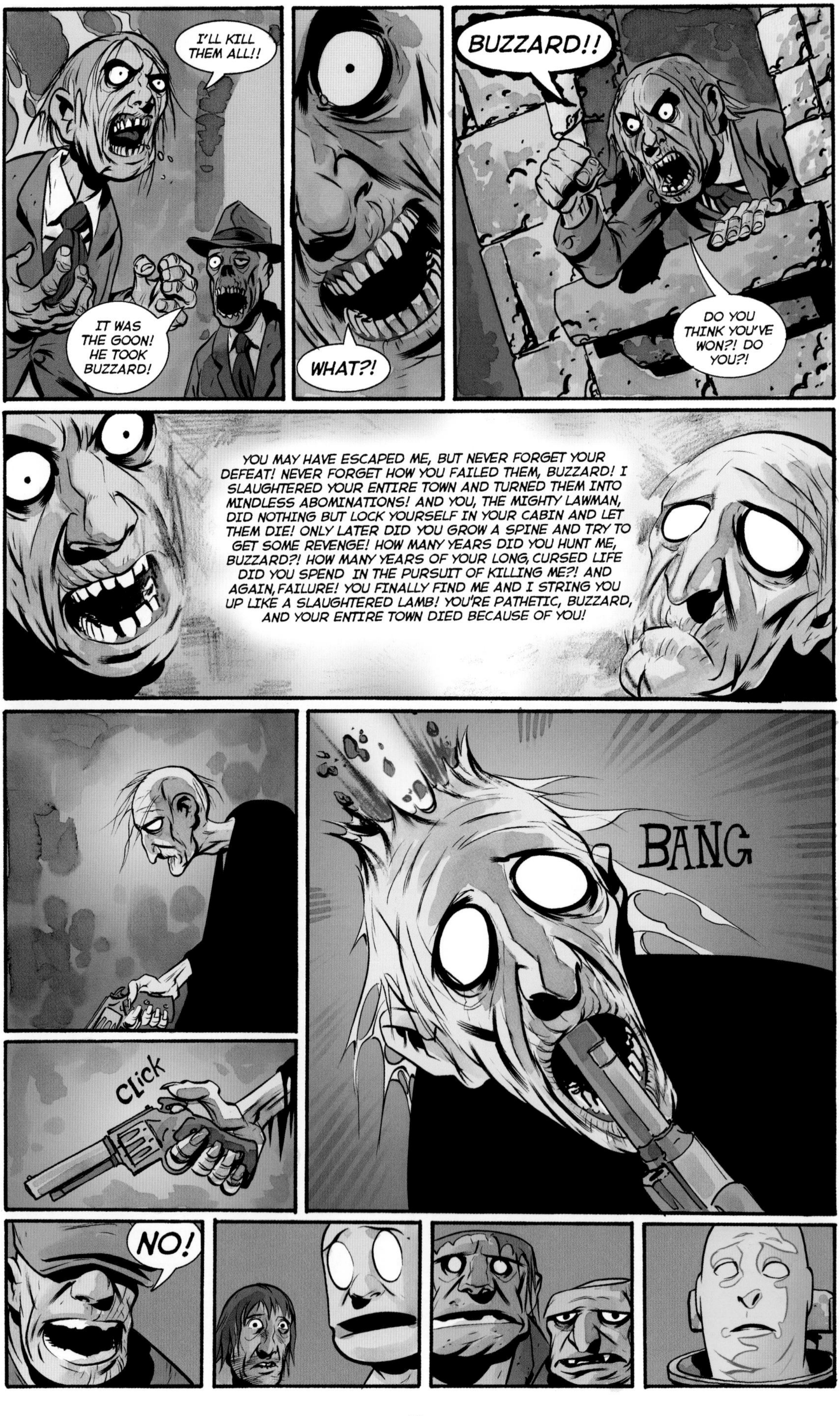
I'LL KILL THEM ALL!!
IT WAS THE GOON! HE TOOK BUZZARD!
WHAT?!
BUZZARD!!
DO YOU THINK YOU'VE WON?! DO YOU?!
YOU MAY HAVE ESCAPED ME, BUT NEVER FORGET YOUR DEFEAT! NEVER FORGET HOW YOU FAILED THEM, BUZZARD! I SLAUGHTERED YOUR ENTIRE TOWN AND TURNED THEM INTO MINDLESS ABOMINATIONS! AND YOU, THE MIGHTY LAWMAN, DID NOTHING BUT LOCK YOURSELF IN YOUR CABIN AND LET THEM DIE! ONLY LATER DID YOU GROW A SPINE AND TRY TO GET SOME REVENGE! HOW MANY YEARS DID YOU HUNT ME, BUZZARD?! HOW MANY YEARS OF YOUR LONG, CURSED LIFE DID YOU SPEND IN THE PURSUIT OF KILLING ME?! AND AGAIN, FAILURE! YOU FINALLY FIND ME AND I STRING YOU UP LIKE A SLAUGHTERED LAMB! YOU'RE PATHETIC, BUZZARD, AND YOUR ENTIRE TOWN DIED BECAUSE OF YOU!
CLICK
BANG
NO!

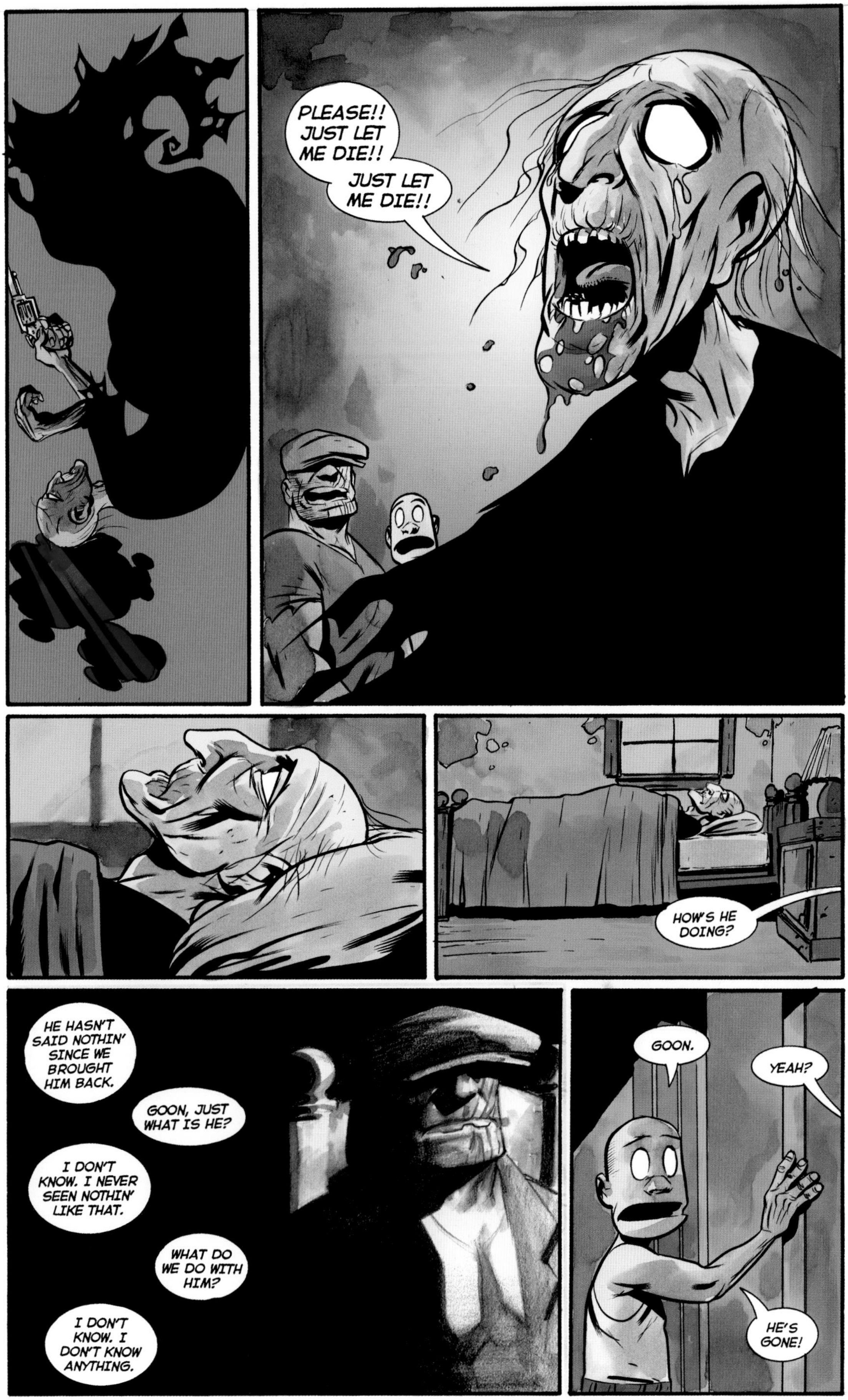

PLEASE!! JUST LET ME DIE!!
JUST LET ME DIE!!
HOW'S HE DOING?
HE HASN'T SAID NOTHIN' SINCE WE BROUGHT HIM BACK.
GOON, JUST WHAT IS HE?
I DON'T KNOW. I NEVER SEEN NOTHIN' LIKE THAT.
WHAT DO WE DO WITH HIM?
I DON'T KNOW. I DON'T KNOW ANYTHING.
GOON.
YEAH?
HE'S GONE!

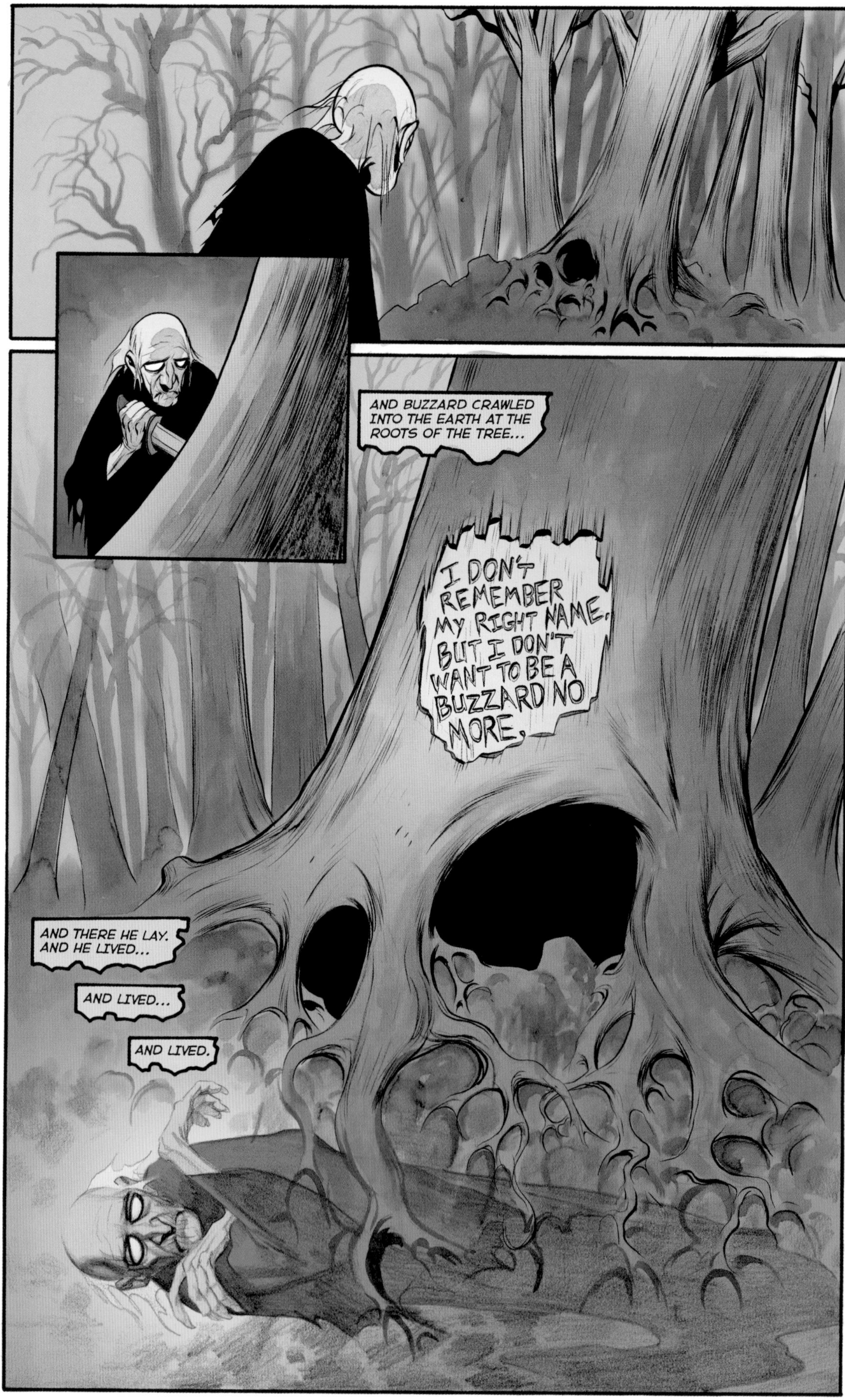

AND BUZZARD CRAWLED INTO THE EARTH AT THE ROOTS OF THE TREE...
I DON'T REMEMBER MY RIGHT NAME, BUT I DON'T WANT TO BE A BUZZARD NO MORE,
AND THERE HE LAY. AND HE LIVED...
AND LIVED...
AND LIVED.

CHAPTER 2

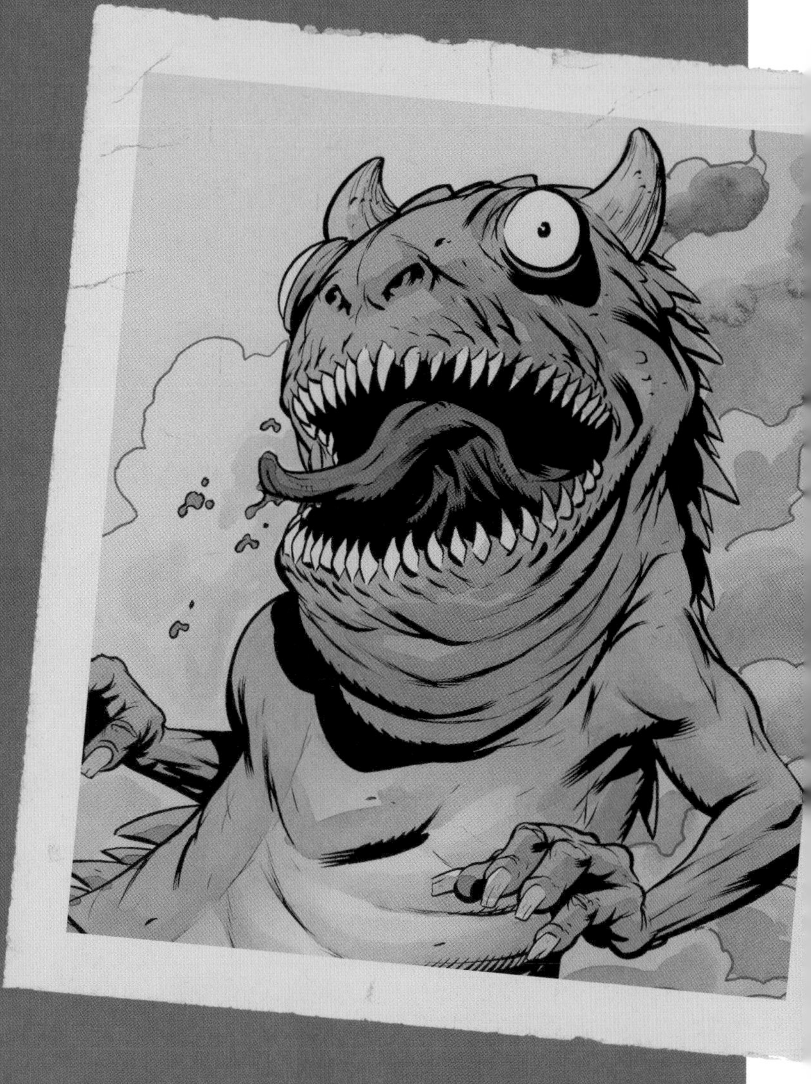

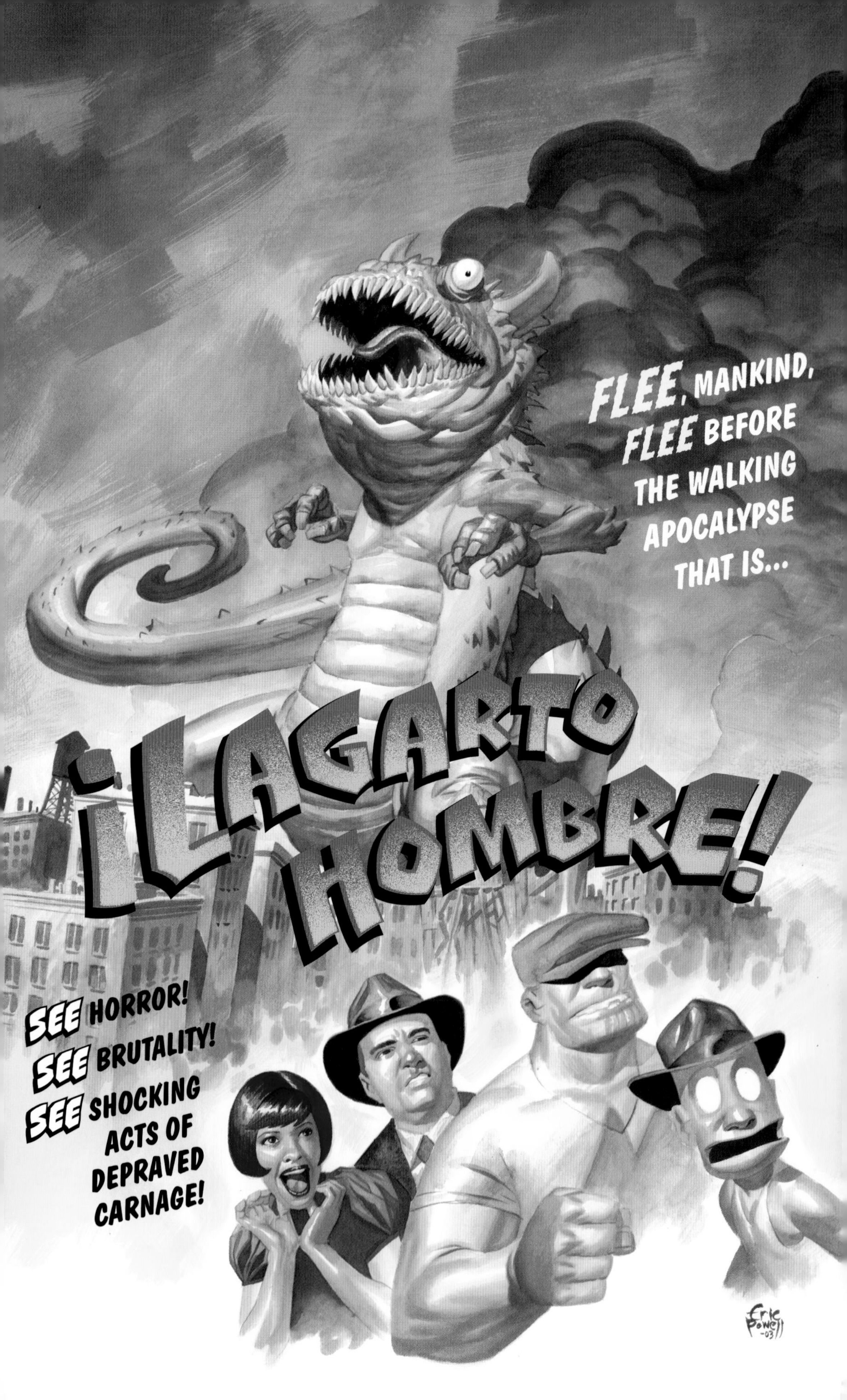

FLEE, MANKIND, FLEE BEFORE THE WALKING APOCALYPSE THAT IS...
¡LAGARTO HOMBRE!
SEE HORROR!
SEE BRUTALITY!
SEE SHOCKING ACTS OF DEPRAVED CARNAGE!
Eric Powell -03

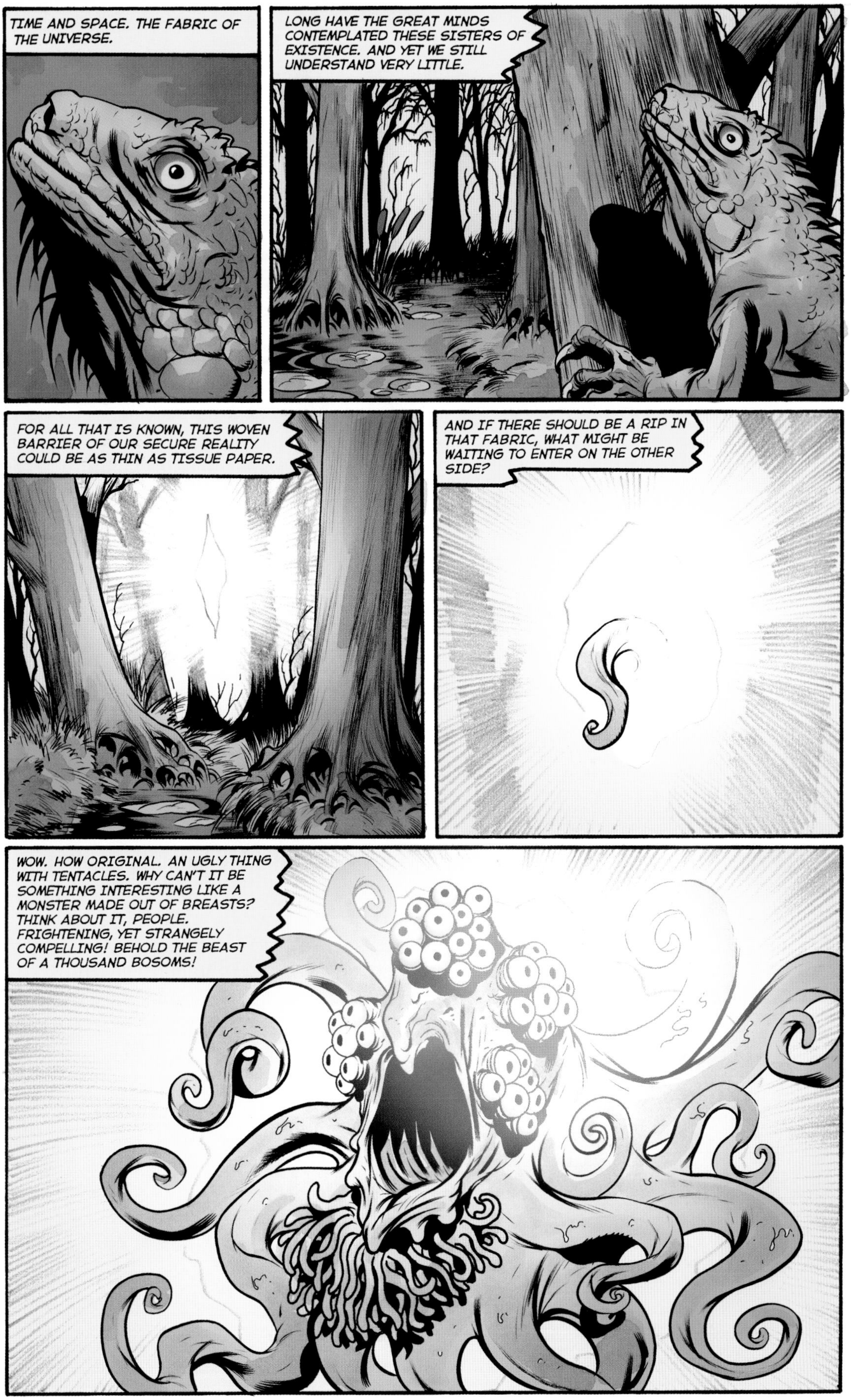
TIME AND SPACE. THE FABRIC OF THE UNIVERSE.
LONG HAVE THE GREAT MINDS CONTEMPLATED THESE SISTERS OF EXISTENCE. AND YET WE STILL UNDERSTAND VERY LITTLE.
FOR ALL THAT IS KNOWN, THIS WOVEN BARRIER OF OUR SECURE REALITY COULD BE AS THIN AS TISSUE PAPER.
AND IF THERE SHOULD BE A RIP IN THAT FABRIC, WHAT MIGHT BE WAITING TO ENTER ON THE OTHER SIDE?
WOW. HOW ORIGINAL. AN UGLY THING WITH TENTACLES. WHY CAN'T IT BE SOMETHING INTERESTING LIKE A MONSTER MADE OUT OF BREASTS? THINK ABOUT IT, PEOPLE. FRIGHTENING, YET STRANGELY COMPELLING! BEHOLD THE BEAST OF A THOUSAND BOSOMS!

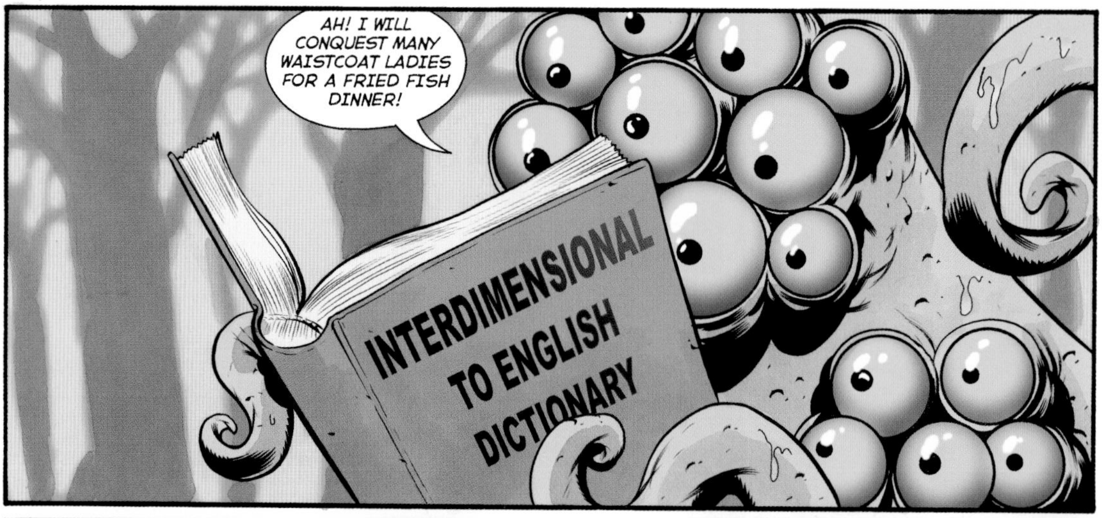
AH! I WILL CONQUEST MANY WAISTCOAT LADIES FOR A FRIED FISH DINNER!
INTERDIMENSIONAL TO ENGLISH DICTIONARY

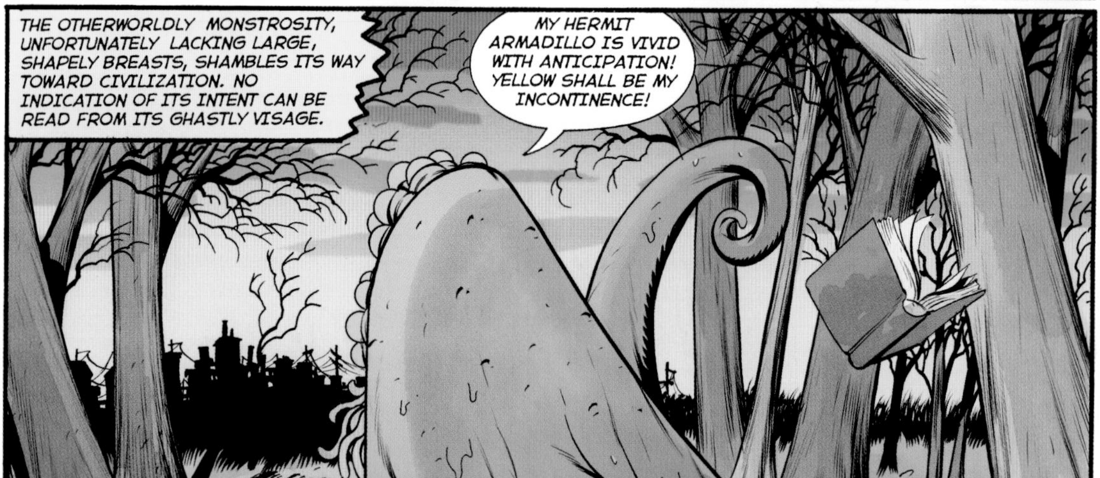
THE OTHERWORLDLY MONSTROSITY, UNFORTUNATELY LACKING LARGE, SHAPELY BREASTS, SHAMBLES ITS WAY TOWARD CIVILIZATION. NO INDICATION OF ITS INTENT CAN BE READ FROM ITS GHASTLY VISAGE.
MY HERMIT ARMADILLO IS VIVID WITH ANTICIPATION! YELLOW SHALL BE MY INCONTINENCE!

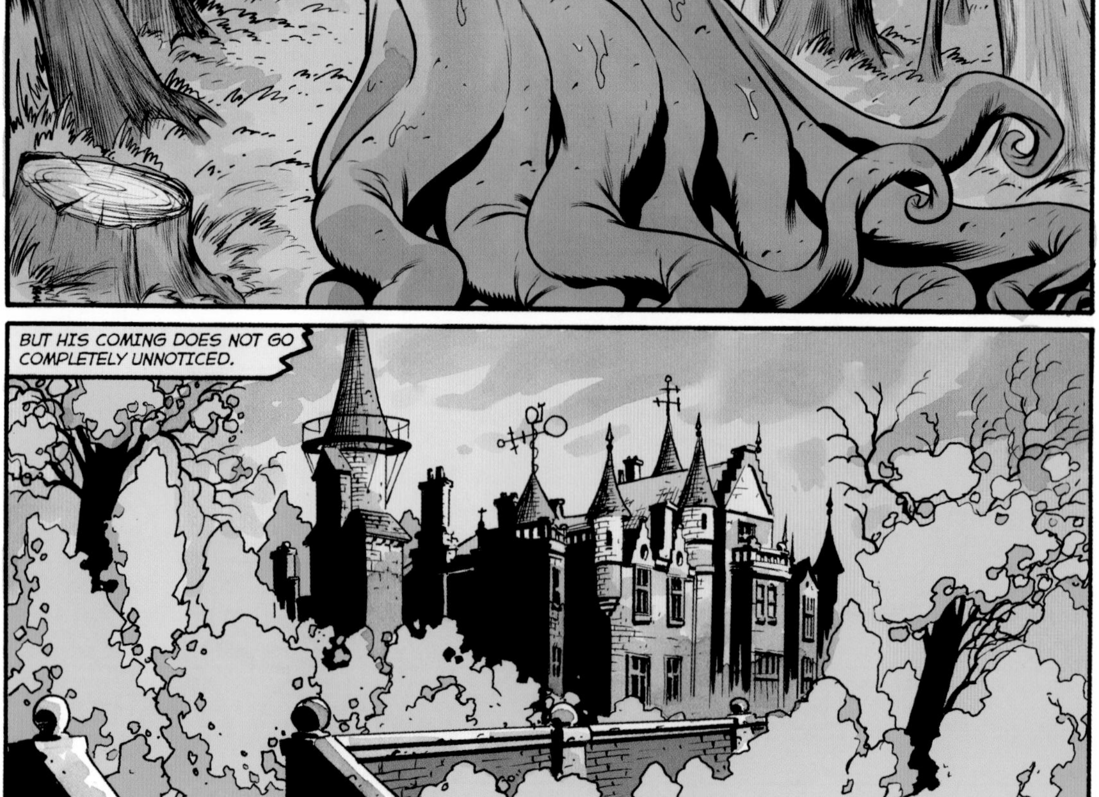
BUT HIS COMING DOES NOT GO COMPLETELY UNNOTICED.

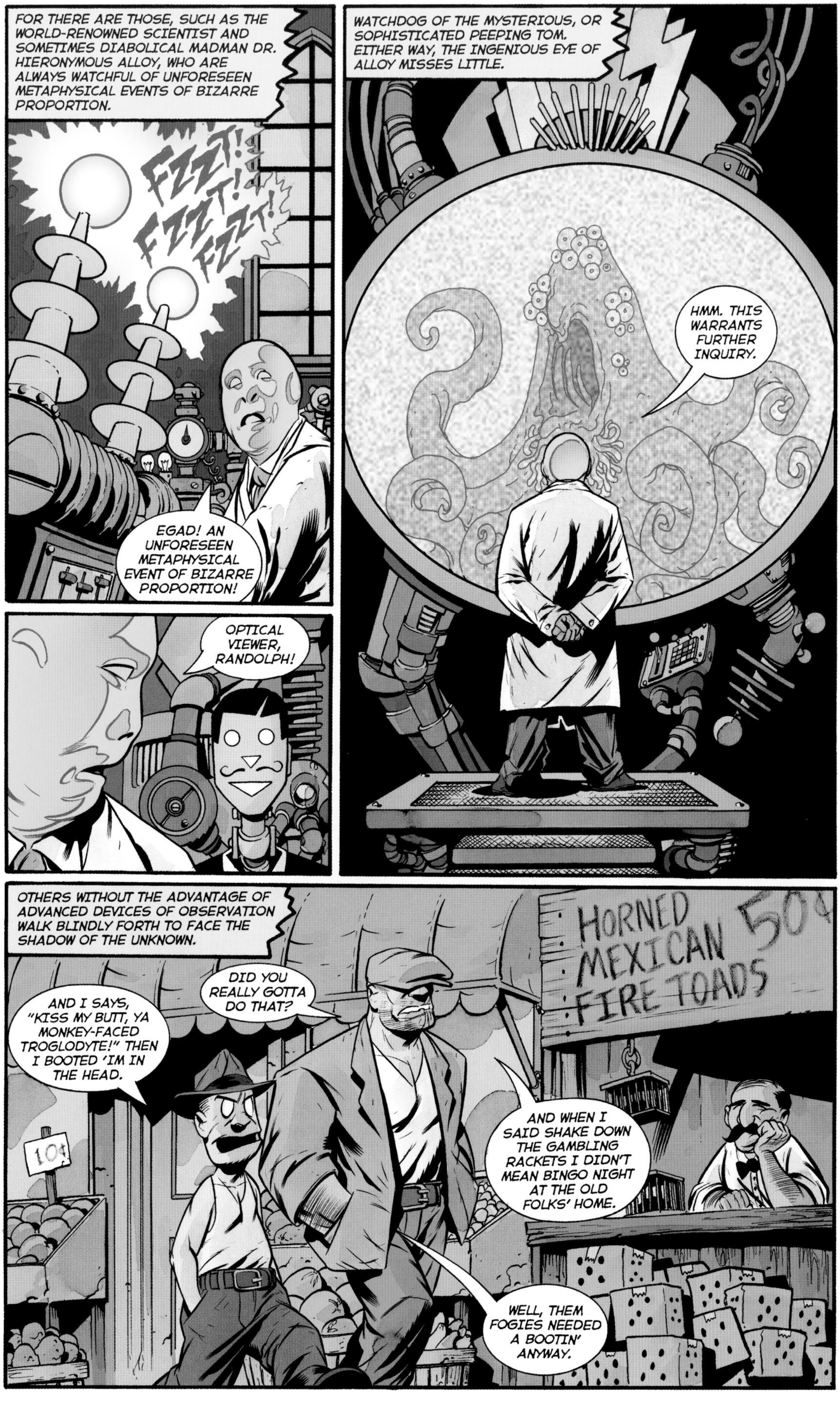
FOR THERE ARE THOSE, SUCH AS THE WORLD-RENOWNED SCIENTIST AND SOMETIMES DIABOLICAL MADMAN DR. HIERONYMOUS ALLOY, WHO ARE ALWAYS WATCHFUL OF UNFORESEEN METAPHYSICAL EVENTS OF BIZARRE PROPORTION.
FZZT! FZZT! FZZT!
EGAD! AN UNFORESEEN METAPHYSICAL EVENT OF BIZARRE PROPORTION!
OPTICAL VIEWER, RANDOLPH!
WATCHDOG OF THE MYSTERIOUS, OR SOPHISTICATED PEEPING TOM. EITHER WAY, THE INGENIOUS EYE OF ALLOY MISSES LITTLE.
HMM. THIS WARRANTS FURTHER INQUIRY.
OTHERS WITHOUT THE ADVANTAGE OF ADVANCED DEVICES OF OBSERVATION WALK BLINDLY FORTH TO FACE THE SHADOW OF THE UNKNOWN.
HORNED MEXICAN FIRE TOADS 50¢
AND I SAYS, "KISS MY BUTT, YA MONKEY-FACED TROGLODYTE!" THEN I BOOTED 'IM IN THE HEAD.
DID YOU REALLY GOTTA DO THAT?
10¢
AND WHEN I SAID SHAKE DOWN THE GAMBLING RACKETS I DIDN'T MEAN BINGO NIGHT AT THE OLD FOLKS' HOME.
WELL, THEM FOGIES NEEDED A BOOTIN' ANYWAY.

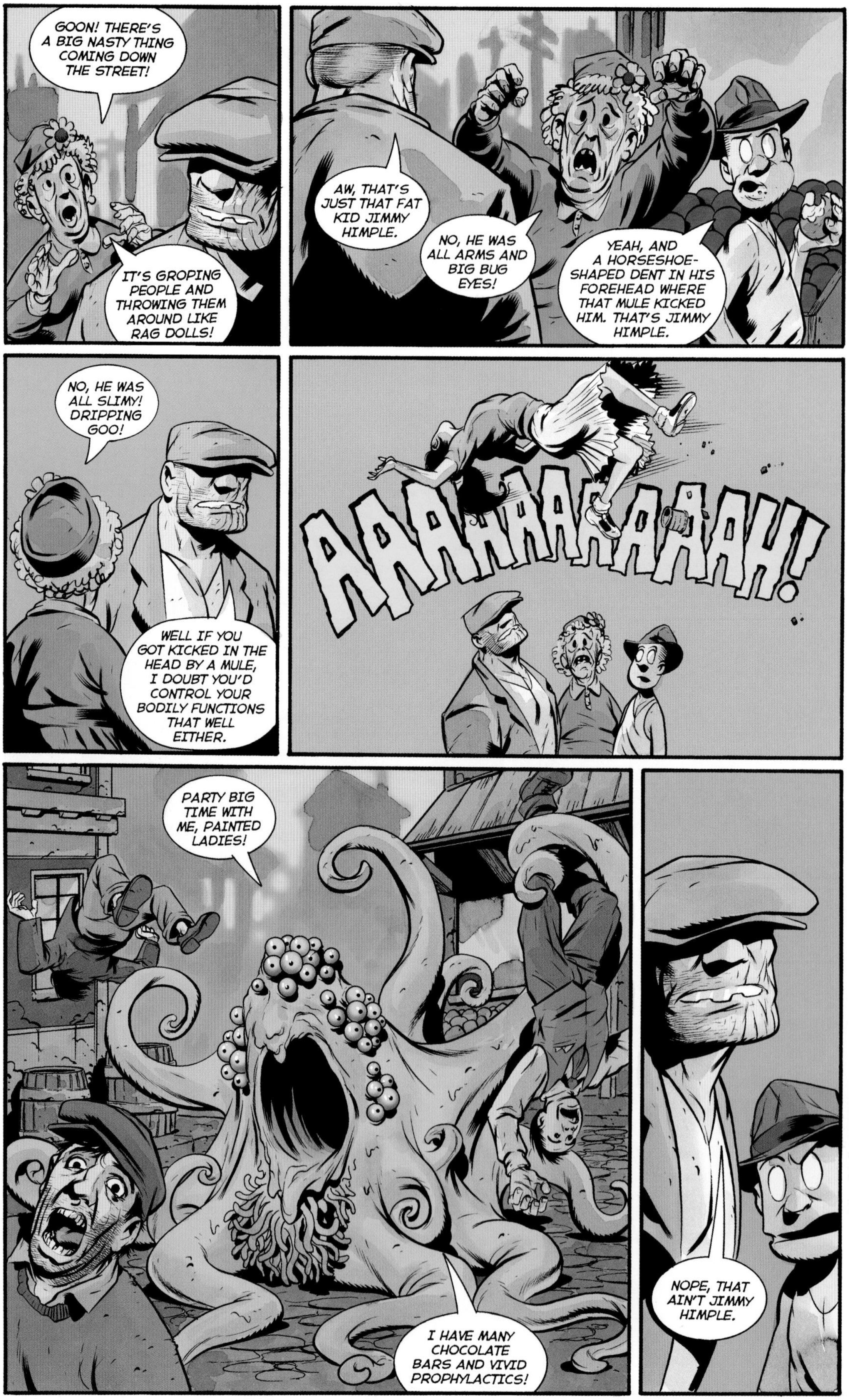
GOON! THERE'S A BIG NASTY THING COMING DOWN THE STREET!
IT'S GROPING PEOPLE AND THROWING THEM AROUND LIKE RAG DOLLS!
AW, THAT'S JUST THAT FAT KID JIMMY HIMPLE.
NO, HE WAS ALL ARMS AND BIG BUG EYES!
YEAH, AND A HORSESHOE-SHAPED DENT IN HIS FOREHEAD WHERE THAT MULE KICKED HIM. THAT'S JIMMY HIMPLE.
NO, HE WAS ALL SLIMY! DRIPPING GOO!
WELL IF YOU GOT KICKED IN THE HEAD BY A MULE, I DOUBT YOU'D CONTROL YOUR BODILY FUNCTIONS THAT WELL EITHER.
AAAAAAAAAAAH!
PARTY BIG TIME WITH ME, PAINTED LADIES!
I HAVE MANY CHOCOLATE BARS AND VIVID PROPHYLACTICS!
NOPE, THAT AIN'T JIMMY HIMPLE.

THE BEAST--REVELING IN THE CHAOS AND DESTRUCTION, OR SIMPLY TRYING TO FIND THE BEST PLACE IN TOWN FOR A TUNA-SALAD SANDWICH WITH THE BREAD LIGHTLY TOASTED, AND A PICKLE ON THE SIDE--DRIVES THE TOWNSPEOPLE BEFORE HIM LIKE RATS FROM A FIRE.

UPSTREAM MY APOCALYPSE SWAYS A CONGEALED SANDWICH! PICKLED DOOM IS BEHELD!

BUT WHILE THE OTHERS SCATTER IN FEAR, FIRM STANDS THE GOON. HIS WILL, HARDENED THROUGH A LIFE OF MISERY AND PAIN, IS SET AND KNOWS NO COMPROMISE.

EYES LOCK AND AN ETERNITY PASSES BETWEEN THEM. THEY EACH KNOW ONE OF THEM WILL NOT SURVIVE THE MEETING.

SOFTLY, DISTANTLY, A LONESOME TUNE FROM A HARMONICA CAN BE HEARD. WAAA WA WA WA!

SUCKLE MY CANTALOUPE. I'M BIG-TIME PARTY BOY.

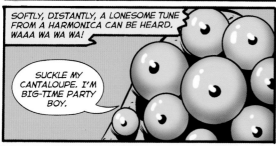

WAAA WA WA WA!

I RECKON.

WA WA WA WAAA!

WE WE WAAA WAAA WAAAAA!

49

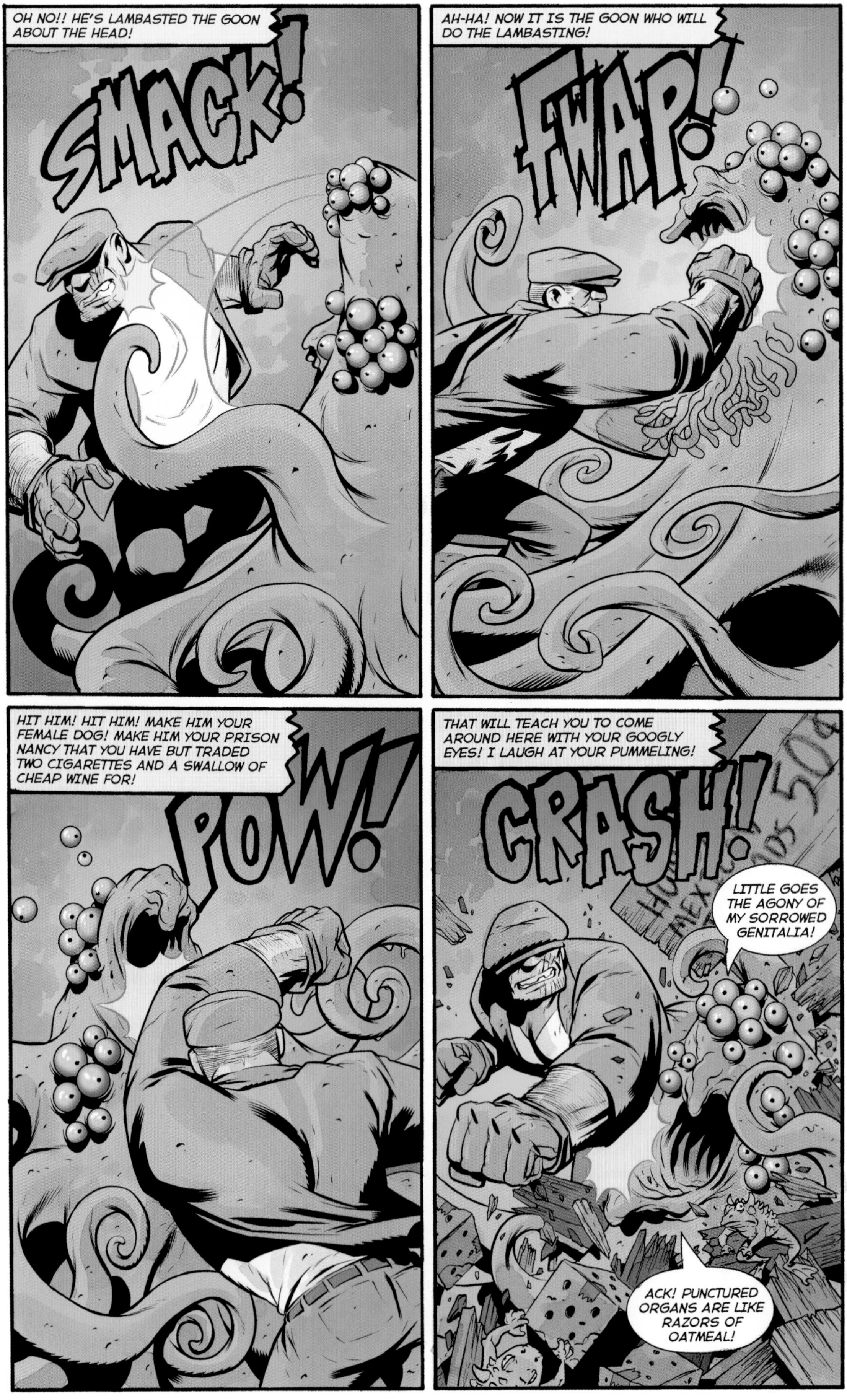

OH NO!! HE'S LAMBASTED THE GOON ABOUT THE HEAD!
SMACK!
AH-HA! NOW IT IS THE GOON WHO WILL DO THE LAMBASTING!
FWAP!
HIT HIM! HIT HIM! MAKE HIM YOUR FEMALE DOG! MAKE HIM YOUR PRISON NANCY THAT YOU HAVE BUT TRADED TWO CIGARETTES AND A SWALLOW OF CHEAP WINE FOR!
POW!
THAT WILL TEACH YOU TO COME AROUND HERE WITH YOUR GOOGLY EYES! I LAUGH AT YOUR PUMMELING!
CRASH!
LITTLE GOES THE AGONY OF MY SORROWED GENITALIA!
ACK! PUNCTURED ORGANS ARE LIKE RAZORS OF OATMEAL!

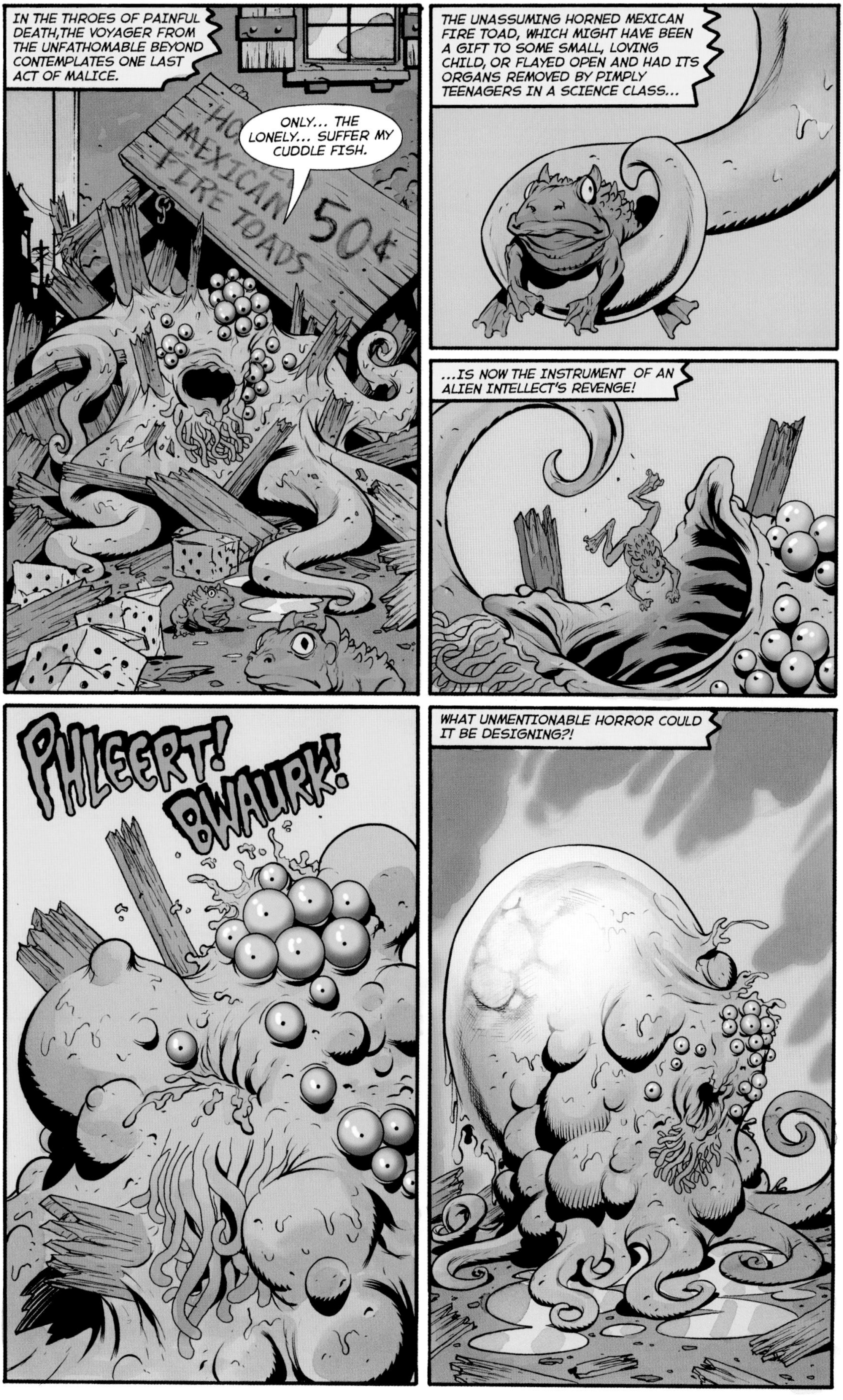
IN THE THROES OF PAINFUL DEATH,THE VOYAGER FROM THE UNFATHOMABLE BEYOND CONTEMPLATES ONE LAST ACT OF MALICE.
HORNED MEXICAN FIRE TOADS 50¢
ONLY... THE LONELY... SUFFER MY CUDDLE FISH.
THE UNASSUMING HORNED MEXICAN FIRE TOAD, WHICH MIGHT HAVE BEEN A GIFT TO SOME SMALL, LOVING CHILD, OR FLAYED OPEN AND HAD ITS ORGANS REMOVED BY PIMPLY TEENAGERS IN A SCIENCE CLASS...
...IS NOW THE INSTRUMENT OF AN ALIEN INTELLECT'S REVENGE!
PHLEERT! BWAURK!
WHAT UNMENTIONABLE HORROR COULD IT BE DESIGNING?!

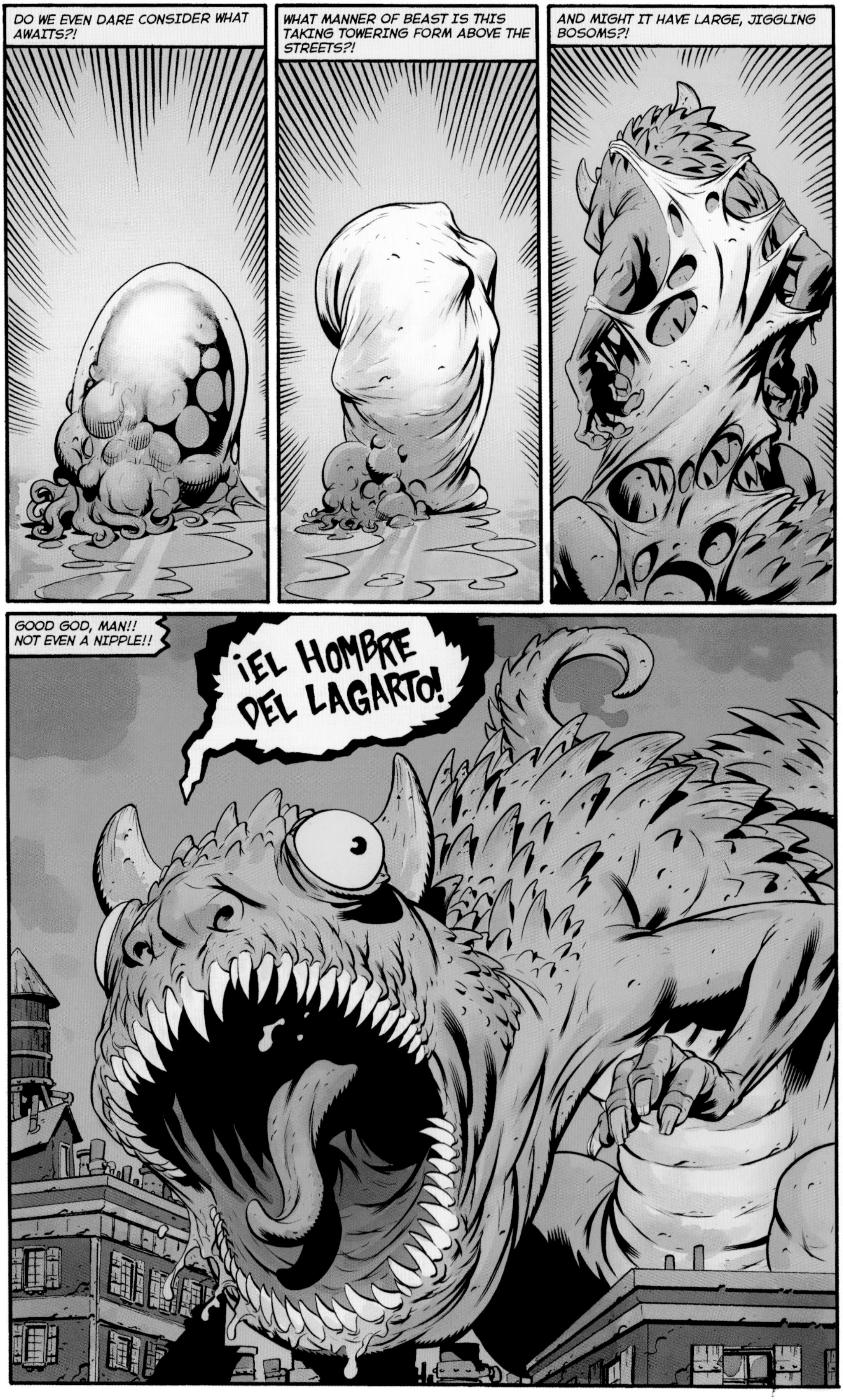
DO WE EVEN DARE CONSIDER WHAT AWAITS?!
WHAT MANNER OF BEAST IS THIS TAKING TOWERING FORM ABOVE THE STREETS?!
AND MIGHT IT HAVE LARGE, JIGGLING BOSOMS?!
GOOD GOD, MAN!! NOT EVEN A NIPPLE!!
¡EL HOMBRE DEL LAGARTO!

THAT'S... UH...

BIG?

YEP.

THE LAGARTO HOMBRE BELCHES FORTH A FUME OF RUIN AS IT SCREAMS CURSES UPON THE MEEK!

¡APLASTARÉ TU PUEBLO DE MONOS ABAJO DE MI TALÓN Y DESPUÉS COMERÉ MI PESO EN TUS CARNES EN CONSERVAS, ASÍ LLAMADOS!

FWOOSH!!

BEWILDERED BY THE SENSELESS CARNAGE TAKING PLACE BEFORE THEIR VERY EYES, NO ONE WITNESSES THE FORTUITOUS COMING OF DR. ALLOY!

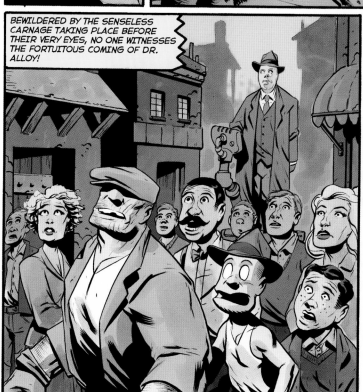

NOT DISTRACTED BY THE UNGODLY BOSOMS A CREATURE THAT SIZE WOULD POSSESS IF IT INDEED HAD BOSOMS, THE STUNNING INTELLECT OF DR. ALLOY ASSESSES THE SITUATION AND QUICKLY TAKES ACTION!

THE GOON WILL DO.

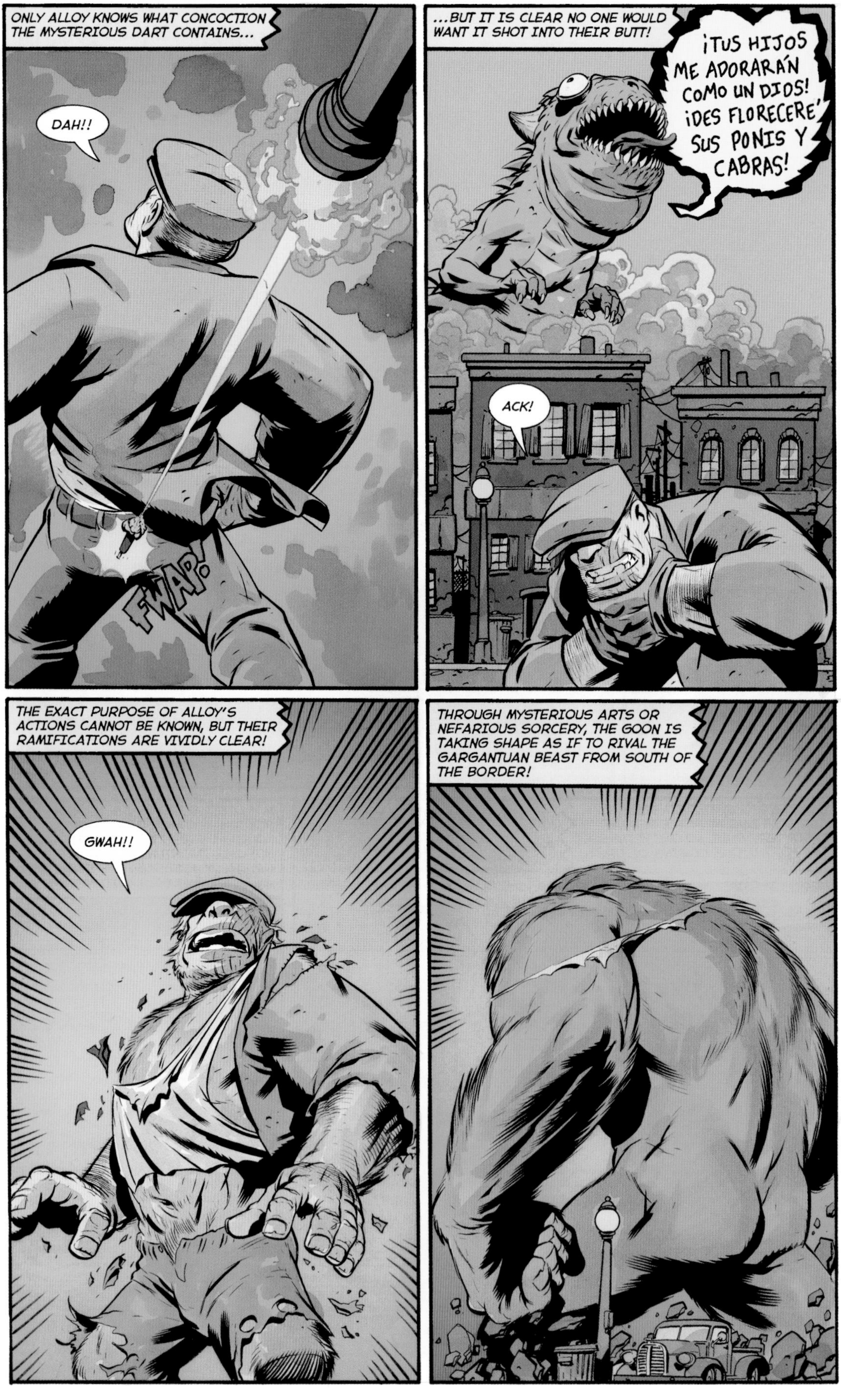
ONLY ALLOY KNOWS WHAT CONCOCTION THE MYSTERIOUS DART CONTAINS...
DAH!!
FWAP!
...BUT IT IS CLEAR NO ONE WOULD WANT IT SHOT INTO THEIR BUTT!
¡TUS HIJOS ME ADORARÁN COMO UN DIOS! ¡DES FLORECERÉ SUS PONIS Y CABRAS!
ACK!
THE EXACT PURPOSE OF ALLOY'S ACTIONS CANNOT BE KNOWN, BUT THEIR RAMIFICATIONS ARE VIVIDLY CLEAR!
GWAH!!
THROUGH MYSTERIOUS ARTS OR NEFARIOUS SORCERY, THE GOON IS TAKING SHAPE AS IF TO RIVAL THE GARGANTUAN BEAST FROM SOUTH OF THE BORDER!

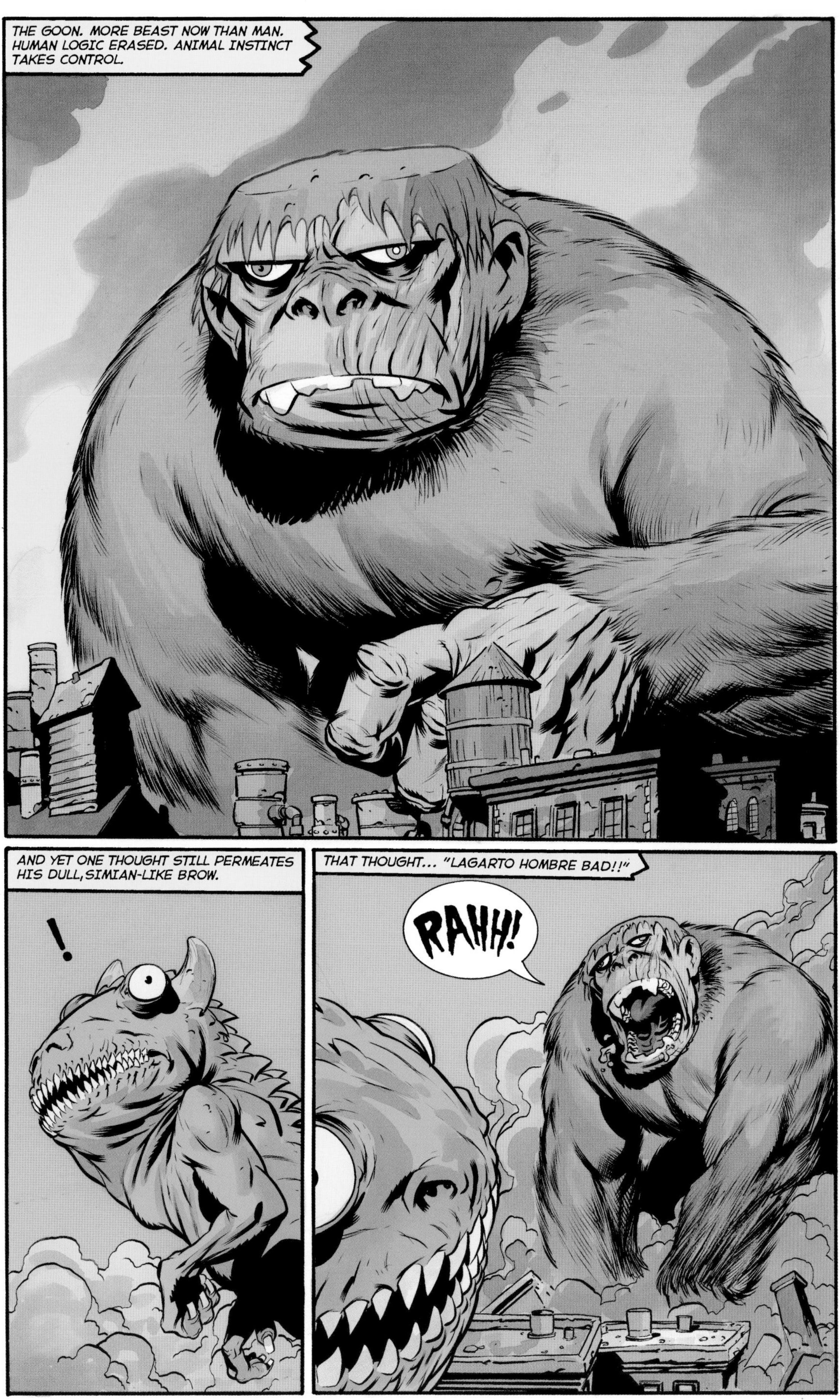
THE GOON. MORE BEAST NOW THAN MAN. HUMAN LOGIC ERASED. ANIMAL INSTINCT TAKES CONTROL.
AND YET ONE THOUGHT STILL PERMEATES HIS DULL, SIMIAN-LIKE BROW.
!
THAT THOUGHT... "LAGARTO HOMBRE BAD!!"
RAHH!

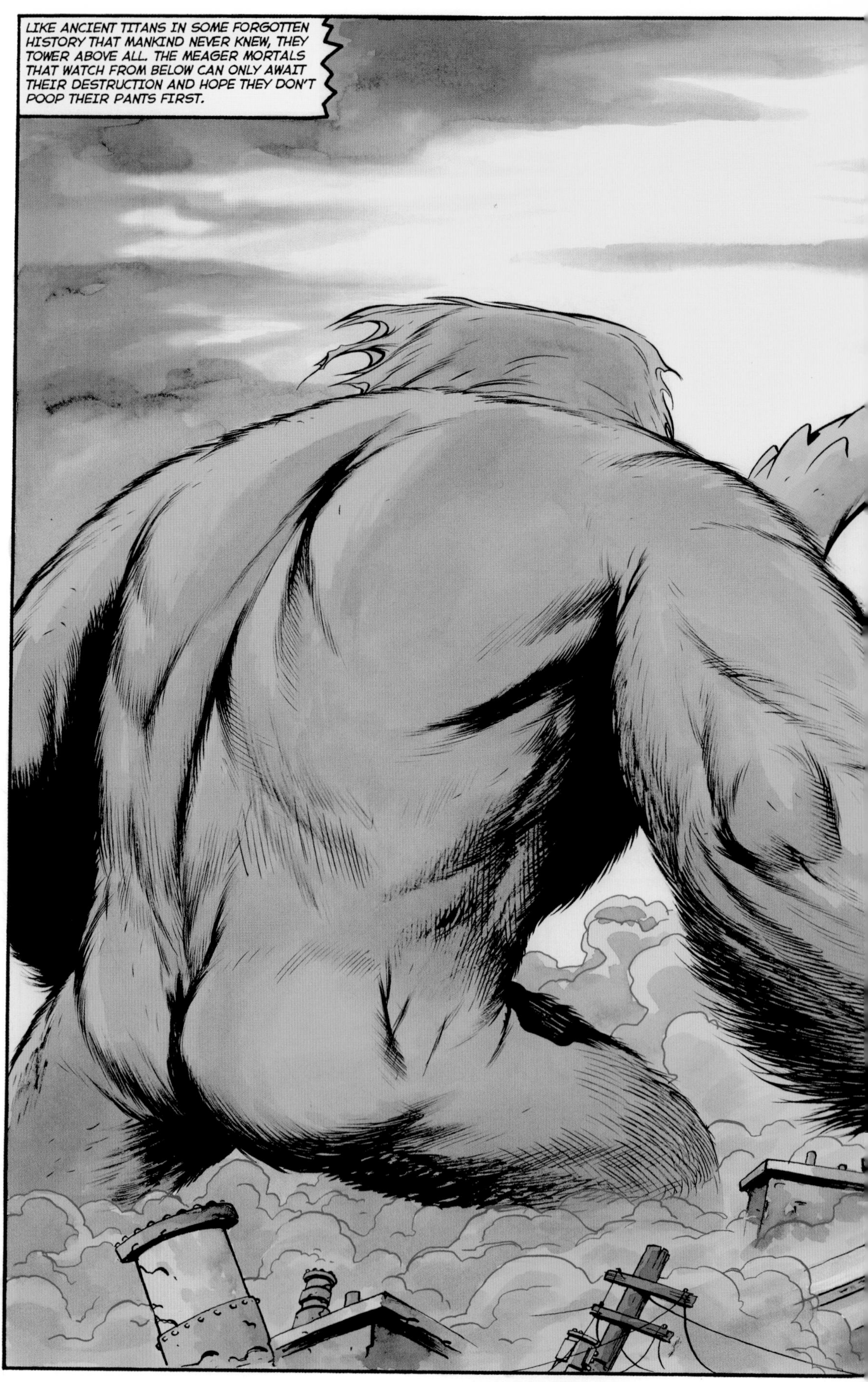
LIKE ANCIENT TITANS IN SOME FORGOTTEN HISTORY THAT MANKIND NEVER KNEW, THEY TOWER ABOVE ALL. THE MEAGER MORTALS THAT WATCH FROM BELOW CAN ONLY AWAIT THEIR DESTRUCTION AND HOPE THEY DON'T POOP THEIR PANTS FIRST.

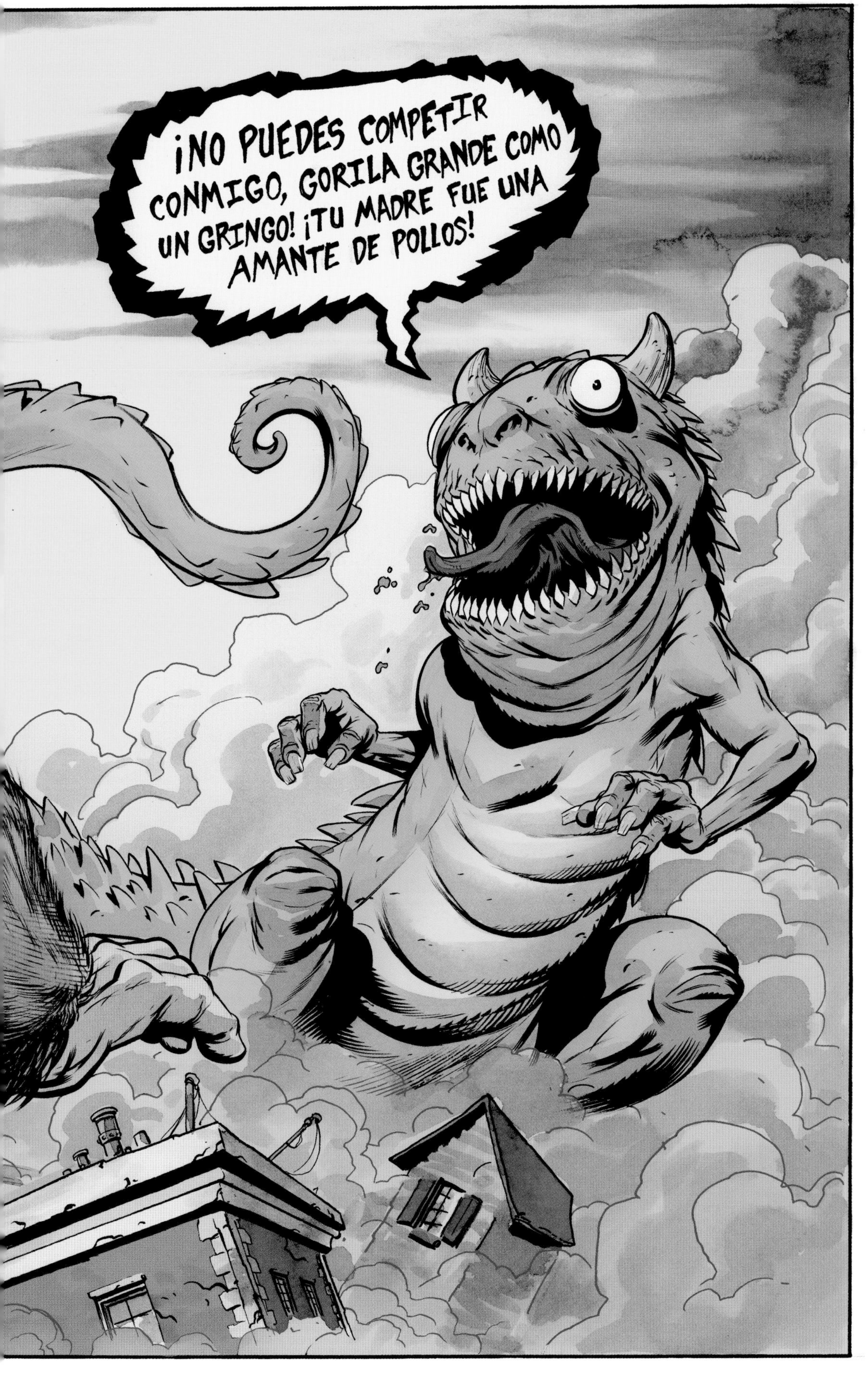
¡NO PUEDES COMPETIR CONMIGO, GORILA GRANDE COMO UN GRINGO! ¡TU MADRE FUE UNA AMANTE DE POLLOS!

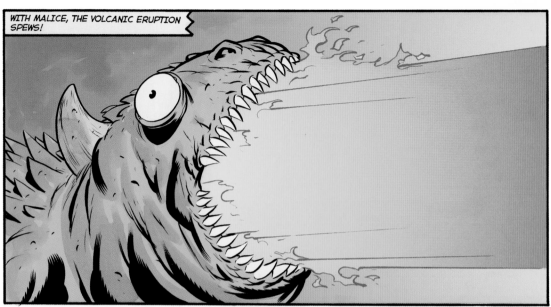

WITH MALICE, THE VOLCANIC ERUPTION SPEWS!

THE BLAST OF HOT LATIN FIRE SMASHES INTO THE GOON LIKE A TORRENT OF WET MOOSE FARTS. HEY! YOU GIVE ME A BETTER ANALOGY AND I'LL USE IT, YOU JUDGMENTAL LITTLE HAYSEED!

AS IF THE VERY HEAVENS WERE BREAKING, THE BLOW LANDS IN THUNDEROUS COLLISION!

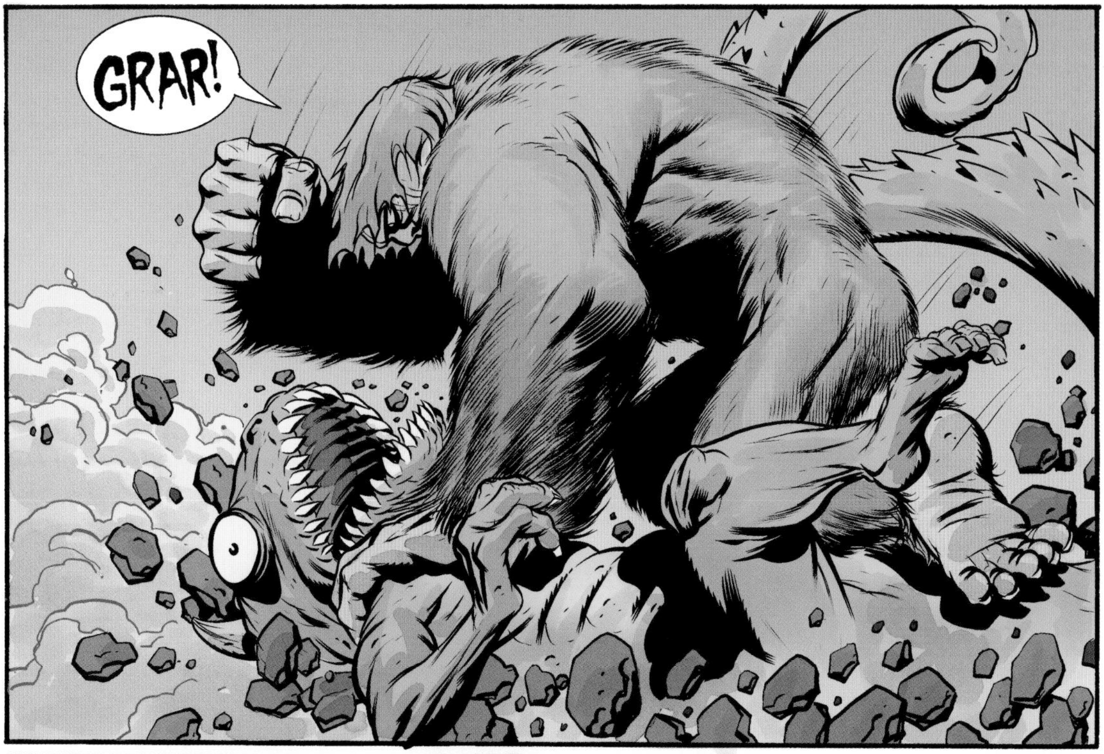
GRAR!

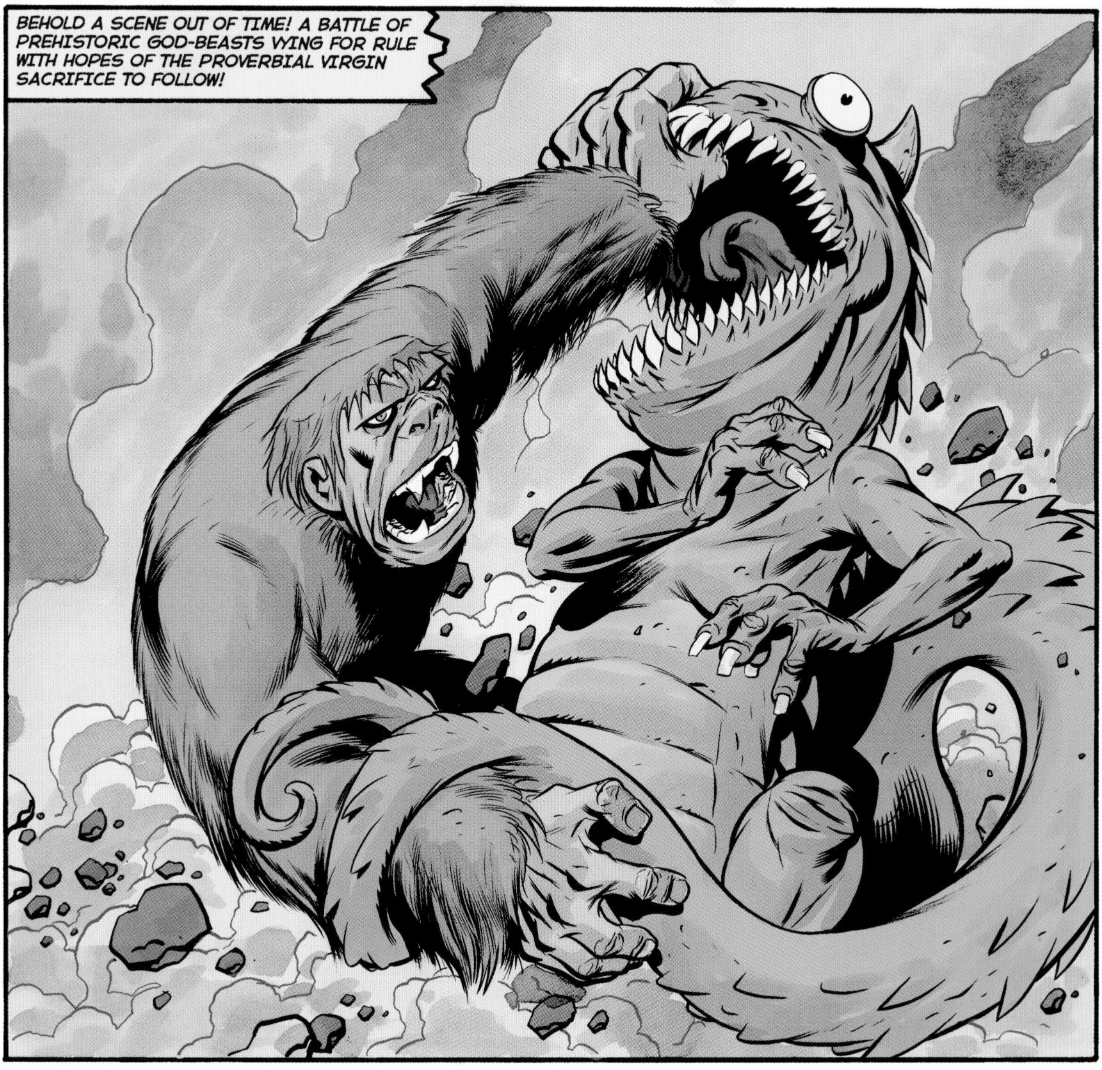
BEHOLD A SCENE OUT OF TIME! A BATTLE OF PREHISTORIC GOD-BEASTS VYING FOR RULE WITH HOPES OF THE PROVERBIAL VIRGIN SACRIFICE TO FOLLOW!

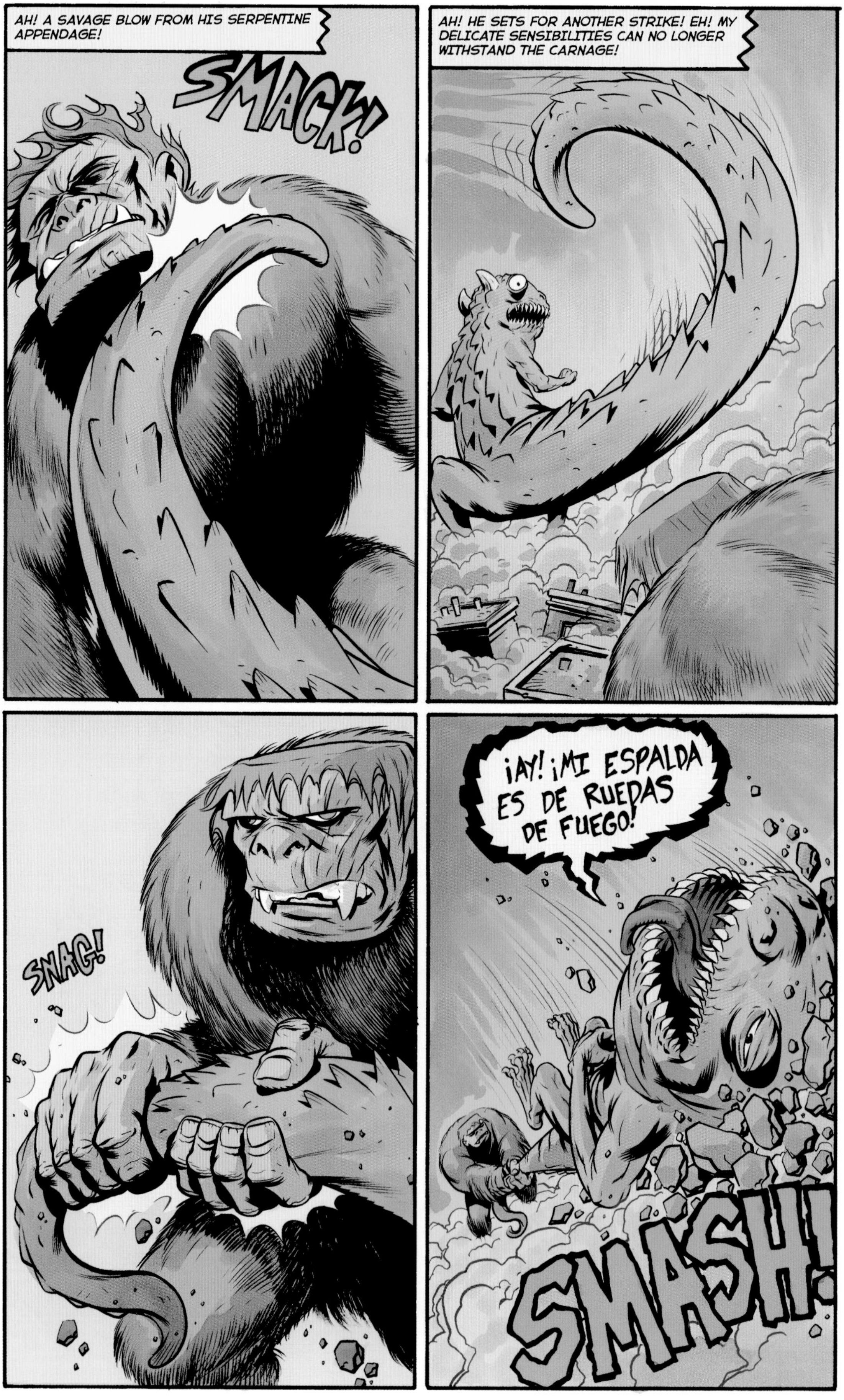
AH! A SAVAGE BLOW FROM HIS SERPENTINE APPENDAGE!
SMACK!
AH! HE SETS FOR ANOTHER STRIKE! EH! MY DELICATE SENSIBILITIES CAN NO LONGER WITHSTAND THE CARNAGE!
SNAG!
¡AY! ¡MI ESPALDA ES DE RUEDAS DE FUEGO!
SMASH!

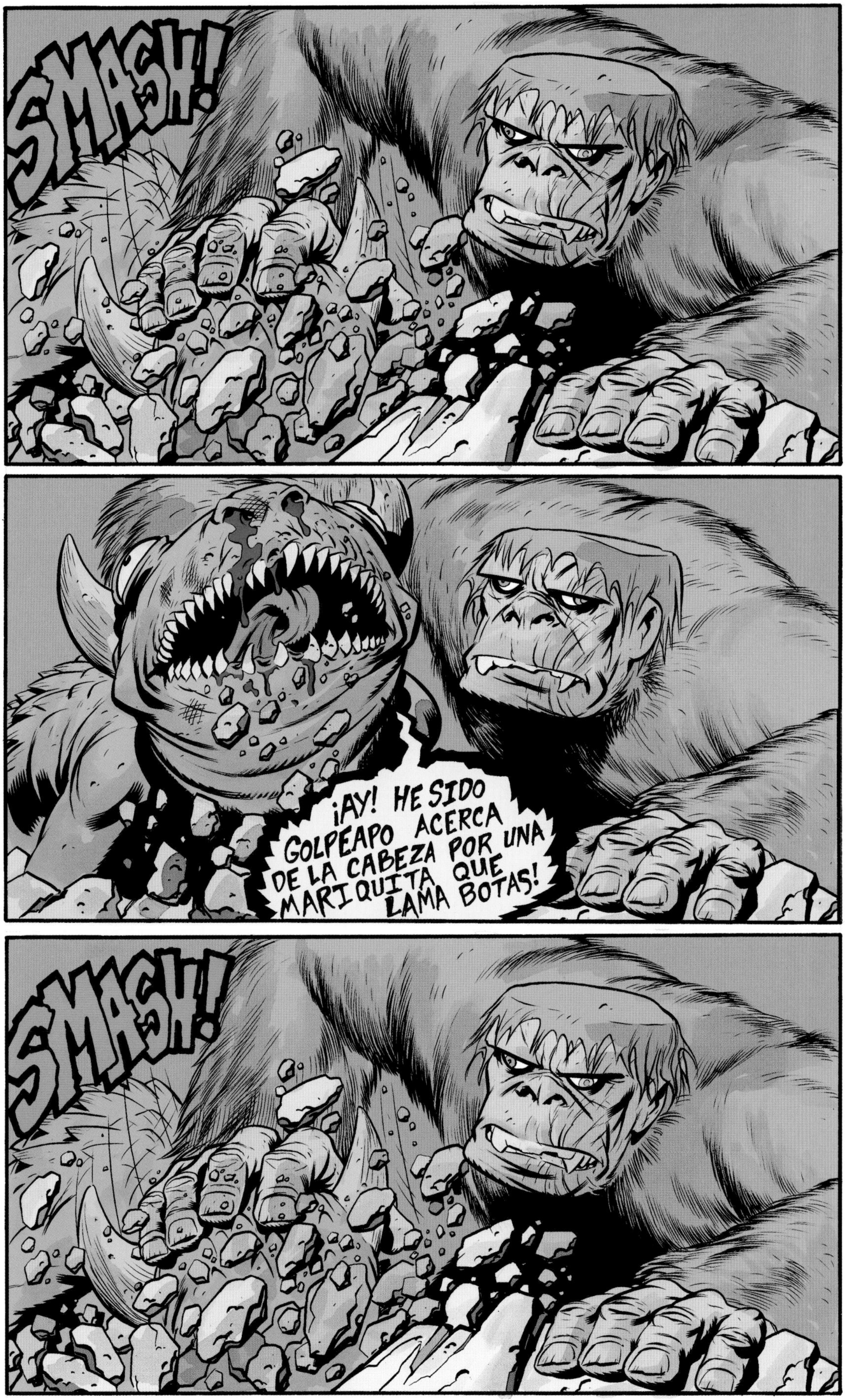
SMASH!
¡AY! HE SIDO GOLPEAPO ACERCA DE LA CABEZA POR UNA MARIQUITA QUE LAMA BOTAS!
SMASH!

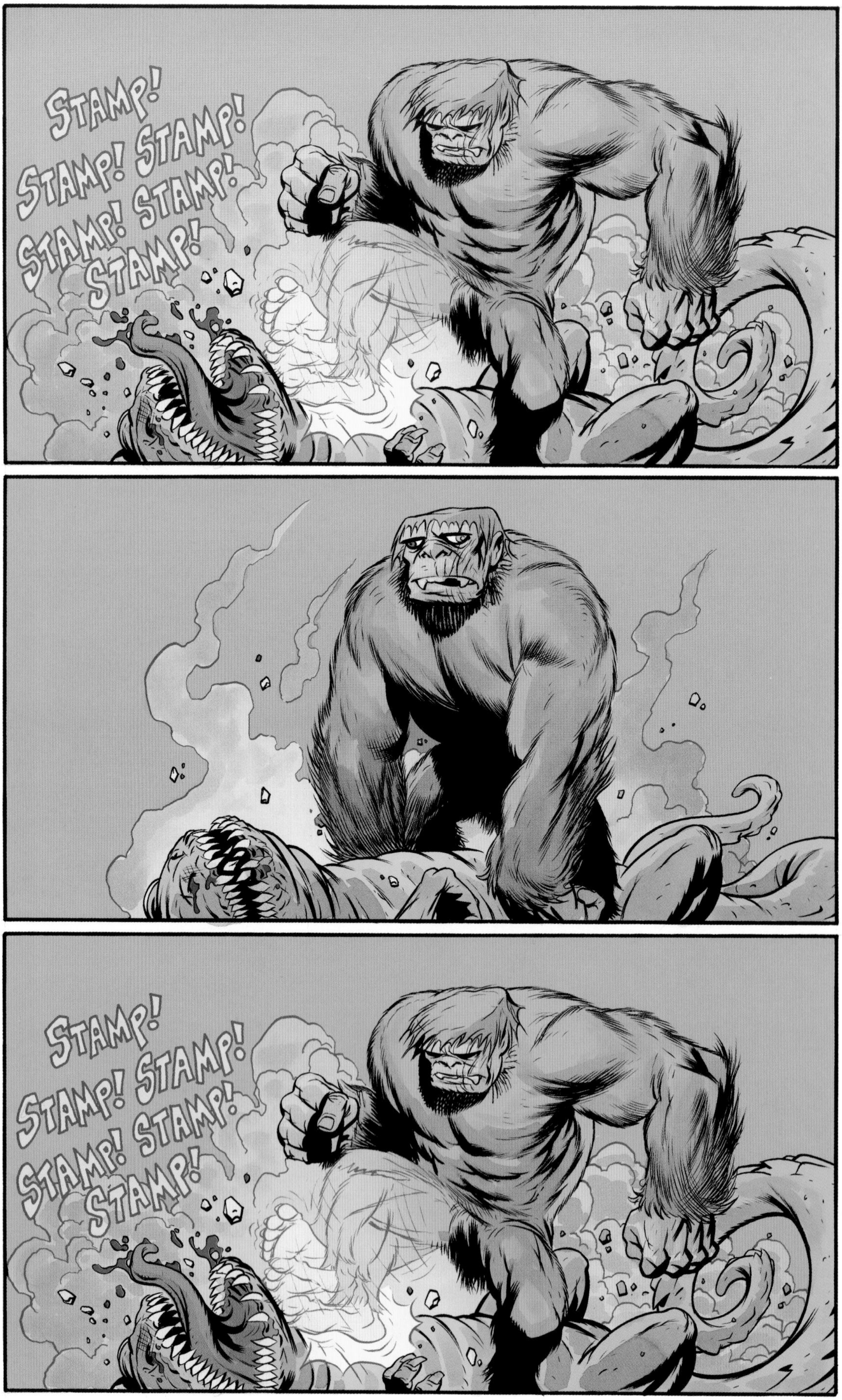
STAMP!
STAMP! STAMP!
STAMP! STAMP!
STAMP!
STAMP!
STAMP! STAMP!
STAMP! STAMP!
STAMP!

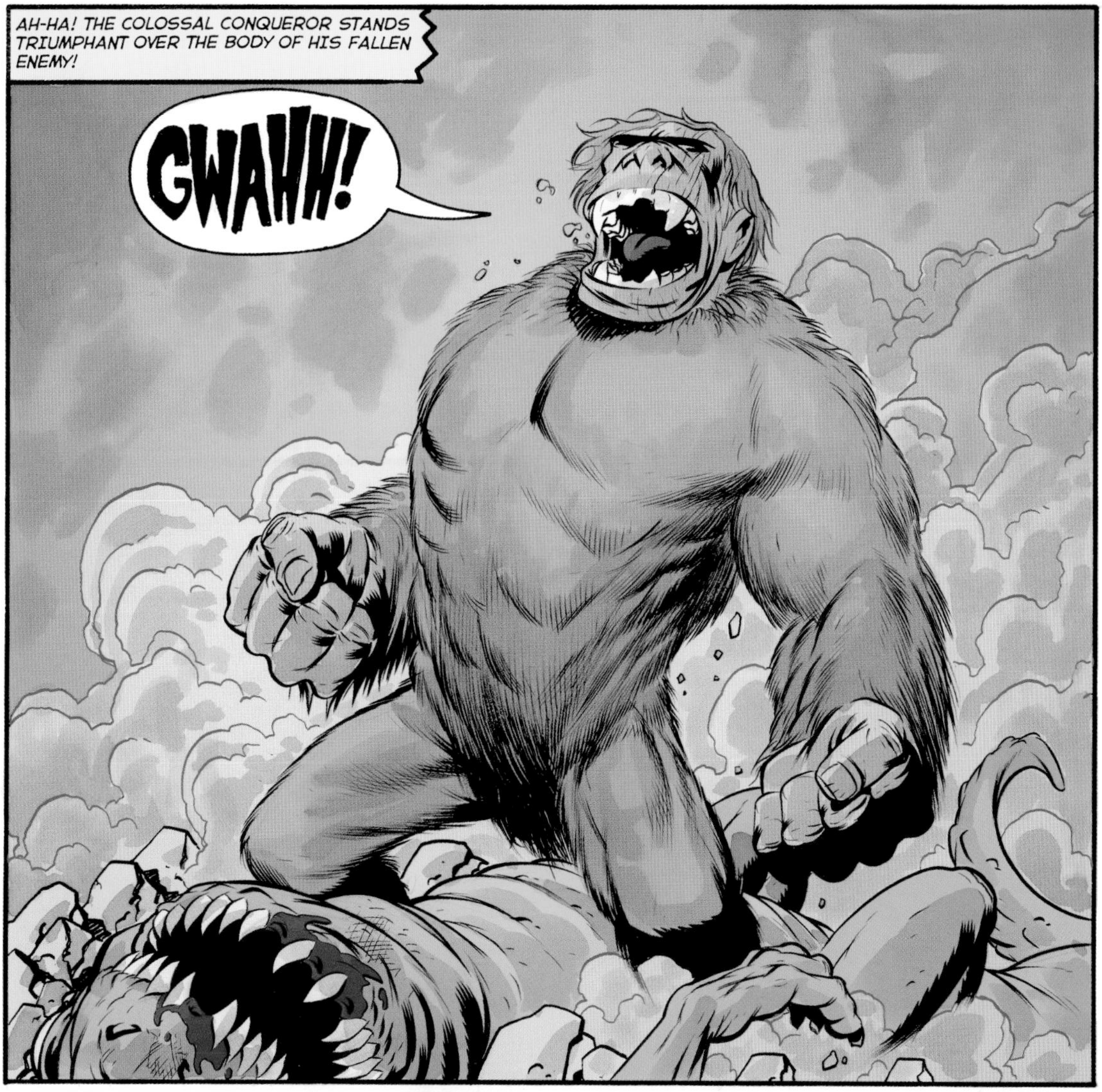
AH-HA! THE COLOSSAL CONQUEROR STANDS TRIUMPHANT OVER THE BODY OF HIS FALLEN ENEMY!
GWAHH!

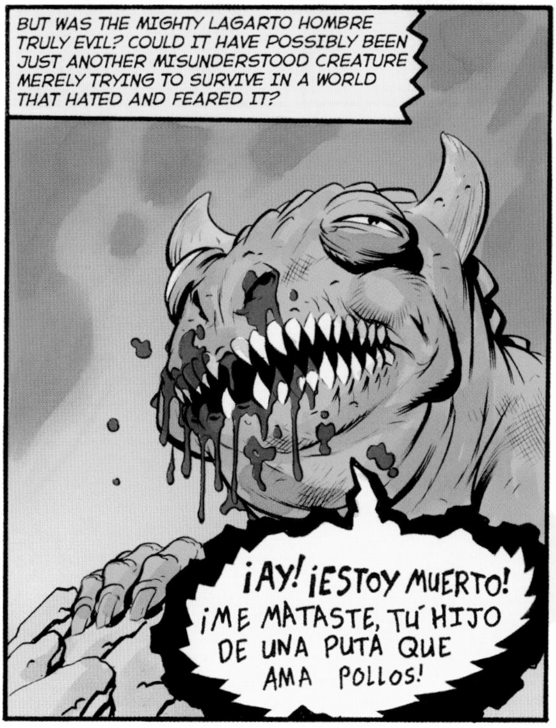
BUT WAS THE MIGHTY LAGARTO HOMBRE TRULY EVIL? COULD IT HAVE POSSIBLY BEEN JUST ANOTHER MISUNDERSTOOD CREATURE MERELY TRYING TO SURVIVE IN A WORLD THAT HATED AND FEARED IT?
¡AY! ¡ESTOY MUERTO! ¡ME MATASTE, TÚ HIJO DE UNA PUTA QUE AMA POLLOS!

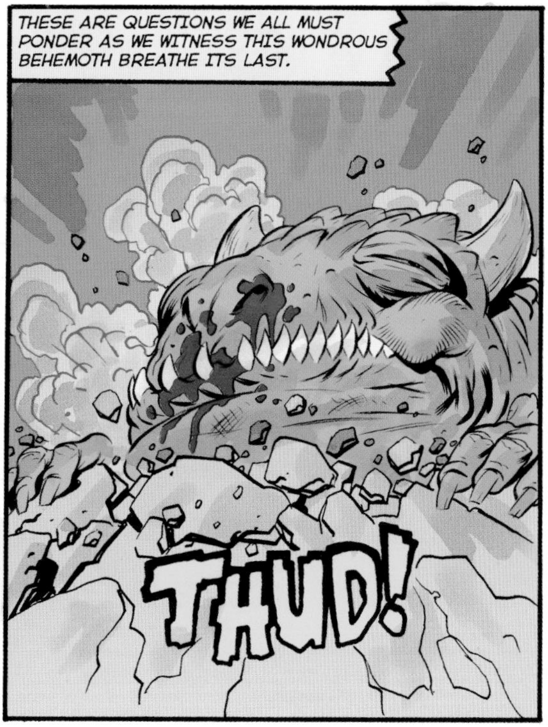
THESE ARE QUESTIONS WE ALL MUST PONDER AS WE WITNESS THIS WONDROUS BEHEMOTH BREATHE ITS LAST.
THUD!

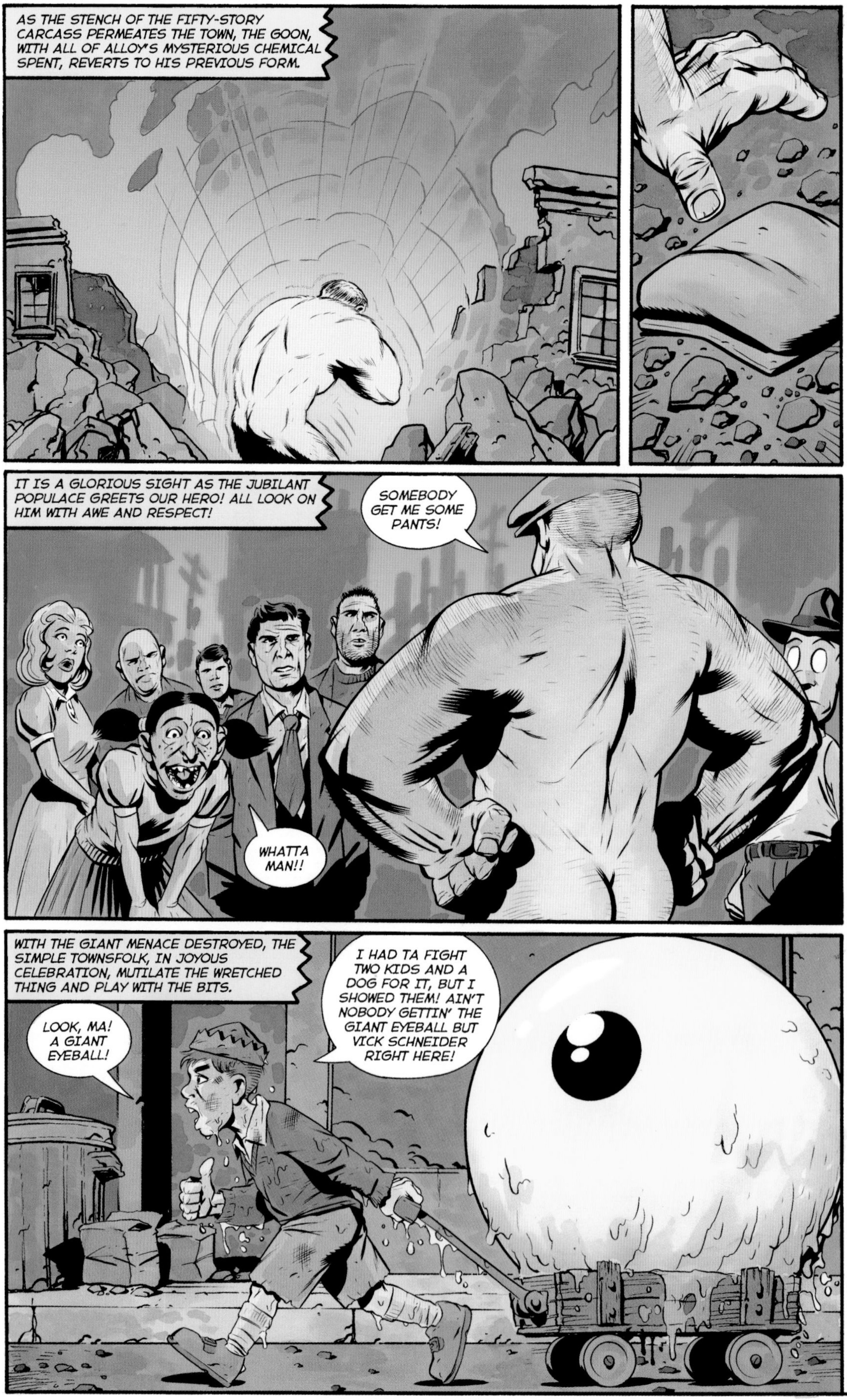
AS THE STENCH OF THE FIFTY-STORY CARCASS PERMEATES THE TOWN, THE GOON, WITH ALL OF ALLOY'S MYSTERIOUS CHEMICAL SPENT, REVERTS TO HIS PREVIOUS FORM.
IT IS A GLORIOUS SIGHT AS THE JUBILANT POPULACE GREETS OUR HERO! ALL LOOK ON HIM WITH AWE AND RESPECT!
SOMEBODY GET ME SOME PANTS!
WHATTA MAN!!
WITH THE GIANT MENACE DESTROYED, THE SIMPLE TOWNSFOLK, IN JOYOUS CELEBRATION, MUTILATE THE WRETCHED THING AND PLAY WITH THE BITS.
I HAD TA FIGHT TWO KIDS AND A DOG FOR IT, BUT I SHOWED THEM! AIN'T NOBODY GETTIN' THE GIANT EYEBALL BUT VICK SCHNEIDER RIGHT HERE!
LOOK, MA! A GIANT EYEBALL!

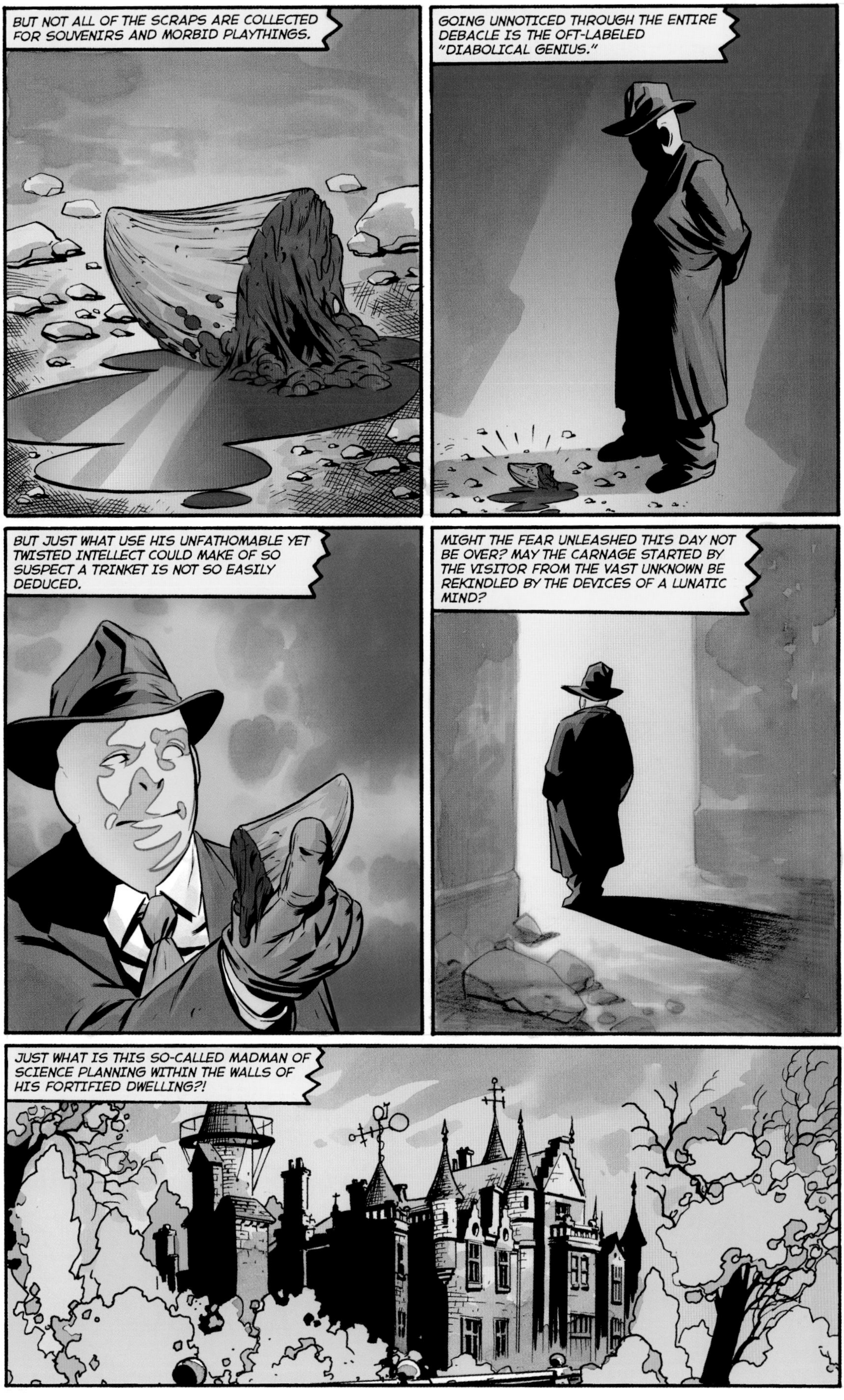
BUT NOT ALL OF THE SCRAPS ARE COLLECTED FOR SOUVENIRS AND MORBID PLAYTHINGS.
GOING UNNOTICED THROUGH THE ENTIRE DEBACLE IS THE OFT-LABELED "DIABOLICAL GENIUS."
BUT JUST WHAT USE HIS UNFATHOMABLE YET TWISTED INTELLECT COULD MAKE OF SO SUSPECT A TRINKET IS NOT SO EASILY DEDUCED.
MIGHT THE FEAR UNLEASHED THIS DAY NOT BE OVER? MAY THE CARNAGE STARTED BY THE VISITOR FROM THE VAST UNKNOWN BE REKINDLED BY THE DEVICES OF A LUNATIC MIND?
JUST WHAT IS THIS SO-CALLED MADMAN OF SCIENCE PLANNING WITHIN THE WALLS OF HIS FORTIFIED DWELLING?!

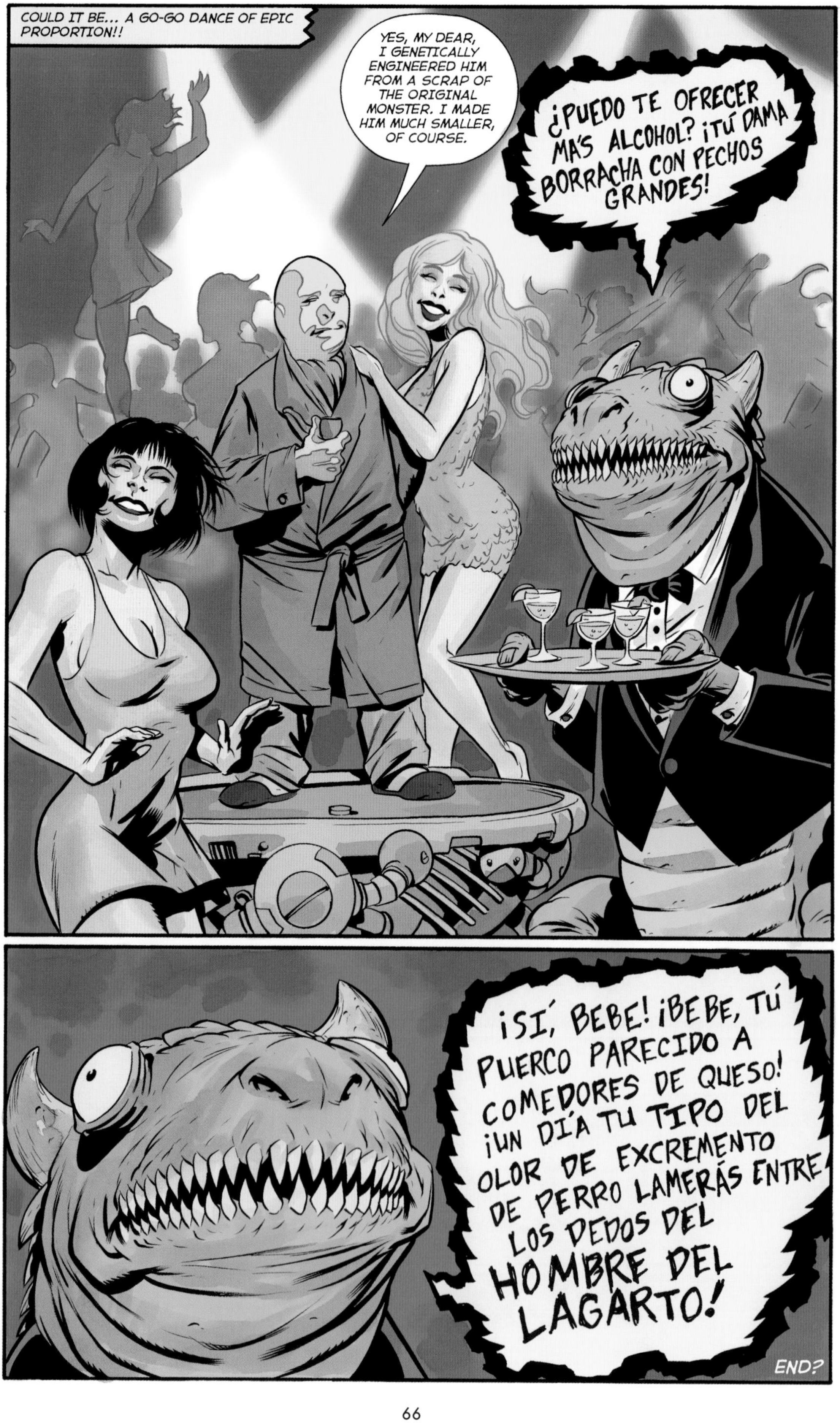
COULD IT BE... A GO-GO DANCE OF EPIC PROPORTION!!
YES, MY DEAR, I GENETICALLY ENGINEERED HIM FROM A SCRAP OF THE ORIGINAL MONSTER. I MADE HIM MUCH SMALLER, OF COURSE.
¿PUEDO TE OFRECER MÁS ALCOHOL? ¡TÚ DAMA BORRACHA CON PECHOS GRANDES!
¡SÍ, BEBE! ¡BEBE, TÚ PUERCO PARECIDO A COMEDORES DE QUESO! ¡UN DÍA TU TIPO DEL OLOR DE EXCREMENTO DE PERRO LAMERÁS ENTRE LOS DEDOS DEL HOMBRE DEL LAGARTO!
END?

CHAPTER 3

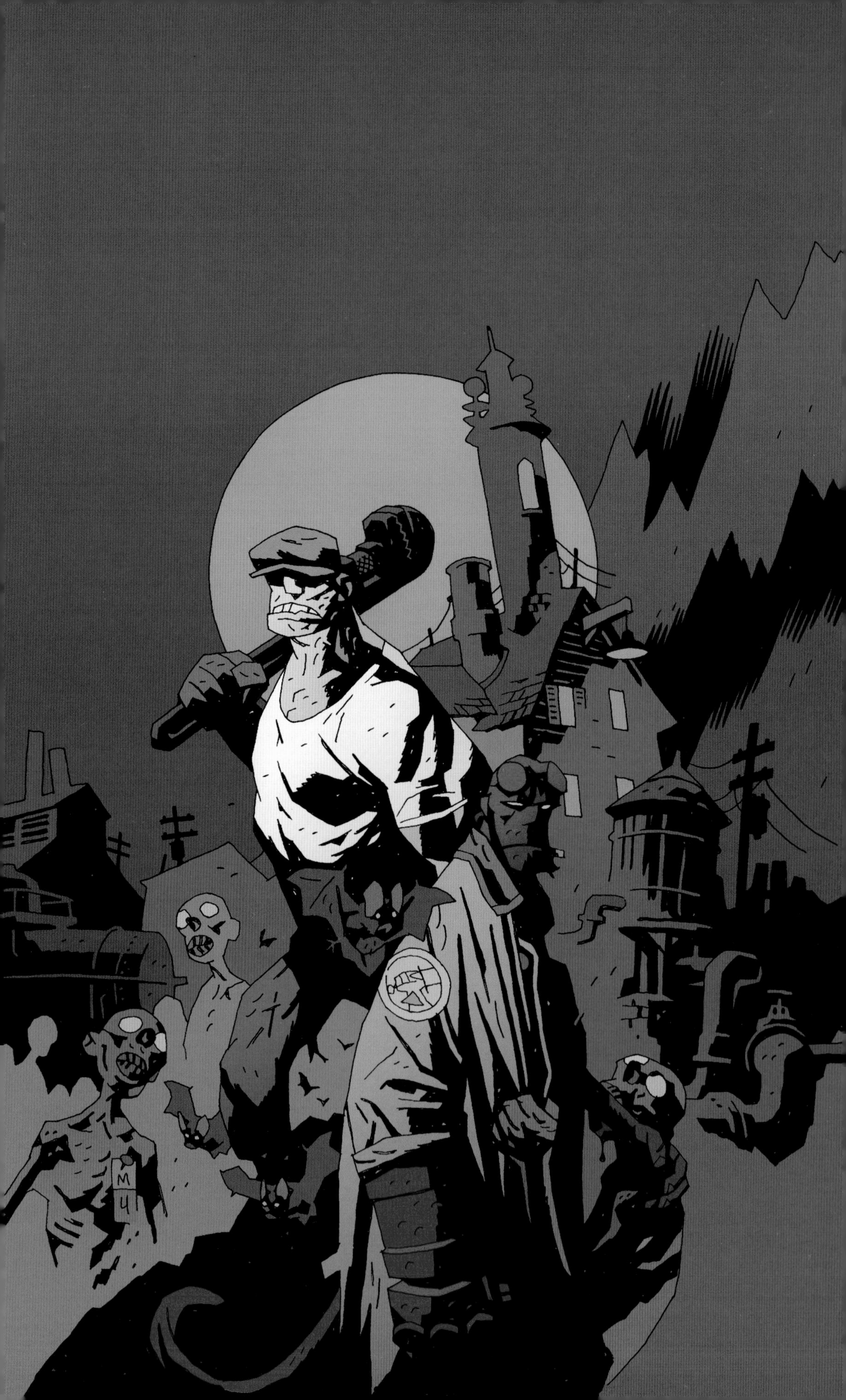

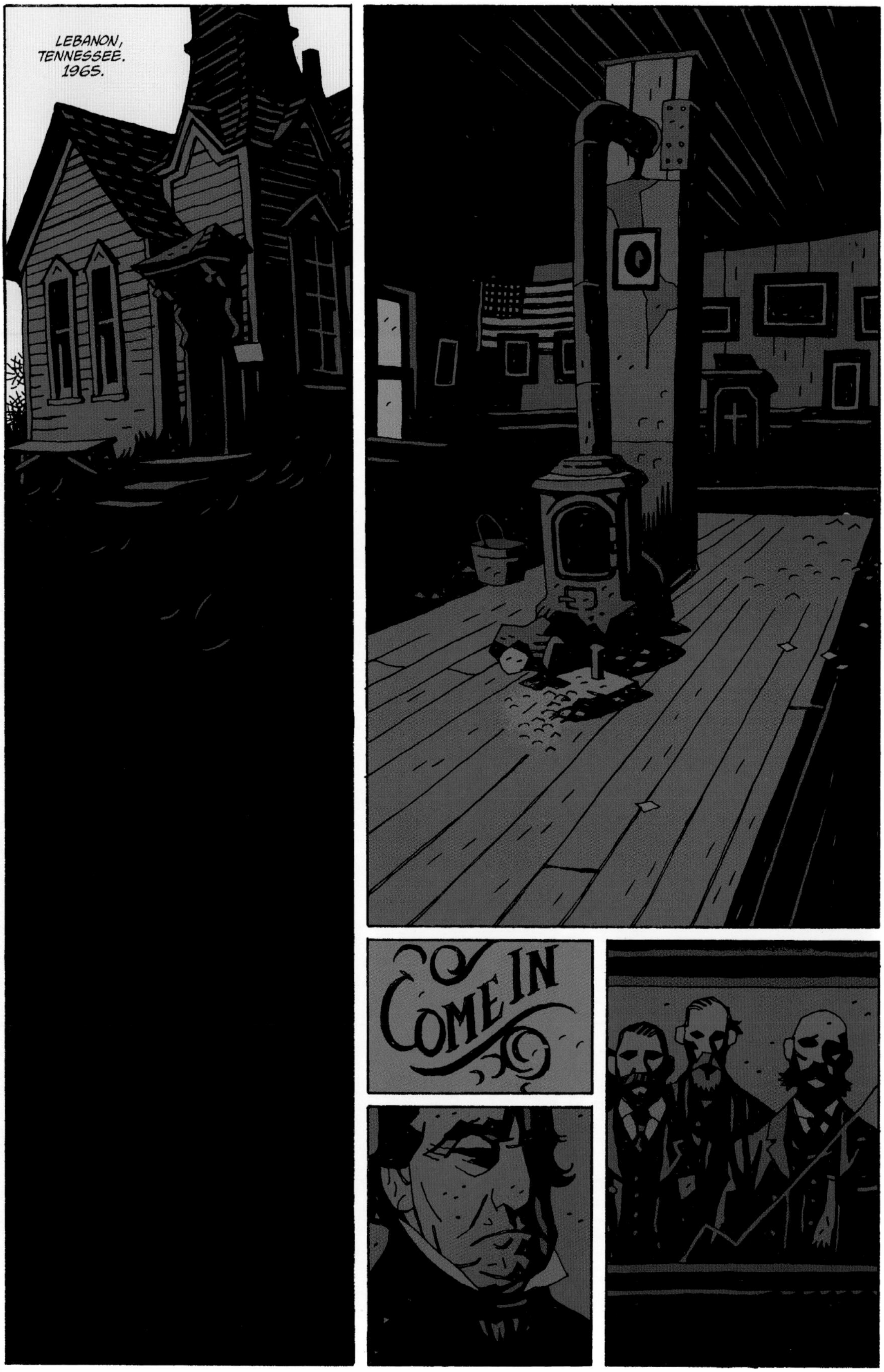
LEBANON, TENNESSEE. 1965.
COME IN

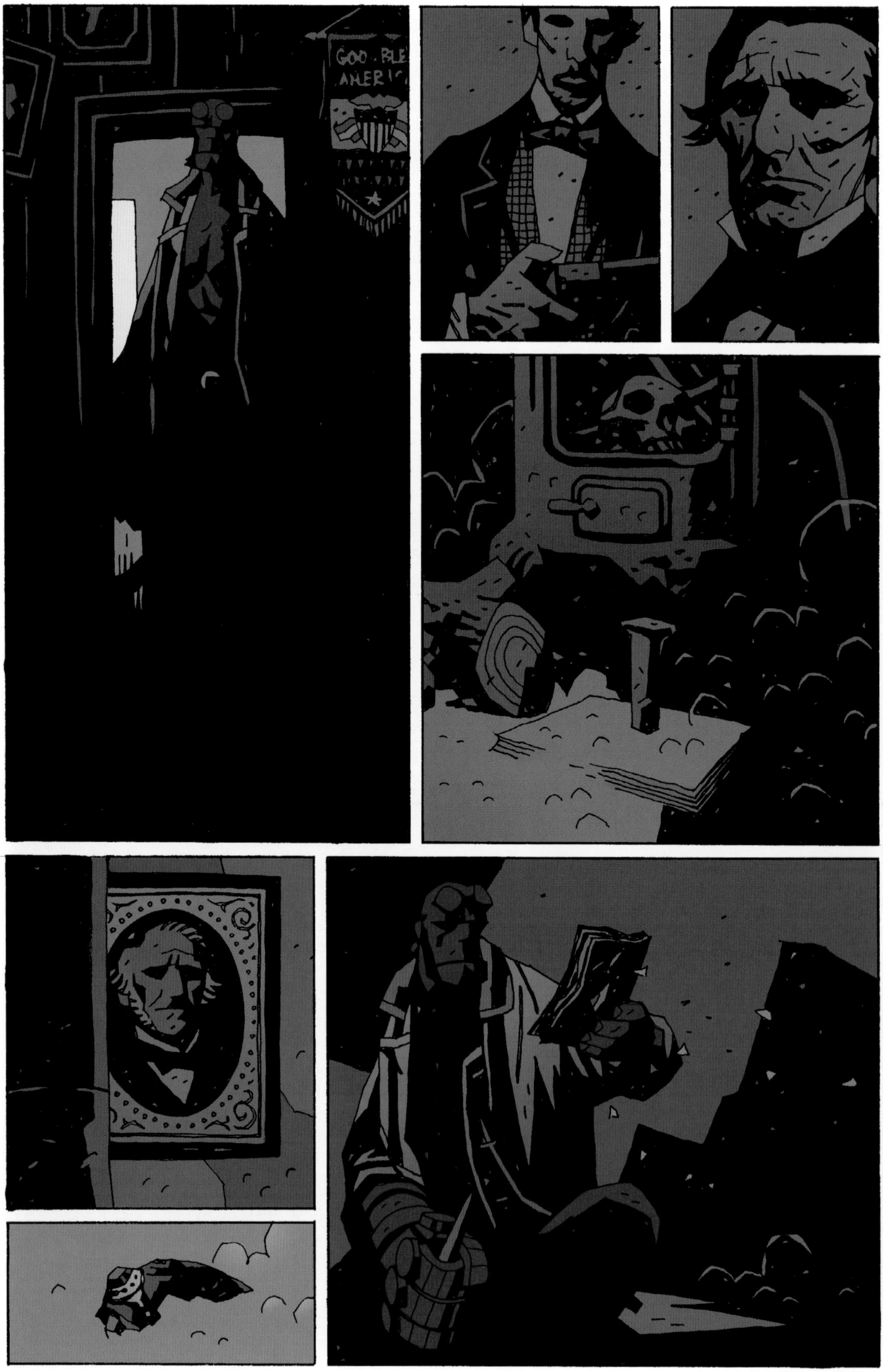

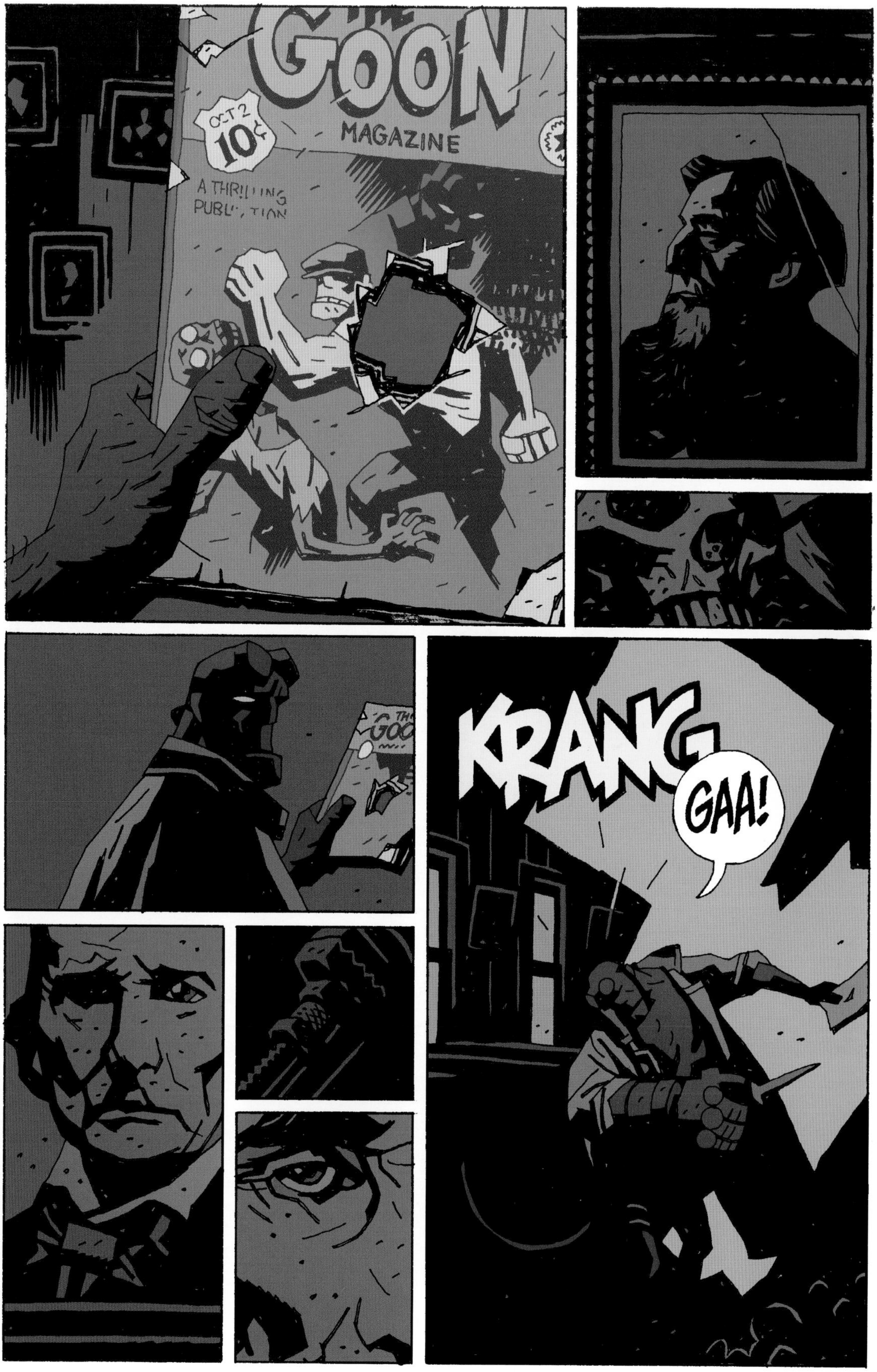
THE GOON
MAGAZINE
OCT 2
10¢
KRANG
GAA!

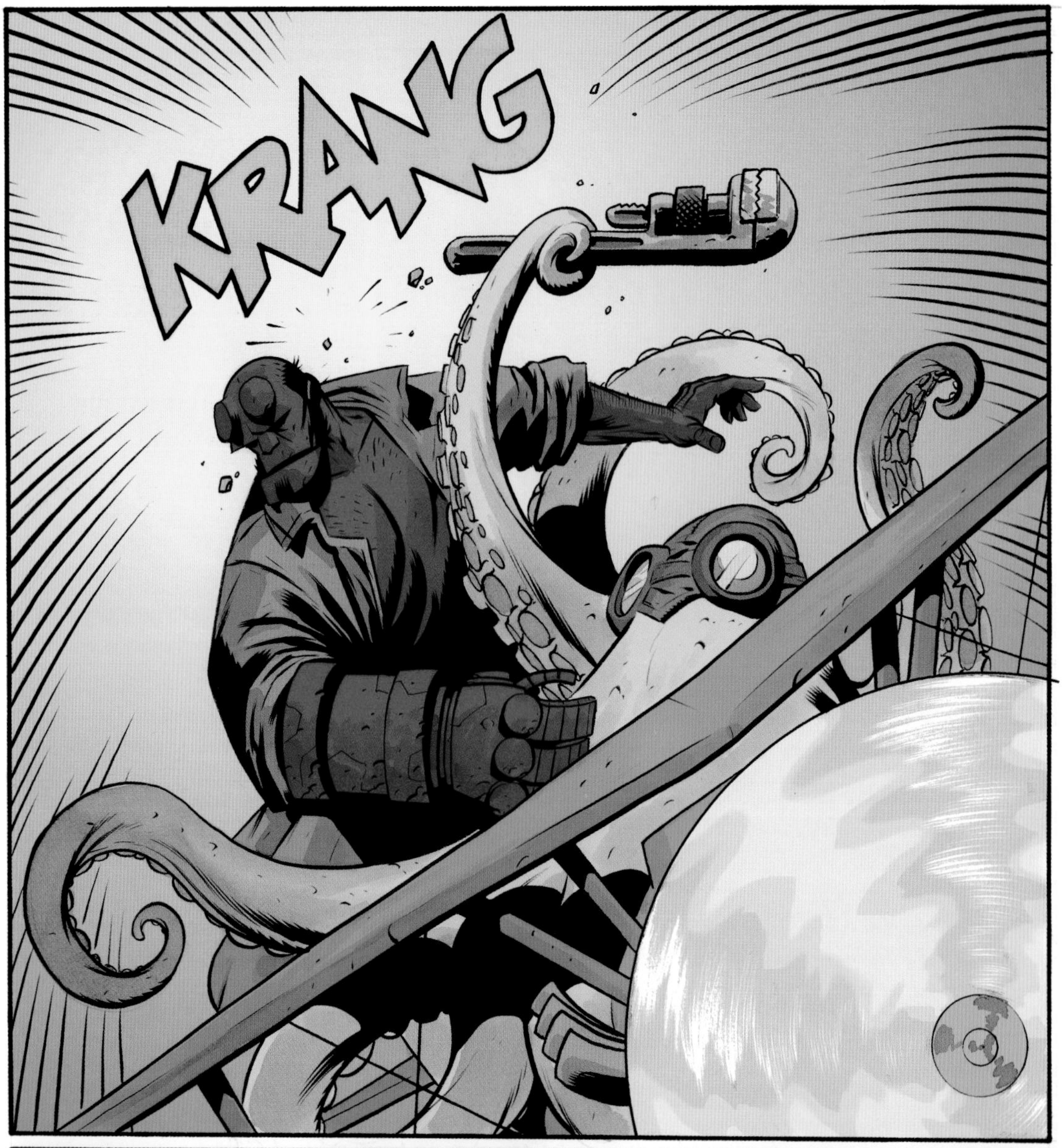
KRANG

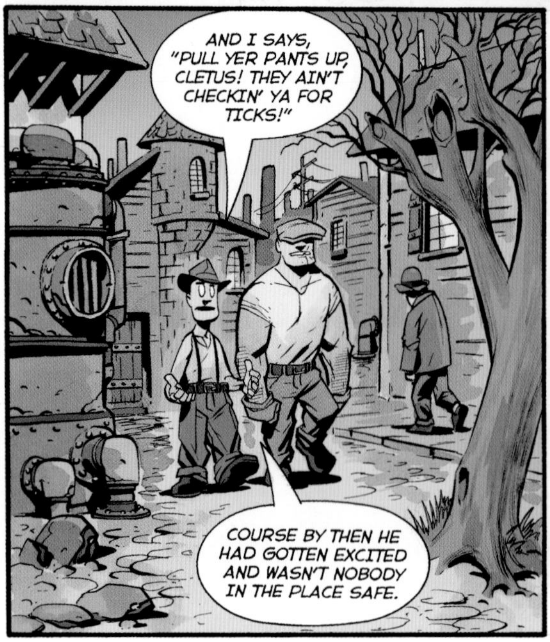
AND I SAYS, "PULL YER PANTS UP, CLETUS! THEY AIN'T CHECKIN' YA FOR TICKS!"
COURSE BY THEN HE HAD GOTTEN EXCITED AND WASN'T NOBODY IN THE PLACE SAFE.

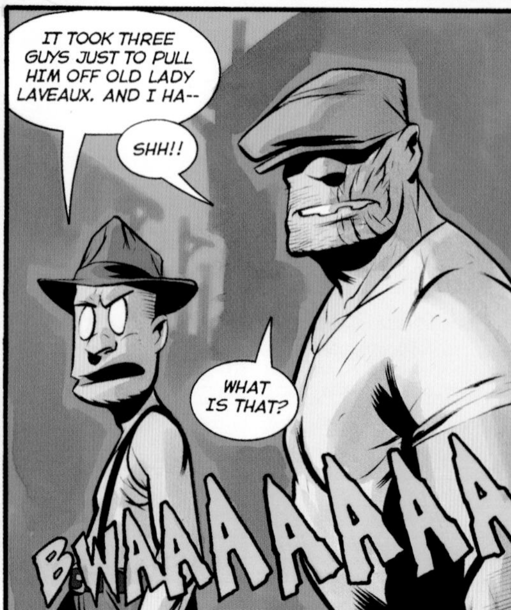
IT TOOK THREE GUYS JUST TO PULL HIM OFF OLD LADY LAVEAUX. AND I HA--
SHH!!
WHAT IS THAT?
BWAAAAAAAA

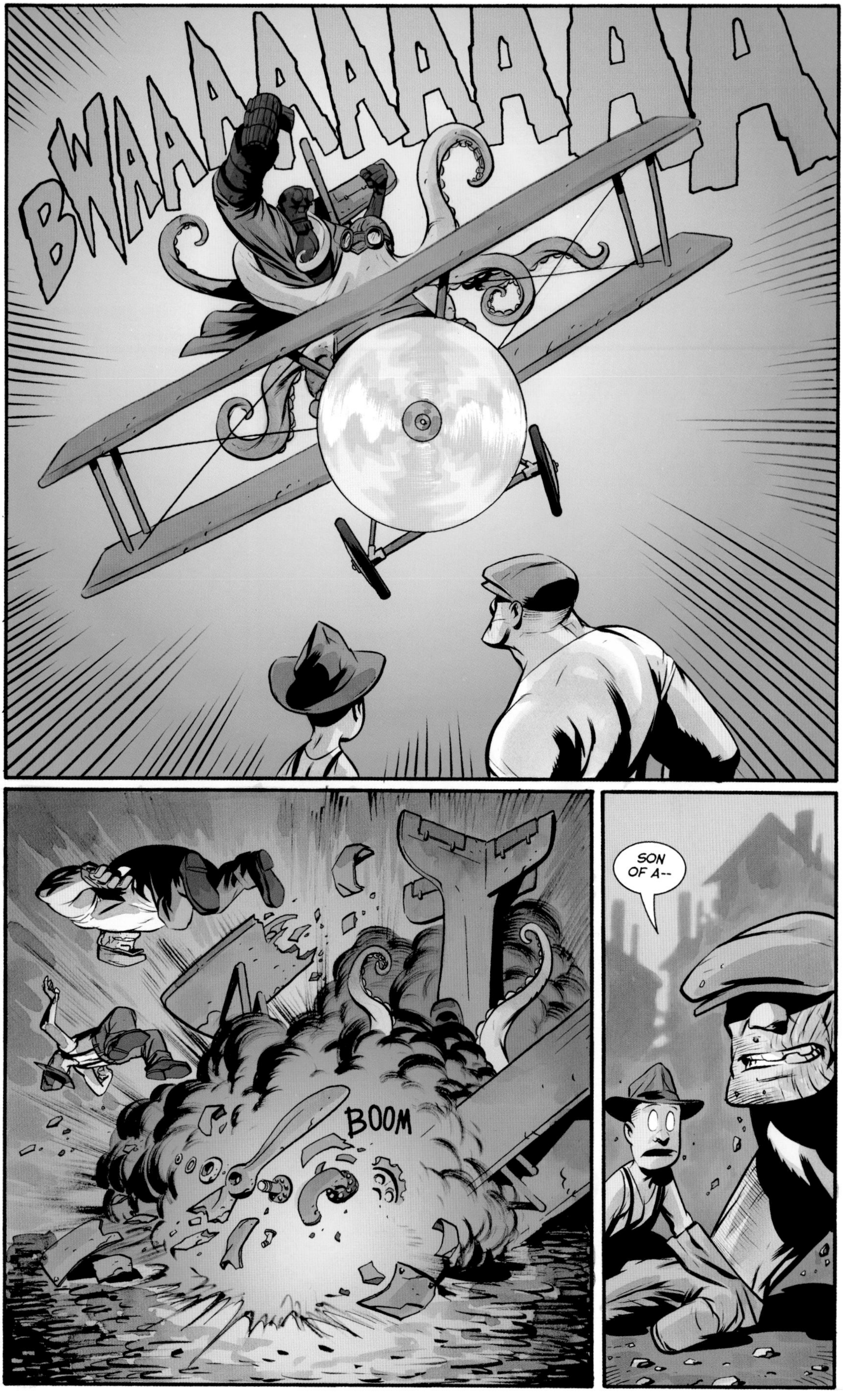
BWAAAAAAAAA
BOOM
SON OF A--

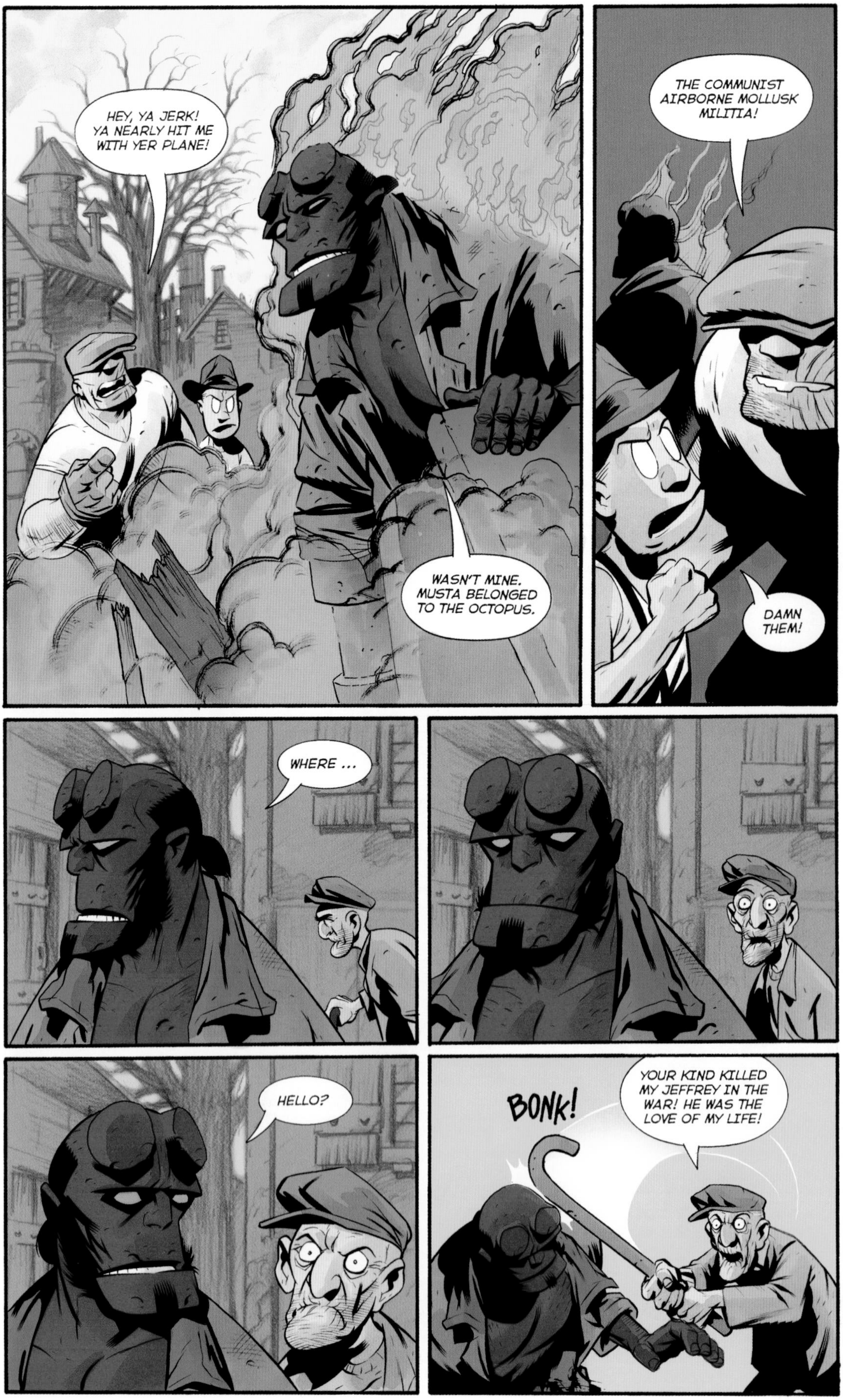
HEY, YA JERK! YA NEARLY HIT ME WITH YER PLANE!
WASN'T MINE. MUSTA BELONGED TO THE OCTOPUS.
THE COMMUNIST AIRBORNE MOLLUSK MILITIA!
DAMN THEM!
WHERE ...
HELLO?
BONK!
YOUR KIND KILLED MY JEFFREY IN THE WAR! HE WAS THE LOVE OF MY LIFE!

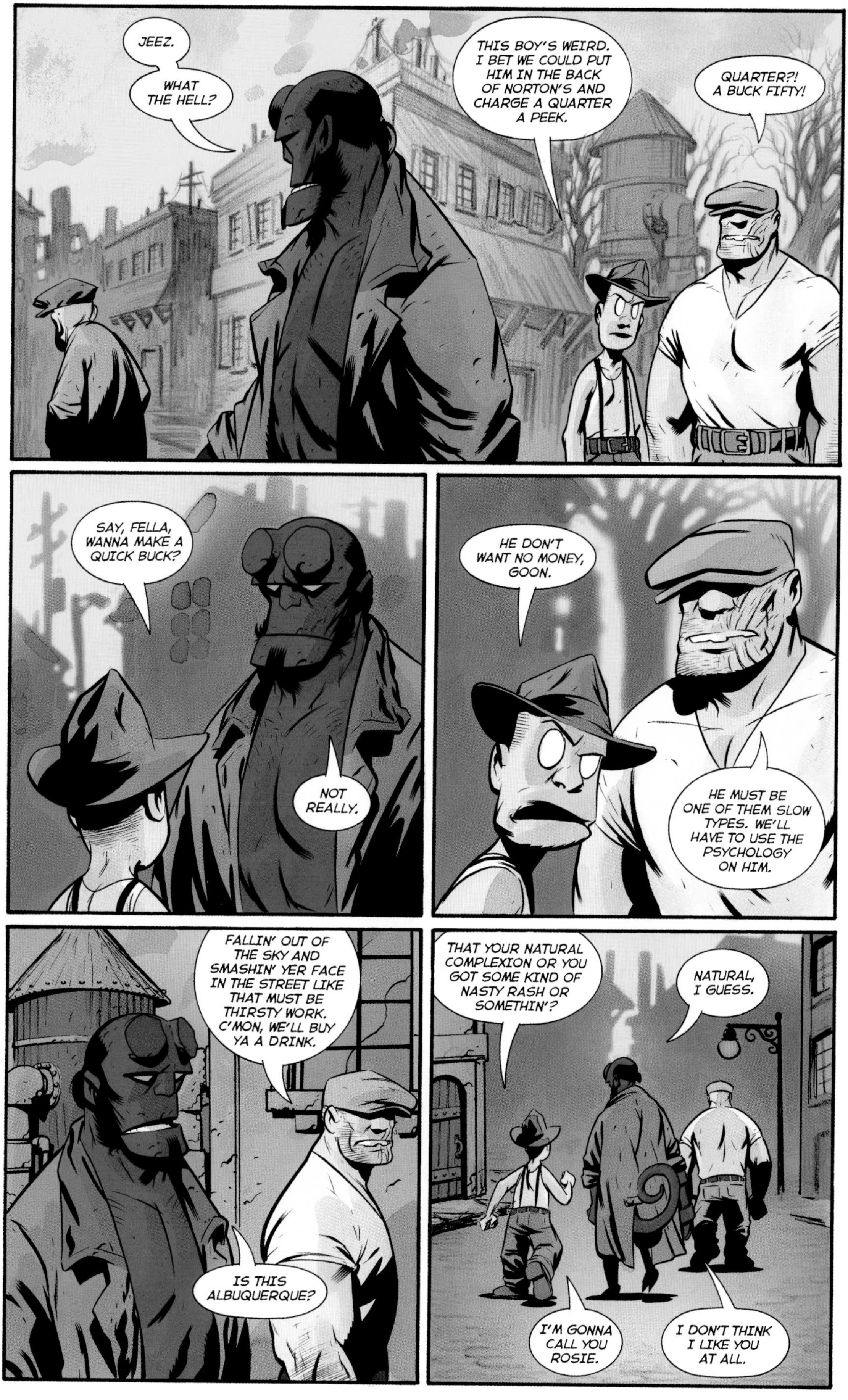
JEEZ.
WHAT THE HELL?
THIS BOY'S WEIRD. I BET WE COULD PUT HIM IN THE BACK OF NORTON'S AND CHARGE A QUARTER A PEEK.
QUARTER?! A BUCK FIFTY!
SAY, FELLA, WANNA MAKE A QUICK BUCK?
NOT REALLY.
HE DON'T WANT NO MONEY, GOON.
HE MUST BE ONE OF THEM SLOW TYPES. WE'LL HAVE TO USE THE PSYCHOLOGY ON HIM.
FALLIN' OUT OF THE SKY AND SMASHIN' YER FACE IN THE STREET LIKE THAT MUST BE THIRSTY WORK. C'MON, WE'LL BUY YA A DRINK.
IS THIS ALBUQUERQUE?
THAT YOUR NATURAL COMPLEXION OR YOU GOT SOME KIND OF NASTY RASH OR SOMETHIN'?
NATURAL, I GUESS.
I'M GONNA CALL YOU ROSIE.
I DON'T THINK I LIKE YOU AT ALL.

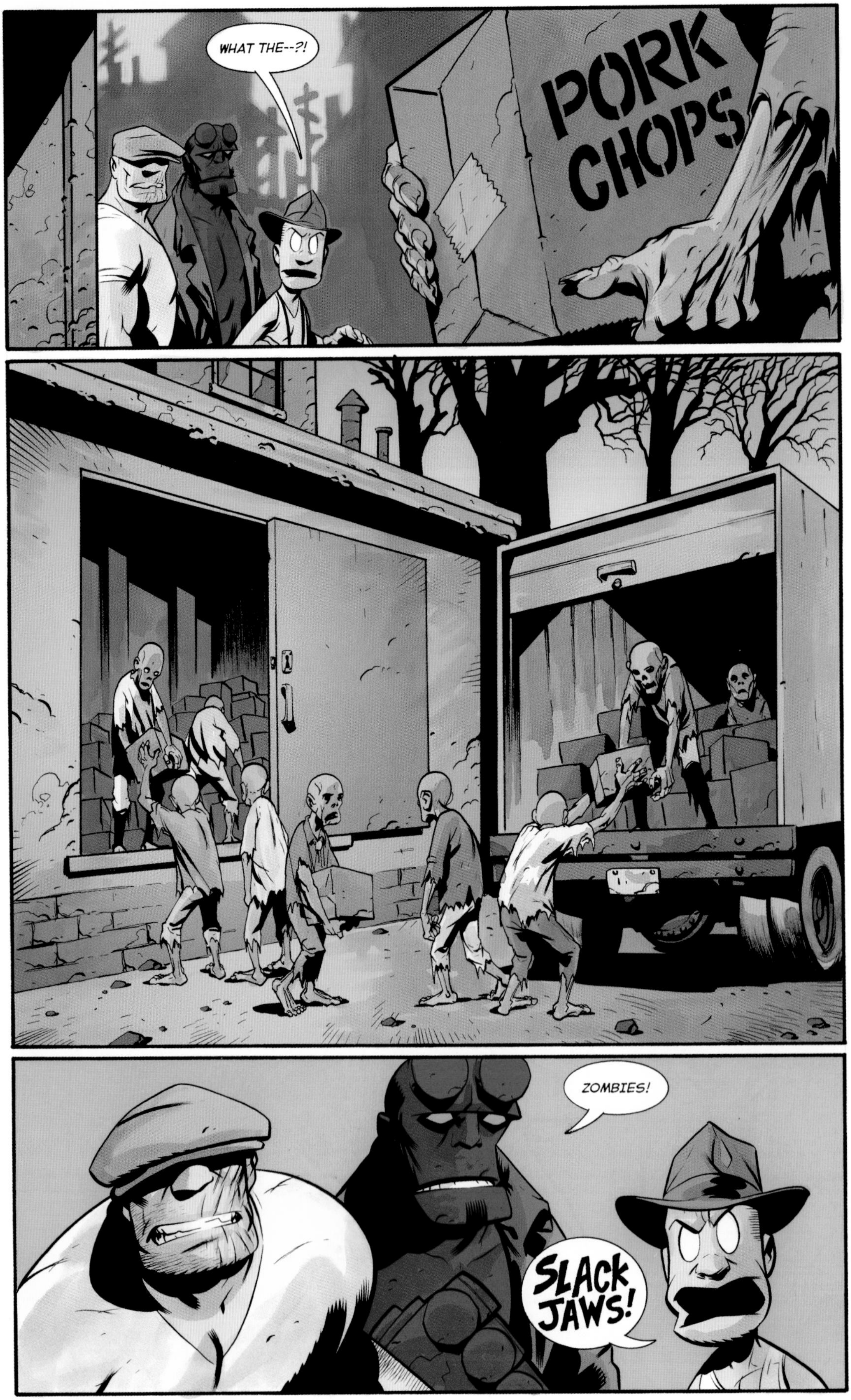
WHAT THE--?!
PORK CHOPS
ZOMBIES!
SLACK JAWS!

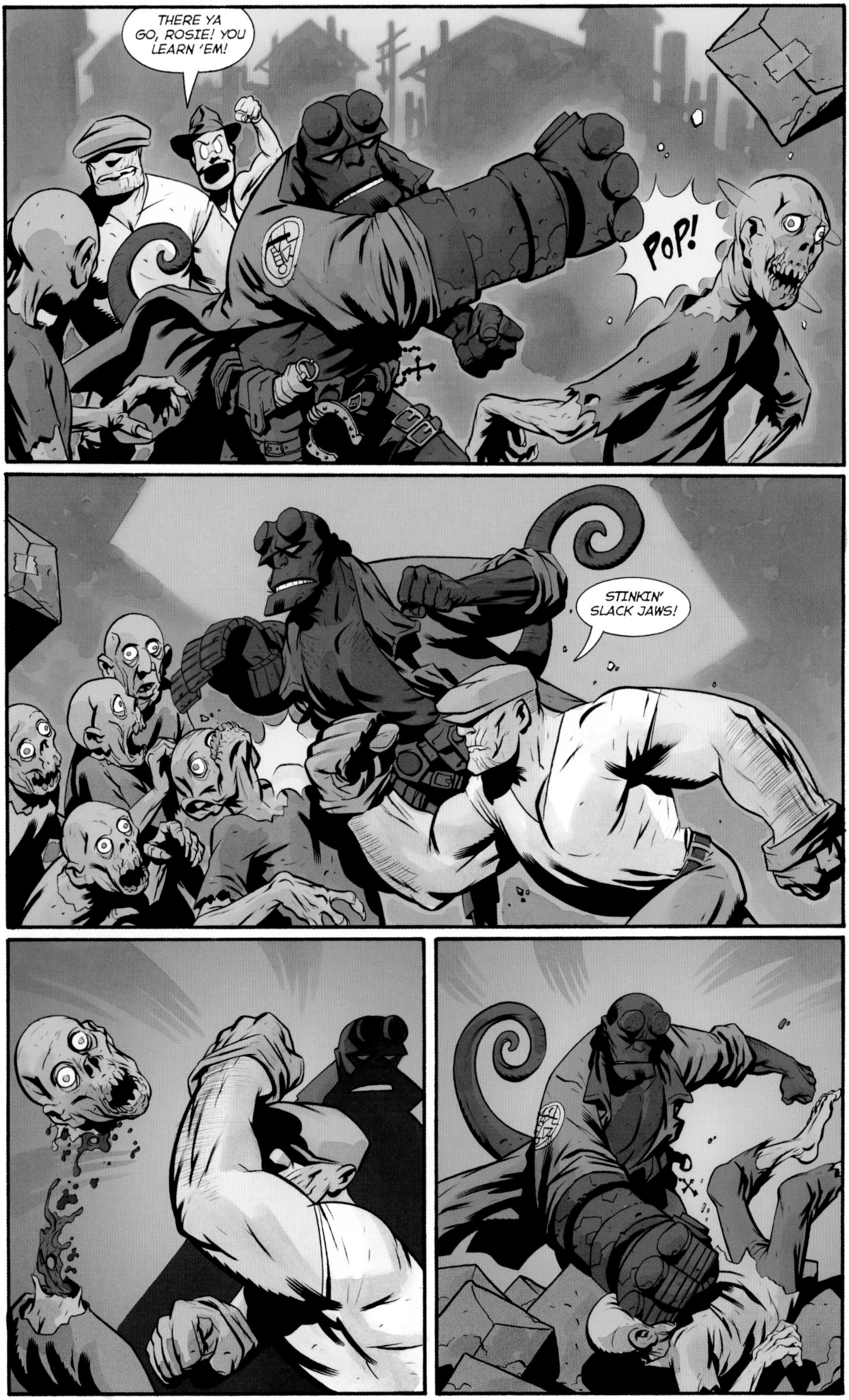
THERE YA GO, ROSIE! YOU LEARN 'EM!
POP!
STINKIN' SLACK JAWS!

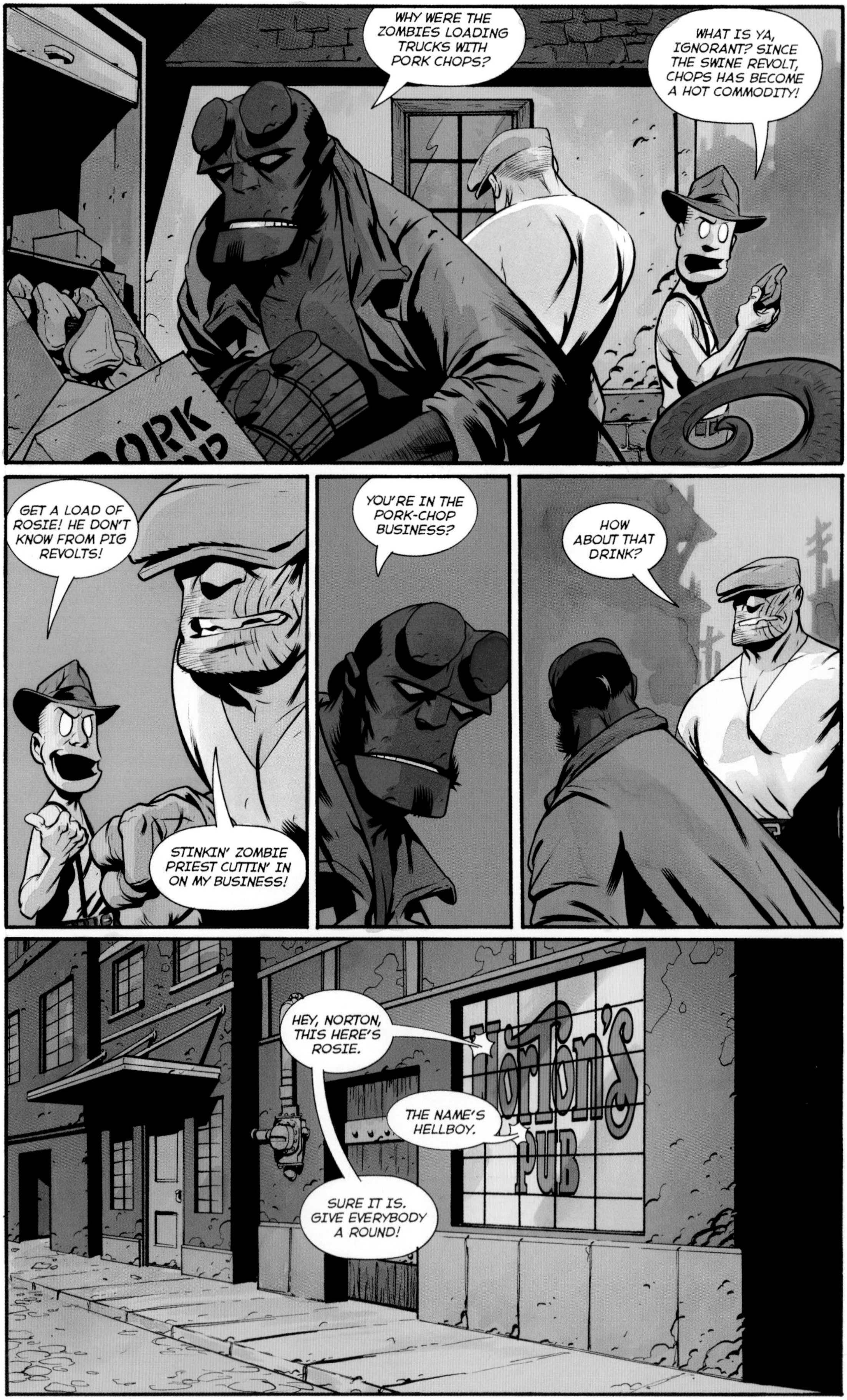

WHY WERE THE ZOMBIES LOADING TRUCKS WITH PORK CHOPS?
WHAT IS YA, IGNORANT? SINCE THE SWINE REVOLT, CHOPS HAS BECOME A HOT COMMODITY!
PORK
GET A LOAD OF ROSIE! HE DON'T KNOW FROM PIG REVOLTS!
STINKIN' ZOMBIE PRIEST CUTTIN' IN ON MY BUSINESS!
YOU'RE IN THE PORK-CHOP BUSINESS?
HOW ABOUT THAT DRINK?
HEY, NORTON, THIS HERE'S ROSIE.
THE NAME'S HELLBOY.
SURE IT IS. GIVE EVERYBODY A ROUND!
Norton's PUB

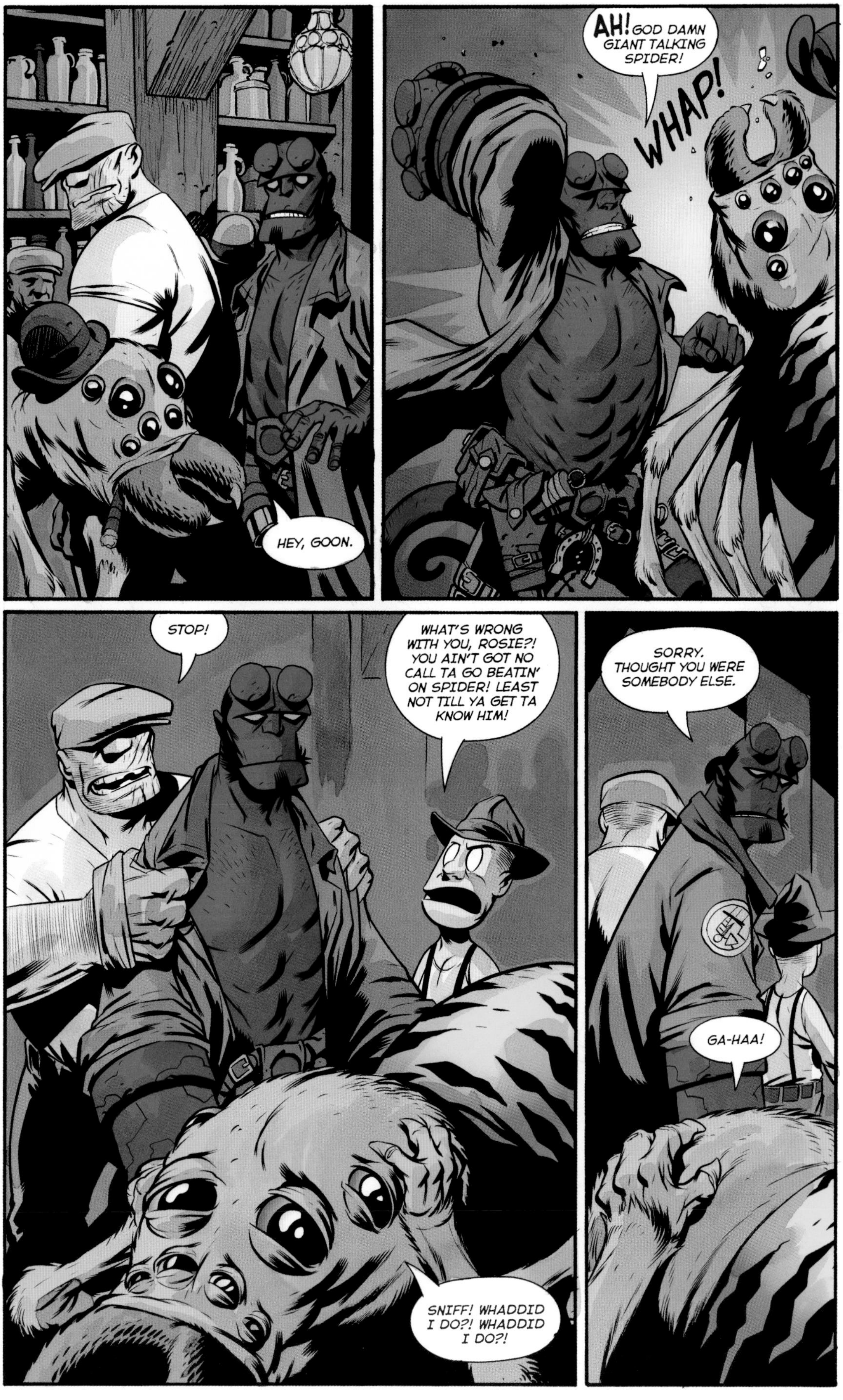
HEY, GOON.
AH! GOD DAMN GIANT TALKING SPIDER!
WHAP!
STOP!
WHAT'S WRONG WITH YOU, ROSIE?! YOU AIN'T GOT NO CALL TA GO BEATIN' ON SPIDER! LEAST NOT TILL YA GET TA KNOW HIM!
SNIFF! WHADDID I DO?! WHADDID I DO?!
SORRY. THOUGHT YOU WERE SOMEBODY ELSE.
GA-HAA!

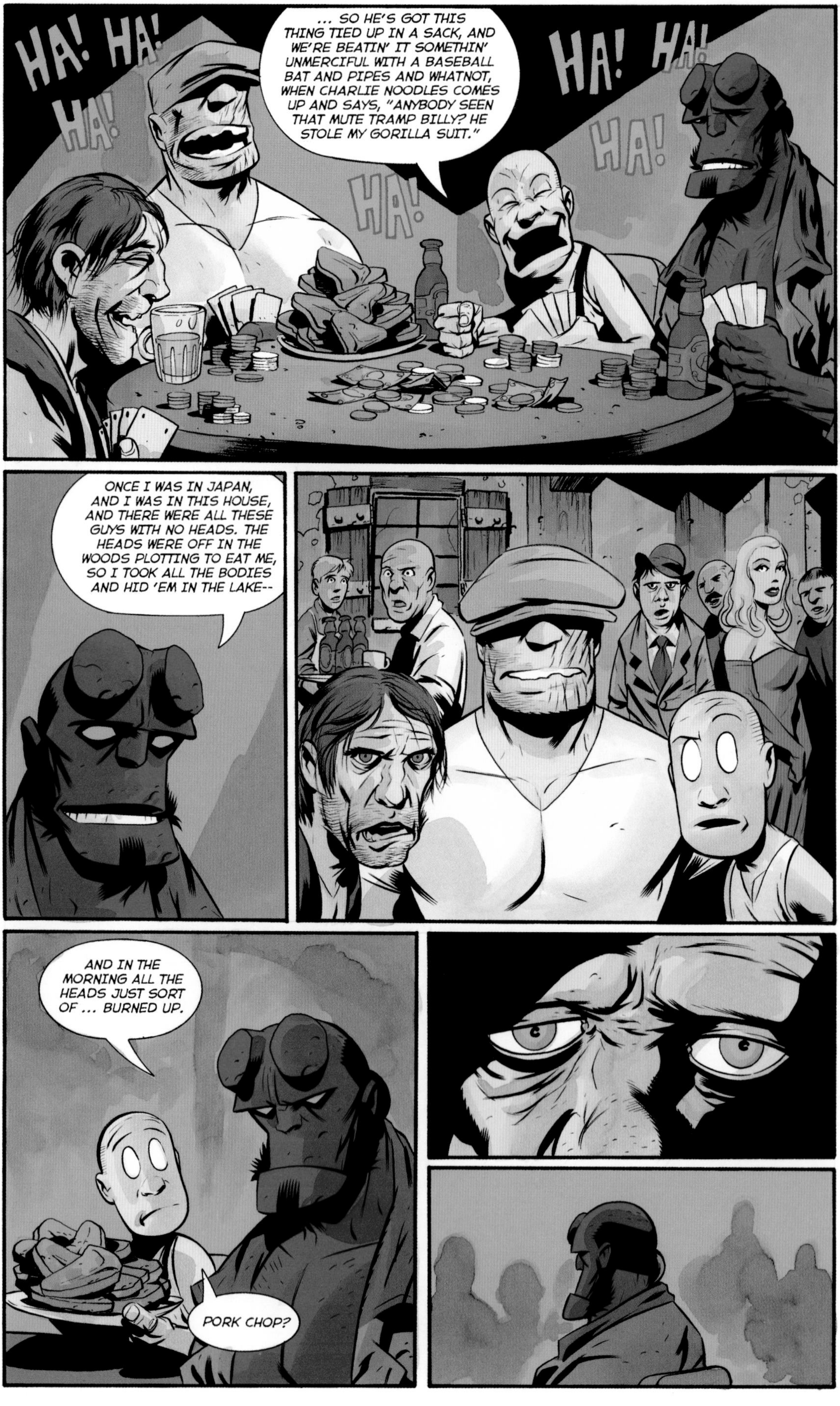
HA! HA! HA!
... SO HE'S GOT THIS THING TIED UP IN A SACK, AND WE'RE BEATIN' IT SOMETHIN' UNMERCIFUL WITH A BASEBALL BAT AND PIPES AND WHATNOT, WHEN CHARLIE NOODLES COMES UP AND SAYS, "ANYBODY SEEN THAT MUTE TRAMP BILLY? HE STOLE MY GORILLA SUIT."
HA! HA!
HA!
HA!
ONCE I WAS IN JAPAN, AND I WAS IN THIS HOUSE, AND THERE WERE ALL THESE GUYS WITH NO HEADS. THE HEADS WERE OFF IN THE WOODS PLOTTING TO EAT ME, SO I TOOK ALL THE BODIES AND HID 'EM IN THE LAKE--
AND IN THE MORNING ALL THE HEADS JUST SORT OF ... BURNED UP.
PORK CHOP?

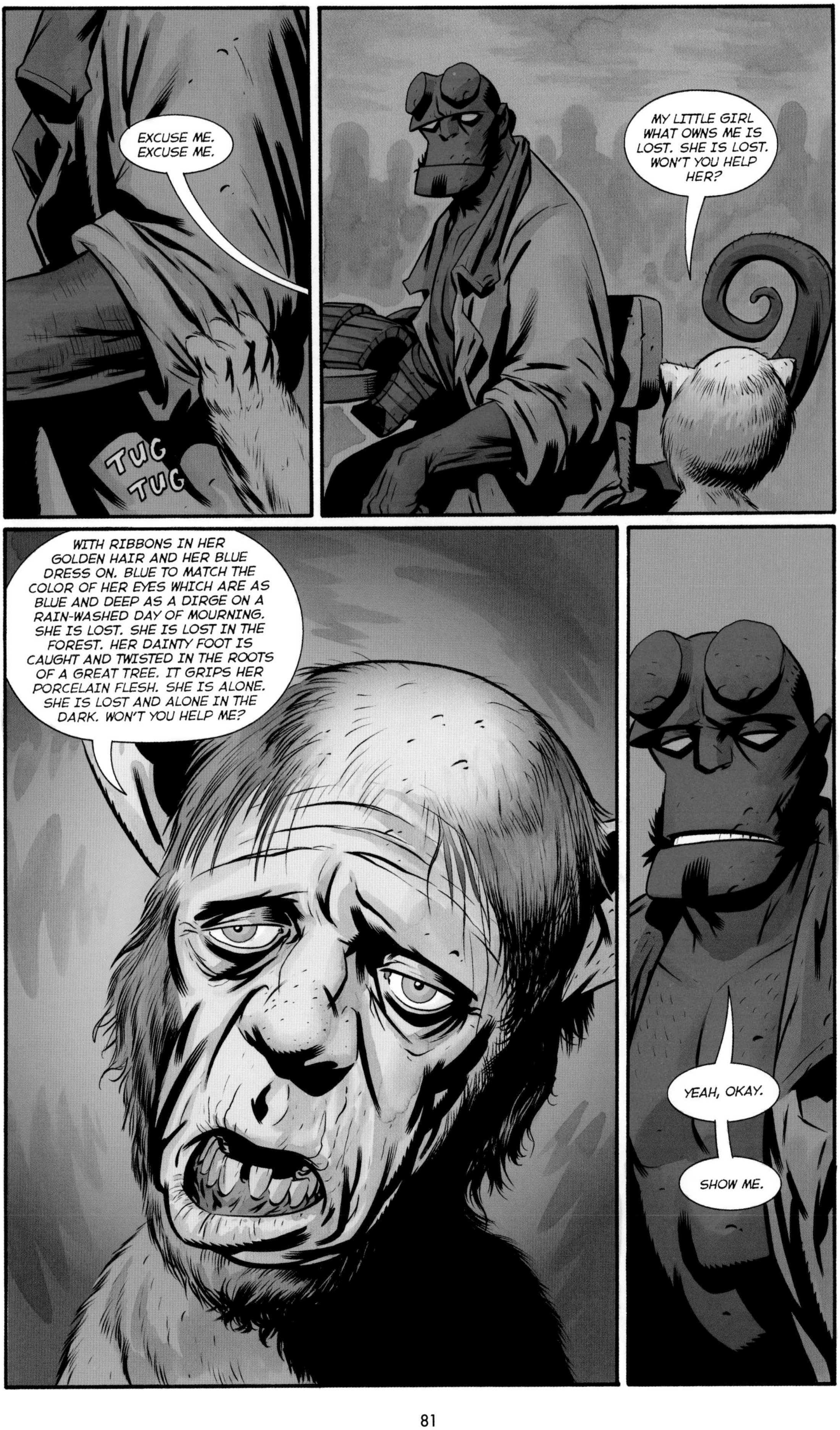
EXCUSE ME. EXCUSE ME.
TUG TUG
MY LITTLE GIRL WHAT OWNS ME IS LOST. SHE IS LOST. WON'T YOU HELP HER?
WITH RIBBONS IN HER GOLDEN HAIR AND HER BLUE DRESS ON. BLUE TO MATCH THE COLOR OF HER EYES WHICH ARE AS BLUE AND DEEP AS A DIRGE ON A RAIN-WASHED DAY OF MOURNING. SHE IS LOST. SHE IS LOST IN THE FOREST. HER DAINTY FOOT IS CAUGHT AND TWISTED IN THE ROOTS OF A GREAT TREE. IT GRIPS HER PORCELAIN FLESH. SHE IS ALONE. SHE IS LOST AND ALONE IN THE DARK. WON'T YOU HELP ME?
YEAH, OKAY.
SHOW ME.

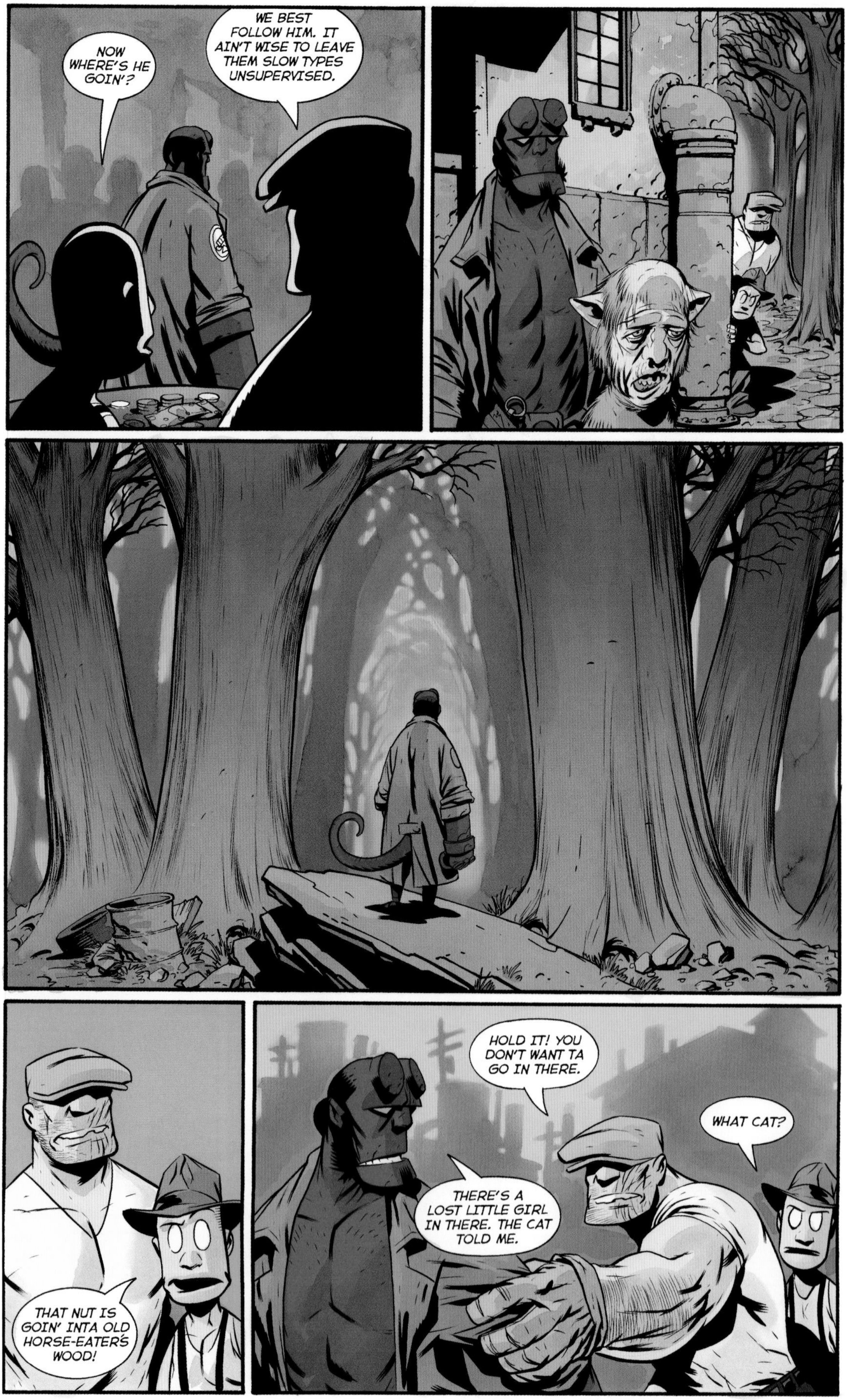
NOW WHERE'S HE GOIN'?
WE BEST FOLLOW HIM. IT AIN'T WISE TO LEAVE THEM SLOW TYPES UNSUPERVISED.
THAT NUT IS GOIN' INTA OLD HORSE-EATER'S WOOD!
HOLD IT! YOU DON'T WANT TA GO IN THERE.
THERE'S A LOST LITTLE GIRL IN THERE. THE CAT TOLD ME.
WHAT CAT?

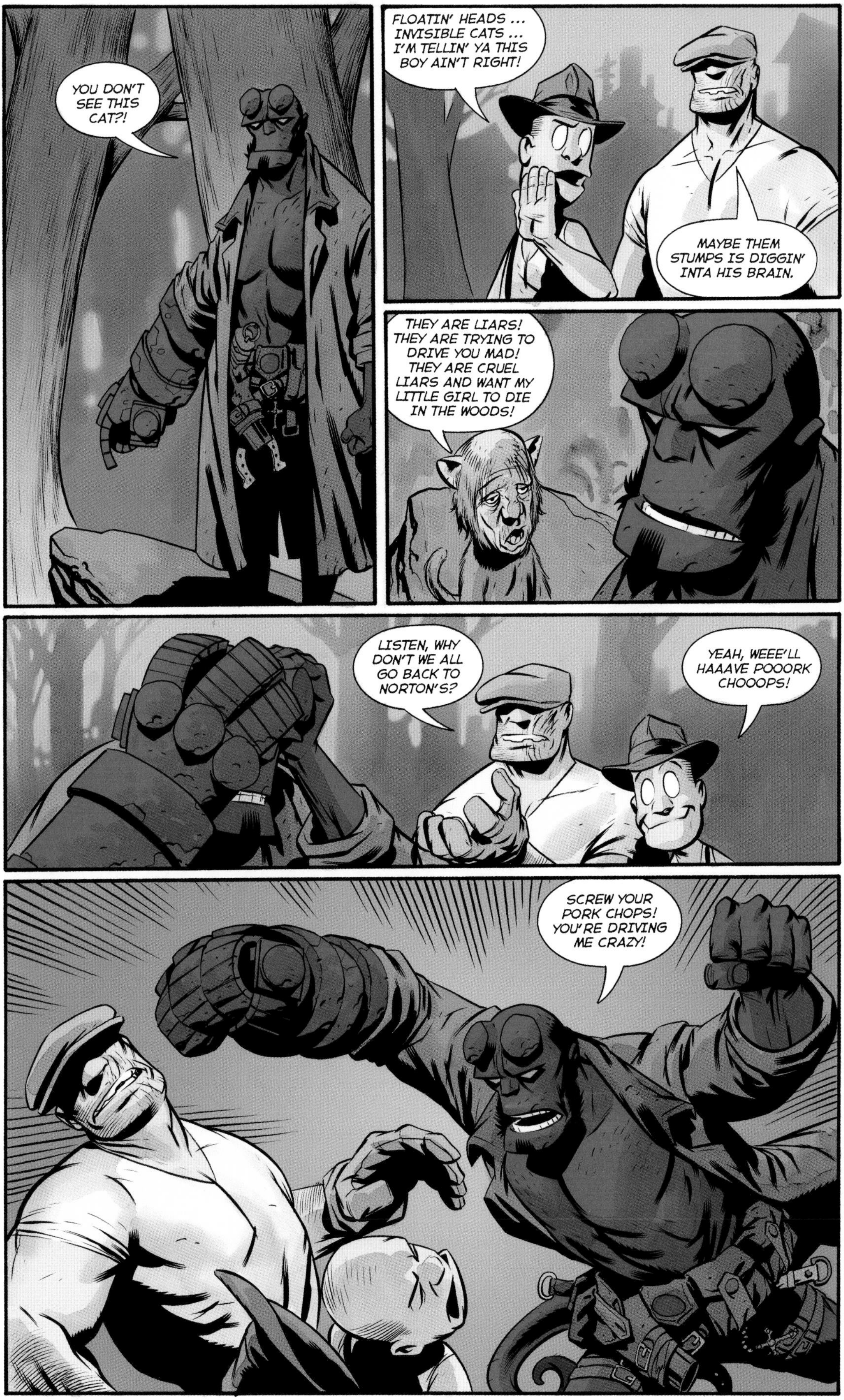
YOU DON'T SEE THIS CAT?!
FLOATIN' HEADS ... INVISIBLE CATS ... I'M TELLIN' YA THIS BOY AIN'T RIGHT!
MAYBE THEM STUMPS IS DIGGIN' INTA HIS BRAIN.
THEY ARE LIARS! THEY ARE TRYING TO DRIVE YOU MAD! THEY ARE CRUEL LIARS AND WANT MY LITTLE GIRL TO DIE IN THE WOODS!
LISTEN, WHY DON'T WE ALL GO BACK TO NORTON'S?
YEAH, WEEE'LL HAAAVE POOORK CHOOOPS!
SCREW YOUR PORK CHOPS! YOU'RE DRIVING ME CRAZY!

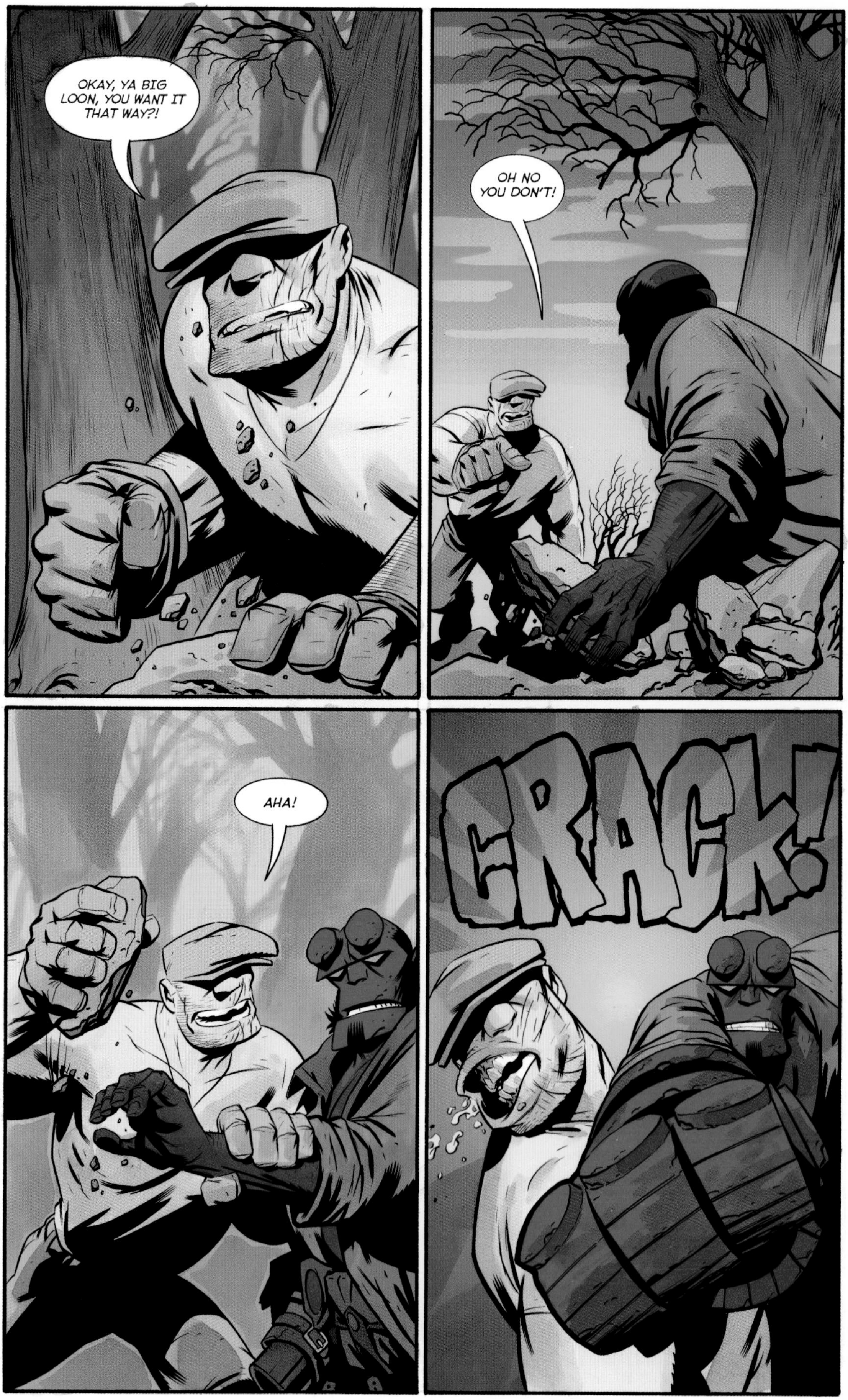
OKAY, YA BIG LOON, YOU WANT IT THAT WAY?!
OH NO YOU DON'T!
AHA!
CRACK!

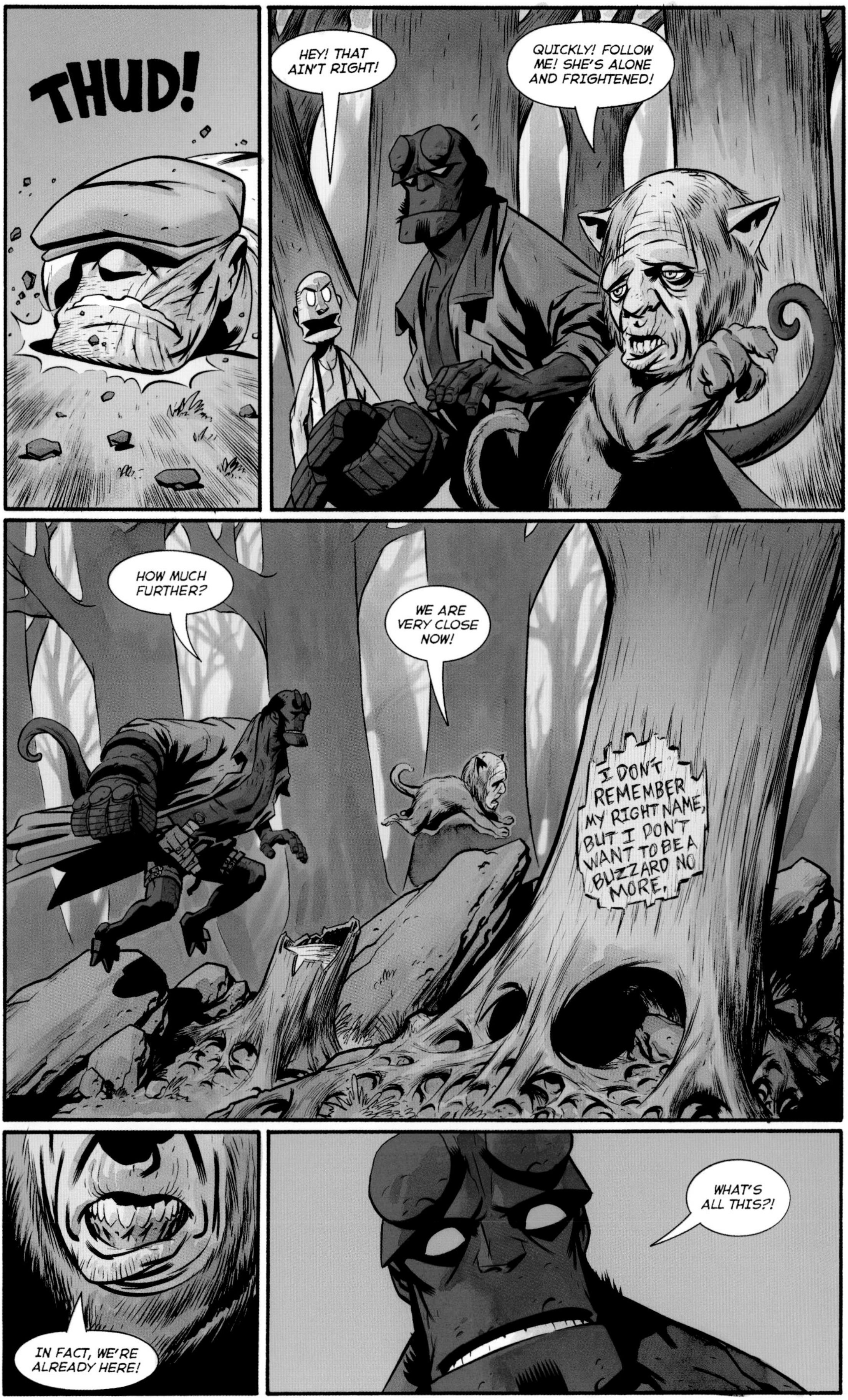
THUD!
HEY! THAT AIN'T RIGHT!
QUICKLY! FOLLOW ME! SHE'S ALONE AND FRIGHTENED!
HOW MUCH FURTHER?
WE ARE VERY CLOSE NOW!
I DON'T REMEMBER MY RIGHT NAME, BUT I DON'T WANT TO BE A BUZZARD NO MORE,
IN FACT, WE'RE ALREADY HERE!
WHAT'S ALL THIS?!

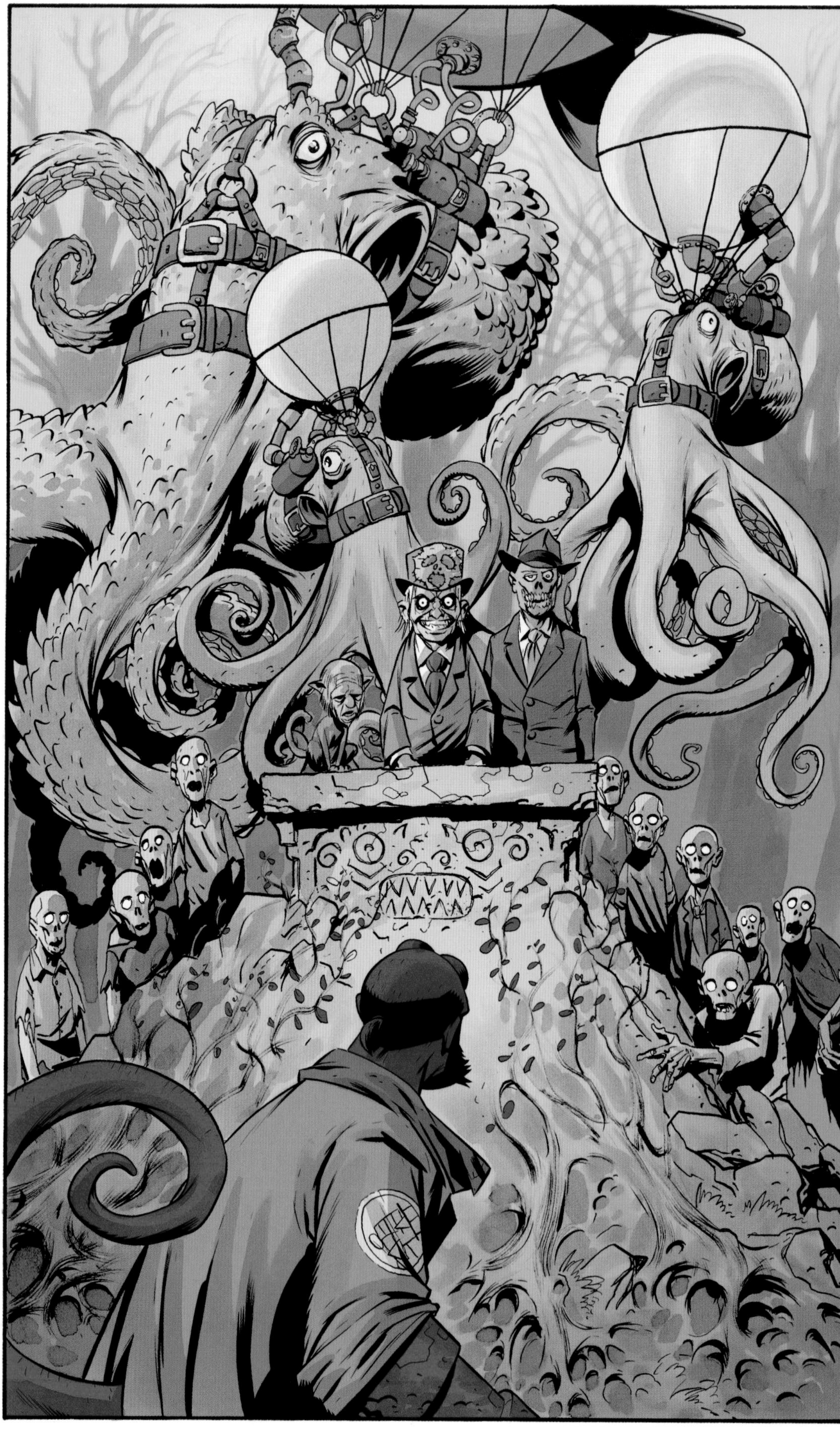

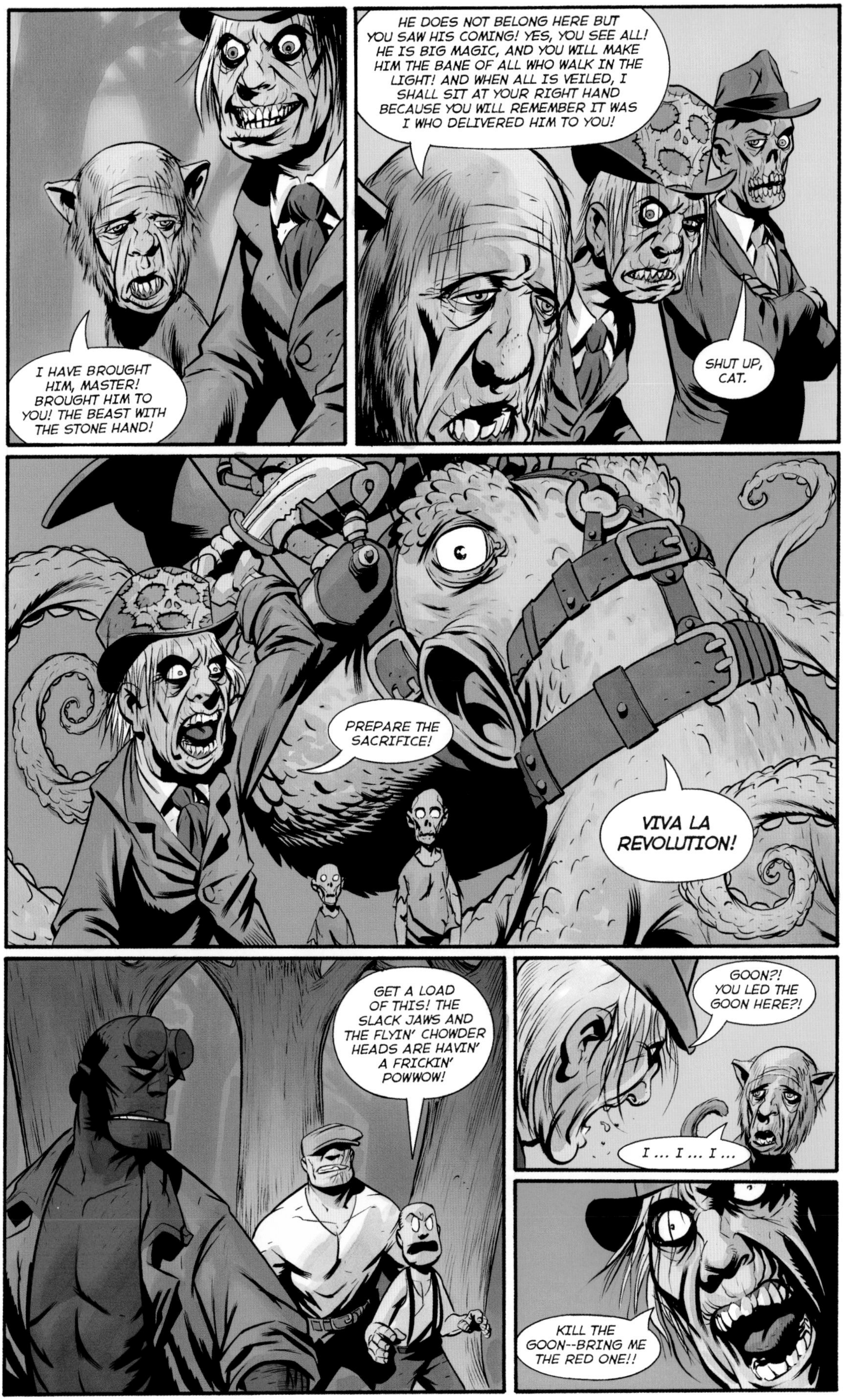
I HAVE BROUGHT HIM, MASTER! BROUGHT HIM TO YOU! THE BEAST WITH THE STONE HAND!
HE DOES NOT BELONG HERE BUT YOU SAW HIS COMING! YES, YOU SEE ALL! HE IS BIG MAGIC, AND YOU WILL MAKE HIM THE BANE OF ALL WHO WALK IN THE LIGHT! AND WHEN ALL IS VEILED, I SHALL SIT AT YOUR RIGHT HAND BECAUSE YOU WILL REMEMBER IT WAS I WHO DELIVERED HIM TO YOU!
SHUT UP, CAT.
PREPARE THE SACRIFICE!
VIVA LA REVOLUTION!
GET A LOAD OF THIS! THE SLACK JAWS AND THE FLYIN' CHOWDER HEADS ARE HAVIN' A FRICKIN' POWWOW!
GOON?! YOU LED THE GOON HERE?!
I ... I ... I ...
KILL THE GOON--BRING ME THE RED ONE!!

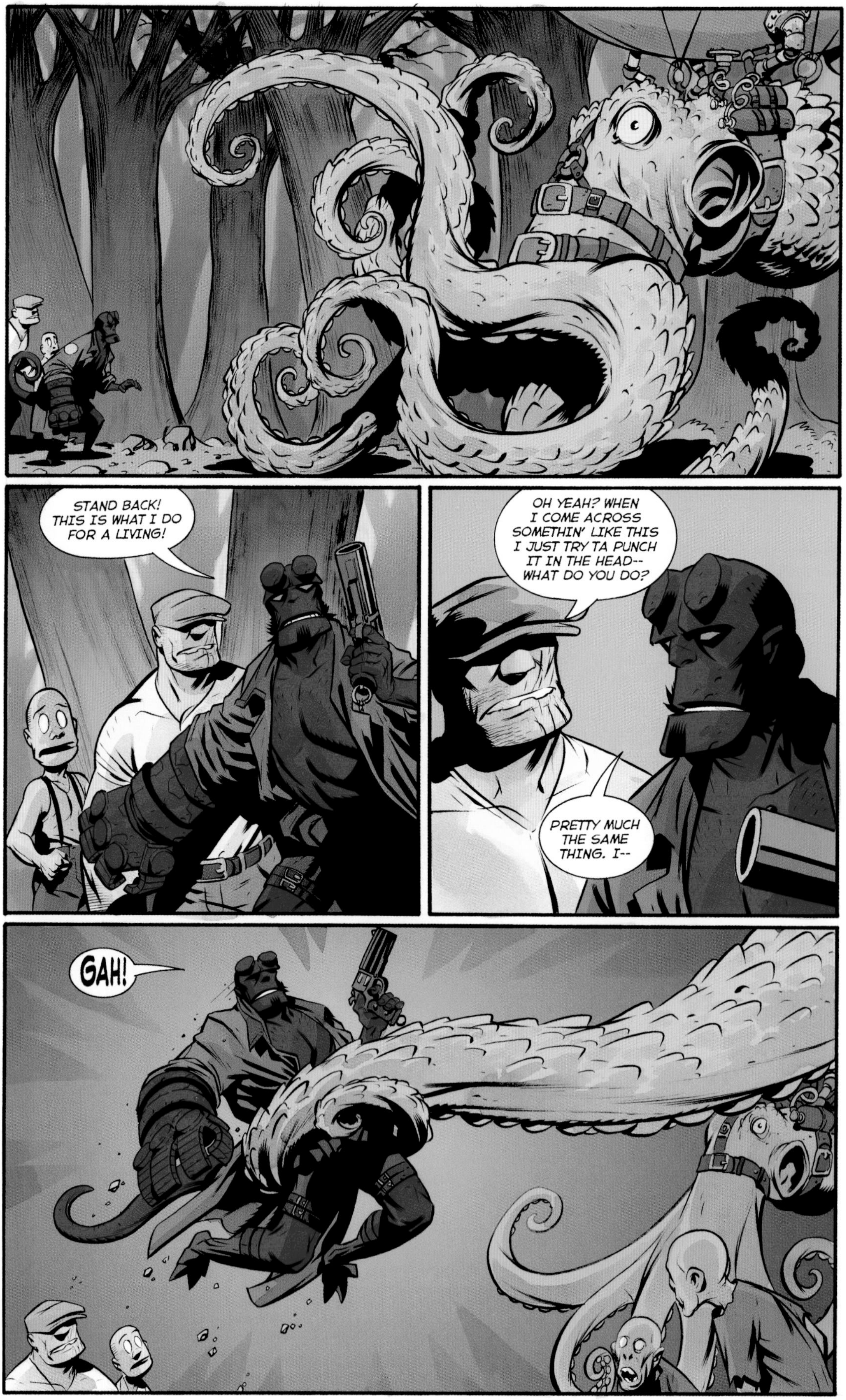
STAND BACK! THIS IS WHAT I DO FOR A LIVING!
OH YEAH? WHEN I COME ACROSS SOMETHIN' LIKE THIS I JUST TRY TA PUNCH IT IN THE HEAD-- WHAT DO YOU DO?
PRETTY MUCH THE SAME THING. I--
GAH!

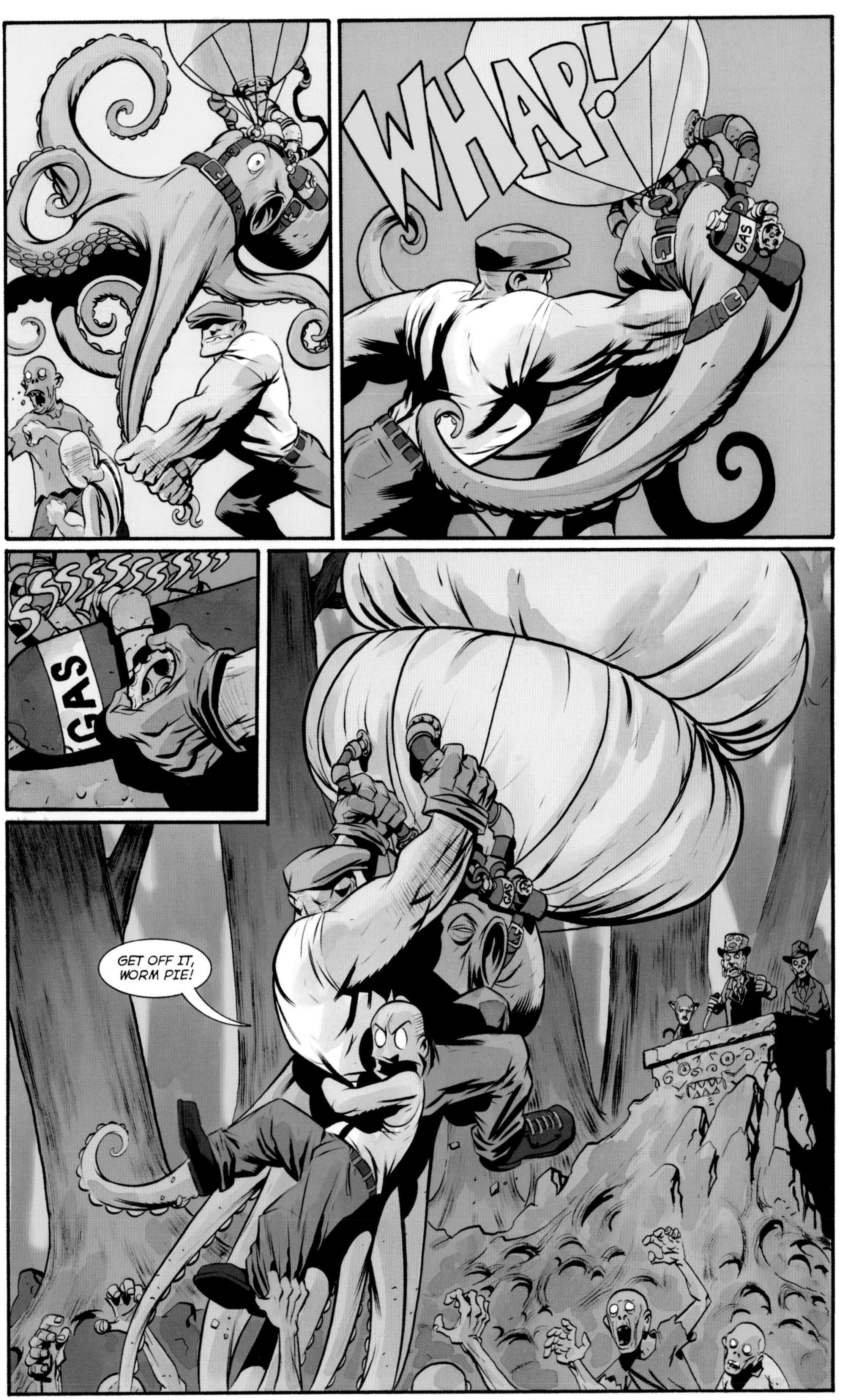
WHAP!
GAS
SSSSSSSSSSS
GAS
GAS
GET OFF IT, WORM PIE!

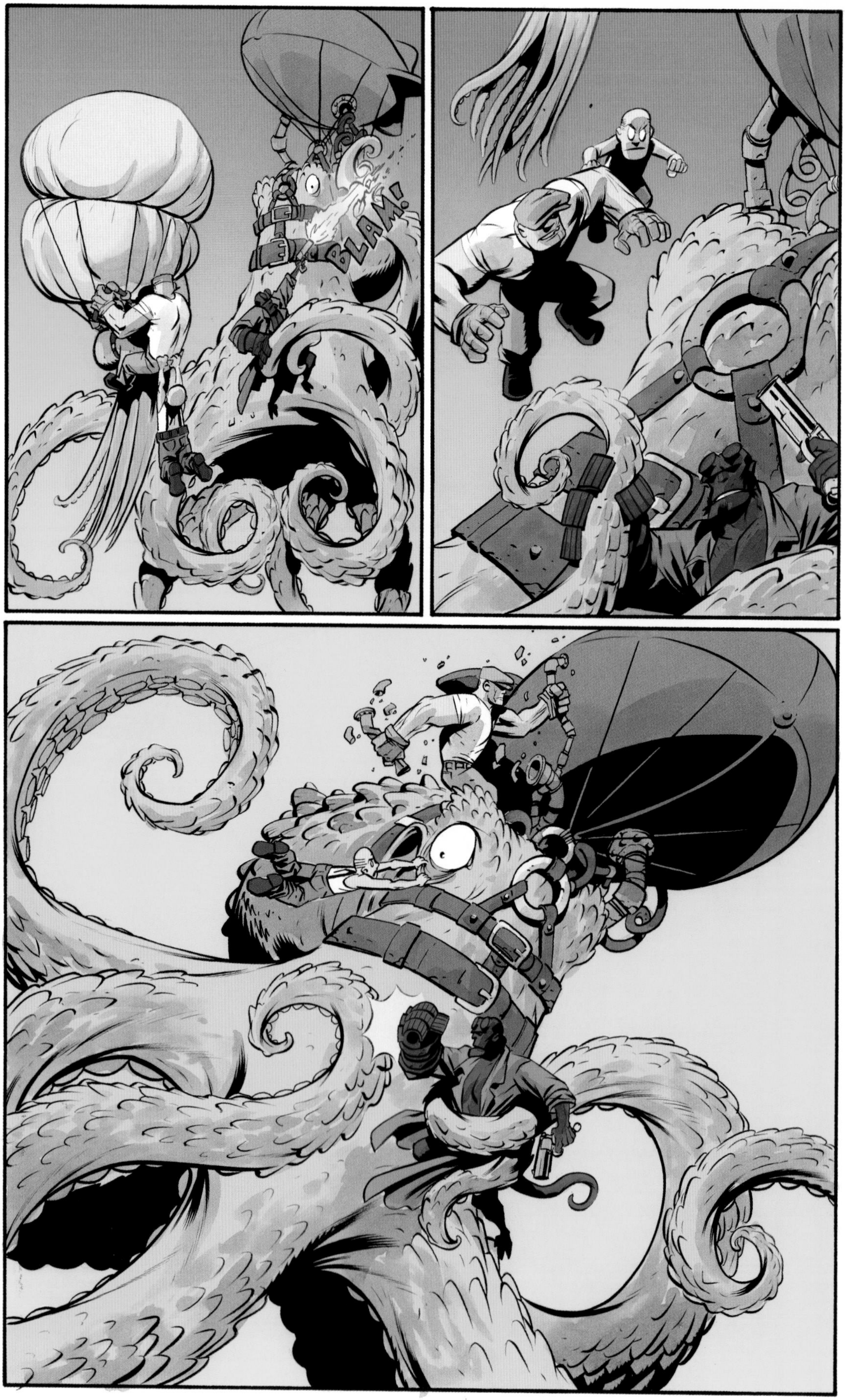
BLAM!

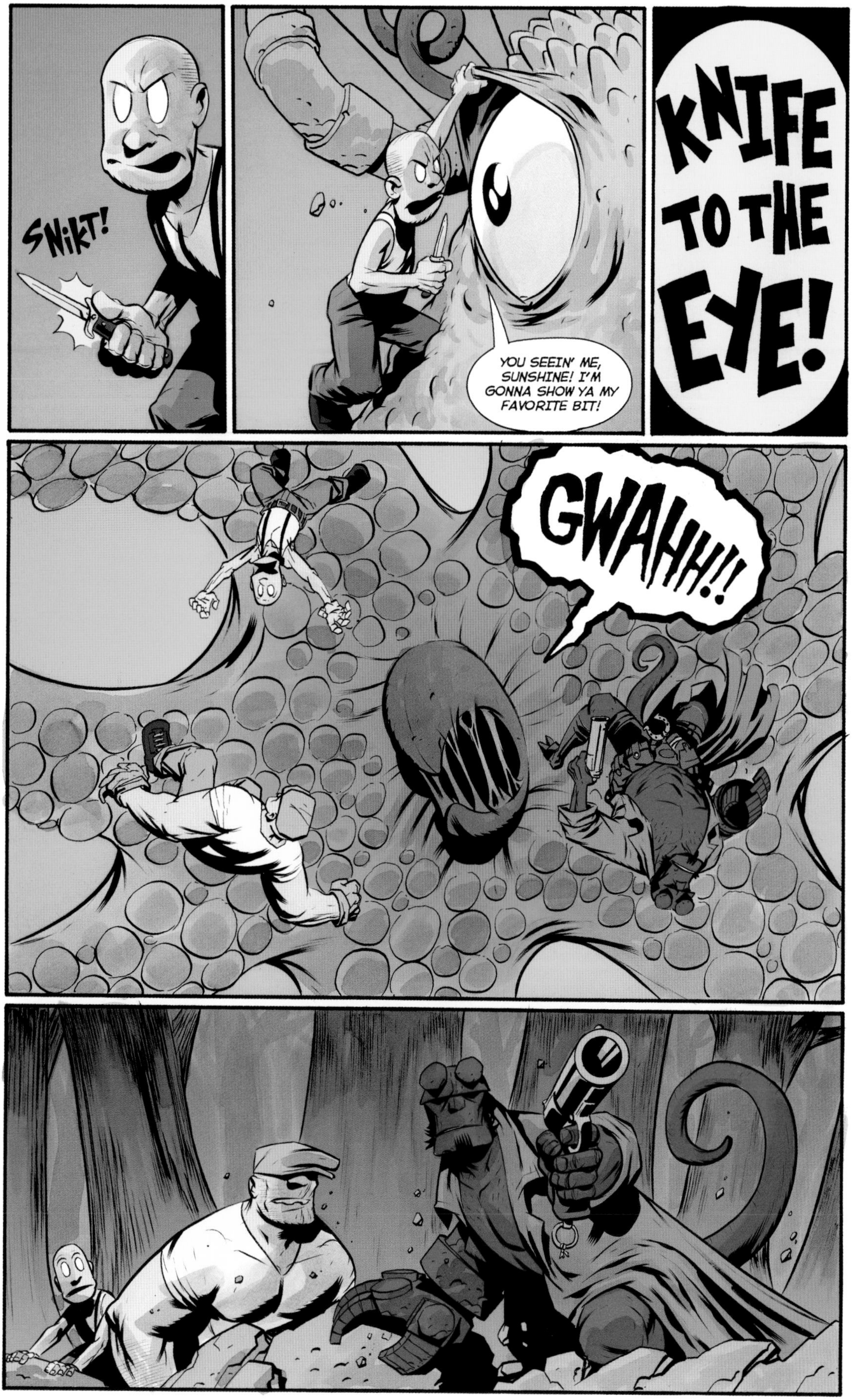
SNIKT!
YOU SEEIN' ME, SUNSHINE! I'M GONNA SHOW YA MY FAVORITE BIT!
KNIFE TO THE EYE!
GWAHH!!!

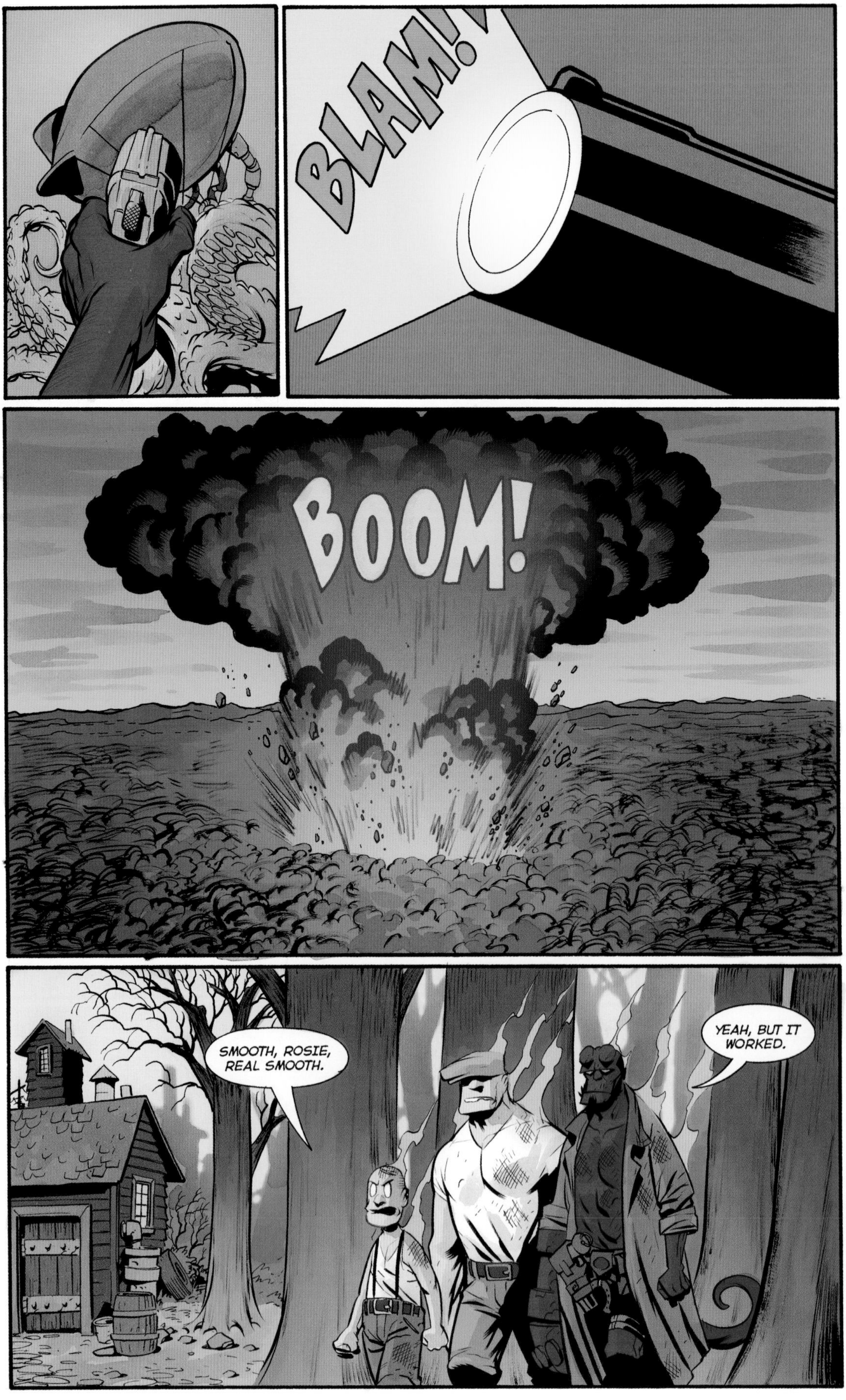
BLAM!
BOOM!
SMOOTH, ROSIE, REAL SMOOTH.
YEAH, BUT IT WORKED.

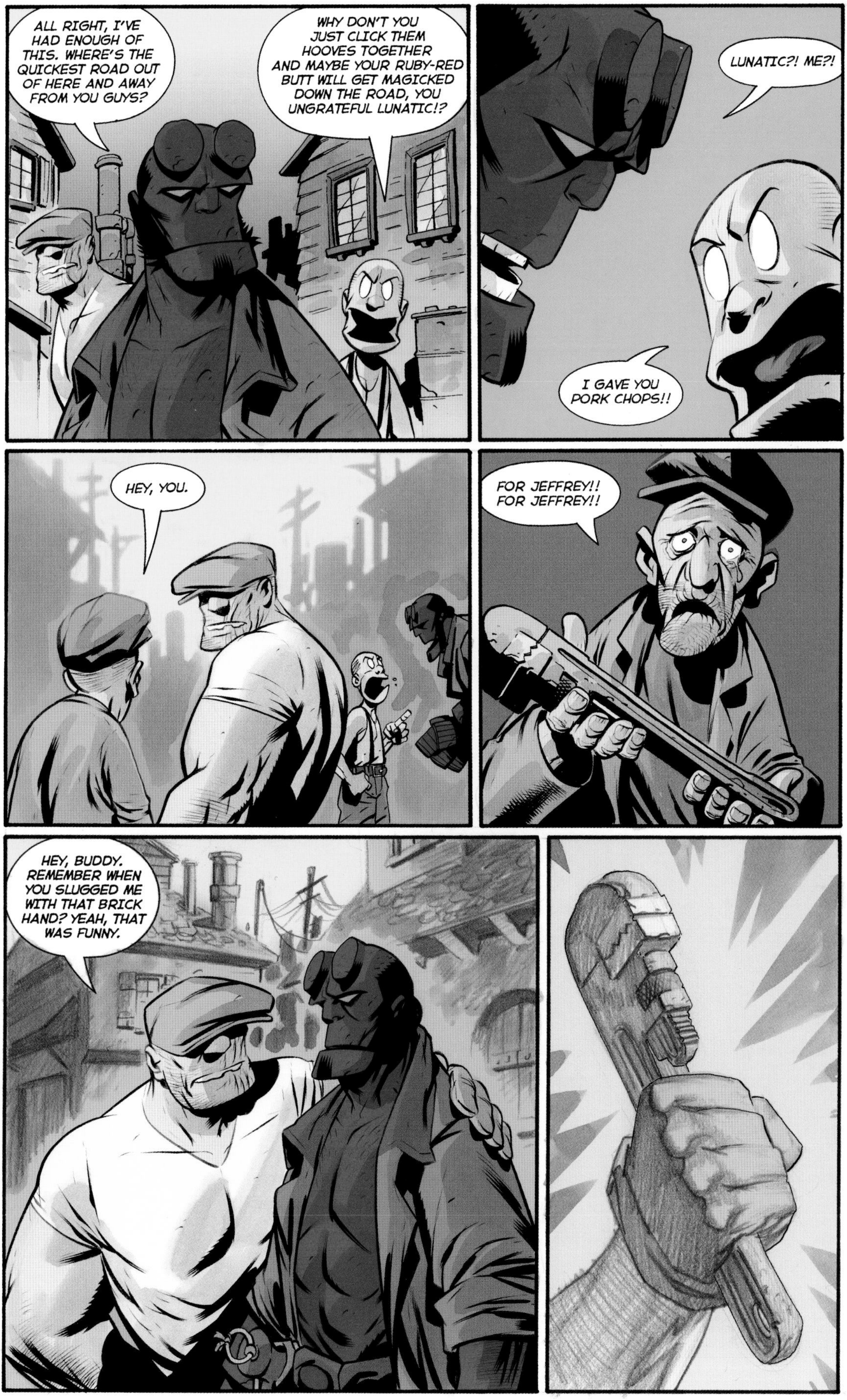
ALL RIGHT, I'VE HAD ENOUGH OF THIS. WHERE'S THE QUICKEST ROAD OUT OF HERE AND AWAY FROM YOU GUYS?
WHY DON'T YOU JUST CLICK THEM HOOVES TOGETHER AND MAYBE YOUR RUBY-RED BUTT WILL GET MAGICKED DOWN THE ROAD, YOU UNGRATEFUL LUNATIC!?
LUNATIC?! ME?!
I GAVE YOU PORK CHOPS!!
HEY, YOU.
FOR JEFFREY!! FOR JEFFREY!!
HEY, BUDDY. REMEMBER WHEN YOU SLUGGED ME WITH THAT BRICK HAND? YEAH, THAT WAS FUNNY.

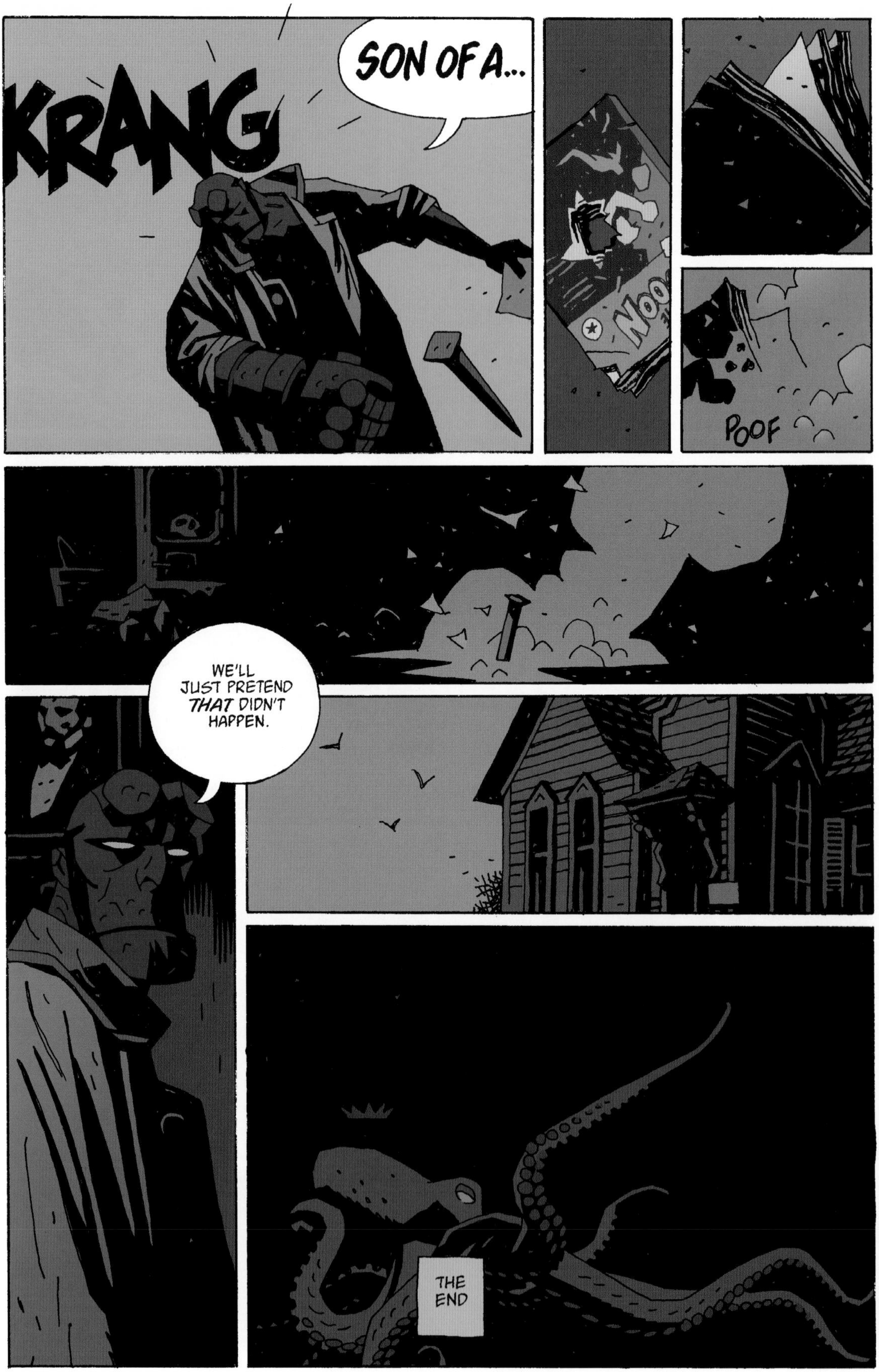
KRANG
SON OF A...
POOF
WE'LL JUST PRETEND *THAT* DIDN'T HAPPEN.
THE END

CHAPTER 4

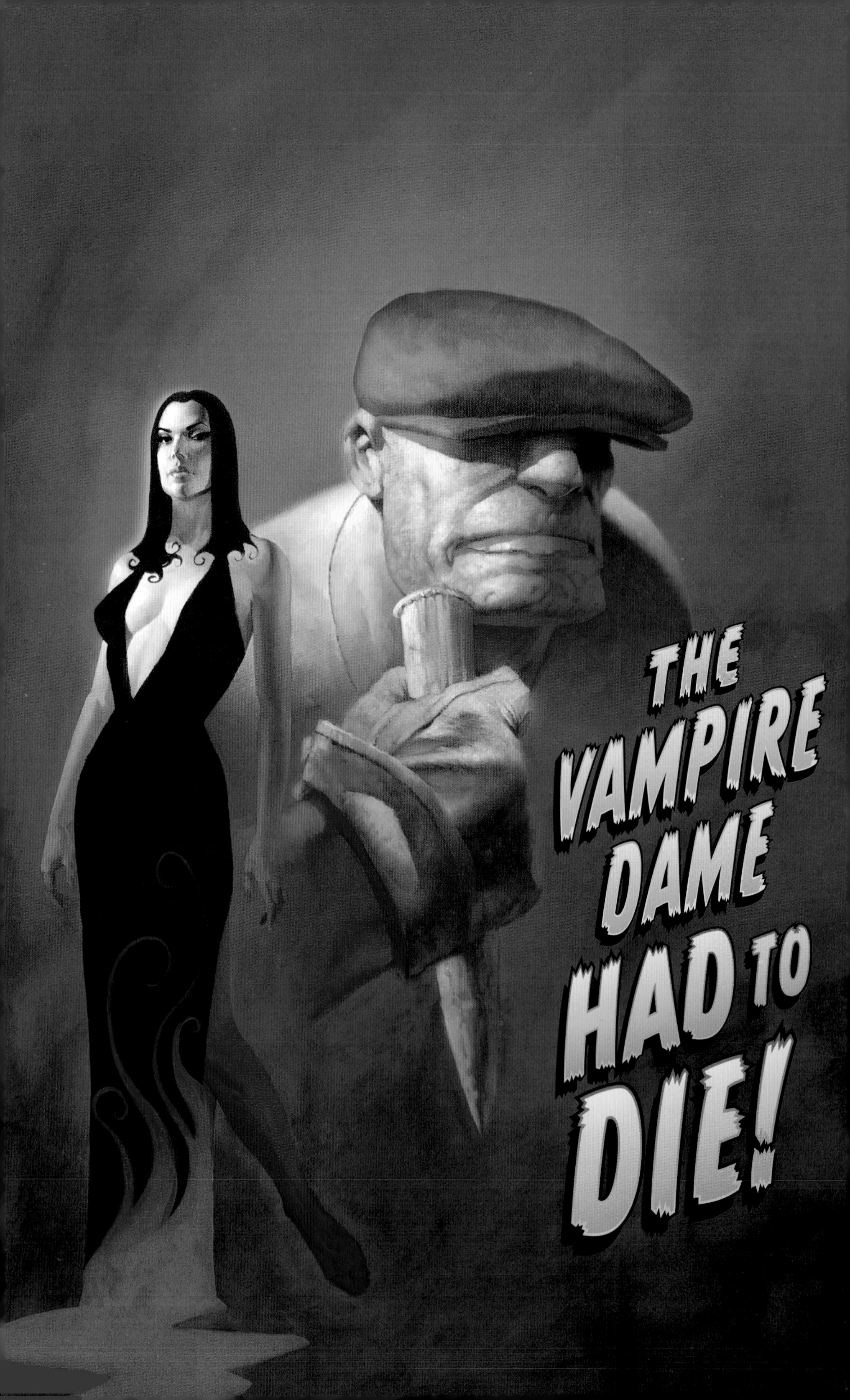
THE
VAMPIRE
DAME
HAD TO
DIE!

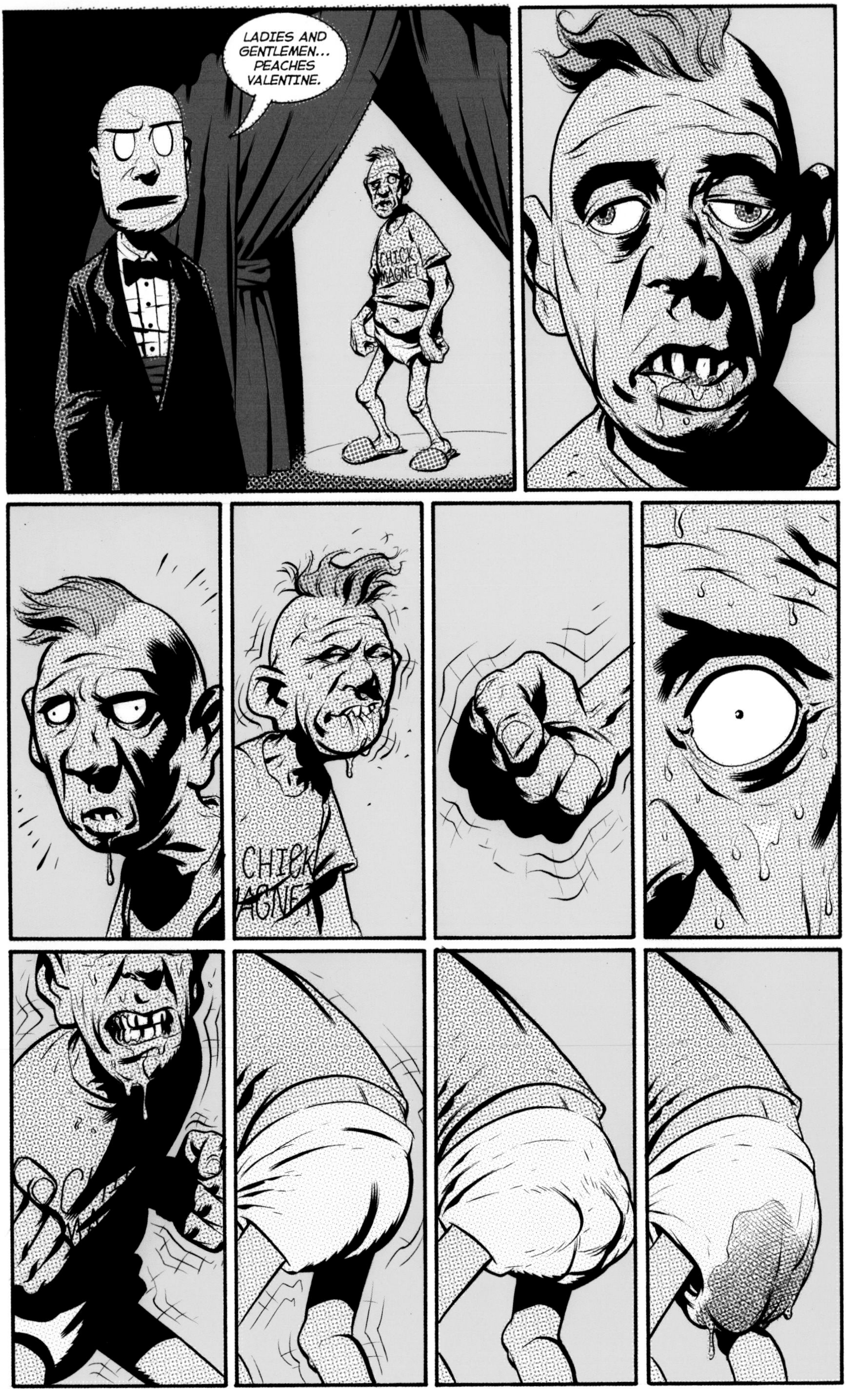
LADIES AND GENTLEMEN... PEACHES VALENTINE.
CHICK MAGNET
CHICK MAGNET

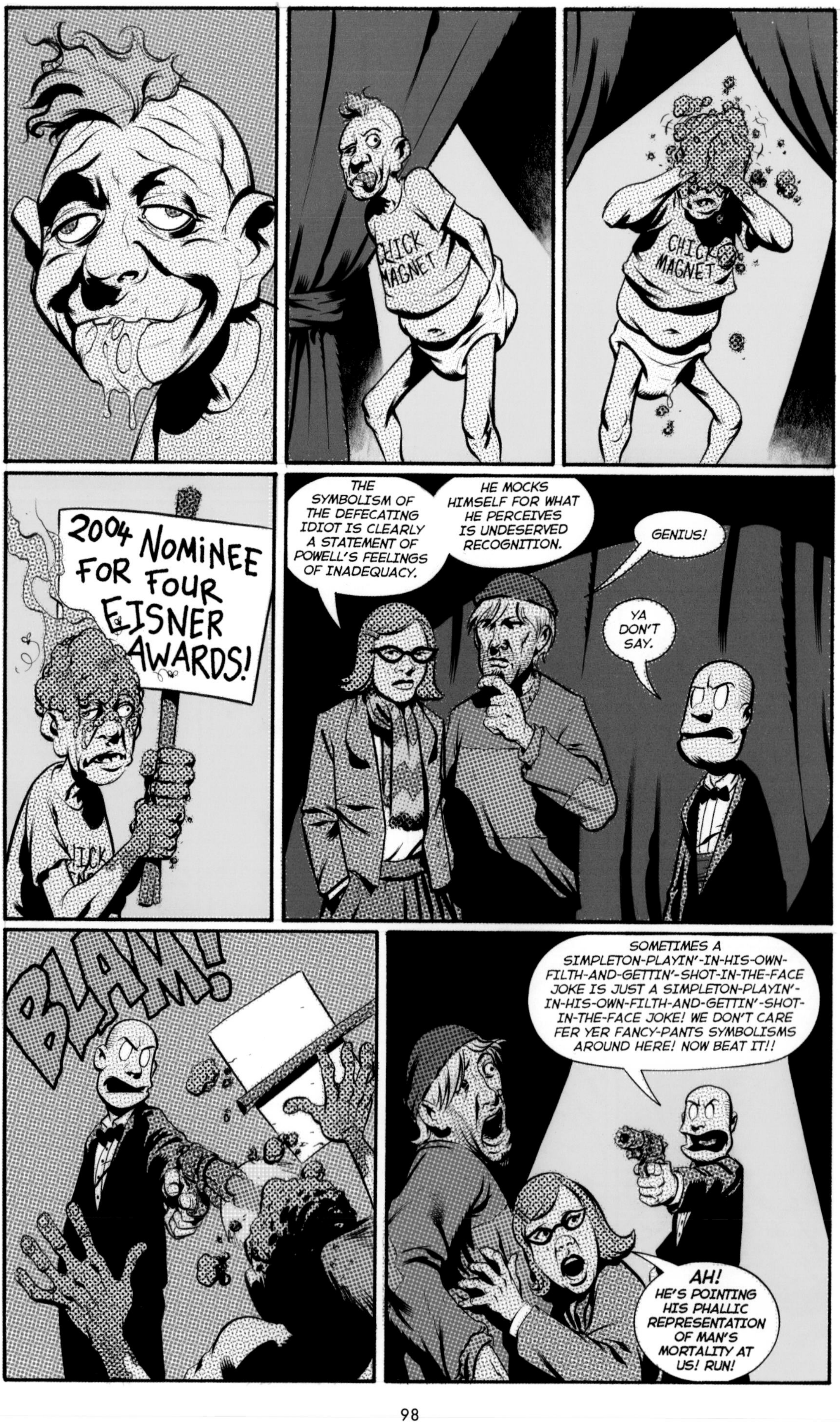

CHICK MAGNET
CHICK MAGNET
2004 NOMINEE FOR FOUR EISNER AWARDS!
THE SYMBOLISM OF THE DEFECATING IDIOT IS CLEARLY A STATEMENT OF POWELL'S FEELINGS OF INADEQUACY.
HE MOCKS HIMSELF FOR WHAT HE PERCEIVES IS UNDESERVED RECOGNITION.
GENIUS!
YA DON'T SAY.
BLAM!
SOMETIMES A SIMPLETON-PLAYIN'-IN-HIS-OWN-FILTH-AND-GETTIN'-SHOT-IN-THE-FACE JOKE IS JUST A SIMPLETON-PLAYIN'-IN-HIS-OWN-FILTH-AND-GETTIN'-SHOT-IN-THE-FACE JOKE! WE DON'T CARE FER YER FANCY-PANTS SYMBOLISMS AROUND HERE! NOW BEAT IT!!
AH! HE'S POINTING HIS PHALLIC REPRESENTATION OF MAN'S MORTALITY AT US! RUN!

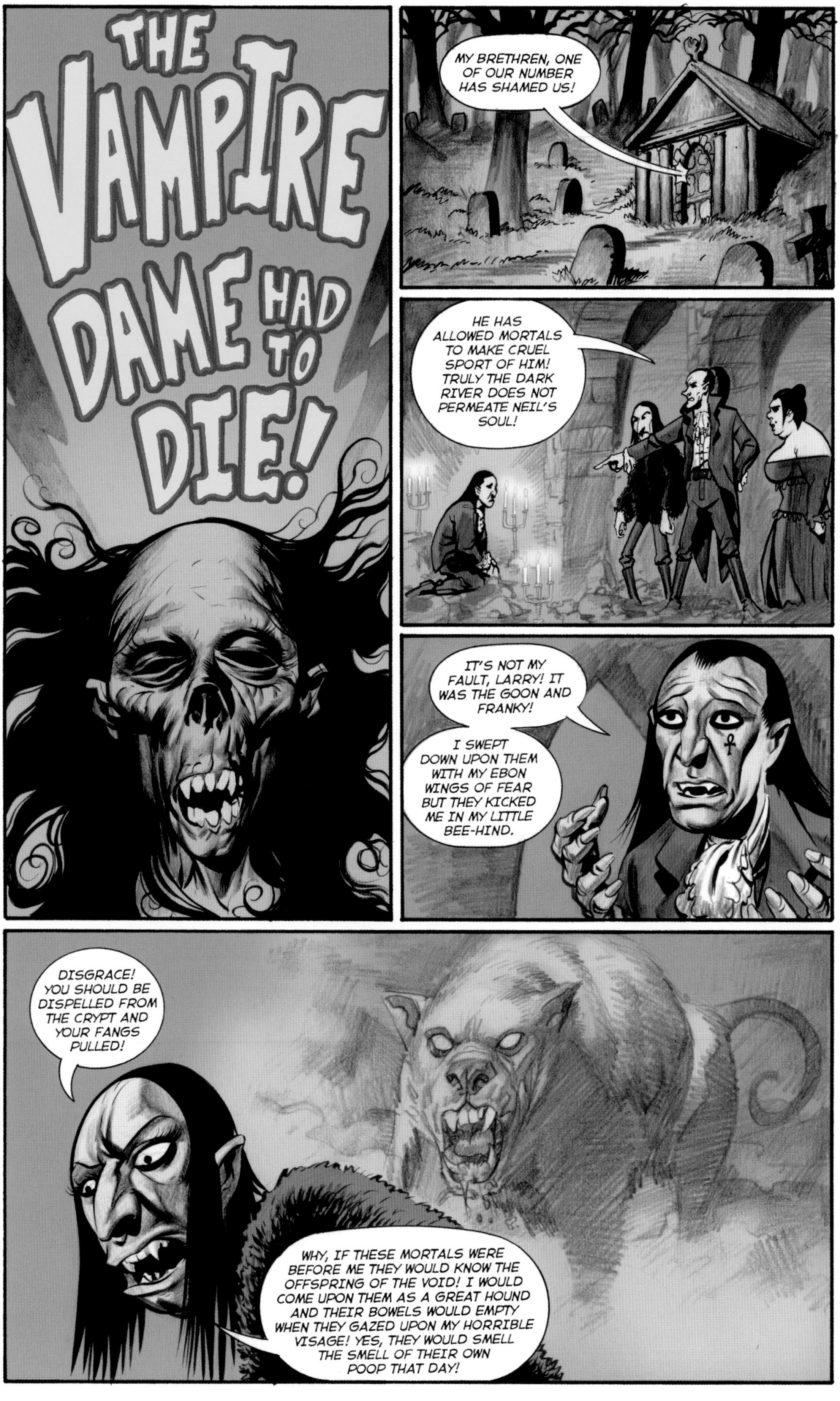
THE VAMPIRE DAME HAD TO DIE!
MY BRETHREN, ONE OF OUR NUMBER HAS SHAMED US!
HE HAS ALLOWED MORTALS TO MAKE CRUEL SPORT OF HIM! TRULY THE DARK RIVER DOES NOT PERMEATE NEIL'S SOUL!
IT'S NOT MY FAULT, LARRY! IT WAS THE GOON AND FRANKY!
I SWEPT DOWN UPON THEM WITH MY EBON WINGS OF FEAR BUT THEY KICKED ME IN MY LITTLE BEE-HIND.
DISGRACE! YOU SHOULD BE DISPELLED FROM THE CRYPT AND YOUR FANGS PULLED!
WHY, IF THESE MORTALS WERE BEFORE ME THEY WOULD KNOW THE OFFSPRING OF THE VOID! I WOULD COME UPON THEM AS A GREAT HOUND AND THEIR BOWELS WOULD EMPTY WHEN THEY GAZED UPON MY HORRIBLE VISAGE! YES, THEY WOULD SMELL THE SMELL OF THEIR OWN POOP THAT DAY!

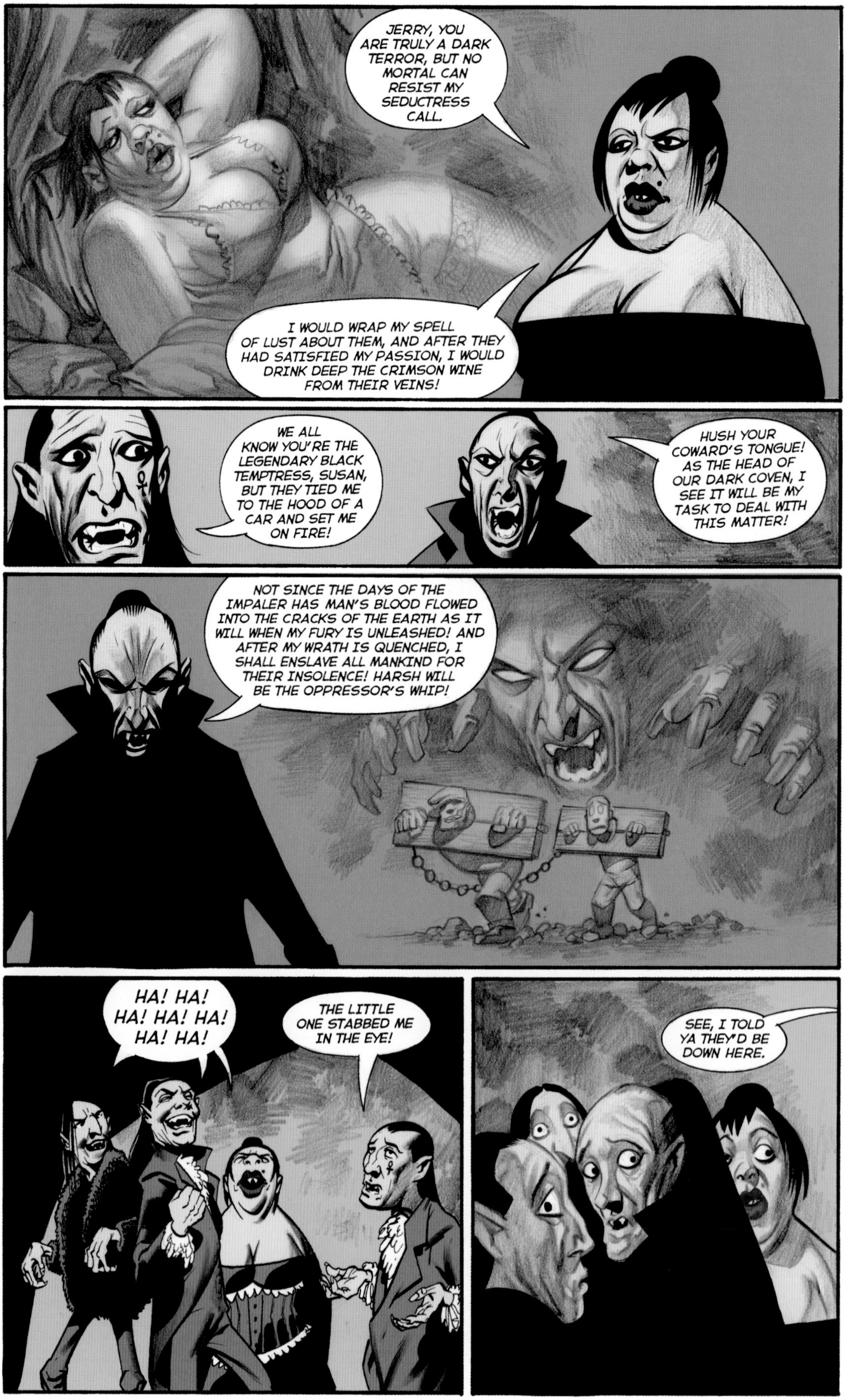
JERRY, YOU ARE TRULY A DARK TERROR, BUT NO MORTAL CAN RESIST MY SEDUCTRESS CALL.
I WOULD WRAP MY SPELL OF LUST ABOUT THEM, AND AFTER THEY HAD SATISFIED MY PASSION, I WOULD DRINK DEEP THE CRIMSON WINE FROM THEIR VEINS!
WE ALL KNOW YOU'RE THE LEGENDARY BLACK TEMPTRESS, SUSAN, BUT THEY TIED ME TO THE HOOD OF A CAR AND SET ME ON FIRE!
HUSH YOUR COWARD'S TONGUE! AS THE HEAD OF OUR DARK COVEN, I SEE IT WILL BE MY TASK TO DEAL WITH THIS MATTER!
NOT SINCE THE DAYS OF THE IMPALER HAS MAN'S BLOOD FLOWED INTO THE CRACKS OF THE EARTH AS IT WILL WHEN MY FURY IS UNLEASHED! AND AFTER MY WRATH IS QUENCHED, I SHALL ENSLAVE ALL MANKIND FOR THEIR INSOLENCE! HARSH WILL BE THE OPPRESSOR'S WHIP!
HA! HA! HA! HA! HA! HA! HA!
THE LITTLE ONE STABBED ME IN THE EYE!
SEE, I TOLD YA THEY'D BE DOWN HERE.

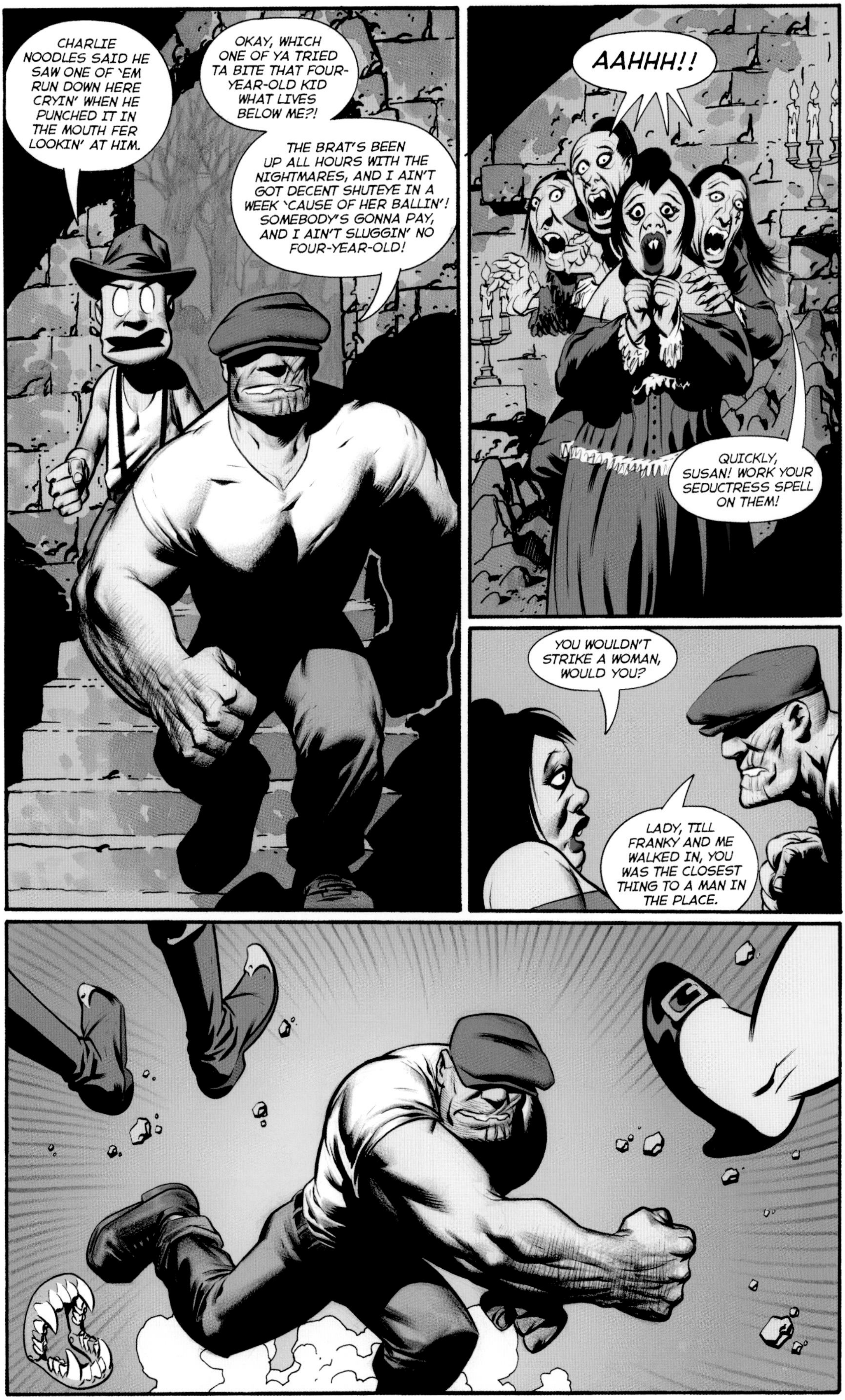
CHARLIE NOODLES SAID HE SAW ONE OF 'EM RUN DOWN HERE CRYIN' WHEN HE PUNCHED IT IN THE MOUTH FER LOOKIN' AT HIM.
OKAY, WHICH ONE OF YA TRIED TA BITE THAT FOUR-YEAR-OLD KID WHAT LIVES BELOW ME?!
THE BRAT'S BEEN UP ALL HOURS WITH THE NIGHTMARES, AND I AIN'T GOT DECENT SHUTEYE IN A WEEK 'CAUSE OF HER BALLIN'! SOMEBODY'S GONNA PAY, AND I AIN'T SLUGGIN' NO FOUR-YEAR-OLD!
AAHHH!!
QUICKLY, SUSAN! WORK YOUR SEDUCTRESS SPELL ON THEM!
YOU WOULDN'T STRIKE A WOMAN, WOULD YOU?
LADY, TILL FRANKY AND ME WALKED IN, YOU WAS THE CLOSEST THING TO A MAN IN THE PLACE.

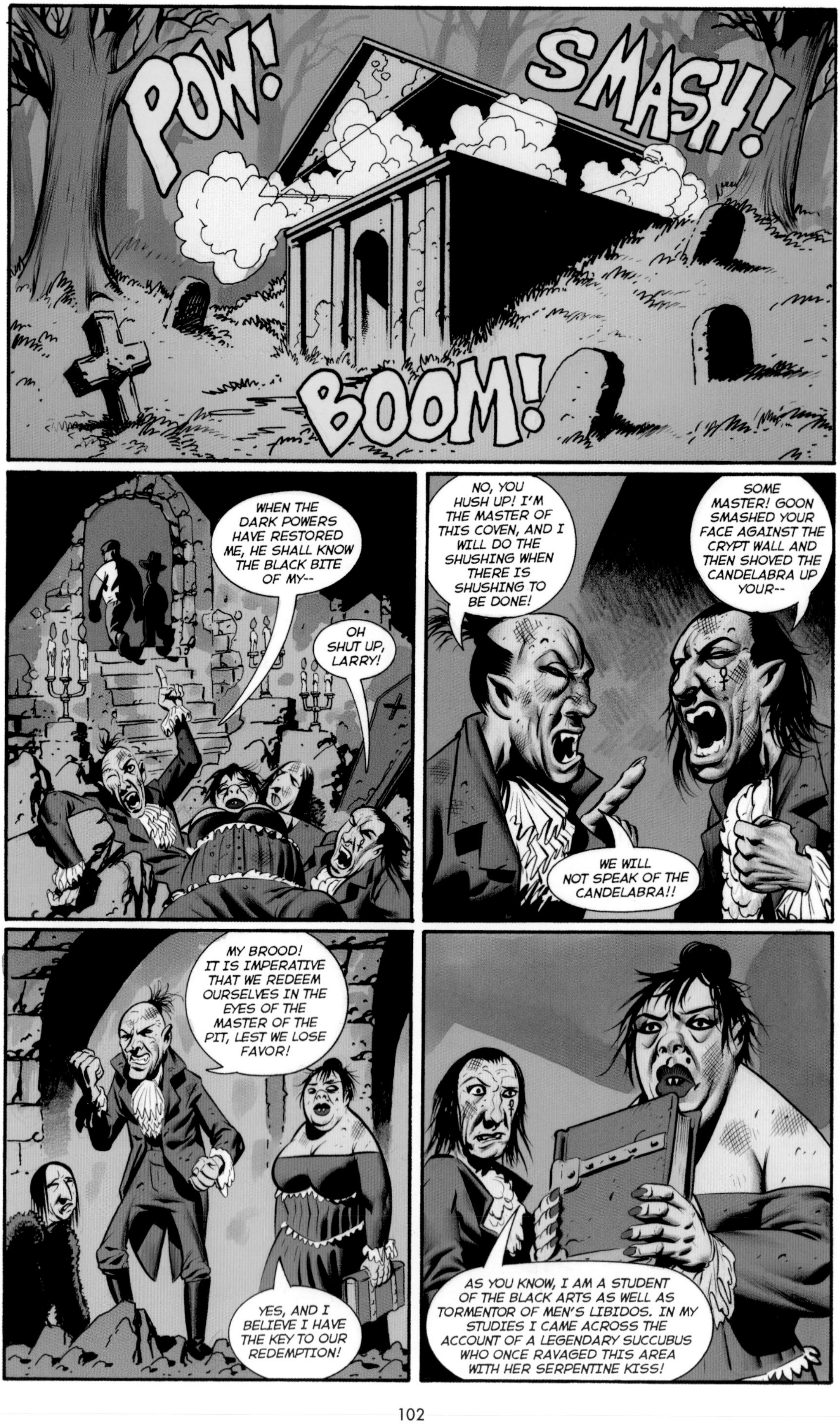

POW!
SMASH!
BOOM!
WHEN THE DARK POWERS HAVE RESTORED ME, HE SHALL KNOW THE BLACK BITE OF MY--
OH SHUT UP, LARRY!
NO, YOU HUSH UP! I'M THE MASTER OF THIS COVEN, AND I WILL DO THE SHUSHING WHEN THERE IS SHUSHING TO BE DONE!
SOME MASTER! GOON SMASHED YOUR FACE AGAINST THE CRYPT WALL AND THEN SHOVED THE CANDELABRA UP YOUR--
WE WILL NOT SPEAK OF THE CANDELABRA!!
MY BROOD! IT IS IMPERATIVE THAT WE REDEEM OURSELVES IN THE EYES OF THE MASTER OF THE PIT, LEST WE LOSE FAVOR!
YES, AND I BELIEVE I HAVE THE KEY TO OUR REDEMPTION!
AS YOU KNOW, I AM A STUDENT OF THE BLACK ARTS AS WELL AS TORMENTOR OF MEN'S LIBIDOS. IN MY STUDIES I CAME ACROSS THE ACCOUNT OF A LEGENDARY SUCCUBUS WHO ONCE RAVAGED THIS AREA WITH HER SERPENTINE KISS!

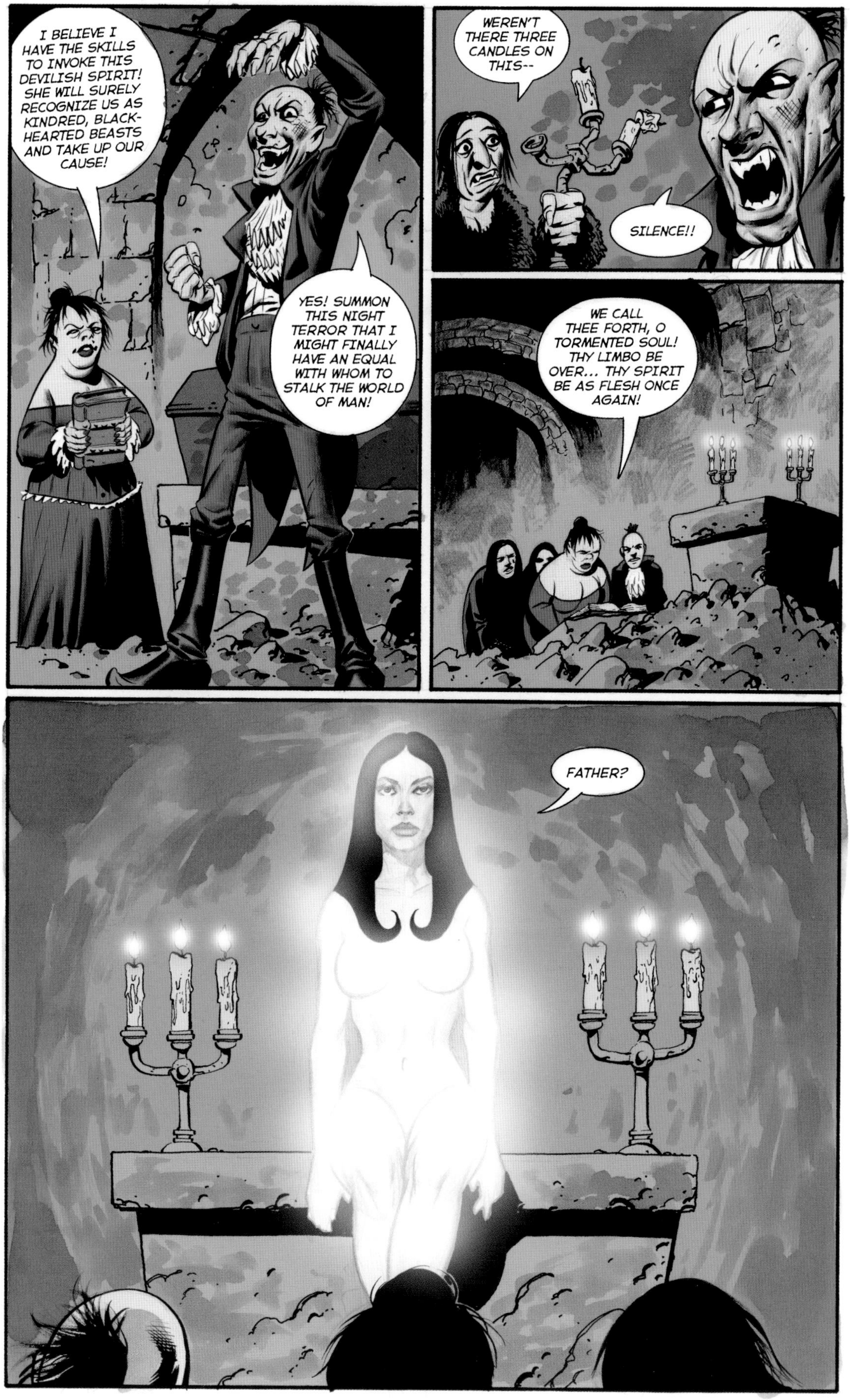
I BELIEVE I HAVE THE SKILLS TO INVOKE THIS DEVILISH SPIRIT! SHE WILL SURELY RECOGNIZE US AS KINDRED, BLACK-HEARTED BEASTS AND TAKE UP OUR CAUSE!
YES! SUMMON THIS NIGHT TERROR THAT I MIGHT FINALLY HAVE AN EQUAL WITH WHOM TO STALK THE WORLD OF MAN!
WEREN'T THERE THREE CANDLES ON THIS--
SILENCE!!
WE CALL THEE FORTH, O TORMENTED SOUL! THY LIMBO BE OVER... THY SPIRIT BE AS FLESH ONCE AGAIN!
FATHER?

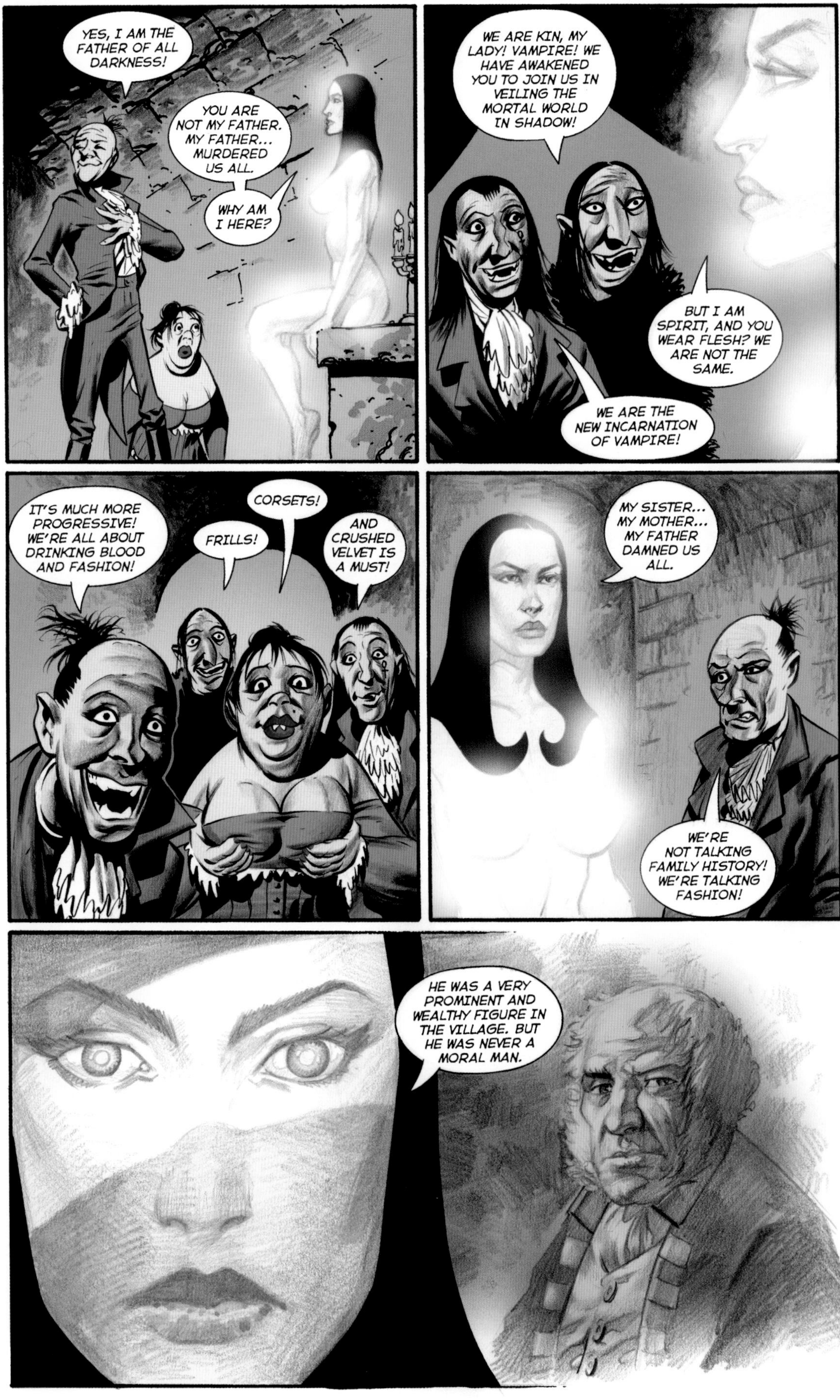
YES, I AM THE FATHER OF ALL DARKNESS!
YOU ARE NOT MY FATHER. MY FATHER... MURDERED US ALL.
WHY AM I HERE?
WE ARE KIN, MY LADY! VAMPIRE! WE HAVE AWAKENED YOU TO JOIN US IN VEILING THE MORTAL WORLD IN SHADOW!
BUT I AM SPIRIT, AND YOU WEAR FLESH? WE ARE NOT THE SAME.
WE ARE THE NEW INCARNATION OF VAMPIRE!
IT'S MUCH MORE PROGRESSIVE! WE'RE ALL ABOUT DRINKING BLOOD AND FASHION!
FRILLS!
CORSETS!
AND CRUSHED VELVET IS A MUST!
MY SISTER... MY MOTHER... MY FATHER DAMNED US ALL.
WE'RE NOT TALKING FAMILY HISTORY! WE'RE TALKING FASHION!
HE WAS A VERY PROMINENT AND WEALTHY FIGURE IN THE VILLAGE. BUT HE WAS NEVER A MORAL MAN.

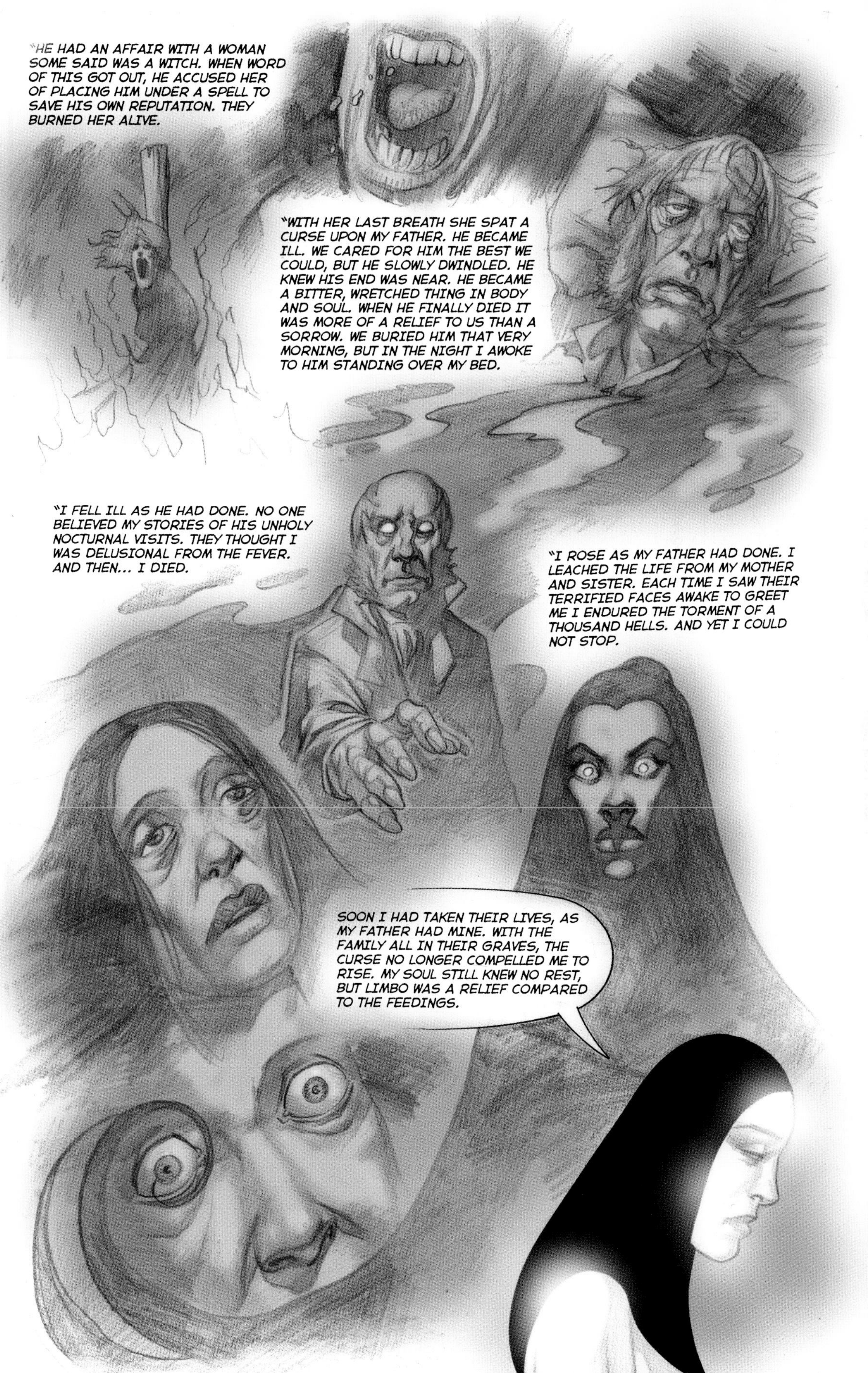
"HE HAD AN AFFAIR WITH A WOMAN SOME SAID WAS A WITCH. WHEN WORD OF THIS GOT OUT, HE ACCUSED HER OF PLACING HIM UNDER A SPELL TO SAVE HIS OWN REPUTATION. THEY BURNED HER ALIVE.
"WITH HER LAST BREATH SHE SPAT A CURSE UPON MY FATHER. HE BECAME ILL. WE CARED FOR HIM THE BEST WE COULD, BUT HE SLOWLY DWINDLED. HE KNEW HIS END WAS NEAR. HE BECAME A BITTER, WRETCHED THING IN BODY AND SOUL. WHEN HE FINALLY DIED IT WAS MORE OF A RELIEF TO US THAN A SORROW. WE BURIED HIM THAT VERY MORNING, BUT IN THE NIGHT I AWOKE TO HIM STANDING OVER MY BED.
"I FELL ILL AS HE HAD DONE. NO ONE BELIEVED MY STORIES OF HIS UNHOLY NOCTURNAL VISITS. THEY THOUGHT I WAS DELUSIONAL FROM THE FEVER. AND THEN... I DIED.
"I ROSE AS MY FATHER HAD DONE. I LEACHED THE LIFE FROM MY MOTHER AND SISTER. EACH TIME I SAW THEIR TERRIFIED FACES AWAKE TO GREET ME I ENDURED THE TORMENT OF A THOUSAND HELLS. AND YET I COULD NOT STOP.
SOON I HAD TAKEN THEIR LIVES, AS MY FATHER HAD MINE. WITH THE FAMILY ALL IN THEIR GRAVES, THE CURSE NO LONGER COMPELLED ME TO RISE. MY SOUL STILL KNEW NO REST, BUT LIMBO WAS A RELIEF COMPARED TO THE FEEDINGS.

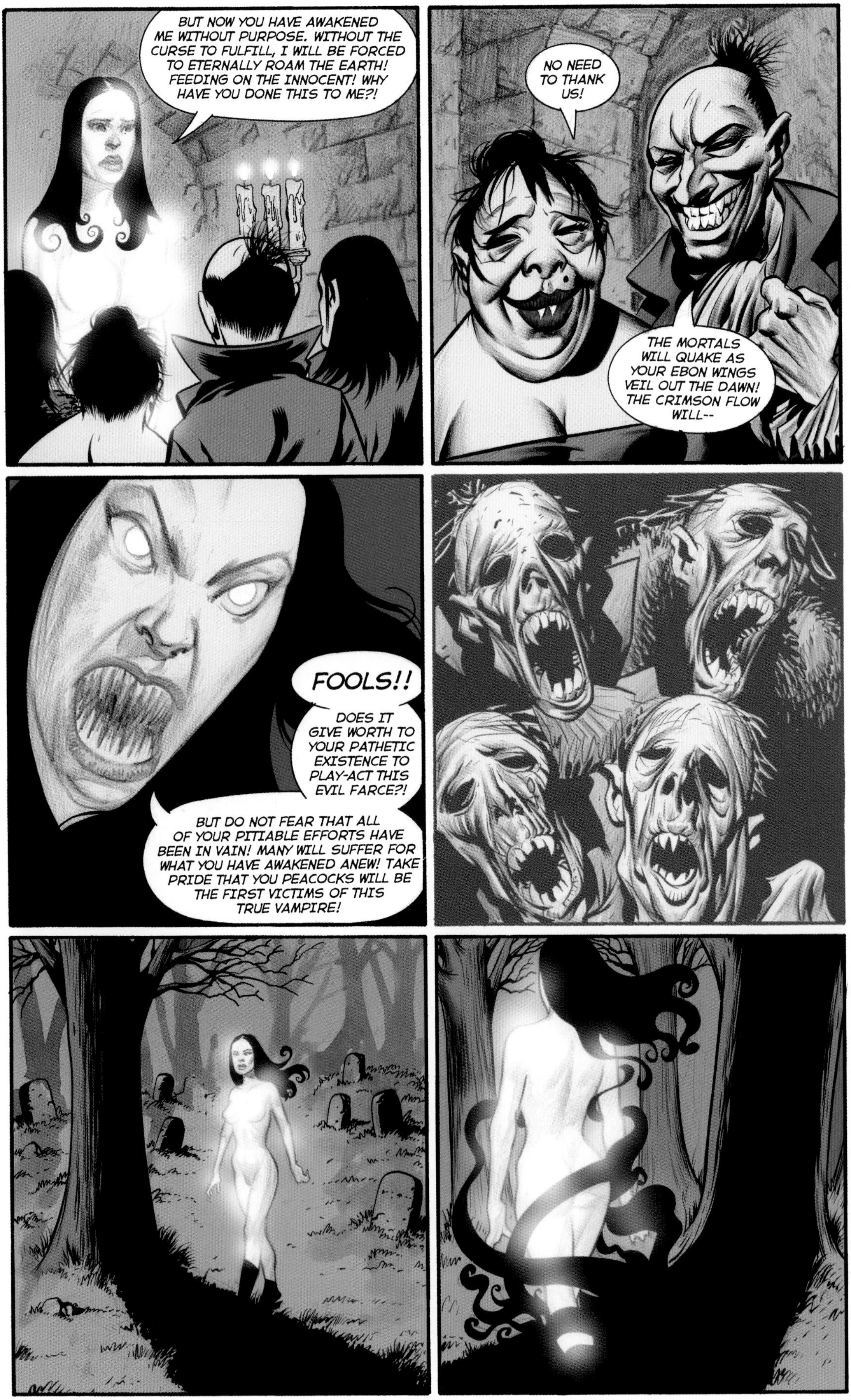
BUT NOW YOU HAVE AWAKENED ME WITHOUT PURPOSE. WITHOUT THE CURSE TO FULFILL, I WILL BE FORCED TO ETERNALLY ROAM THE EARTH! FEEDING ON THE INNOCENT! WHY HAVE YOU DONE THIS TO ME?!
NO NEED TO THANK US!
THE MORTALS WILL QUAKE AS YOUR EBON WINGS VEIL OUT THE DAWN! THE CRIMSON FLOW WILL--
FOOLS!!
DOES IT GIVE WORTH TO YOUR PATHETIC EXISTENCE TO PLAY-ACT THIS EVIL FARCE?!
BUT DO NOT FEAR THAT ALL OF YOUR PITIABLE EFFORTS HAVE BEEN IN VAIN! MANY WILL SUFFER FOR WHAT YOU HAVE AWAKENED ANEW! TAKE PRIDE THAT YOU PEACOCKS WILL BE THE FIRST VICTIMS OF THIS TRUE VAMPIRE!

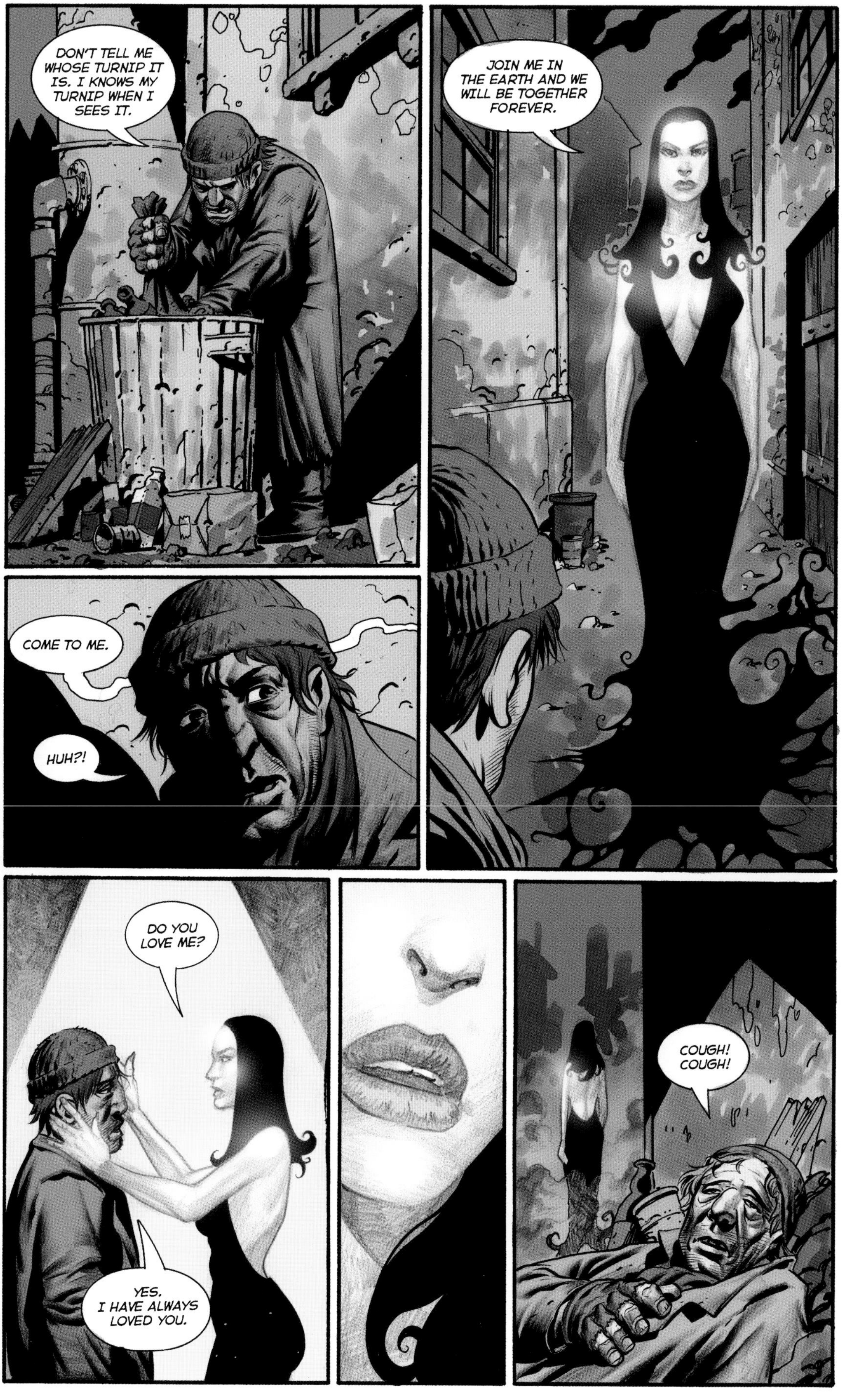
DON'T TELL ME WHOSE TURNIP IT IS. I KNOWS MY TURNIP WHEN I SEES IT.
JOIN ME IN THE EARTH AND WE WILL BE TOGETHER FOREVER.
COME TO ME.
HUH?!
DO YOU LOVE ME?
YES. I HAVE ALWAYS LOVED YOU.
COUGH! COUGH!

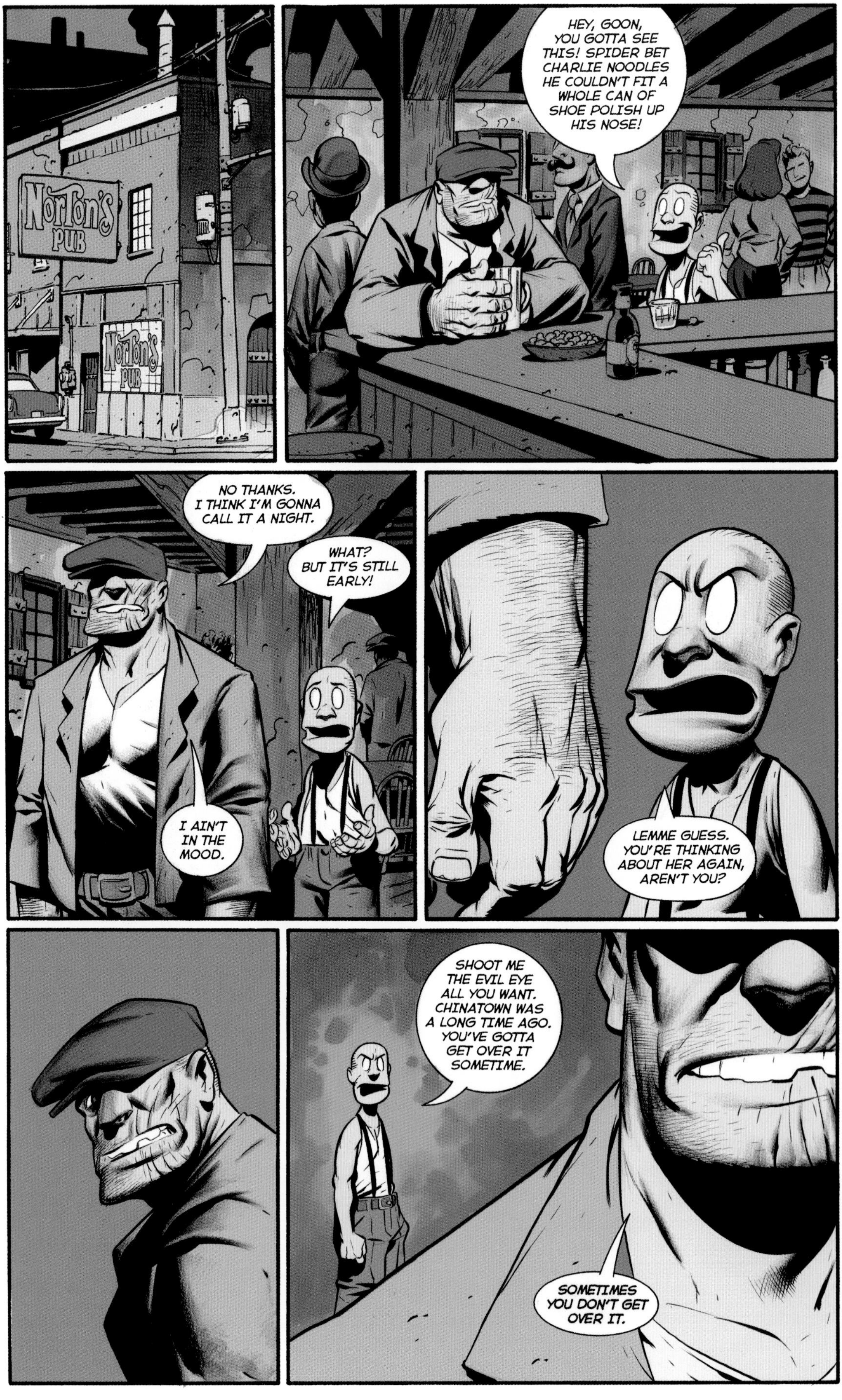
Norton's PUB
Norton's PUB
HEY, GOON, YOU GOTTA SEE THIS! SPIDER BET CHARLIE NOODLES HE COULDN'T FIT A WHOLE CAN OF SHOE POLISH UP HIS NOSE!
NO THANKS. I THINK I'M GONNA CALL IT A NIGHT.
WHAT? BUT IT'S STILL EARLY!
I AIN'T IN THE MOOD.
LEMME GUESS. YOU'RE THINKING ABOUT HER AGAIN, AREN'T YOU?
SHOOT ME THE EVIL EYE ALL YOU WANT. CHINATOWN WAS A LONG TIME AGO. YOU'VE GOTTA GET OVER IT SOMETIME.
SOMETIMES YOU DON'T GET OVER IT.

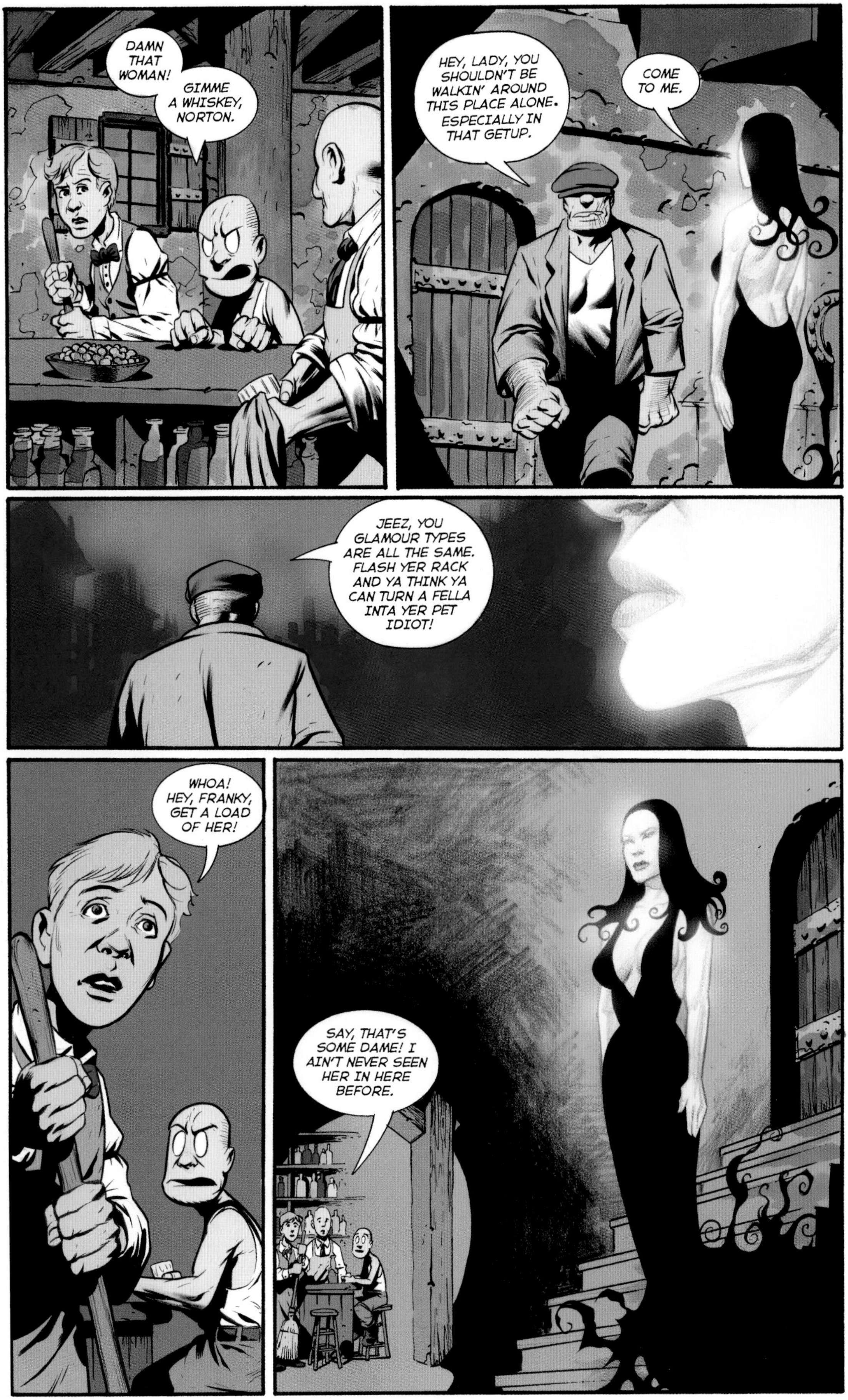
DAMN THAT WOMAN!
GIMME A WHISKEY, NORTON.
HEY, LADY, YOU SHOULDN'T BE WALKIN' AROUND THIS PLACE ALONE. ESPECIALLY IN THAT GETUP.
COME TO ME.
JEEZ, YOU GLAMOUR TYPES ARE ALL THE SAME. FLASH YER RACK AND YA THINK YA CAN TURN A FELLA INTA YER PET IDIOT!
WHOA! HEY, FRANKY, GET A LOAD OF HER!
SAY, THAT'S SOME DAME! I AIN'T NEVER SEEN HER IN HERE BEFORE.

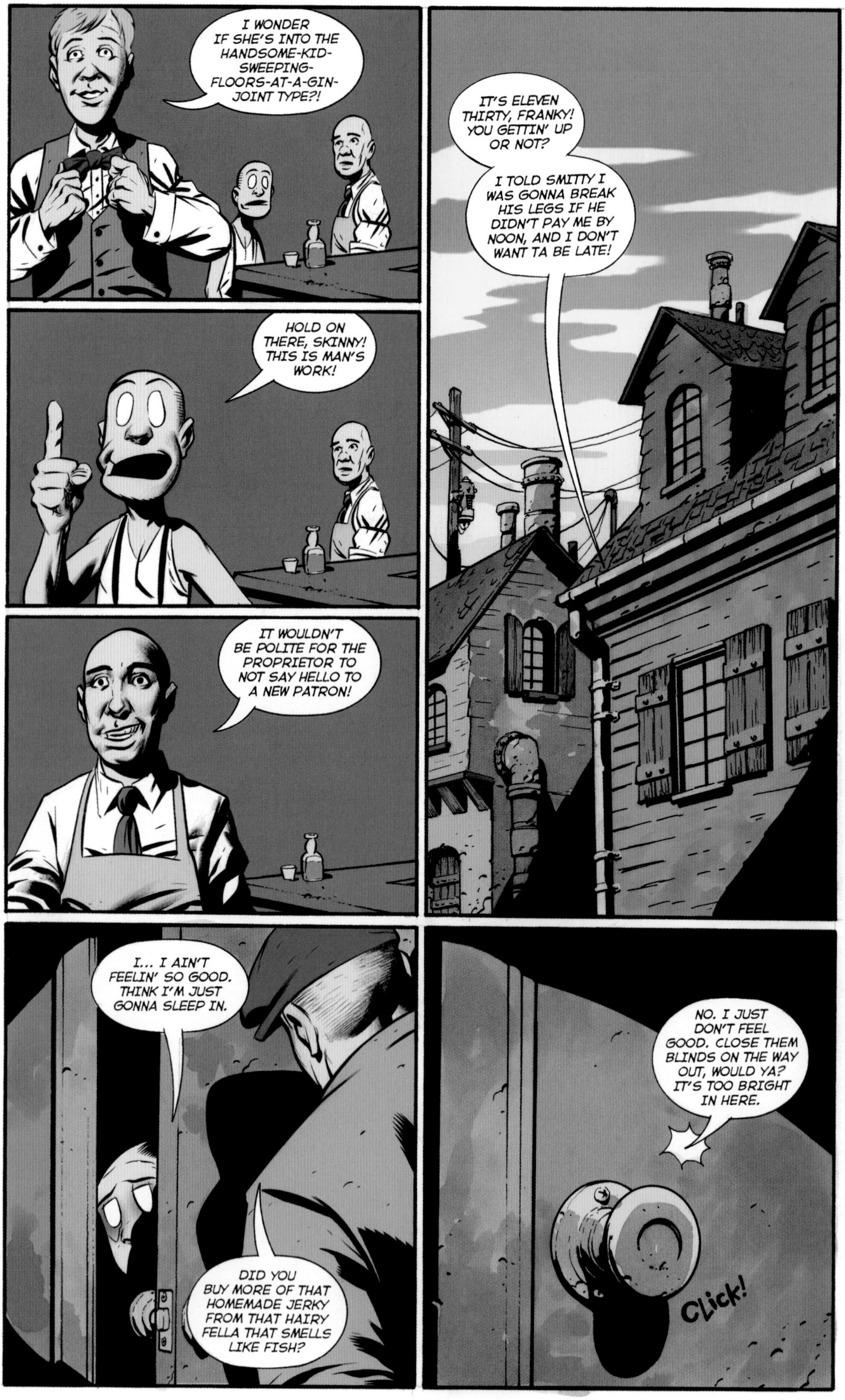
I WONDER IF SHE'S INTO THE HANDSOME-KID-SWEEPING-FLOORS-AT-A-GIN-JOINT TYPE?!
HOLD ON THERE, SKINNY! THIS IS MAN'S WORK!
IT WOULDN'T BE POLITE FOR THE PROPRIETOR TO NOT SAY HELLO TO A NEW PATRON!
IT'S ELEVEN THIRTY, FRANKY! YOU GETTIN' UP OR NOT?
I TOLD SMITTY I WAS GONNA BREAK HIS LEGS IF HE DIDN'T PAY ME BY NOON, AND I DON'T WANT TA BE LATE!
I... I AIN'T FEELIN' SO GOOD. THINK I'M JUST GONNA SLEEP IN.
DID YOU BUY MORE OF THAT HOMEMADE JERKY FROM THAT HAIRY FELLA THAT SMELLS LIKE FISH?
NO. I JUST DON'T FEEL GOOD. CLOSE THEM BLINDS ON THE WAY OUT, WOULD YA? IT'S TOO BRIGHT IN HERE.
CLICK!

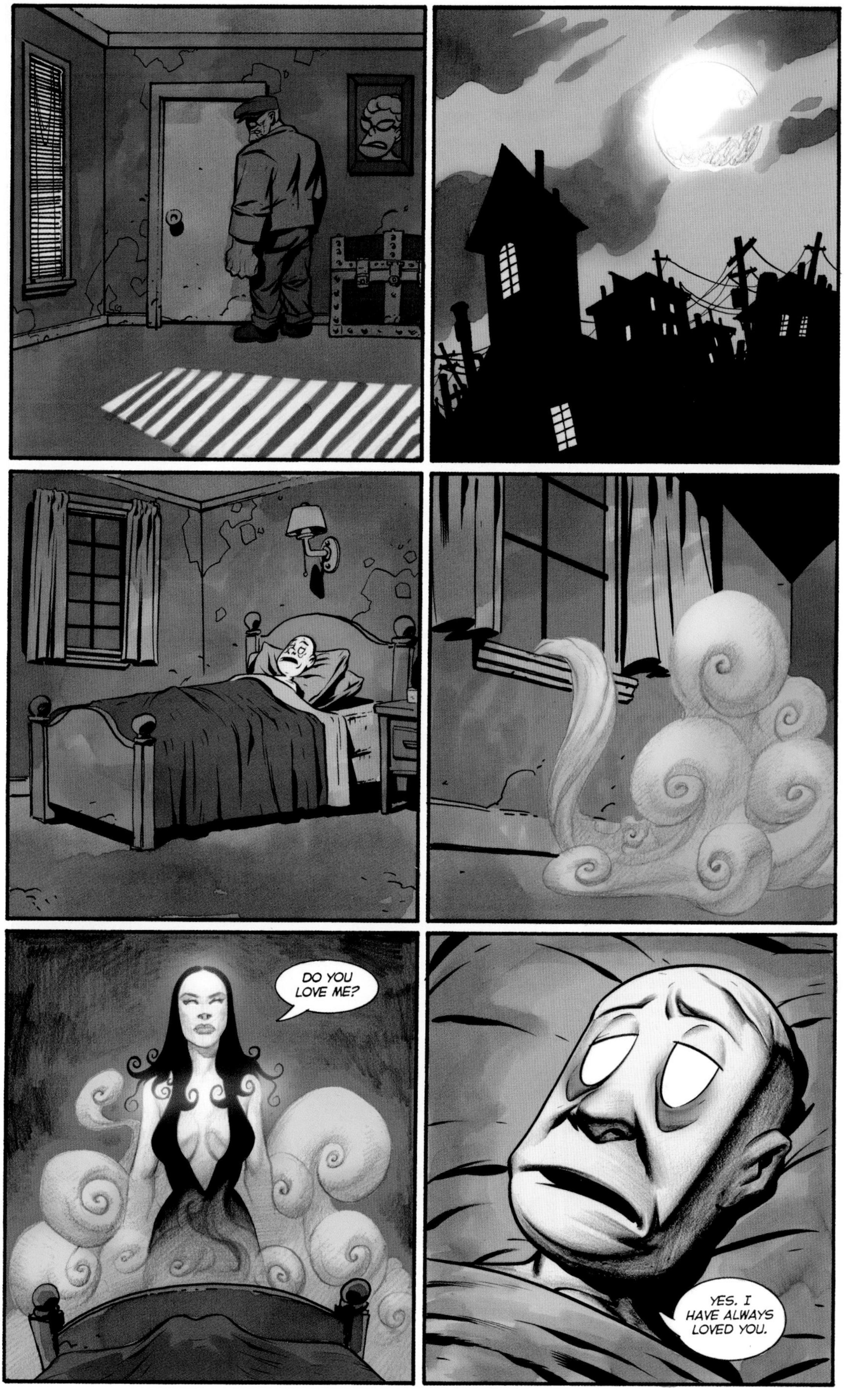
DO YOU LOVE ME?
YES. I HAVE ALWAYS LOVED YOU.

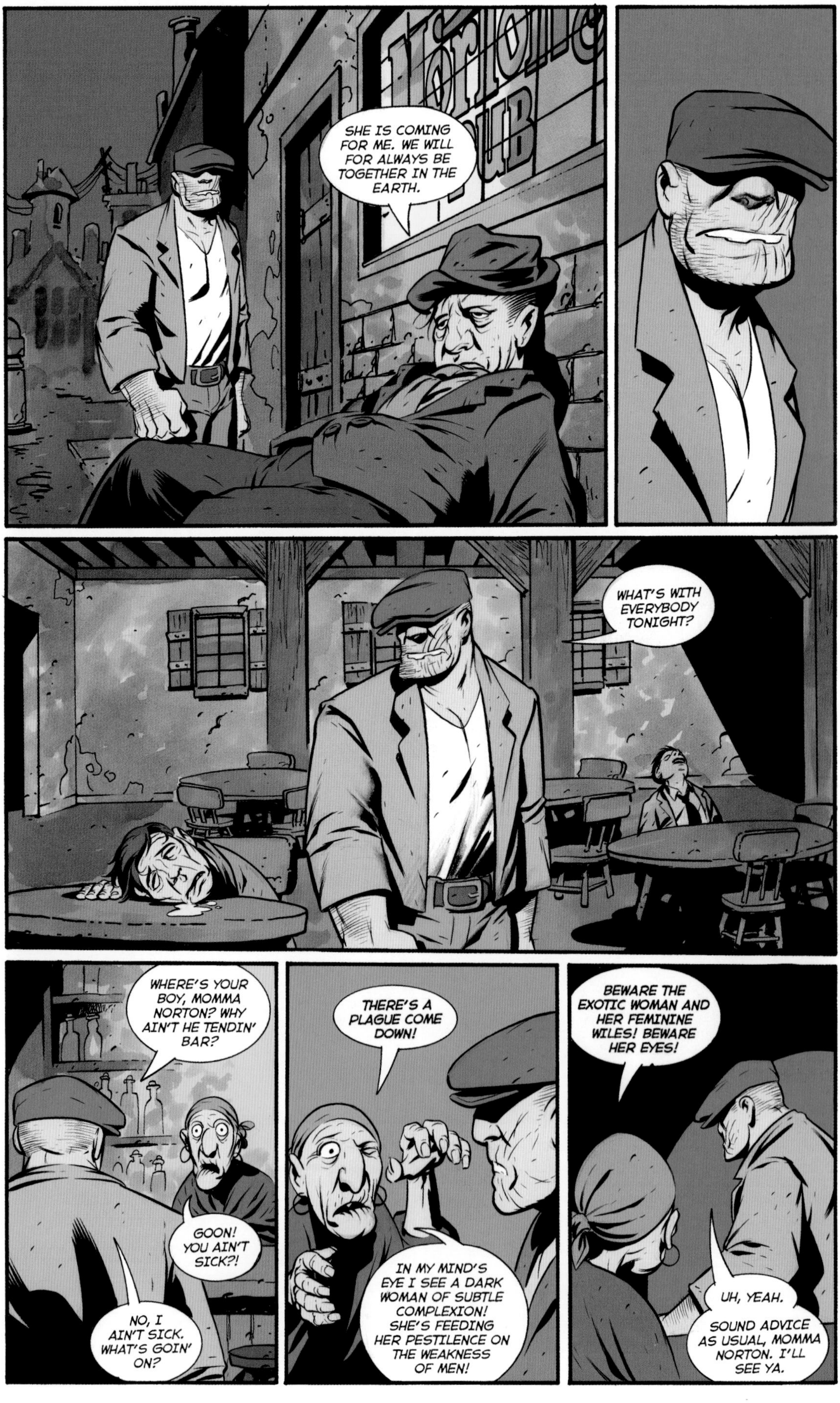
SHE IS COMING FOR ME. WE WILL FOR ALWAYS BE TOGETHER IN THE EARTH.
WHAT'S WITH EVERYBODY TONIGHT?
WHERE'S YOUR BOY, MOMMA NORTON? WHY AIN'T HE TENDIN' BAR?
GOON! YOU AIN'T SICK?!
NO, I AIN'T SICK. WHAT'S GOIN' ON?
THERE'S A PLAGUE COME DOWN!
IN MY MIND'S EYE I SEE A DARK WOMAN OF SUBTLE COMPLEXION! SHE'S FEEDING HER PESTILENCE ON THE WEAKNESS OF MEN!
BEWARE THE EXOTIC WOMAN AND HER FEMININE WILES! BEWARE HER EYES!
UH, YEAH.
SOUND ADVICE AS USUAL, MOMMA NORTON. I'LL SEE YA.

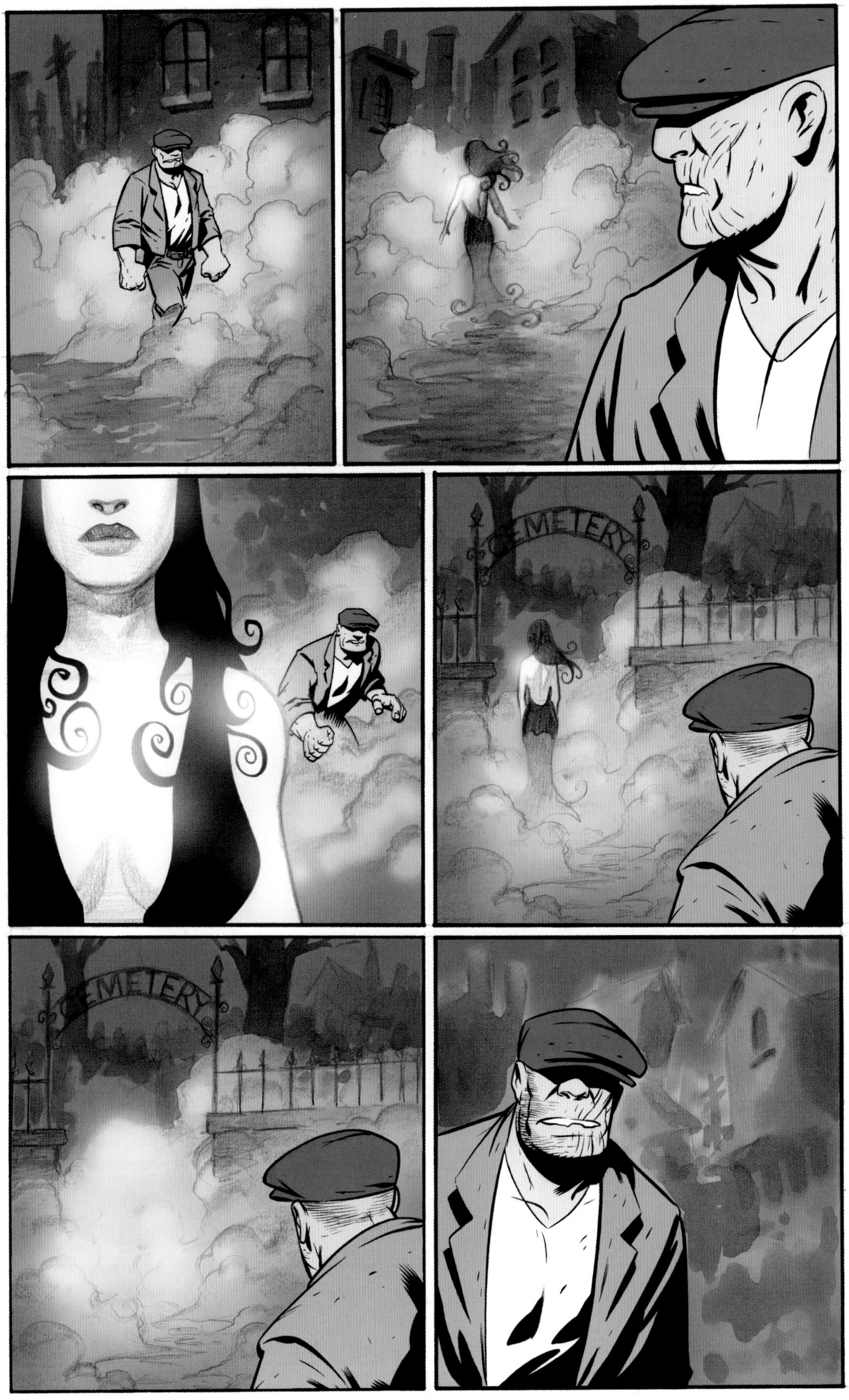
CEMETERY
CEMETERY

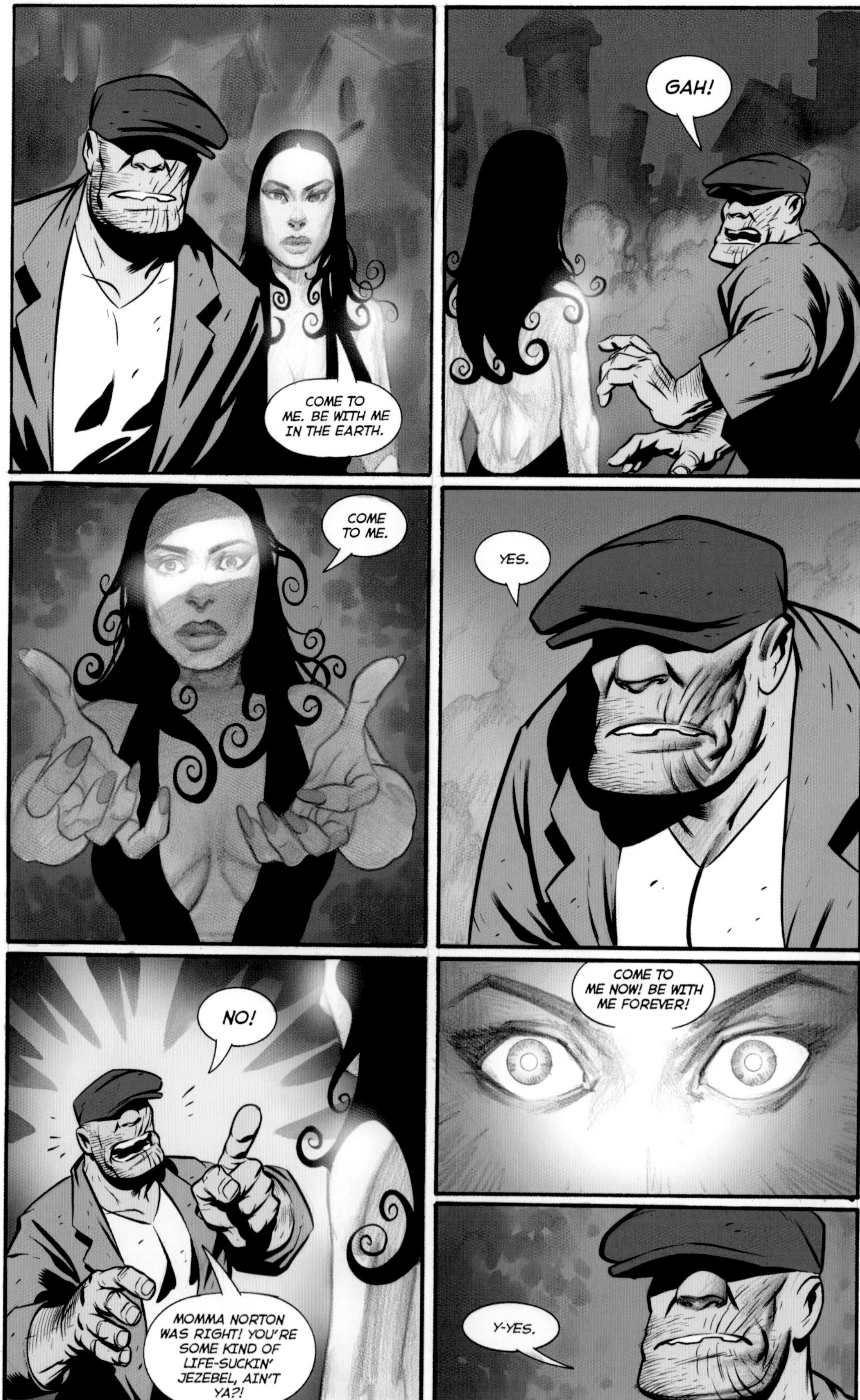
COME TO ME. BE WITH ME IN THE EARTH.
GAH!
COME TO ME.
YES.
NO!
MOMMA NORTON WAS RIGHT! YOU'RE SOME KIND OF LIFE-SUCKIN' JEZEBEL, AIN'T YA?!
COME TO ME NOW! BE WITH ME FOREVER!
Y-YES.

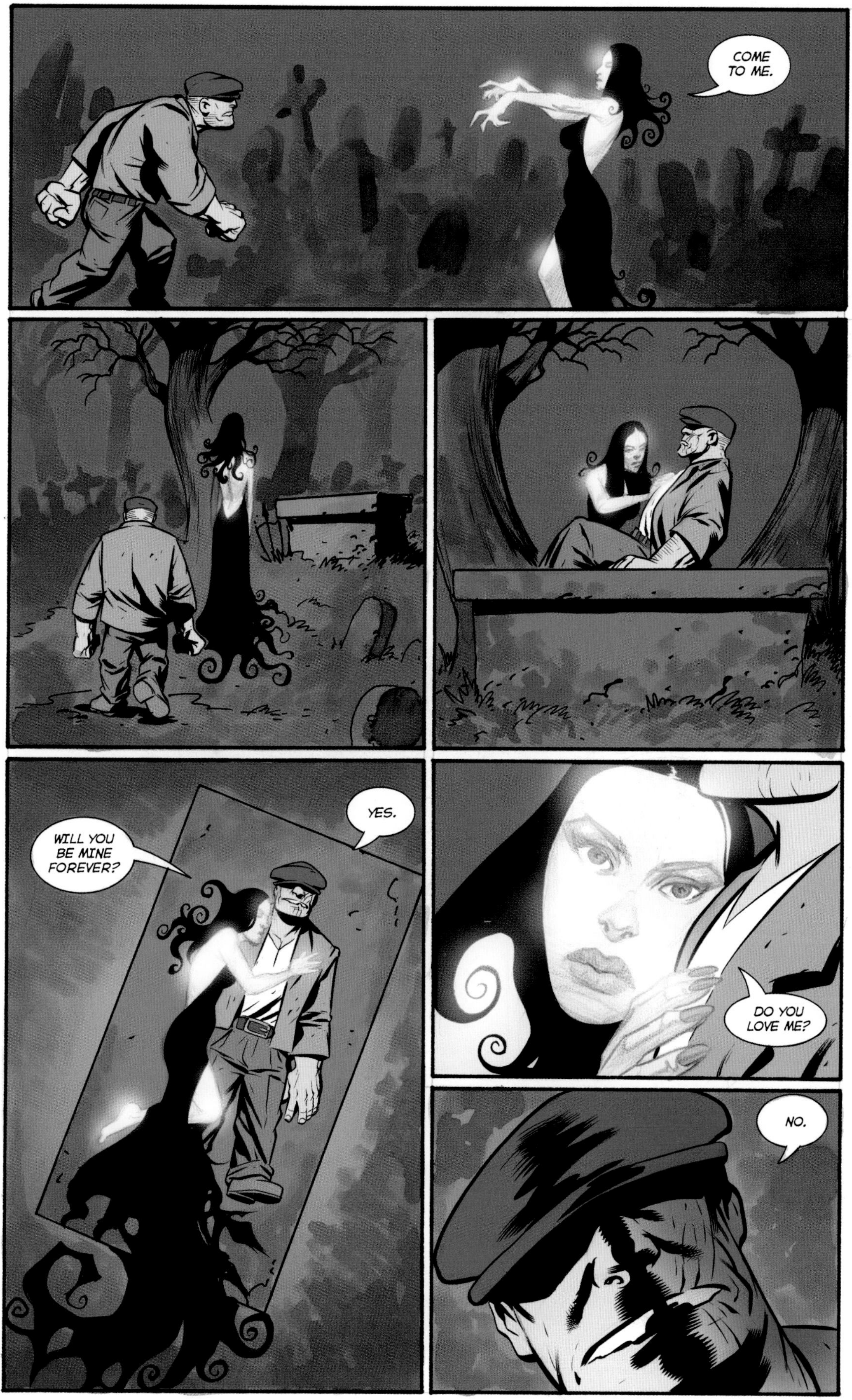
COME TO ME.
WILL YOU BE MINE FOREVER?
YES.
DO YOU LOVE ME?
NO.

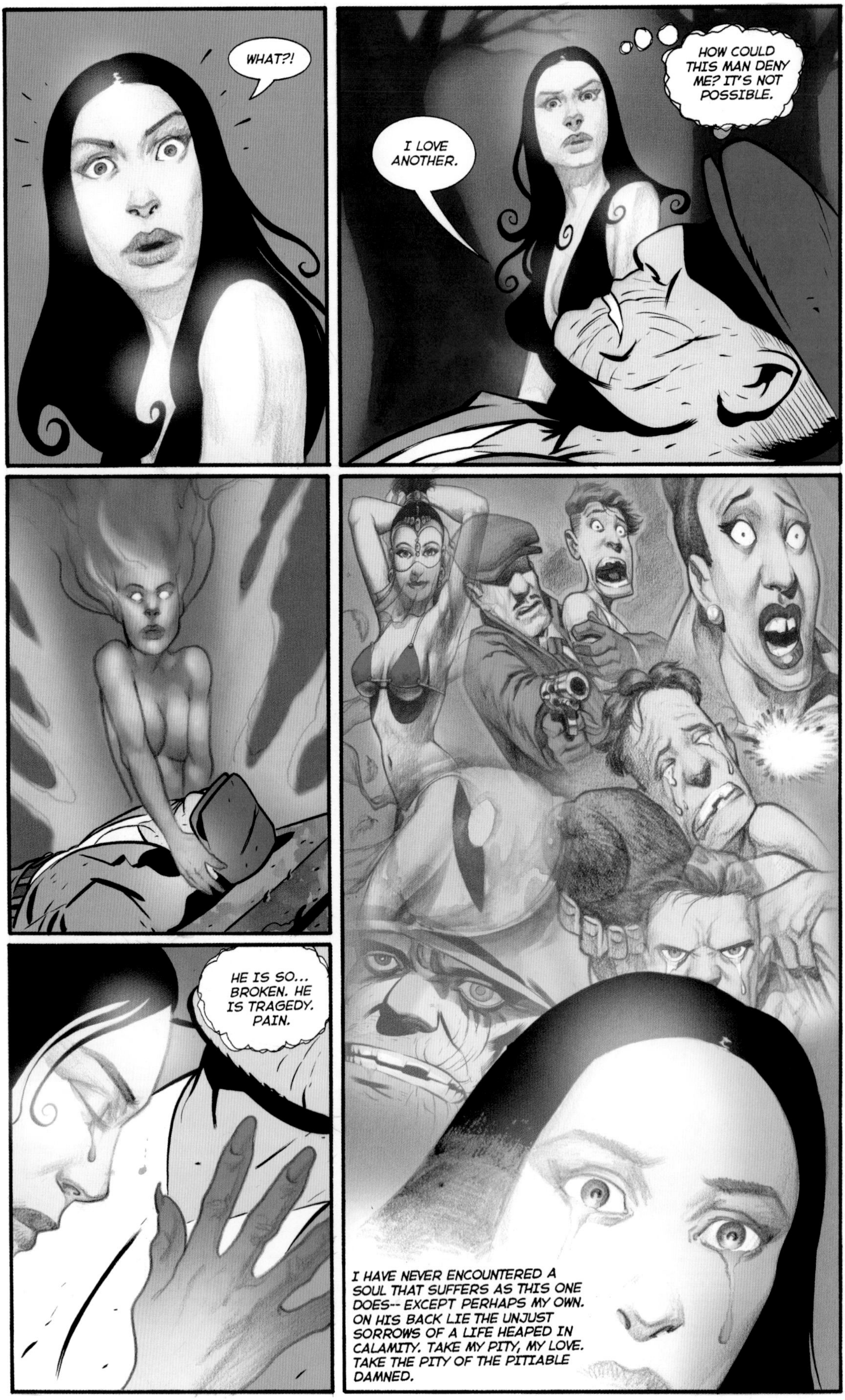
WHAT?!
HOW COULD THIS MAN DENY ME? IT'S NOT POSSIBLE.
I LOVE ANOTHER.
HE IS SO... BROKEN. HE IS TRAGEDY. PAIN.
I HAVE NEVER ENCOUNTERED A SOUL THAT SUFFERS AS THIS ONE DOES-- EXCEPT PERHAPS MY OWN. ON HIS BACK LIE THE UNJUST SORROWS OF A LIFE HEAPED IN CALAMITY. TAKE MY PITY, MY LOVE. TAKE THE PITY OF THE PITIABLE DAMNED.

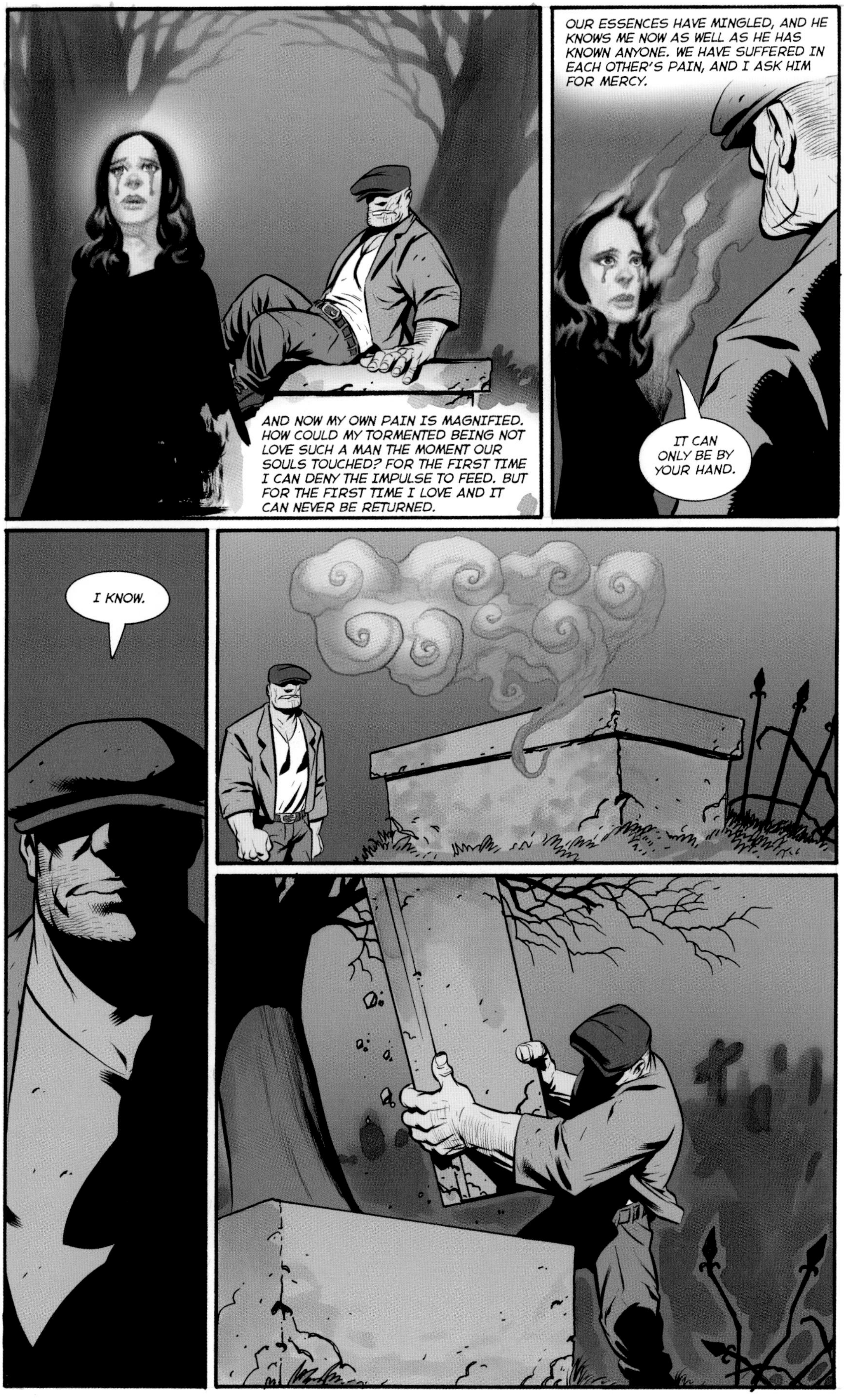

AND NOW MY OWN PAIN IS MAGNIFIED. HOW COULD MY TORMENTED BEING NOT LOVE SUCH A MAN THE MOMENT OUR SOULS TOUCHED? FOR THE FIRST TIME I CAN DENY THE IMPULSE TO FEED. BUT FOR THE FIRST TIME I LOVE AND IT CAN NEVER BE RETURNED.
OUR ESSENCES HAVE MINGLED, AND HE KNOWS ME NOW AS WELL AS HE HAS KNOWN ANYONE. WE HAVE SUFFERED IN EACH OTHER'S PAIN, AND I ASK HIM FOR MERCY.
IT CAN ONLY BE BY YOUR HAND.
I KNOW.

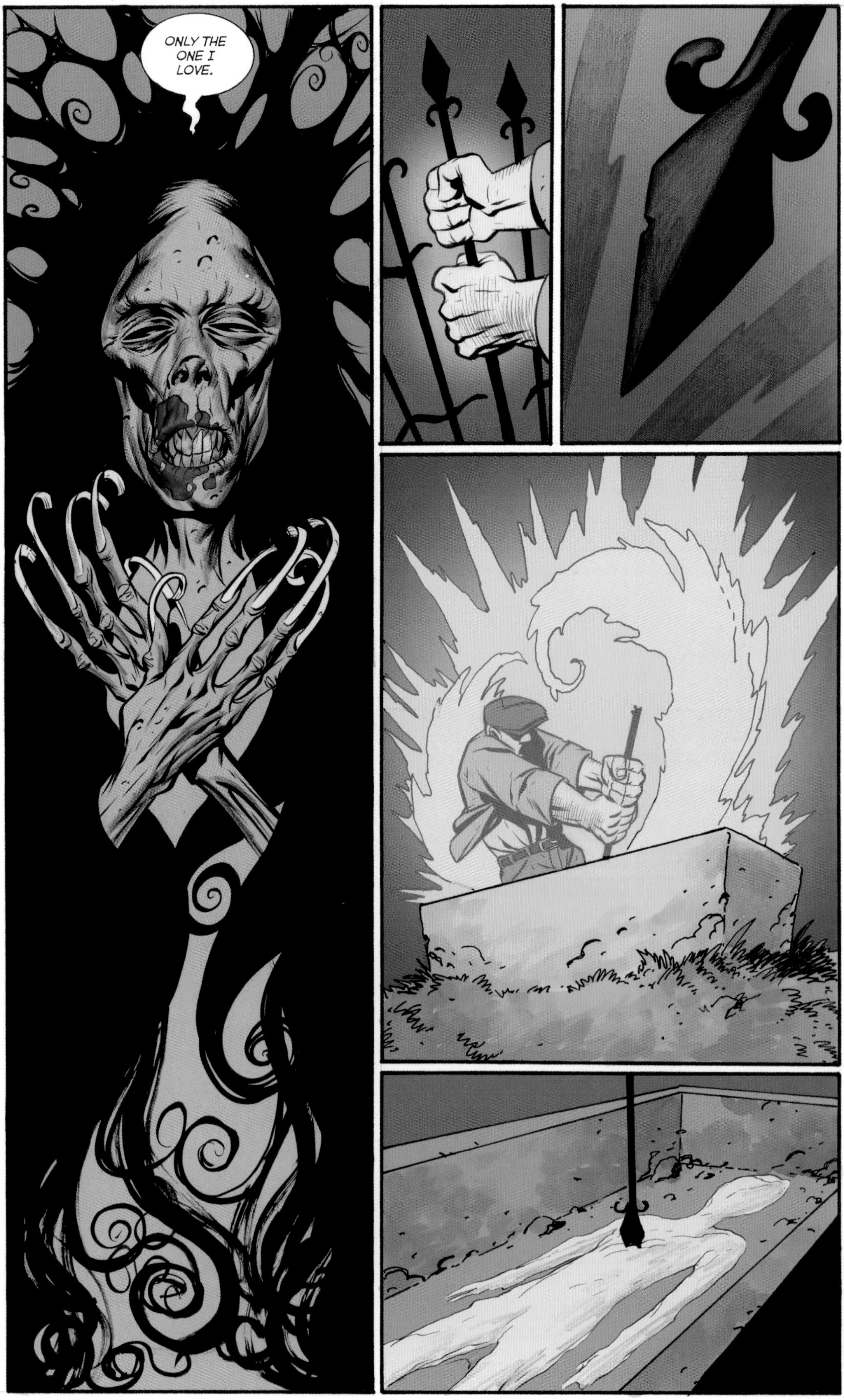
ONLY THE ONE I LOVE.

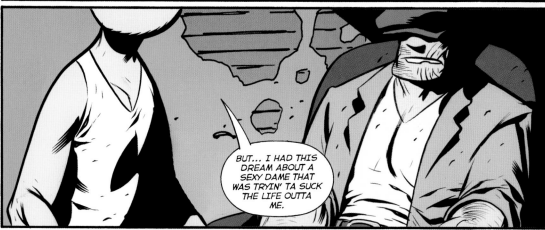

WHEW! IT'S A WONDER WHAT A GOOD NIGHT'S SLEEP WILL DO FOR YA! I FEEL LIKE A NEW MAN!

BUT... I HAD THIS DREAM ABOUT A SEXY DAME THAT WAS TRYIN' TA SUCK THE LIFE OUTTA ME.

WONDER WHAT THE HEAD SHRINKERS WOULD HAVE TO SAY ABOUT THAT. PROBABLY THAT I WAS AFRAID OF WOMEN OR SOMETHIN'. WHATTA YA THINK, GOON?

THE GOON

SKETCHBOOK

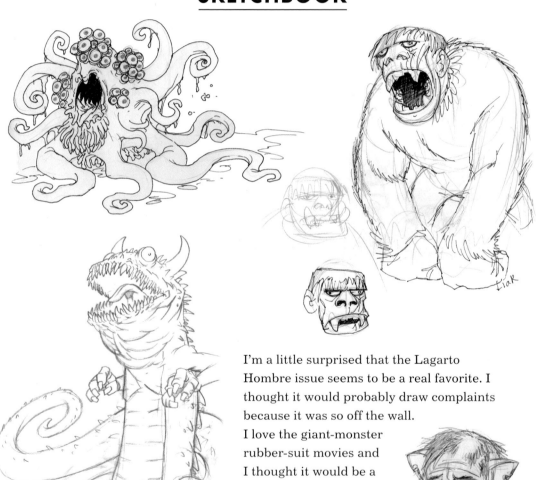

I'm a little surprised that the Lagarto Hombre issue seems to be a real favorite. I thought it would probably draw complaints because it was so off the wall. I love the giant-monster rubber-suit movies and I thought it would be a lot of fun to spoof them in an issue of *The Goon*.

The cat in the Hellboy story was actually going to be used for another issue but I decided to throw him in #7. It wasn't until later that I realized (I think Mignola brought it to my attention) that it was like a mangy Cheshire cat and the issue was like "Hellboy in Wonderland" . . . my retarded, flying-octopus Wonderland.

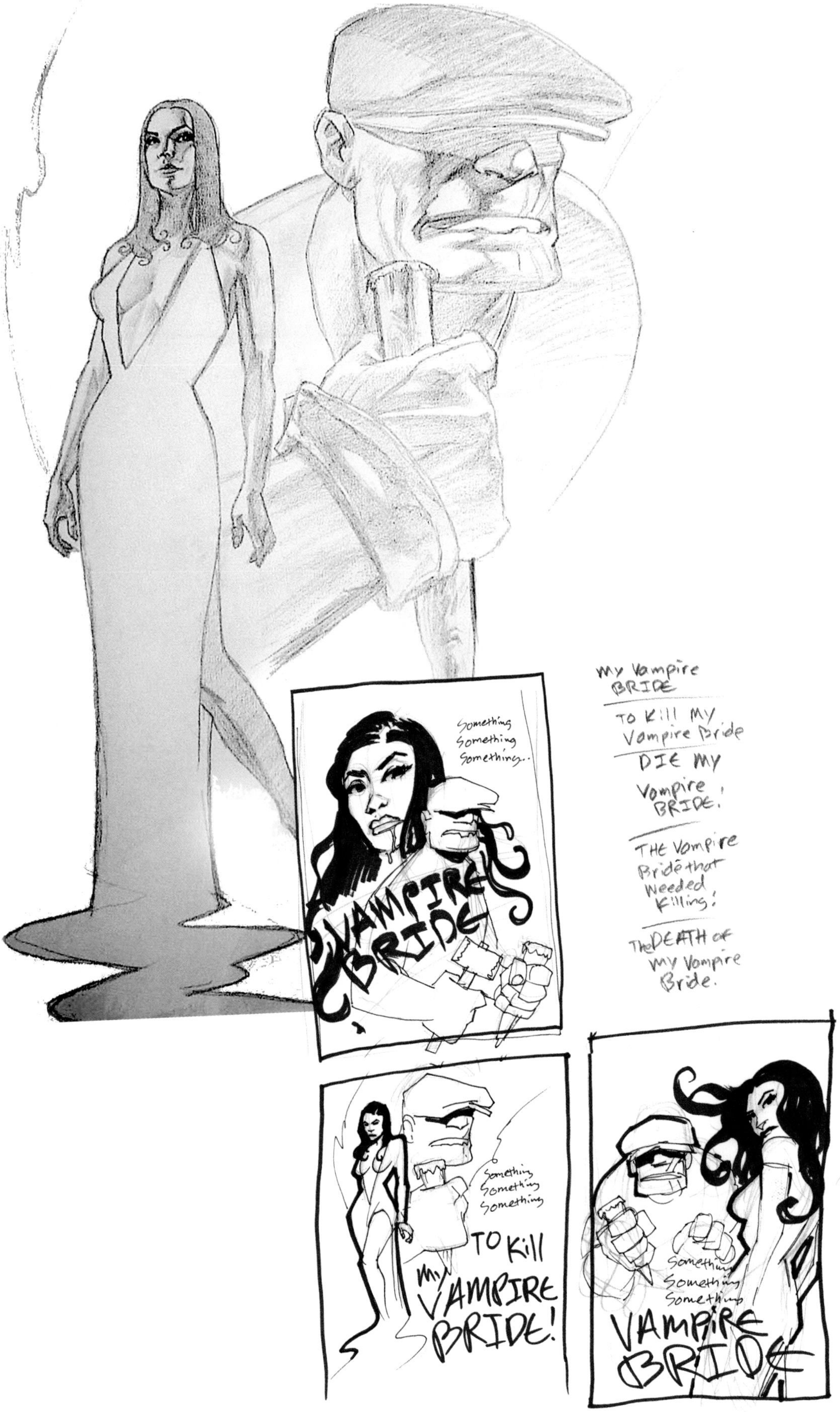

My Vampire BRIDE
TO Kill My Vampire Bride
DIE MY Vampire BRIDE!
THE Vampire Bride that Needed Killing!
The DEATH of My Vampire Bride.
Something Something Something...
VAMPIRE BRIDE
Something Something Something
TO Kill My VAMPIRE BRIDE!
Something Something Something
VAMPIRE BRIDE

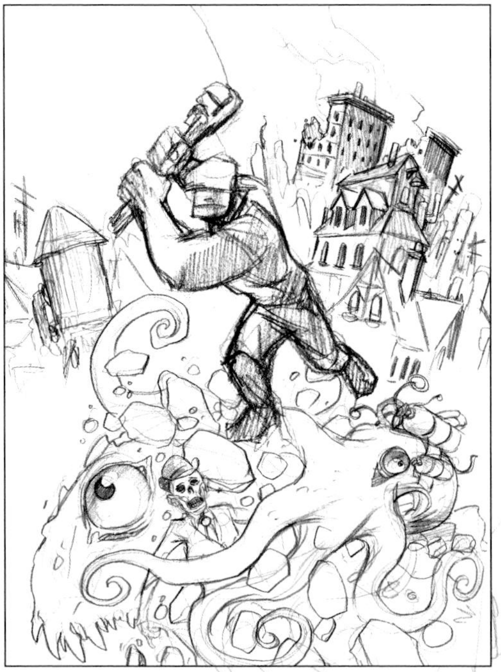

Sketch, pencils, and final cover of the first edition of *Heaps of Ruination*

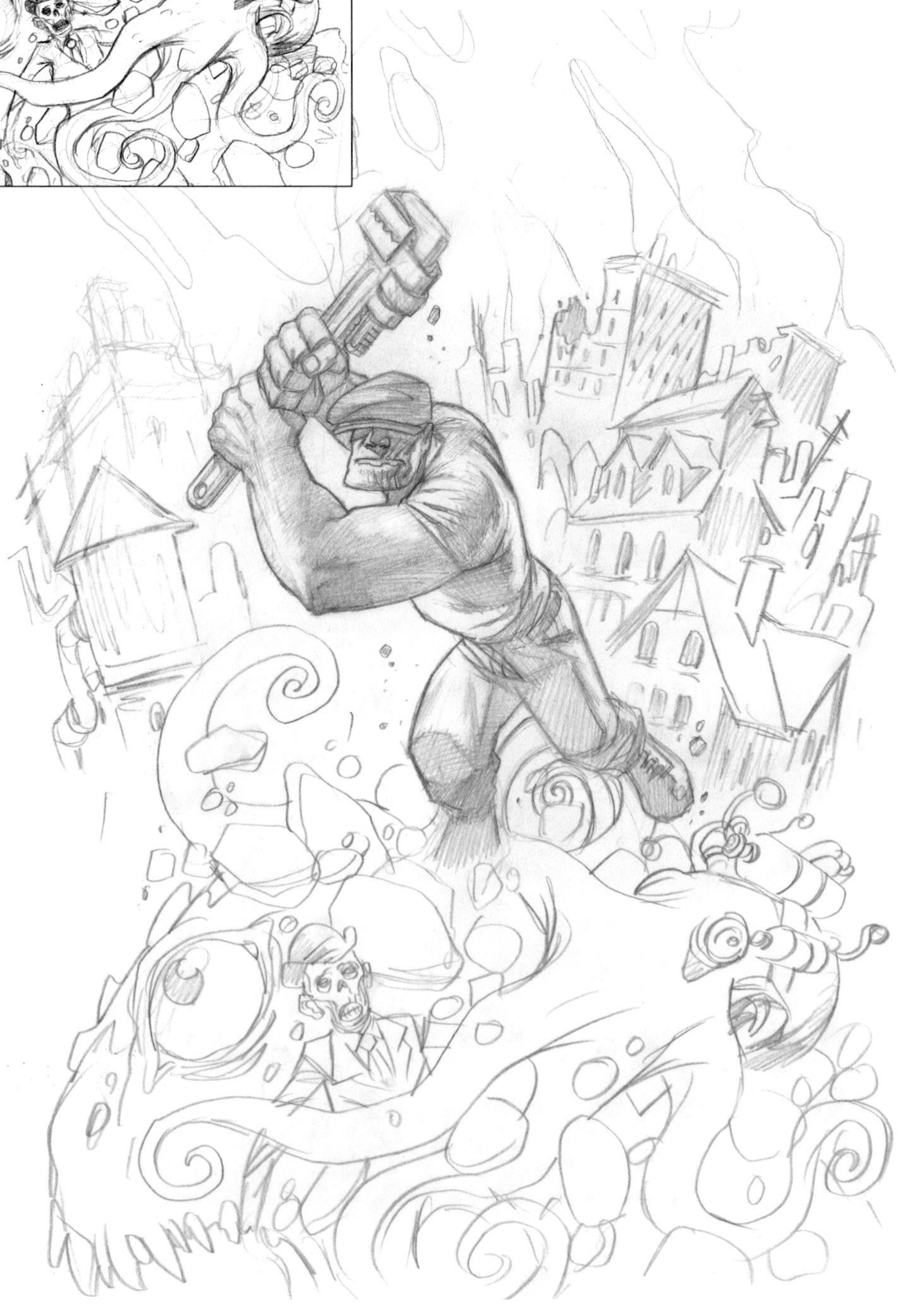

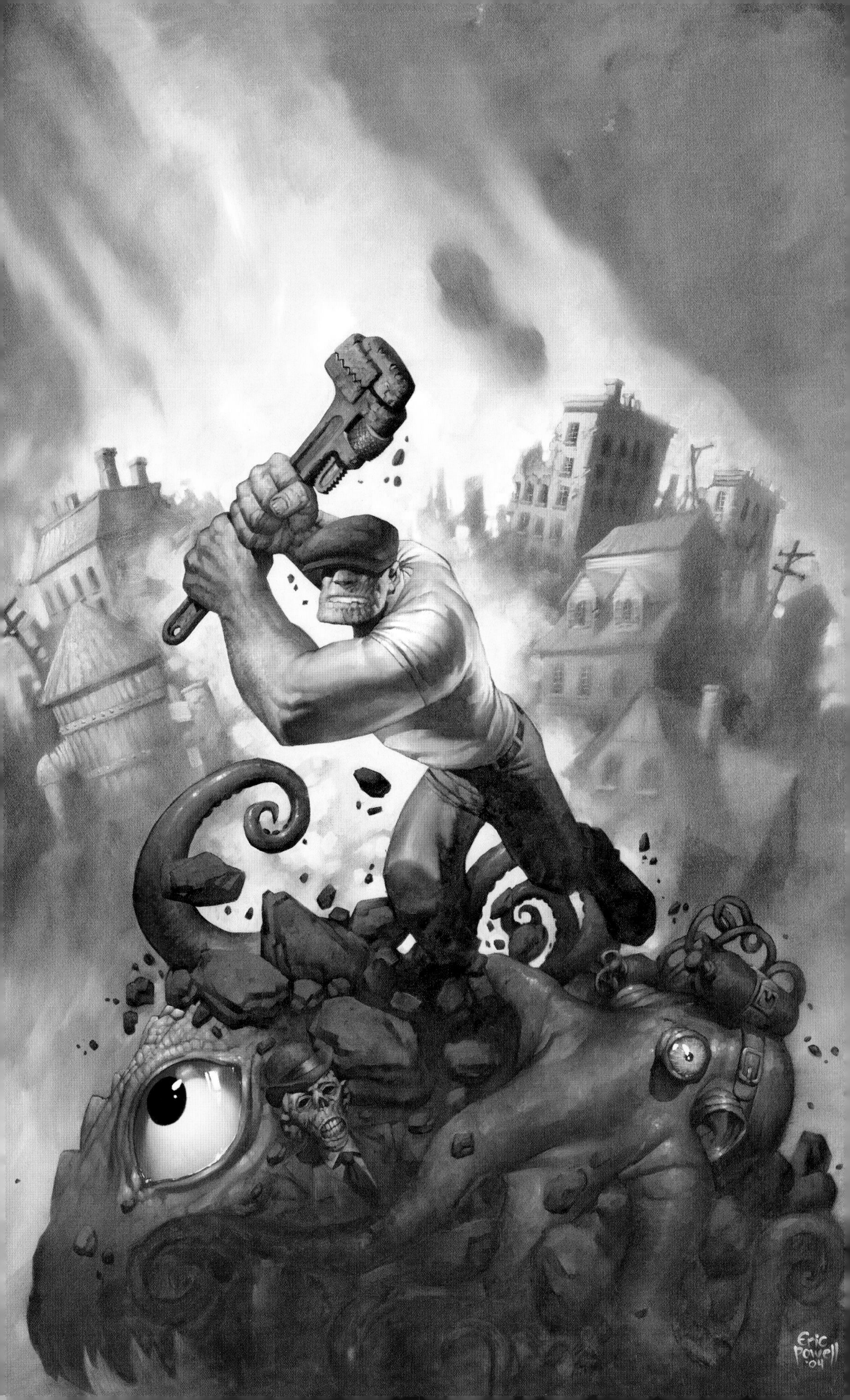
Eric Powell '04

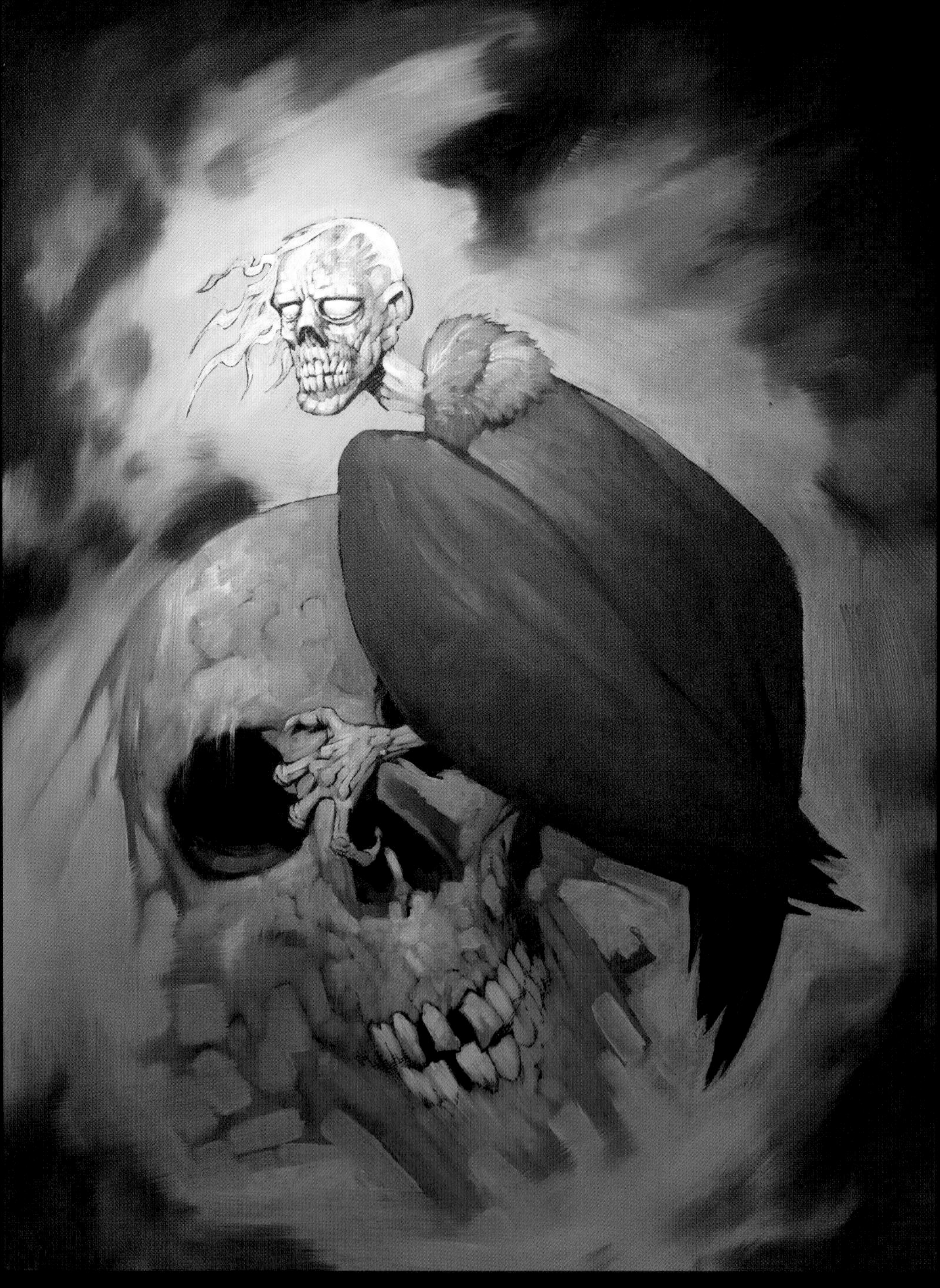

THE GOON GALLERY

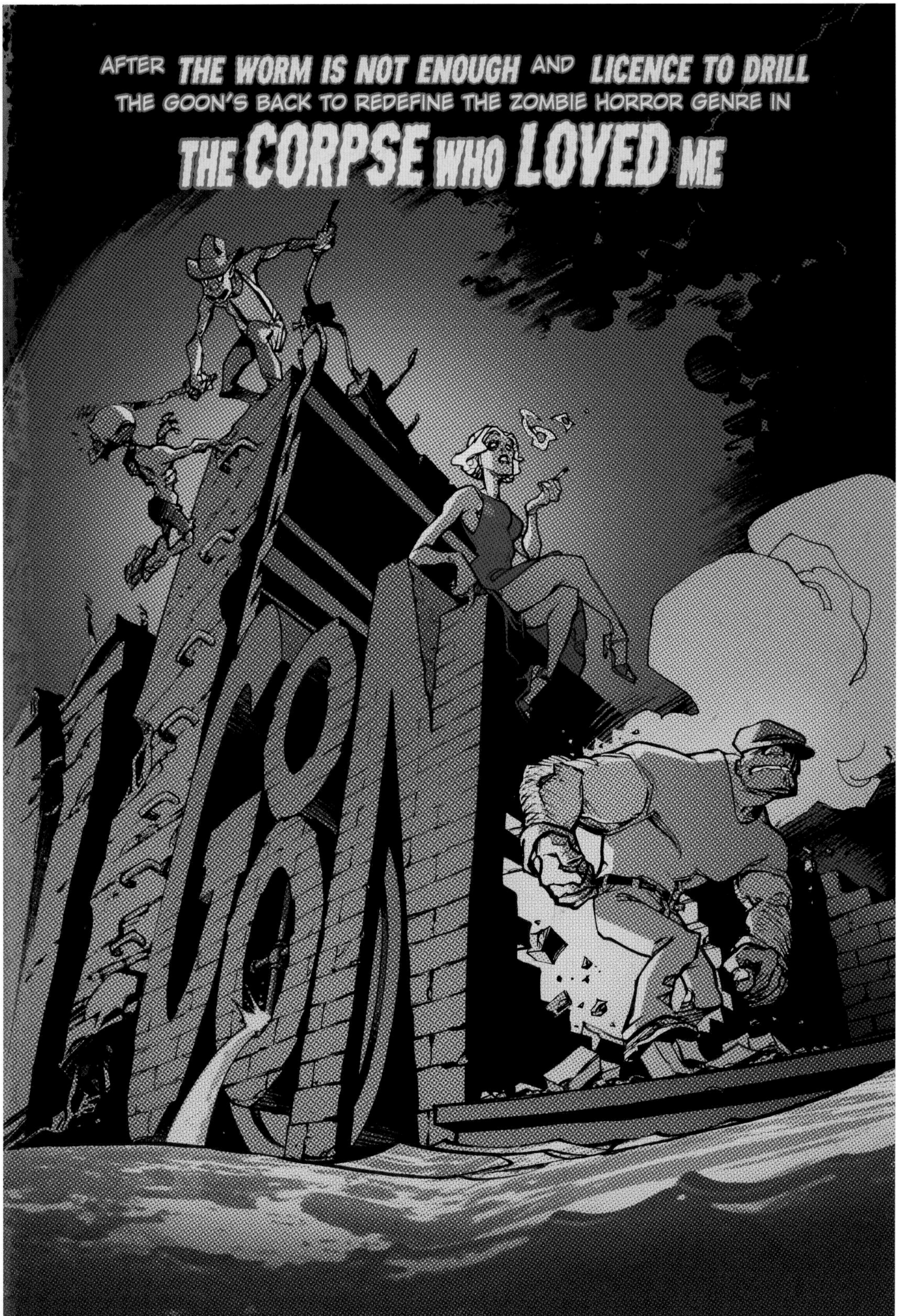

AFTER THE WORM IS NOT ENOUGH AND LICENCE TO DRILL
THE GOON'S BACK TO REDEFINE THE ZOMBIE HORROR GENRE IN
THE CORPSE WHO LOVED ME

OLIVIER VATINE

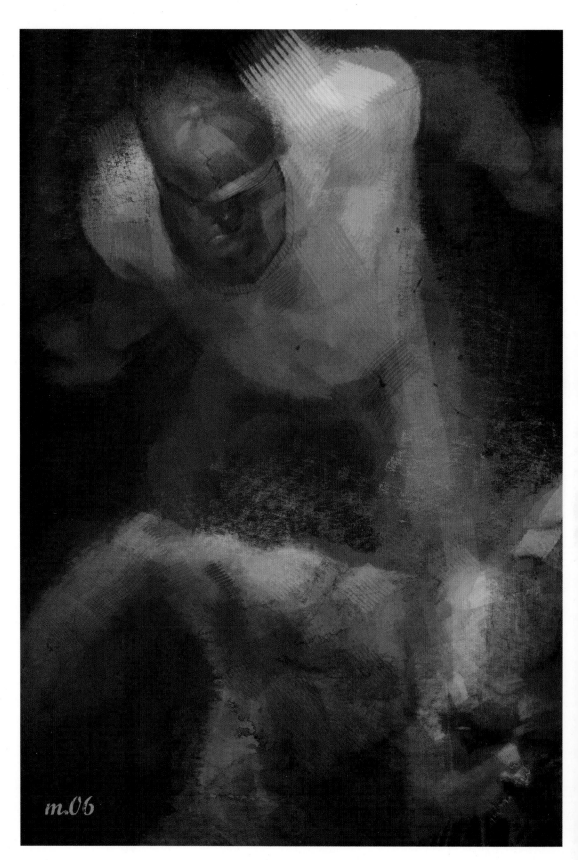

m.06

MIKAEL BOURGOUIN